Penguin Books

JOINING THE GROWN-UPS

Christine Park, daughter of Labour life peer the late Lord Cohen of Brighton, was born and brought up in Sussex. She took a London external degree in English Literature and subsequently an MA (in nineteenth- and early-twentieth-century literature) at the University of Sussex.

Her life experience includes: marriage, bringing up a child, running a successful business as a housing agent, housing researcher for the Inner London Probation Service, working in the editorial department of André Deutsch and, most recently, spending some years as a literary agent.

She is currently working on her next novel as well as doing some freelance editing, including co-editing a volume of short stories to be published by Virago in 1988.

She lives in London with her daughter Nira.

CHRISTINE PARK

Joining the Grown-Ups

Penguin Books

To the memory of
my mother, Sonya Coleman,
and my father, Lewis Cohen

Penguin Books Ltd, Harmondsworth, Middlesex, England
Viking Penguin Inc., 40 West 23rd Street, New York, New York 10010, U.S.A.
Penguin Books Australia Ltd, Ringwood, Victoria, Australia
Penguin Books Canada Ltd, 2801 John Street, Markham, Ontario, Canada L3R 1B4
Penguin Books (N.Z.) Ltd, 182–190 Wairau Road, Auckland 10, New Zealand

First published by William Heinemann Ltd 1986
Published in Penguin Books 1987

Made and printed in Great Britain by
Richard Clay Ltd, Bungay, Suffolk
Typeset in Sabon

Part I

JOSIE

I looked down. Mushroom soup. Over-blended. Too much corn starch. No give, no elasticity. And what underneath? The shape of houses, whole streets, the river, Windsor Park, lights of the runway, tarmac, the . . . I gripped the armrests.

'How I hate these landings,' said the woman sitting next to me, 'scare the death out of you.'

Negative sod, I thought, feeling the rush, the spill, the wild ferment, feeling death in my mouth and with it life, like conjoined fruits. Feeling the crunch of wheels, the speed, the wind, the escalation.

She put her hand over mine. Loose flesh billowing round taut tense bones. The plane veered wildly. Gusts of wind, God knows how many knots an hour. I tried to imagine how the sensation could be re-created on a fairground. Hundreds of midget planes veering like this. What great stuff. And Bowie singing and –

'Visiting relatives did you say?'

'Yeah, my mother.'

We touched down. She let out a long groan ending in a shudder.

'Geeze, that was great.' I claimed. But I was sick inside; sick and

1

elated and suspended – a great whirl of emotions. Somewhere outside, somewhere in that fog was Sylvia. And God damn it I didn't even know if I would recognise her. Or if she would recognise me.

Minutes later we were walking along the endless corridors, my companion panting beside me, shoulder-level. Rucksack on my back, grasping only my purse and the bottle of brandy Dad suggested I bring to Sylvia (peace offering?) my hands were free. I offered to carry one of her bulging holdalls. Her wavy greying hair jerked up and down in acknowledgement.

She moved at a snail's pace, keeping up a barrage of chatter and questions. She was in her late sixties, slowed down by the two-metre-high heels on her shoes. Three daughters she told me she had, five lovely granddaughters. All hobblers? I wanted to ask.

Then as I was pushing the trolley with our joint luggage through 'Nothing to Declare', she had to be the one they pounced on.

Look, do you mind if I leave you? My mother is a busy woman; not the type to be kept waiting. I'm sure someone else would – But how could I be that churlish. So there we were ages after everyone else from our flight had cleared off, manoeuvring our way into the Arrivals Lounge.

'You being met, dearie?'

'Yeah.'

'Always makes such a difference being met. Now, my Albert . . .'

'Yeah.'

'Did you say it was your mother?'

'Yeah.'

I looked into the space beyond the railing. Looked like a UNESCO poster. Faces of every colour. Souls of every credo. And one of them Sylvia. How the heck was I going to know which was she?

'This is Albert. Albert, this nice young woman . . .' We shook hands. Albert took my two cases off the trolley and handed them to me.

'What are you carrying?' he asked. 'Guns?'

I laughed. 'My friends. I brought them all with me. Reckoned I'll need them.'

'Friends?'

'Books.'

I had a vision of her recognising me, walking up and claiming me while I was saying 'books' and smiling at a retired farmer from Hadlow Down, East Sussex. So I let the smile stay on my face for a moment too long till the corners of my lips yanked with an ache. Let something happen before I have to do anything. Let her happen upon me while I'm still pretending that I'm preoccupied. Don't let me have to go and find her. I can't bear to be that vulnerable.

'What a crowd. So many people waiting for someone. Airports make me quite sentimental. Do you think you can see her, dearie?'

'Yeah, yeah, I can.'

'Oh well, ta-ra then. We'll be moving along. Hope you enjoy your time here. With all your . . .' she laughed, 'friends!'

Quite a wit. They inched out of sight.

I looked again at the UNESCO poster which had thinned and sharpened into a different kind of perspective. The Chain of Mankind. Lugging my cases, I weaved my way between them, as if in a dance. But who was for me, I wondered. Who was my partner? Who hers?

*

She was going to have another baby. When? When? Dad was at home and we were hopping around him, pulling his arms, clutching his trousers at the knee and twisting them around and around, as our 'au pair' Anna did when she wrang out our clothes.

'Today,' he said, smiling and brushing us free.

'But today, how today?' I hopped up and down on one foot and then the other, wanting to pee, but wanting to ask questions even more.

'Will the baby just pop out?' Angus asked. We exploded into laughter. Pee dripped into my pants. Wet, hot, reassuring. It was funny, and exciting, but nervous-making too. And then there were so many of us already. I wasn't sure I wanted another brother or sister.

'Couldn't she change her mind? Make it go back where it came from?' Angus giggled.

We all giggled. I pulled on Dad's hand. 'Dad?'

'Silly billies,' he teased.

In the room off the kitchen, Angus doodled with plasticine and William played with his cars.

'She's insisting on having it crouching,' Anna was telling a friend on the phone. 'Crazy, if you ask me, but she's certainly someone with views of her own.'

How? I wondered. I crouched myself, and tried to imagine it. Push. Push. But now I'd have to have a pee. Would there be time? I shot through the kitchen into the bathroom leaving the door open.

It was easier to imagine. Would it be like this. Would it. . . . I could hear Anna putting down the phone. Noise, commotion. Karen came running through the kitchen. She took her thumb out of her mouth. It made a 'plopping' sound.

'C'mon,' she said, 'c'mon.'

Her thumb went back in but her other damp hand clutched mine. Anna headed the procession up the two flights of stairs from basement to first-floor bedroom. Close to her was Angus, with William on his heels. I brought up the rear with Karen still clutching my hand. From the half-landing onward we could hear blood-curdling noises. Our mother panting and moaning, and worse. Dad came out from inside the room.

'You can come in now, but I want you all to be very good. The head's just appearing. Mummy thought you'd like to be there when she gives the last big push.'

We hung back.

'5p,' he said, 'for the first to say whether it's a boy or a girl.'

'How'll we know?' William whispered.

'See if it's got a penis, stupid,' retorted Angus, grandly.

'Dad . . .' Anything to put off the moment. Was she really squatting on the floor while she made all those horrible noises?

But she was not. Rather she was lying in the centre of the enormous bed, her black hair clinging to the pillow, clumps of it, damp, sticking to her forehead, which the lady doctor was sponging. Her cheeks were hollowed more than I had ever noticed before.

'Hello. Here you all are. Come closer. (We were hovering by the door.) Look, can you see your new brother or sister?' Her feet were drawn up under her. She opened her legs wide, laughing. But the laugh turned into sounds of distress. 'Oh, oh, hold on now everyone. I believe – baby – is – coming out.' These last words were said in a rush. Her hands clutched the sheets. The knuckles five red blotches. Her face contracted and unrecognisable all of a sudden. Then that horrible panting.

'Gently does it,' said the doctor.

Karen began to cry quietly. The doctor put her fingers to her lips. 'Now you must all be quiet and help your mother push.'

How? How could we do it? Oh. Oh. Oh.

'It's coming,' she said. 'I'm sorry, Dr Jennings, I can't . . .'

'I can see it,' squealed William. 'I can see it.'

'Me can too.' Karen at my side was timorous, yet triumphant.

'Dash!' said Angus. 'Blast!' loud and angry.

4

'What's the matter, darling?'

'It's not a boy after all.'

She looked at the doctor for confirmation, and at Daddy. I felt I'd never seen, that I'd never see – ever – ever, a sweeter smile.

'Is it . . . Is it a little girl?'

They nodded.

'There. You all have a new sister. A very special one.'

Dad bent over to kiss her. She let herself be kissed. Her eyes focused on the ceiling and it was as if she were talking to herself. 'I knew it would be,' she whispered.

I'd managed to keep my eyes fixed on her face almost entirely. Like the times I stare at a spot on the wall above the telly, when there are faces I don't like. Those scary ones. But now I felt I had to look at my sister. Say hello. There was blood and water and yuck everywhere.

'I'm going to be sick,' I said.

'Me too,' echoed Karen.

'Anna,' said Dad (Anna had posted herself at the door during all of the preceding), 'take the children out now. When the baby's had a clean-up you might take to your sister rather more!' he said to us.

'Quick, quick,' I said. I ran to the door which Anna opened, hand over my mouth.

But once back in the safety of the kitchen and playroom it suddenly seemed thrilling. We hung round Anna asking impossible questions, 'Do you *think*, but do you *think* . . .' She couldn't say whether she thought Sylvia would choose this name or that. Whether our new sister would in time go to the same school as Angus and me. How soon Karen would have to give up her cot. Whether the shawl that Grandma Miller had knitted and sent from Aberdeen would be used or the one that Aunt Jesse had brought yesterday – pale primrose yellow. So pretty. I hoped it would be that one. No, Anna was completely disappointing when it came to our questions. But she cut bread and made our favourite sandwiches. And I begged her to let us finish the apple cake. And when she reminded me that I'd said I was going to be sick, I realised I'd quite forgotten. That seemed ages ago.

When we opened the door next there were roses everywhere, pink ones, and deep red, and some white ones with a pale yellow glow like the pages of Dad's old books. Three vases were filled with the roses. The smell was sweet and heavy. Through the open window the wind was making the curtains billow. The heads of the roses in the vase on the window-sill nodded vigorously.

All the horrid bits and pieces which belonged to the doctor had disappeared.

In the bed she was lying back on two plump pillows. White cotton with a blue daisy pattern. Her hair had been brushed. It no longer looked wet and funny. I wanted to put my hand in its dark mass and cuddle up to her.

'Come here, moppets,' she said, 'onto the bed with you.'

We clambered up cautiously. Sitting in an awkward semi-circle as if we were preparing for a picnic.

She put out her hands and clutched one of William's and one of Karen's.

'Now isn't this lovely?'

'Yes, yes,' we mumbled.

'Where's Dad?' I asked.

'Back at the hospital. Seeing his proper patients,' she laughed.

'Where's the baby?'

'You'll see her in just a moment. Tell me what you've been doing downstairs.'

The boys fought each other for her attention. I kept looking at the door. Wondering. Surely it wouldn't be as horrid as last time I saw it. I'd just have not to look. No one would notice. The inside of my tummy felt as if it was a rock pool with lots of little crabs crawling round the surface.

'Josie, darling,' she said to me.

'Mum?'

'Why don't you just pop to the bathroom and see how Dr Jennings is doing.' I slid off the bed. Pleased of action, direction.

But I didn't have to get as far as the bathroom. In the corridor Dr Jennings was coming towards me; the yellow-shawled bundle in her arms. She bent down. 'Do you want to see her properly now, Josie?'

I shut my eyes.

'No.'

'She's rather like you, you know.'

'She's not. Besides she's not a baby at all. She's a mistake. All bloody and things.'

'She's a little doll now she's had her bath. You'd be surprised. Go on, open your eyes and have a look, then perhaps you'd like to carry her in.'

'Me!' I squeaked, hoarse with the very thought of the responsibility. Maybe I'd drop her. Maybe I could drop her. Then she'd die. Go away and all this wouldn't be happening. I determined to risk opening my eyes. Just take a quick peep.

'You promise, you do promise she's not yucky?'

'I do.'

I opened my eyes, in one 'pop', while I had the courage. And there she was, pink face, brown hair, tiny little toes stretching out of the shawl.

'Did I look like that?' I whispered, awed.

She laughed, and bent lower. 'Here, you take her in.'

'Really? Really?'

The baby seemed heavy and shapeless. Nothing to grab onto. But warm and sweet-smelling. My sister. Dr Jennings held her too. Just one arm in case I tripped.

'My!' said Sylvia as we walked through the door. It took ever so long to get to the bed. All the others were bouncing up and down and saying, 'Hurry, hurry'. Sylvia patted the space in front of her and we got the baby there at last.

I crawled up into the semi-circle and sat there, cross-legged, with my shoes on – I reckoned Sylvia wouldn't complain at a time like this.

Everyone peered. The baby opened her eyes. They were deep blue like Sylvia's. But she told us that all babies' eyes are blue at first and that later they may go brown like Dad's or the boys' and mine, or remain blue always like hers and Karen's.

I wanted them to be like mine.

'She's saying hello to us,' said Angus.

'She can't see you yet,' Sylvia explained. 'But in a week or two.'

'Can we put her in my pram?' Karen asked. We went on asking questions. She went on answering. I was thinking I don't mind really then. Us being so many . . .

The door creaked. She stood there looking at us all. And we her. She'd come to the house once or twice before but I'd never really noticed her. Never focused on her till that moment.

She must have been in her mid-thirties then. Sylvia's age. Of course she just looked old to me, a grown-up. She had on brown lace-up shoes, not unlike my own. I'd never seen a grown-up woman wear them before; not Sylvia or any of her other friends. She was carrying flowers that made me think of dead butterflies' wings. I hoped they weren't for Sylvia. I thought they'd look horrid amongst the roses.

'I phoned from work,' she said. 'Your "au pair" gave me the news.'

'Snapdragons,' said Sylvia, 'my favourites.' She looked towards this stranger and her face wore that smile again. 'God, am I pleased

7

to see you. It makes my day that you've come.'

'Out, out, every last one of you.' This to us. She wriggled her legs. So that suddenly her inexplicably angry toes were jabbing at our bottoms and thighs.

'Move,' she said. 'Quick. Alison hasn't got all day to waste.'

With hindsight I think she said it with pride. The working woman. The woman who didn't have time to waste. Despite all that domesticity – or perhaps because of it – the other was what it was all about. I'm going to have so much time to waste. I vow whenever I can, I'm going to do nothing but waste time.

*

I stood around, looking loopy, waiting to be claimed. I peered at any dark-haired woman who might be Sylvia, but nobody peered back at me with welcoming enthusiasm. Since the cases, as old Albert had already discovered, contained like a ton of books, they didn't encourage movement from the original spot where he'd off-loaded them. On all sides people pushed by. I stood astride the luggage, occasionally moving a few degrees to left or right. A revolving clock. A beacon of New World energy. You bet!

At 5 foot 10 inches I could see over most heads. To more heads. I kept checking my watch. I kept trying not to look disgruntled. Forty-five minutes. An hour and a half since the plane landed. She's not coming.

'Say, could you just keep your eye on these?' A huddle of saried Indian women, grandmothers, kids, the lot, looked at me dubiously. 'Yeah, well I'll only be two minutes. Promise. Just want to go to the Information Desk for a sec. Thanks.'

The message board was apparently inside the Arrivals Lounge and no, I hadn't thought to look at it. But after a whole bunch of calls, and waits and waves to the saried group and repeating my name and spelling it out, and spelling it out yet again and deciding that give or take an 'l' or two there could be a communication – Miller/Minter give or take – 'Yeah,' I said, 'you've got it straight on. That's me.'

*

It's cold, even for here unusual. I'm guessing it's reached the twenty below mark. No one wanted to collect the wood with Dad; least of all me.

'Come off it, Dad,' I growled. I let the hair out of my pony-tail, shook it, then tied it back again. It had felt too tight before. One of those days. Everything tight. A tight knot of resistance in me when he pulled me to my feet, teasing, flirting, and in front of Anna too.

'Come on, Josie, help your old Dad. Put that down. Too much reading . . .' I sighed, glared at him, knowing I'd give in. I could have said, 'Why not one of the others?' But I knew what he'd say. It was always the same on these awful 'family weekends' he was so keen on.

Outside the log cabin the snow came in flurries, lighter white on an already grey/white packed and freezing environment. He took my hand; through three layers of gloves I could still feel his warmth and strength. I could feel too my affection and confusion.

'Why so moody, Josie?'

'Oh, you know,' I shrugged.

'No I don't.'

'God damn it!'

Mom, [I wrote] Mother, Sylvia. What you will. It's cold. You can't imagine how cold. My reckless family (yours too) are skiing, every last one of them. But yours truly, Josie by name, eighteen now and in her first year at UBC, has taken it into her head to sit by the fire – as near as one can decently or safely get – and write to her old Mom.

Thing is – and I'll rush straight to the point – for a whole bunch of reasons too complicated to go into unless you absolutely insist, I just can't get into the whole university thing. Maybe I'm not ready, or maybe my talents lie in another direction or something. Anyway – deep breath here. Gosh, my toes incidentally are beginning to melt like broiled marshmallows. A delicious sensation. Now where was I? Yeah, the crunch, the bite, said extra speedily, like all in a rush. I was wondering, hoping that you might look positively on the idea of giving your long-lost daughter a job in that literary agency of yours for a year. I could arrange to drop out in the second year and go back in the third – if I hadn't taken the agency over by then. Only a joke. But more seriously, I can type (took a course last semester), can speed-read. Ditto, another course. Love books. Got straight As all through high school. So, you see, your eldest daughter is super-bright plus

9

has cheery personality and is extra-helpful. I know I'd be good at any menial jobs the agency would need doing – or anything else for that matter. Would love to see England again. Have missed it for ten long years. Would like to see you again. There, I've admitted it.

Must finish. Must get this to the post before I lose courage. And the others will be back soon. Write soon, to the college address I'll put on the bottom. In anticipation, plus a general state of fingers and toes crossed, your loving daughter, Josie. P.S. I can live with that other matter: I'm sure I can.

Josie, what a surprise to hear from you! And forgive me for the length of time it has taken to get down to responding. Don't take it as a reflection of my interest in all you have to say, but rather the last month has been a particularly busy one, the World Book Fair and its aftermath taking up the major part of it. Immediately after which my secretary Sally rather inconveniently took her holiday and only now are things beginning to revert to some state of normality.

Hence the delay. I was of course surprised that you wrote. Even curious to know whether your father supplied the address. And naturally was delighted to hear that you had achieved 'A' grades all through high school and are now studying at the University of British Columbia (an excellent university, I understand). Is your major to be English literature?

I do hope, Josie, that you'll continue to fulfil the potential that you obviously showed at school. We are living in an age where the world is an open book for a young woman who works hard and diligently. I urge you to settle down and make the very best of these next years. Don't allow yourself to become too carried away by your emotions. You sound a rather emotional girl. Try to throw your energies into your work. You won't regret it later.

What are your courses this year? Which writers are your favourites? Do you have any particularly exciting teachers? Have you a group of like-minded friends? It helps so much if you can find such.

No doubt the snow is beginning to thaw now, and you are able to get outside more. How lucky you are to have the benefit of all that outdoor life. I send you love, and thank you again for your letter. I do hope your brothers and sisters are thriving. And your father. All the best, Sylvia.

Gosh Sylvia, you don't know me at all — which is hardly surprising. I hate the outdoor life, ugh, awful. HATE IT WITH A VENGEANCE. One snow-covered mountain looks just like another after a time. I bet you'd feel the same. After all it's not really quite your thing, is it. Why should it be mine?

Right, well let's start at the beginning. Your letter was a bitter disappointment. Really. Went to the donut diner (not with a group of 'like-minded friends', incidentally, but by my god-damn self). Ate two wholewheat and one caramel-coated donut, a king-size glass of juice, three coffees, and cried buckets. Emotional? But so what. It's got to be a good thing sometimes.

Sylvia, everyone else has got a mother and I haven't. And she's not dead or anything conclusive like that. She just doesn't want to see me. Right? And why do you say so formally 'hope your brothers and sisters are thriving'? Is that England for you? Why don't you want to know about them? Still I'm not telling till you ask.

Nope, Dad never did give me your address. The mind blows at the thought of asking him. Poor Dad. Nope, it was super simple; just went into the University library and looked you up in the register of overseas publishers and agents. There you were as large as life — geeze, all these years I've been wondering about it — snug between Julian Finney and Futon Brown Associates, whoever they both are. And I plan to know in time. But there you were. Fisk, Farmer & Tickle. It had to be you. Two literary agents with the name of Fisk: not likely, I reckoned.

Now what's all this guff about working hard, making the most of opportunities. I'm getting enough of that from my year tutor. Not from you too. I don't need it. I used to like studying. It was something to get my teeth into. And then Dad was so pleased, and I had to set an example to the others. But this university lark, it's quite something else. Stuffy buggers here. And I'm just not interested in more study at the moment. Seems like some mammoth waste of time; okay for all those who want to be academics, but a dead duck for me. All that analysing. Dry. Dry as chick peas. Nope, I want to live. I want to work. I want to love. I want to write. I want to know you. And not necessarily in that order.

Oh, I'm in the middle of such a great book, incidentally. One of the greatest. *Under the Volcano*, Malcolm Lowry. All that thwarted passion, that deep despair. The urgency, the pace, the descriptions of Mexico. There's a real writer for you. Did you ever read his work?

Well I'll sign off now. Back to Lowry. There's nothing like those guys to cheer me up. Bob Marley, Sibelius, you know. Your loving fille, Josie. P.S. Tell me about your authors. Go on, do.

Sylvia. Syl – or is that too intimate, too cheeky? I'm writing this in the cafeteria here. Excuse the exercise book notepaper. Got yours this morning. Nope, read Lowry for pleasure, not course material. But he is an author who is covered in some of the 3rd-and 4th-year courses. And in the library, as you say, there is next to nil reading material on him. Just one or two really weirdo-sounding books. Nothing that sounds like my reading of that masterpiece. Spent this morning checking. Don't worry, no classes till this afternoon. Well, only one, and that most missable. Bet your client would find his book wanted here. Lowry is very big at the moment. Especially because of the film. Is he good, anyway? Your client, I mean. Not Lowry. Lowry's amongst the greats.

Tell me some things. Where do you live? Anything. Are you super successful. Are you fabulously wealthy? Do you still go to the opera and ballet like you used to with Dad? Have you got grey hair now? Perhaps you could send me a photo. I'd like that.

Spring, Spring, Spring. Last of the snow melted away. Early flowers beginning to bloom. Campus looking good with its green grass and vibrant borders. The poor old sods at home, though, are still frozen in for another month at least.

About my weight or the donuts or whatever, you're a restraining old stick for someone I don't even know. I don't believe in all that guff about being slim for the blokes. And in answer to your question, no I haven't got one – a bloke, I mean. I did have, my last year in high school, but that's another story. They say, or least someone has, that I'm like you. Take that as you like. I'm not half as pretty anyway. Go on, *please* send me a photo. Even if you just get that secretary of yours – what was her name – Sally – to 'pop' one in an envelope. You don't even have to sign a compliments slip. Incidentally, if I was over there next year, I could take over from Sally every time she grabbed a vacation at an inconvenient time. How about that for an idea. Got myself a deal, have I?

Oh Sylvia, how wrong you are yet again. You sound quite muddle-headed if you'll excuse me saying so. I don't want to be fobbed off with a holiday with you. Two weeks bombing around Europe in and out of art galleries and the like. I want to work, work, and live with you for a bit. It's like every letter is a rejection and so painful. You can't go on doing it. Doesn't your heart just break to think of your poor daughter sitting in the donut diner 'toute seule' munching her way through several varieties of donut and crying buckets into her coffee because her distant mother writes such *distant* letters.

To use a favorite expression of Dad's, it's been raining cats and dogs for days here. Which does nothing of course to help a person's mood. 11 a.m. Am studying in the library – or supposed to be. Almost black outside. All the lights are on. Don't you hate fluorescent tubes? Hope your staff are well cared for, incidentally. None of those Dickensian conditions. You wouldn't be one to go in for those, would you? I wonder what kind of a boss you are. Amusing to speculate. Wonder if I shall ever know. Seeing your mother at work, you know, just as in earlier ages one might have wanted to see her in the process of cooking or knitting or some other aspect of homemaking, is all part of the new feminine consciousness.

Course I can hardly remember you in the homemaking role. Only just. Anna's done pretty well by all of us. But it's not the same (she cries theatrically); it's not the same. Are you involved in any part of the feminist movement, by the way? Or don't you need to be, having upped and done it – in every way – by yourself? So many questions I'd like you to answer. Still. Still, let's not get too maudlin.

Doing a course of 19th-Century English Lit. plus the social history of the time. We've got a number of Marxist students in my year. Do they just go to town on some of the 19th-Century bit. To say nothing of what the feminists have to say. All my old favorites, Dickens, George Eliot, the Brontës, etc., being turned on their heads by these new interpretations. But don't race away with the idea that your daughter is getting stuck into the courses at last. Just whiling away the time. Still planning to leave this summer whatever. Maybe take a boat to Mexico . . .

It was, I suppose, decent of you to offer a vacation. Just caught me off balance because it was so little when I want so much. But don't think I'm not grateful. I am. Even if I have to admit it grudgingly. You could have offered nothing after all. So thank you. My exams are next month. Could you think of me then. Your daughter, Josie.

Geeze, darling, darling Sylvia. What can I say. You're a honey, a poppet, a real darling. That's just great, great, great. I can hardly believe it. This is written at 5 a.m. by the way, so if I sound kind of wild, blame it on the hour. Plus the message incorporated in your letter. Plus the general state of exam fever. Started yesterday with the three-hour papers (your letter waiting for me on my return from second). Two more today. Plus another ten after the weekend. Ugh!

Won't do brilliantly this year, but on the other hand hope at least for a row of comfortable Bs. Worse is just super stupid. But since I haven't worked I'll need all my wits about me. Hard in the circumstances. My wits are every which way. Though I'm not blaming you – she adds with a rush – I'm thanking you. It's a great scheme. June 20th, you say, till end of August. Two and a half months. And yes, okay. I won't sign out for next year. I'll keep my options open, as you say. And I'll brave it with Dad. But will you write to him say it's okay with you, that you'd actually *like* to have me. I'll need all the help I can persuading him.

I'm so excited I can hardly write coherently. Except to say thank you. Did I say that already? Except to say you won't regret it. Honest. Honest. Except to say I'm longing to see you.

*

In the Arrivals Lounge I tore at the envelope. 'Important last-minute meeting. Impossible to meet plane. Take a cab. Sally will pay on arrival if you haven't the cash. Till later, Sylvia.'

Geeze, oh geeze.

Along the motorway the black taxi sped. England was as grey as I remembered it. That's why I'd liked the weather so much better in

14

BC than all the endless blue sky you get where we live in Edmonton: it reminded me of home. Home, I told myself, home girl. Home, home. But looking out of the taxi window, I felt pretty funny, pretty rasping inside.

It was beginning to drizzle. I wound down the window and felt the soft pats of water on my wrist and spraying gently the back of my hand. I opened the window some more. The spray hit my neck and face. Damp it was but good. London, I told myself. Where's all that excitement gone? Find it and hold on to it. And then since homely remonstrations like that, the Dad variety, were having zero effect on my state of mind, I tried something stronger. Man, I told myself, the University of Life; are you so puny that you're going to quit at the first deck?

'You smoke?' I pulled back the dividing window and asked.

'Thanks. I wouldn't say no.'

'I haven't got any. I meant – could I have one of yours?' Through the mirror I felt his eyes appraising me.

'I need one.'

'Do you? The flight made you nervous?'

'Nope, but getting here sure did.'

Geeze, the silence of the English. I could have kissed him for saying nothing. He passed a packet and lighter through the window.

'Help yourself.'

I lit up and passed them back.

'Cancer,' he said, 'none of us should, according to the doctors.'

'We think so much about death,' I said, 'while we're living. Cigarettes, butter, sugar, meat, drink, drugs: turns out everything's dangerous. Everything that's enjoyable.'

'Not everything.' He smiled into the mirror. Don Juan of the taxi-cab drivers. And all for the price of a cigarette.

'I wouldn't know about that. Do you often – you know?'

'What?'

'With your female passengers?'

'Aren't you a one!'

'No, tell me.'

I thought this just wouldn't be happening in a street in Edmonton. For one thing, straight out, I wouldn't be asking. He hummed a tune. I followed the tube stations. Hammersmith. Shepherd's Bush. Watching the people in dark macs, holding dark umbrellas, loom out of the blanket of grey continuous rain for brief seconds and then disappear back into it. Simple things struck me now we were off the motorway: the dirt, the litter, the seediness; the narrowness of the roads, the congestion: the advertisements, that in Britain an adman would risk the general public understanding a pun.

Through the driving-mirror I took a shifty at the driver, his profile, the part of his eyeball, his chin, the slight movement of the throat that precedes speech. I wondered, would he be forthcoming?

On that one topic, though, he never was, but he became communicative on many others. So that for a time Sylvia slid right off my mind.

Highbury, Islington. A row of shabby houses. Old like they had the weight of history behind them. And across the way a rectangle of green with tennis courts at one end. The rain had abruptly ceased. There was an eerie pink-grey light.

The taxi drew to a standstill. Raindrops melted on the windows and bonnet. Through a cleared section of the pane the brass plate of Fisk, Farmer & Tickle jumped in front of my eyes. I've made it. Half way across the world.

'You want to pay the fare then?'

'Sure, sure.' I opened the glass partition and pushed through a bunch of notes.

'Sure you can manage those?'

'Yeah.'

'Cheers, then.'

'Cheers.'

From a partially opened window a Mozart piano concerto sounded. Your house is shabbier than the rest, I see. But someone has polished your name-plate. Only yours. Not Messrs Doban and Doban, nor Brian Austen and Partners. All these people whose daily lives intermingle with your own.

With an arm as limp as a ripe banana, I reached up for the doorbell.

*

'Waiting in Vain.' Yeah, the right kind of noise for a hot blue day. The sun bouncing off the hot red metal. The glare of the gravel. The

16

heady, pungent hibiscus scent from the borders of the high school grounds.

Dad had lent me the Porsche.

'I'd like to give you a treat, Josie. I think you deserve something special.'

'Hold on, Dad. What's all the fuss?'

'Your last term's grades were quite exceptional.'

'Oh that!'

'Well, come on, old thing, don't "oh that" it. Not everyone does as well.'

Anna came into the room. I was relieved. Since when had I become embarrassed when it was just him and I. He always tried so hard. It gave me an uncomfortable and hopeless feeling.

'We're discussing Josie's treat.' Dad turned to Anna for help.

'What about clothes, Josie? A new dress, trousers, jeans?'

'There's no need,' I said.

'Come on,' she went up to him and slipped her arm through his. 'Give your Dad that pleasure.'

I looked at them both. I was just going to say, honest there's nothing I want, when a thought struck me.

'Yeah, I've an idea. It's not anything to buy me, mind.'

'Well, come on. Out with it.'

'Let me take the Porsche to school.' (I'd passed my test six months before.) Silence. 'Just once. I'd be super careful. Promise.'

Sign language between them. He saying, 'What do you think?' Her eyes signalling back, 'Go on, trust her.' Nice gentle Anna.

'Okay. You win. When'll it be?'

'Geeze, thank you, Dad.' I swung my arms around him. 'First day of school?'

'First day of school. It's a deal.'

Early September. End of first day of last year at school. A great feeling revving that sassy engine then letting it purr away to a wimpy death. Then starting it again. Prolonging the moment, the pleasure of easing the foot pedal, feeling the engine escaping like a racehorse.

'Hi-ya, Dave.'

'What a pose! That your Dad's?'

'Ya. Want a ride?'

'Who says no to a red Porsche?'

'What about me? Don't forget the girl that goes with it.'

We laughed.

So it was as simple as that, I thought, as we sped along the highway. Geeze, and I'd been waiting for it to happen for most of the last year.

With my left hand I switched the tape back to the beginning of 'Ghost Town' for the third time.

'Where'll we go?' he asked.

'I could drop you at your place. You live on 52nd, don't you? Fact is I've promised to take the other kids to swim in the reservoir.' I looked at his face.

'What kids?'

'You know, all my awful brothers and sisters. Wish I hadn't now. But Dad's only letting me have the car this one day, and I promised them.'

We drove in silence.

He chose another tape and put it in the tape deck.

'I could come too.'

'You're joking? You're not? With all my lot? You don't know what you're letting yourself in for. You can't mean it.'

'Shut up, Josie. I mean it.'

That car purred along.

The clatter of knives and forks. Family dinner time. Anna feeling sick. Not eating. Third time this week, I noticed.

'– and Dave came with us,' explained Angus to Dad, with his mouth full.

'Who's Dave?'

'Kid in Josie's class, dummy.'

'Angus, I've told you before. Don't say that to me and preferably don't say it to anyone.'

'– and I can dive now. He taught me how to,' Angus continued. 'You ought to see, Dad –'

'He played great games with us,' William wanted to say his bit 'and I chased him and I . . .'

That's what it's like in a large family, I thought. If you're one of the poor sods in the middle you just never get to the end of a sentence.

'But Anna,' said Karen, 'Anna, Anna!' She waved her fork to get attention. 'You should have seen his legs.'

'What's wrong with his legs?' The words had left my mouth before I had time to think. Damn these kids! And I could see the look of amusement on Anna and Dad's faces.

'They're such spindly spidery legs. And hairy!

The two girls went into peals of laughter, spluttering and rocking on their seats.

A retort had already formed: 'fat lot of thanks I get for taking you lot with me; I can tell you it'll be a long time before I offer again . . .' Then I caught Anna's eye. Friendly, calmly appraising the situation. There was a slight shift of her head. Let them be, she was telling me, they're just children. And with it, by implication: welcome, you're a woman too, you've crossed the line, Josie. Then, that's how I read it.

*

Late afternoon when I awoke. Dreams of home, of Dad, Anna, and the others. Then waking up to this whitewashed attic room with its old-fashioned furniture, flowered curtains, cracked blue bowl in which someone (Sylvia?) had arranged wallflowers and large white daisies.

I was off the bed in an instant and back into jeans and shirt. Despite it being late June it was cool so I opened one of the bags and rummaged through until I found a sweater, shut the lid and on second thoughts opened it again. Her present. Bow flattened and paper creased. Like me it had come a long way. I did what I could with the bow and left it beside the bed.

Felt odd. Was she around now? After all, how long can a meeting go on? Had she been watching me sleep? I opened the door and listened for sounds. None. I left the room and stood in the corridor. A cool breeze came from somewhere. The silence was peopleless, I felt sure. I started opening doors, inspecting, getting a handle on these surroundings.

The apartment was on the fourth floor, situated directly under the roof. Sloping walls, curtains. Recently-fixed windows cut right out of the roof to create light. Exposed beams. White walls. Polished wood floors. Gay colours of Afghan and Mexican rugs. Plants and bowls of flowers everywhere I looked.

The breeze was coming from the sitting room, a long narrow room facing down over the park and the rows and rows of houses, the density of London. The mind-boggling variety of roofs, of chimney stacks, of square shapes and curved, of spires and arches and turrets and I don't know what.

A low window opened into a valley between this house and the next and on it two white cats were stretched out asleep. The sun was trying to get out from behind the clouds. But failing. Too much of an effort. Yet the clouds themselves were glistening, sparkling, great puffed-up self-satisfied pillows, taking all the sun and refusing to pass any of it on to the Londoners who were no doubt forever hopefully in wait. Particularly those two cats. The thought of it took me slap-bang back into my childhood. 'If the sun comes out,' I can hear her saying, then she would fill the paddling pool, then we could have our strawberries and cream in the garden, then she would walk with us through the park to the swings, then she would make us soap bubbles and we could blow them from the top of the hill. So much magic if, if, the sun came out.

It came out now. Quite suddenly, heightening the rich colours of the room. Making me think how much I liked it. How it was strange, an adult room. Not a sign of a kid, not a toy anywhere. Not an item out of place. Not a room I'd had any part of. And yet everywhere there were resemblances to that other house, the house we'd all lived in together. In the colours, the flowers, the shells, the clumsiness of silver objects, her love of art nouveau, the decadence of the paintings, the way objects were grouped together, making me think why did no one else think of grouping them like that. Her style. So easy. So casual. It was overwhelmingly familiar. All of it. Like I'd always been here living amongst these objects. For two jello crackers I could have collapsed onto the sofa, and howled into red and grey cushions.

Moments later I heard the door open and someone with brisk steps make their way towards the room in which I was sitting. This is it, then. I drew breath.

It wasn't. 'Oh hi-ya, Sally.'

'Feel refreshed?'

'Yeah.'

'You certainly had a good long sleep. You'll be up till all hours tonight, I suppose.'

I wanted to say, 'Where is she?' but who'd be that gauche, that direct.

'I'm closing up now. So thought I'd pop up and see how you were making out before I left.'

She was a couple or so years older than I. Small, neat, languid. The regular English type, right out of a book. Tailored lilac skirt with a slit showing a part of neat, shapely leg. Deep yellow sweater, white blouse, a small row of pearls.

'Nice of you,' I said. 'Guess I was pretty bleary-eyed when I arrived this morning. Must have seemed a real dummy not even knowing she lived on the premises and that. But I've got it all together now. Ready for pretty much anything. So what do you suggest?'

'What do you mean?'

'Well – er – shall I start preparing a meal – or – this meeting will it be – I mean do they tend to go on into the evenings?'

'Oh golly,' she laughed. 'Thanks for reminding me. I'm terribly sorry.'

'S'okay.'

'No, but you see I forgot to give you her message. I'd have gone home still forgetting if you hadn't reminded me.'

I looked at her. I took my hair out of its braid and shook it out. Sally was in the process of straightening a crooked picture. Get it moving kid. Out with it. Sylvia's given you a bummer, that much is obvious. No wonder you almost forgot it. Who wants to be the unfortunate one to tell your boss's daughter that – come on. Step on the gas, kiddo, let's have the worst. Throw it me, straight. I'm a big girl now, you know. I can handle it.

When she turned to face me her cheeks were pink. Squeamish about emotions. I could see her trying to find the right words. Could imagine Sylvia saying to her, drop it as tactfully as you can.

'Let me guess. It's a meeting that's going to last till the end of August?'

She laughed and shook her head. 'It's just that, well, she is tied up this evening. She told me to give you some money for a meal from petty cash.'

I retied my plait. 'It'll be fun exploring the area.'

'It's just . . . I know how I'd feel in your place. And your first night here. It's not like her. It must be something especially important that's come up.' She glanced at her watch. 'Listen, there are a couple of extra keys for you in the top lefthand drawer of my desk. I'll leave my office open and you can collect them before you go out. You'll be okay, won't you?'

'Sure.'

'Cheers, then. See you tomorrow.' Then she was gone.

The apartment suddenly seemed painfully empty.

Sylvia, Mother, literary agent extraordinaire – for that is what someone called you in the course of yesterday evening – who would have thought that having got here I should still be wanting to write letters to you. I see now how very long it is going to be before I am

21

able to talk to you; really talk to you. Will these two and a half months be sufficient? Who knows. Maybe I shall write this out and leave it for you to read after I've gone. (Not dead and gone, but you know, gone gone.) You who read so many pages of written material, so I presume.

The time is the early hours. Can't tell when. Too lazy to get out of bed to go and look. Too warm also.

Last night I lay awake, listening. Waiting for your key in the lock. Then finally I heard it. My light was out, my eyes closed. Just in case. Your step. Quick, decisive, came nearer and nearer. Hesitated outside the door. I wanted to call out 'Come in', but I couldn't. Then I heard you making off along the corridor to your room. Or yours and Alison's. Do you just have two rooms to keep up appearances? All will no doubt become clear in time. Where is she, incidentally? Are you both hiding from me? That's what it feels like. And is it her you still live with?

Two years ago someone Dad knew from England – you might have known him too, his name is Alex Bruton – brought with him the English Sunday papers he'd been reading on the plane. The next morning over breakfast I heard him say to Anna, 'Look at this, that woman of Sylvia's has done pretty well for herself.' Do you remember? It was when she became editorial director of Harper & Wiskert. There was a full-page profile of her in the review section. No mention of you, of course. I read it greedily, in case. Very little, next to nothing, about her personal life. She hadn't married. Was married to publishing. A 12-hour working day. A charming flat – I can't remember if it mentioned Islington. A close circle of friends. Enjoyed travelling and escaping to the country at the weekends. Was often a guest at various weekend houseparties, etc. Most of the article was to do with how she became where and who she was, you know the sort of thing, by which I don't mean sexually.

Now I come to think of it, it was a clever article. Clever of her. For you were kept right out of it. Nothing was exposed. And reading it sitting on at the breakfast table after everyone had long since upped and left, all of sixteen, I remember I tingled with voracious nerve-racking excitement. Hoping yet dreading to find among the pages some sort of a scandal. Your name exposed. Something to make me angry and sorry for Dad and furious with you. Something that would draw the emotions like a needle being driven into the body to collect fluid. But there was nothing, nothing at all. The relief was compounded by a sensation of being terribly let down. I went out into the garden. The snow lay inches thick. I made snowballs, many of them, and smashed them against the snowbound trunks of the trees.

Past history. And now I'm shit scared. Of meeting with you over the breakfast table this morning. After all, we've got to meet sometime. Can't get out of it for ever. Of meeting you, of meeting her. Of taking in and becoming accustomed to your intimacy. Of a thousand things. And I guess, certainly all the signs point that way, that you must be feeling the same.

Let me describe for you last night's strange interlude.

Sally had told me to collect the keys from her desk. Apparently you'd left them for me and she'd forgotten to bring them up. I was in her office when a noise behind startled me. For you must know how spooky the building appears in the evening. Except, sorry, I forgot, you're not the emotional type.

It had begun to rain again. And a wind was working up to something of a gale, I reckoned. Doors were banging down empty corridors. I thought I heard someone come into the room behind me. I could sense a presence. Felt myself being observed. But I sure couldn't turn round and face whoever it was. In case it was you, perhaps. For you were everywhere in the building. In my thoughts, on the walls, in each individual book jacket pinned to the wall. It was you, and only you I was ready and waiting to throw my arms around. To claim.

'Rifling desks — is that your bag?' a low male voice — oh so English — said to a spot mid-way down my spine. I swung round. Stood with feet slightly apart, hands in my pocket, facing him.

'Just another part of the ever so friendly welcoming brigade, are you?'

I reckoned him to be about your age. He is of course a big man. From one over-eater to another there was an instant recognition. Wonder what his kick is. Not donuts in this country, you bet. His chin was covered with a fur of stubble. Stray wisps of his amazing white hair, appearing below his ears, made me want to get out the scissors straight away. A session in the kitchen like I do for the kids back home once every few months. A touch disreputable, wouldn't you say? That's how one could describe Jeremy Farmer. He's a state, wouldn't you say? Particularly with his clothes creased. Travelling all night, he said. Left wife and kids on in France for another week's holiday, while he had to get back. Popped in to look at the post.

'And was it interesting?'

He looked at me surprised. 'Disappointing.'

23

'Oh. Why's that?'

'Welcome to Fisk, Farmer & Tickle,' he said. 'You'll find out.'

'So you've worked out who I am?'

'Chip off the old block,' he actually said. And I could have hugged him. But restrained myself. Wait till I'd hugged you, I reckoned.

'Am I?' I couldn't help asking. I wanted to hear it all over. But the pleasure was denied me.

'Let's just say from the frontal rather than the posterior view, even after twelve hours in a train, and under a tenth of that asleep, I can still make out who you are.'

It was distinctly disappointing. I wanted to ask, what bits, you know. What bit particularly resembles . . . but I bit my lip. This time I shut up. Soon enough I'll see for myself. Soon. Soon.

'So, my new assistant,' he asserted.

'Your what?'

'Didn't Sylvia tell you? She's seconded you to my side of the show. You can type?'

'I can type.'

'Yes, well it suits me quite well since I happen to have just sacked my secretary.'

'Why's that?'

'Inquisitive, aren't you?'

'Interested.'

He laughed but said nothing. Then, 'I hope you're not planning to make it a holiday. Work load's heavy, you know.'

'Okay by me.' We appraised each other.

'The last time I saw you you were a little nipper with a skipping-rope.'

'Then we know each other already?'

'In a manner of speaking.'

'You look as if you could use another meal,' I said.

He laughed. 'What you mean is you could use one, and wherever Sylvia is I get the impression she isn't round to feed you.'

I nodded. Felt it then, from a vital place – why do they say 'bones' – that we were going to be pals, he and I. We're all going to be pals, darling mother. See how easy it'll be. Just get up now and make a first gesture towards me. Knock on my door.

We walked out into the light summer drizzle. He put up a large black umbrella which covered us both. In the park opposite the houses kids were kicking at a ball. An old guy in a grey track suit was running on the spot. Dogs were chasing one another while their owners chatted. Above, large silvery blue clouds moved swiftly.

Yesterday I was up in that. I felt light-headed.

'Here,' he touched my arm to guide me, 'this way.' I followed where he led. 'Your mother tells me you like books.' Now what kind of an opening was that? Skirting the Green we made a kind of zig-zag trail down one after another of the narrow streets, arriving finally at a dive I think he described as a neighbourhood Greek restaurant. He knew what to order and I just said, 'Ya, ya, okay with me' to any suggestion he made.

'Tell me about your holiday,' I said. And he did.

He sure knows how to entertain a person. After the second glass of rough red wine – I'm mostly into cokes back home – I wondered if he'd entertain me with stories of you. 'She's a literary agent extraordinaire,' he said. 'And for the rest, you've got the whole summer to find out. You don't need me to tell you, Josie.'

'Nope, I suppose I don't. It's just that –'

'Tell me about Canada. About your brothers and sisters. About life back home.'

'Nope,' I said, 'shut your eyes, and tell me if you can imagine what your wife is doing right this minute.'

'Christ,' he said.

'Why? What?'

'Christ,' he said again.

So I did tell him about Canada, about the kids, about the cold in Edmonton, about the lodge, about breaking the ice and collecting the firewood at 30 degrees under, while we ate sweet pastries and settled into a second bottle of that rasping, grapey wine. And the more time went by the more he laughed and the more he laughed the more I talked; recounting incident after incident of our family life which had never struck me as funny or in any way out of the ordinary until that moment. 'Geeze, what an audience!'

'Are you talking about me?'

'They don't come like you in Canada,' I told him straight.

'You know,' he said, as we walked back along the dark wet streets, 'you've got a gift.'

'Yeah?'

'A gift,' he said, 'and it wouldn't be hard to see where it comes from.'

'Yeah,' I said again.

I wasn't for pressing him. Nor on that other raw nerve I'd exposed. There was I walking back under his large black umbrella, with my chum – and yours – who'd just said I had a gift, who'd just for the second time linked me with you. Nothing so good has happened all this last bleak year at UBC. Hugging my 'gift' I said goodnight to him and put my key in the lock. And now suddenly I think I'll go back to sleep again. I think I have no choice. See you later. Yours with a gift, ha! Josie.

'Josie.'

I was a kid. Lying in bed, snug and warm. My two blankets and eiderdown made the perfect shape over my body. I moved down into the depths of the bed (it was always just a bit scary) so that not even one strand of my hair would give the clue to my existence.

'Josie, you little rabbit,' she laughed. 'Come up this instant.' I felt light firm fingers tickling my rib cage through my blankets. I wriggled and squirmed and giggled. I felt her beginning to pull on the bedclothes and from inside the bed I grabbed them and with all my might held them tight. Pegging them down as we had that summer in the garden. 'Josie,' she said. 'I'll count to ten.' Of course I waited till the nine and three-quarters. If nothing else, for the fun of having her there, waiting for me. Of hearing the sing-song voice of her counting. Of having her there. Besides, who wants to go to school one's first day? 'Nine and three-quarters.' Now we were daring one another. Would she call my bluff? No, she settled for nine and seven-eighths. 'That's the very last, Josie. Either the rabbit comes out of its hole, or I'll have to –' I threw the blankets back.

'I'm coming, I'm coming.' I woke out of a deep sleep. I groped for my watch. 8.15. Pushing the hair out of my face, feet cold on bare floorboards, I made for the door.

'Did anyone call?'

'I did.'

'You did?'

'I'm making breakfast. Will toast and coffee suit you? Or do you like a full cooked breakfast?'

'Toast and coffee. Please. Sylvia . . .'

'Are you dressed?'

'No.'

'Hurry then.'

'You haven't got all day to waste?'

There was silence from the kitchen. I could have kicked myself. But I did hurry; racing into my jeans and pulling out of the case a clean if somewhat crumpled blue and white check shirt. Shoes could be left till later. Hair too. On second thoughts, catching sight of myself as I was about to leave the room, I brushed it swiftly and tied it back in a band at the nape of my neck. I opened the door a second time and listened cautiously. There were only sounds of one in the kitchen. Maybe she'd asked Alison to stay in bed for an extra half an hour. Give her a headstart. Give us time to be reunited. Something like that. Would they kiss good-morning? Of course I could cope.

'I'm a woman too,' I'd said to Dad. 'It might be disgusting to you. But not to me,' I'd nodded, nonchalant, like I'd become this last year away from home. 'You see that kind of thing all the time at UBC.' Liar. But he wasn't to know. His eyebrows had shot up. And sometimes I wondered why they just didn't stay like that permanently. Poor decent Dad. All of life seemed to have surprised him. Sylvia, us kids with our ways he called 'North American' or 'new-fangled', Anna becoming pregnant when he'd set his mind on us five being quite enough for him to handle – not to mention support. And now my determination to come to England, and far worse, having had the effrontery, the temerity, to go ahead and more or less arrange it without even consulting him. So the image of women disporting themselves in front of his daughter's eyes on the campus of UBC was just one more shock along the line. And though it was a lie, it helped my cause.

It was a long corridor. Making my way down it towards the kitchen I felt like a bride walking up the aisle. As if it's taking for ever. She had the radio on. A Mozart violin concerto. I regretted that I'd stopped practising last year. Oh well, just one more part of my life that had gone overboard. I stood at the kitchen door. I held on to it. And it moved on its hinges and I found myself in a stupid gangly position moving with it.

There she was. My mother. Tall, dark, faint first traces of silvery white in her very deep brown hair. Upright, graceful, slender. Beautifully outfitted in coffee-coloured suit with cream silk shirt and cream shoes. Slender and beautiful and contained and penetratingly remote.

'You'll pull the door out of the wall if you hang on like that. Come to the table. The toast's only been out of the toaster this last minute or two, so you'll find it quite warm, I think. Orange juice before coffee? Or just coffee?'

I sat down at the table. The impossibility of hugging her hit me forcefully. I looked away out of the small long window at the skyline. Lighter today, more translucent. A pearly grey. I didn't *think* it was raining. Give me strength, I prayed. Give me a way of seeing what to do.

27

She poured orange juice and coffee and, sitting opposite me, gestured to the toast rack.

'Do take some.'

'Thanks.' I tried to imagine her joking around with Jeremy as I had been last night. I tried to imagine her having a cosy breakfast with Alison. I tried to imagine her in any other situation.

'Well,' she said.

'Yeah, well. Should we shake hands?'

It was over her eyelids rather than her brow that I noticed tension, the lines of a frown. Her nails were well manicured, elegant, in perfect keeping with the rest of her. Carefully, she sparingly buttered her brown toast and spread marmalade. Homemade. One of Alison's country weekends?

'I do apologise for last night, Josie.'

'It's okay, honestly. No hassle.' I tried to smile at her reassuringly.

'It's just that business takes precedence. You'll find that's something you'll have to accept. I can't just down tools, just because . . .'

'It's okay, it's okay.' Now why did she need to say that? We sat on in silence.

'You're not eating anything.'

'Despite my reputation with the donuts!' I laughed.

She looked at the clock on the wall behind me.

'Look, there's a phone call I have to make. I'll be back in a moment. Pour yourself another cup of coffee if you like.'

When she returned to the table the lines in her eyelids had smoothed themselves out.

'Actually I had a great evening.'

'I'm delighted to know that.'

'Yeah, Jeremy took me out to dinner. He came in for some post, he said, and – and we were both hungry so he took me to a Greek restaurant. We got on ever so well. I'm looking forward to working for him. Though of course I'd much prefer to work for you.'

'That's excellent.'

'I'm sure I can be a help.' Oh stop this fawning, Josie.

'I'm sure you can, Josie.'

'My flight was good, by the way.'

'Fine, fine,' she picked up the newspaper and started to read.

When Alison appeared I could have hugged her. Anything to break that earth-shattering silence.

She must be in her mid-forties. Smart now. Wearing tweed trousers and loose-fitting jacket. Battered but polished lace-up shoes. Longer nose than I remembered. Lively grey eyes. She used glasses to read the paper. They took *The Guardian* and *The Times* and swapped them around. Alison reading avidly while she ate. Her voice was gruff but not unattractive.

She had the air of success. Of someone who'd arrived. Or was I just influenced by the newspaper article? She did ask about the flight. She listened while I answered. Her eyes seemed wise. As if she'd seen a hell of a lot of life. Was it all those screwy authors, I wondered? She looked different to Dad and Anna and all their lot. She looked different to all those stuffy professors at UBC. She looked the real thing. Someone one could talk to. Whereas Sylvia. Geeze.

Faintly strange sitting between these two women — faintly! Waiting for something to happen like a hug, a kiss, something I could take exception to. Something that would prove Dad right. 'You'll hate it, you'll feel horribly uncomfortable, darling.' 'Oh Dad, I'm grown-up now.' Join the grown-ups.

Is that what I'm doing sitting between these women? Two women. With their cats and their secrets. Their work and their love. And all being observed by fresh eyes. All right, critical eyes. Eyes of one too close, in some ways, for comfort. Okay, I give it to you, Sylvia, it can't be easy. For you perhaps more than for her. You who left us all, you who didn't want us all, you who made a choice: you who must feel I've come back partially to judge you. And who wants to be judged? A deal then. I won't judge. I'll try not to. But will you accept? Could you help me? Or is that too much to ask?

The breakfast seems to take for ever. And the quiet, heh! And now again the sound of gentle rain on the panes. No storm this. Just pretty much continual drizzle.

Childhood impressions are stronger. Hot days and cold, sunshine, wind, downpours. The fun of getting caught out as we trudged over heath and hill. One or perhaps two being pushed by Sylvia in the increasingly worn pram. A downpour meant excitement. She too loved moments like that. Caught our thrill of the unexpectedness. Or perhaps created it and transposed it onto us. Her 'small adventures' she'd term them. Before the large one. She loved to get her hair wet. I remember that so well. No scarf or woolly hat for her. She'd look up at the darkened sky, her face full of relish. Shaking her hair this way and that as large drops fell fast. 'Quick, Josie,' she'd say. 'Help me push this pram.' And I'd push with her, the others laughing and running behind us, faster, faster. How gay we were. We would wave at other families also running to avoid the outburst. And home we'd arrive, triumphant and exhilarated. She was so swift. Within instants clothes had been changed, hair dried with warm towels, crumpets were heating under the broiler, to be spread with strawberry jam and honey —

The quiet consistent relentless rain, on the other hand, that's nothing and everything, I don't remember at all. But now it penetrated as persuasively as salt in the cooking-water.

Breakfast like this I had not known. At home it is always one hell of a scramble. Kids late for school; Dad hunting for something or other he's mislaid, tears over eggs too runny or too hard; tears over homework not done; everyone clammering for everyone's attention, most of all Anna's. At college, the cafeteria was a riot of noise. Shuffling, pushing, sweaty unwashed bodies. Tables wet with juice slopped and sticky with crumbs. And that continual buzz of students describing their last night's activities. And then there was the donut diner.

Here in this long low attic kitchen the surfaces were so clean. So much space. So little of it populated. I had the kind of feeling these two characters weren't messy enough. Almost as if having done something so well and truly messy they had to be entirely the other way in their personal life. I tried a few comments. A joke. A what I was sure was a brilliant analysis of Lowry's *Ultramarine* which I had just finished reading, concluding with, 'he made his first voyage too, you know, when he was eighteen.' But any ideas I might have had for livening their breakfast, for making contact, fell to the rain, like pellets of chocolate sinking into not yet hardened icing. Alison smiled. Sylvia did not. Okay ... okay, like I know for some breakfast can be a sacred time. I'll adapt. I can handle silence too.

When they made a move, so did I. And I was quicker on the draw than either of them.

'Beat you to the washing-up.' A look passed between them. Something that almost passed for a real expression in her face. But I couldn't yet tell what it was.

'That's good of you, Josie.' Alison.

'Of course, I do it at home. We all help. I don't want you to think I'm in any way going to be a burden.'

Another exchange. Invisible mysterious sign language.

'I'm sure you won't be.' This time Sylvia.

Half an hour later I was following Sylvia out of the apartment and down to her office. Alison had left minutes earlier. Back in my room after our abortive breakfast, while making my bed, I had left the door open. Heard the two of them talking in low voices in the

30

corridor. Heard the turn of the latch. Alison's 'Have a good day then, both of you.' Sylvia's 'Bye. Thanks, Alison.' Two middle-aged women. 'We just liked each other best' I remembered some aged writer on a programme I once saw, saying about her life-long female companion. We just liked each other best. Was that all it was? Was that sufficient to tear her away from us and turn her into this person whose brittle taut body now preceded me downstairs towards the office of Fisk, Farmer & Tickle? Oh Sylvia, you're my *MOTHER*, I wanted to shout, *REMEMBER*? For a moment I seemed to be propelled towards her, to touch her – Then she had opened the door and was safely inside the outer office with Sally smiling attendance and I was being directed to go and find Jeremy further down the corridor.

The first day set the pattern for the days that followed. Silent breakfasts. The three of us reading the two papers. The small radio on top of the fridge turned to the classical music programme. When the sun shone, the window was open. The sky always seemed part of the breakfasts. All three of us drank orange juice (freshly made by Sylvia the previous evening just before she went to bed) and coffee, home-ground (supplied by Alison who passed a very good coffee shop on her way to work), and ate toast with marmalade or Alison's homemade jams. Sometimes croissants or brioches. Often peaches, plums, cherries. There was a continual change of flowers in the pewter bowl in the middle of the table, and in my room, I noticed.

These breakfasts, neo-silent affairs except for a grudging comment on the subject of coffee or a reference to the book reviews (always read with eager concentration – by myself too, from the first I was determined to be in on everything), I began to adapt to. Silence, I could handle. And gradually I began even to welcome it, for without the noisy chatter which had so far accompanied almost all eating occasions, everything else became clear and sharp in relief.

As I ceased to try for a breakfast joke, ceased to attempt to engage the others, so they relaxed into what I took to be their general pattern. Though Sylvia in the mornings rarely looked in my direction, nor did she withdraw, ward off. And gradually I felt less clumsy, less of an imposer. I heard my chair squeak less. I stopped fearing that I would slop my coffee or break the marmalade pot. We left the table at the same time. I no longer needed to say 'I'll wash up.'

31

Shortly after breakfast, Alison would leave the apartment. Her firm was in the centre of town. Sylvia would then take an extra twenty minutes or so grooming herself. This was a vital part of her appearance and performance. The mother I had once known in those far-off days, which were fast becoming nothing more than the realm of nostalgia, had been naturally and carelessly beautiful. Tall, dark, vital, very beautiful skin, I seemed to remember. Her clothes were often scruffy. Mauve trousers, open-toed sandals, long skirts and narrow close-fitting bodices. I remembered a kind of look of a faded gypsy. Even the same musky smell, the large heavy silver bracelets and amber beads. A long casualness of limbs. A sexuality, I suppose, though I didn't think of it like that then.

What I was aware of was that around her there was a buzz. Dad was noticeably affected by it. Us children. Other parents. She always seemed to be in the centre of admiring friends. And indolent, as if only half contained in action.

Now her looks, though still magnificent, no longer had the same indolence. On the contrary they were being used for effect. Every last drop of them. And that, to the mind of this daughter, suited her less well. Gave a sharpness, a prostitution to those looks. I wanted her to keep them for me, for us. Was it simply that her looks were part of her job, no different to that of an actress or film star, in that they took on some other quality: the quality of unnatural use? Or was it that as Jeremy had said to me laughingly at the end of my first week, 'But agency is a kind of prostitution, what can you expect, Josie?' But I am getting ahead of myself.

Her wardrobe was legion. Usually having retired from the breakfast table she firmly shut the door of her bedroom, but on my fourth day – was it because she was less frightened of what I would do; jump on her, shout at her, accuse her, even fling my arms round her neck, make, in effect, any undignified emotional gesture; did she feel sufficiently reassured after our fourth incident-free breakfast that such would not be my method, despite the emotional high drama of the blackmail of my letters – she called out to me through her now opened door.

Her voice was low and sonorous. Made me think of church bells. For years, simply years, against all our new accents I had heard her voice in my sleep, woke to find that she hadn't returned after all. And her voice was the same now. Painfully alluring, calling one to it like a mermaid enticing one to the sea. Only like every other bit of her it was now contained at the edges. Where previously the hum of the word just finished would trail off into an ever-receding horizon, now the end of each word would cut off as if it had been clipped, as if messiness of any kind had once led her into disaster areas and now always she had to be on her toes.

'Josie, come here a minute, will you.'

I entered her bedroom for the first time. The first official time. I had, of course, nosed around that first solitary evening in the apartment. Just to get the feel of the place. In Sylvia's room I had not stayed long. Not because it wasn't alluring, and unexpected. But because I wanted to come into Sylvia's presence, into her life, through the right means. Not sneakily. I had two and a half months to know my mother and she to know me. This wasn't a one-night affair, as they say. We had time.

The unexpectedness of the room stemmed from its monkishness. It was in direct contrast to the sitting room and the country prettiness of the kitchen with its deep red mugs and pottery and pewter vases and candlesticks and sycamore wood table and chairs. The room was large and plain. The walls were a pale terracotta and the duvet cover on the large double bed the same colour. On the walls were one or two black and white drawings (by the same artist), abstract and intense, making me think of heaven and hell, but for all that rather lost to the overall colour of the walls, unless one peered closely as I did now. For I was nervous in her presence. Nervous that I would do something unseemly. Nervous, crazy as it might seem, that I might cry, cry out, 'Oh why did you forsake us?'

On both sides of the bed were low white shelves, containing, of course, many books. On the floor, the wooden floorboards were uncovered except for two small, square gaily coloured rugs, oatmeal with bright strange animals, unicorns, rhinoceroses, and others I couldn't make out but took to be mythical animals.

'Tibetan,' she said, seeing my glance.

'Oh, oh.'

Very little else. A window facing over the house's delightfully unruly backyard, where roses climbed metres high, morning glory, out now with its large white flowers suffocating a number of bushes whose species I couldn't make out. Pear and apple trees were beginning to make their this year's fruit. Huge marigolds, holly-hocks and some kind of wild poppy grew in clusters. My room and the sitting room both looked out over the park in the front. The kitchen set at the side of the house, gave a view of skyline and roof tops. This was the first time I had looked down on the garden.

'Do you use it?' I asked.

'What's that?'

She was through an arch in a small inner room, where three enormous cupboards all had their doors open. I moved nearer so that she could hear what I was saying. Dresses, skirts, shirts, pant suits, every conceivable garment greeted my eye, and in the bottom of these cupboards in their legions, her shoes. She was looking at herself critically in the mirror which was the entire door of one of the cupboards.

'Josie, can you sew?'

'More or less.'

'More or less?'

'Kind of the basics. Anna taught us some.'

'Yes, I remember Anna's sewing.' She gave a little private laugh. 'Is it a tear?'

'I've caught my hem. See here. Damned annoying.'

She looked at her watch and as if it was catching I looked at mine.

'I have just a few minutes, and still haven't quite finished my eye make-up. Otherwise I wouldn't ask you. Could you . . .' She didn't look at me, but at my reflection in her large mirror. And I, speaking at her back but hoping that it would penetrate through to where it would matter, said I'd try to do as neat a job as possible.

She stepped out of her skirt and standing in black and white shirt and black satin slip she passed over to me first the skirt and then delving further into one of the cupboards, a wicker sewing basket. There was something about her in this state of undress that raised my heart and troubled me deeply. Troubled me and drew me. Only she, I thought, can create such a chord inside and cause such distress.

After the wrench most of my childhood life had seemed simple as apple pie in comparison. I had not been a bad-looking child, with some of my mother's features, tall too and dark, though not as dark as her. My face was broader, more of Dad. Features that were perfect on her face were cast in a different mould on mine. But as Dad always used to say when I dressed up for my first high school dances on those far-away Saturdays at the Barn Club, 'Josie darling, let me look at you. You can certainly pass muster. Keep that dimple in your cheek, just keep smiling and they'll all be falling at your feet.' That was it, I could pass muster. Beyond that I didn't give the matter much thought. We were outdoor kids, mostly wearing jeans and sneakers, daring each other to feats on bikes, in trees, on horseback.

Then in my teens I became less interested in these things, sat around reading, had to be ferreted out of the house by Dad, as one

34

might a pickle out of a jar. By Dad, never by Anna. For a load of reasons: because she was only twelve years older than myself, because her temperament was placid and domestic, because, perhaps, I was my mother's daughter, and the eldest, she played the role more often of a big sister than made any attempt to take me over or become a second mother. And then there were so many of us and so much to do. Impossible almost to have time for individual quirkiness. Perhaps too, it was discouraged. The healthy outdoor environment, few pretty clothes, most of the artistic sense we had in our London home, most of that sense of whimsy and faint decadence, most of the allure too, strictly ruled out, kept at bay, even in the way Dad for a long time tried to guide my reading and my tastes, kept at bay just in case.

I would lie if I didn't say that for the most part it was happy and harmonious. Except for some of those nightmares. Having lost wretchedly we were lucky in what we were left with. We were lucky over Anna. She could have been mean, devious, jealous, bitchy. Except for the all-vital once she was none of those things. Except for the all-vital one time she was an approving and positive force. It was then as if I could stay asleep cocooned in our Edmonton life all would be simple enough. School was enjoyable. Friends came readily, though superficially. Buddies were easily available. One just had to keep that little bit of oneself back. At home it wasn't hard to be the good daughter. Actually I liked hard work, it suited my nature. And more or less I liked the other kids and felt a special responsibility for them because I was older than them, had seen more when it happened to us all, felt they looked to me and I had to help them through.

'Try and set a good example, darling,' Dad would say. 'Anna's been so good to you and you know well that what you do the others will follow.' And as long as I stayed firmly planted in the easy-rolling North American life that they had established for themselves it wasn't hard. Their life was like their sitting room, I thought. Fitted carpets, surfaces of tables and chairs that were cleanable, comfortable, utilitarian. No need for much care and polish. No hidden corners, no areas lit with a darker glow than the rest. The same light picked up evenly every aspect, every contour. Rooms they would say were for sitting in, talking in, playing games of Racing Demons and Irish Rummy in, for family occasions; not for dreams.

As long as I planted my loyalty with all that, the essence of my days was unruffled. Perhaps that's why I was reluctant to grow up.

35

A large armchair with anglepoise light over it, perfect for evening reading, was almost the only furniture in my mother's room other than the bed. Sitting in it I set about the task of sewing as neatly as I possibly could the part of the hem of her skirt that had come unstitched. The room was quiet. She remained throughout in the inner room, under two large bright lights, applying her make-up.

She and I were about the same height. Her limbs would touch the same parts of this chair while she sat reading. And yet what a difference. I felt myself, as never before, gangling, awkward, outside – for ever – the charmed circle. I also felt that she remained in the inner room not only because it was necessary for the task in hand but because my presence made it inevitable.

During my first year at UBC I had eaten with relish, stuffed with vengeance. After Dave it seemed almost the only thing I could do. And once I started there was no stopping. The girls who dormed with me teased me but I breezed through, making jokes that kept them at bay. At home it was a different matter. Dad was concerned, from a medical point of view, as he put it. 'As to your looks that's your own business, Josie.' 'You're bloody right it is!' 'No need to swear,' he'd said sadly, like almost all of Dad's utterances to me these days, as if he was in defeat.

But now my heavy thighs, my jeans that felt as if they'd been filled too full, my sweaters stretching over tummy and bottom, even the new way of walking, standing, sitting which had evolved with this added weight, felt so at variance with her presence that it added to my discomfort. And cutting across the dash and determination of the front that I liked to think that I presented consistently to the world, the devil may care, haven't you read *Fat is a Feminist Issue*, geeze what a restriction, food is good, let it all happen, don't tell me anything, sort of attitude, was a longing to belong, to be of her world, to be drawn in, to be loved by Sylvia. As if harmony, any harmony that followed would only come from that impossible task.

Sitting across from her, watching her back as she surveyed herself in that large mirror, I put the last stitch in her skirt and cut the remaining thread as close to the material as I could. I felt myself praying that I wouldn't always be like that, that I wouldn't always go through life speaking to her back.

My little task over, I handed the skirt back to her.

'Thank you.'

It was flat. But it was there. We left the room and I followed her down to the office.

My early days were not with Sylvia. She had skilfully arranged this and, as time went by, I became grateful for her forethought. Wanting to please, eager as I was to please, being in the position in those early days of being drawn to her presence, drawn to make any kind of gesture of supposed helpfulness, only to fail over and over again. Knocking perpetually on a door that wouldn't open, though sometimes it seemed to quiver, was exhausting.

That being the case, though I was cross and disappointed to be fobbed off with Jeremy, and in some ways, counted it quite impatiently as wasted time, I was also relieved. Had I had more wisdom I could have even commended the instinct for survival that led her to this decision. Or was it chance, just the facts of the business, just that she didn't need any extra help and Jeremy clearly did? How hard to dislodge oneself from the centre of the universe.

The offices of Fisk, Farmer & Tickle were on the first floor of this gigantic and rather strangely built early Victorian house which Jeremy called a 'folly'. The offices didn't make up a self-contained unit but rather all rooms opened directly onto the central landing in the middle of which was a huge stairwell. In any North American building an elevator shaft would have been fitted into the central pit. But not here. Fun it was to look over the carved banister down to the oak floor and enormous potted plants that occupied the ground floor. Any of my brothers and sisters would have been tempted to throw sweet papers down. I know I wanted to myself. For I had at this early stage discovered English toffees. 'Plain Jane' with almonds in them. What a lift!

Over the front of the building on the first floor, then, was Sylvia's gracious office, with a dividing door into Sally's smaller one. On the other side of the corridor were four more rooms. Two were offices, Jeremy's and Alan Boddington's. Then something they called the 'library', around the walls of which manuscripts were meant to be kept in alphabetical order under the author's name. In the centre of the room, a conference table. And at the back of the building down a few stairs and on a half landing, the minuscule kitchen and equally minuscule washroom.

This then was Fisk, Farmer & Tickle; Tickle, by the way, was nowhere in evidence. Alan Boddington, in his thirties, I guess, a good ten years younger than the other two, came in the afternoons only. For a time no one was willing to say what he did in the mornings and I fantasised quite a number of black possibilities. For a time no one was ready to say anything much. Not even Jeremy. But then I asked a lot of questions, and they were all very busy. So there was no way I could have suspected it was anything more than English reticence. At its best. And worst.

Sally, at the point when I arrived, was the only secretary. Jeremy had recently sacked his. Alan mostly did his own work, sometimes twisting Sally's arm to type a long letter or 'bung out a contract'.

The corridor seemed to act as a natural division. In the front, rather grandly, 'her majesty's office' which is how, when they let their hair down, they laughingly referred to her. She and Sally, symbiotic in their working unity, provided a distinctly superior female air. The better equipment and standard of decoration across the corridor was noticeable. In small things too: attractive ashtrays whereas our lot shared one gigantic one that seemed to have been pinched from a pub, an up-to-date *Writers' and Artists' Yearbook* (our camp had one two years old), the only *Writers' Market Place*, the only *Who's Who*, the only good dictionary; all of which I was from time to time requested to cross the corridor to collect for the men. And each evening, no doubt sent by my meticulous mother, Sally would invariably come back to retrieve them before leaving.

Our rooms were shabbier, more down-beat. It was hard to find the basics, like an extra pencil or rubber. The typewriter on the desk to which I had been assigned struck me as being as old as the building. 'Is this an heirloom or what?' I asked Jeremy. 'Surely you don't expect me to type on this thing?' But apparently he did. There were coffee cups still a quarter full dotted around on the window-sills, looking as if they had definitely not been drunk from the day before. Two cactus plants whose earth was as dry and as crumbly as bread crumbs seemed to be expiring their last breath, having given up on all hope of receiving water.

There was about these rooms to the back of the building something of the atmosphere of a boys' club, not so much the sophomore boys' halls at UBC but something which had affinities with that. Somewhere between that and the kind of men's clubs that Dickens or Pepys or one of the eighteenth-century English writers might have described. Down-beat it might be, but relaxed and matey in a way that the front rooms were not. The pressure not as pervasive. The camaraderie of good jokes, the smell of pipe (Alan's), lack of time-keeping, of which Sylvia noticeably disapproved. (Like more important things of which I was in ignorance then.)

Sometimes she would forage her way into this domain of ours. More often meetings were held in her room, and for conferences the library was used. It was much more often that those from the back rooms stepped over the corridor and entered her domain than she entered theirs.

But it didn't always work that way. And when she entered our domain there was a quickening of pace, a sitting in a more upright posture, legs off desks, etc. Books usually piled on every surface, even on the two low chairs that made up a kind of sofa, were cleared so that she could perch somewhere. And once in this atmosphere, perching lightly like a kind of glorious rare bird, she seemed not out of place, or if so not in a way which made her uncomfortable, but which seemed to suit and heighten her specialness. Her eyes would quicken. Her own colour would glow underneath her skilful make-up. Again the thought would occur to me, a touch of gypsy. As if one had escaped years ago, done something as unlikely and highly romantic as found in the pages of some of the trashy manuscripts I was now having the honour and dubious pleasure of being asked to peruse: something as unlikely as marrying a duke. Only to return years later and be pleasantly tempted by those same gypsies, or kindred souls.

Tempted she might have been, but every bit the duke's wife, so to speak. And with an iron will. Which drew the men towards her. She it was who held the purse strings. I could see that from the first. Without any need to look at the accounts. She who seemed to make the two men (all of us) jump to her tune. She who caused a stir when she appeared in our quarters, caused things to be done, appointments to be kept, made decisions which from the start struck me (with no knowledge of business at all) as eminently more business-like than those emerging from some of the rambling discussions between Alan and Jeremy. She was the boss, that was for sure. And she liked it that way. She must. And yet. I don't know how soon it was that I first sensed an underlying unease, sensed it and was sufficiently unparanoid to be able to recognise it as not necessarily having anything to do with myself.

The large building had five floors, that is if you counted the basement – which most of the buildings' inhabitants appeared not to. The basement held the same number of rooms as each of the other main floors. But was unused. All the doors hung open on their hinges. The walls were running with damp. The paint was peeling. There were cracks in the plaster. 'Wet rot, dry rot, woodworm, you name it,' Jeremy said when I asked him about it.

'But why doesn't anyone do anything about it? They're all good rooms. Must be a waste. Besides, won't the whole building be affected? Why, I know at home when –'

'Yes, yes, of course you're right. It's just one of those things. You don't understand; and then it's not really our problem, but the landlord's.'

'Oh, the landlord's. How do you mean?'

'Josie.' He would turn back to reading with the utmost concentration. With the air of someone who was working hard. Contemplating great things. And I would type another letter on that typewriter that punched a hole where every 'o' should be – amongst its many eccentricities.

The ground floor was rented by two more literary agencies. The first floor us. The second, the apartment (residential) of the freeholder who was rarely in evidence. The attic floor us. Such was the building. Such was this domain into which I had plunged with such urgency, such determination.

'Hi, Jeremy.'

No answer. Jeremy was reading his post, his eyes glued to the letter he was holding, his face more intent and serious than I had yet seen it. This was somewhere towards the end of my first working week at Fisk, Farmer, etc. I had noticed that nobody pronounced the Tickle. It was as if he (or she) had indeed become an etc.

The working days had begun to fall into something of a pattern. I liked patterns and tended to create them even where there weren't any. Jeremy, as I quickly fathomed, was erratic in many ways. Firstly his hours. If you were sitting at your desk at nine-fifteen you might wait till eleven or afterwards for his entrance. Almost never before half ten. Though there was one day when I breezed in to find him sitting at his desk and groaning 'Where the hell have you been? I've been needing some help' (by which he meant someone to dictate to).

'Hold on. I'm not a moment late. You know my family; punctual as clockwork. How long have you been here?'

'Hours. Listen, be a honey and go and buy me a roll and some coffee, will you?'

I couldn't help wondering if he'd been there all night. And for a moment my mind went back to that outburst in the restaurant.

He seemed to work in fits and starts. Between the two there were periods of what I can only describe as active non-production. During these he would stare fiercely out of the window, sometimes for hours on end, and be deaf to any comments made, even on the 'would you like some coffee?' level. He would assume the air of a man contemplating great things, brilliant strategic ploys perhaps, which needed the concentration of a chess player.

If the phone rang at such times, which it did continually, he would appear to hardly notice its urgent call. Sometimes I would move over to his desk and pick it up for him. 'The phone for you, Jeremy,' I would say. 'Bruce Hall from CBT wanting a word.' I would hold the receiver out to him and still he would look out of the window. Time would go by. I would wonder if he'd heard, whether I should repeat my announcement, whether I should apologise to Bruce Hall. But just then he would with an enormous sigh give up his contemplation and pick up the receiver. And stare into it. 'Bruce . . .' I'd whisper. More seconds went by. I found myself holding my breath. And then his voice, urbane, easy. And I would hear him fitting back into his agent's groove or whatever it was, pleasant, concerned, the nice chap, the joker.

After these conversations he might take me into his confidence, he might be sufficiently fired up to shoot off a shower of letters, or he might leave his desk in a hurry in order to find Alan or Sylvia and not be seen again for hours, or he might lapse back into silence.

Of course there was a lot that I wanted to ask, a lot that I wanted to know (everything). And sometimes he partially obliged. Sometimes not at all. I had difficulty gauging the whys and wherefores. But that was all right. Not a problem, as they say. His erratic changes of moods suited my own. And since the pace for any secretary was not exactly hot by any standards, my inadequate typing was adequately covered for in the many slack periods I had, when letters could be re-typed two or three times if necessary. It did occur to me to wonder what his last secretary could possibly have been fired for. It seemed on the face of it such a very easy job.

Naturally I was keen to be as much use as possible. Sylvia had on my first day mentioned the conference room. 'Whenever Jeremy doesn't need you,' she'd said, 'you can make yourself useful by sorting the scripts in the conference room (library). They're meant to be filed alphabetically but, as you'll see, to the right of the door as you go in are quite a pile of manuscripts now that we haven't had time to sort. So that's something you might like to work your way through.'

So it became my pattern to spend the first hour or so of every day in the conference room, sorting, collating, re-labelling. The system that had grown up, if it was a system, could only be described as unique to the firm of Fisk, Farmer & Tickle, like the legal system or the English language, grounded in precedent rather than any overall view. Whenever I asked why one thing was done one way or another, some historical incident in the firm's much varied past was called to account. Which made it nigh impossible for anyone who hadn't been there since the firm's inception to do anything as normally simple as find a script. Neither Jeremy nor Alan seemed to be able to find their way around it. Both asked Sally whenever they wanted anything. As did I. And she asked Sylvia.

I was convinced the system could usefully be changed. And broached it with Sylvia my third morning, not over breakfast – hopefully I was learning my lessons – but once she was safely ensconced behind her desk and her roses and had already given her morning nod of acknowledgement to Sally, who was busy opening the post. I'd already taken Jeremy's post into our room and laid it on his desk. Ready for the moment some two hours later when he would no doubt make his appearance. Now I darted back into Sylvia's room past Sally's raised eyebrows.

'Sylvia, have you got a moment?'

'What is it?'

Hating to stand gaggling by her desk I sat on one of the comfortable armchairs and faced her with my suggestion for innovation. I used words like 'systems' and 'time-effective' and 'efficiency'. I had it all planned.

She appeared to frown, the way she did, creasing up her eyelids. And I hated it and felt sickened that I should once again be the one to make this happen. But dared myself on, knowing super sure that she'd be pleased in the long run. I wanted to leave a trail of legacies, Josie's super-efficiencies making their mark on Fisk, Farmer etc.; it was as simple as that. I wanted to help. Frankly I was dying to help. She must be going to let me.

'How thoughtful of you, Josie.'

'You think it's an okay scheme then?'

'I've said yes. Sally, pop in here for a moment will you. Josie?'

'Oh – okay then. Okay. Thanks.' It was as if something I'd picked up on my shoes when I'd gone out earlier to smell the roses (and to pick some surreptitiously so that our office enjoyed them too) stuck my feet to the floor. I was sure there was more to be said. More we should say. But I couldn't think what. And hated Sally to observe all this from under her fair and finely pencilled eyebrows. Somehow I picked up my feet and left the room.

In the library I set to work with vigour. The project, I was determined, would give point and purpose to the first hours of each morning.

It was Friday. The last day of my first week at Fisk, Farmer. A whole week. I was hung up on the cliché, Canada seems a lifetime away. A lifetime. And UBC further. The working life, geeze I knew it'd be for me. And here in London in this funny old house, all these books, all these authors, and all this business, this hurrying and scurrying, this doing something in the real world. This even pretending to be pooped in the evening, this lazing back with Alison and Sylvia as they sipped their whisky and soda and gin and tonic respectively.

I didn't actually say, as they did, 'What a hard day.' But as they sipped their drinks and I munched at the peanuts, I mouthed it to myself, imagined saying it to my mates, if I had any. Imagined saying it to the kids at home. I was sufficiently close to real work, I reckoned, to know what it was like. And it was heady. Fisk, Farmer seemed the centre of the universe, the most exciting place. Besides I'd hung through the first week and no one seemed like pushing me out yet.

'Jeremy, do you reckon I'm a good thing?' No, no hope from him this morning. He was still looking at the same letter with a glazed look on his face. I sensed something was wrong.

I'd been counting on a bit of bonhomie this morning. It was Friday and ahead loomed the weekend. Work was one thing, I could handle that. But the prospect of the whole weekend up in the apartment was scary. I couldn't help wondering if Sylvia was planning to bolt, suddenly find she had a client down in Cornwall, or up in Edinburgh perhaps. A client who had an urgent wish to see her. Something last-minute of course, something that would surely take her till Monday morning. I'd sensed something like that at breakfast this morning. And the thought made me nervous. Sick inside. As if I always had to keep my eye on her. In the work routine we'd now got to know where we were. But the weekend, even if she didn't run away, was panic stations for me. So I supposed I could imagine what it was for her.

The more so because Alison wouldn't be around. She was delivering a lecture in Oxford tomorrow, and staying over with friends. Tonight she was taking me to the theatre. Just the two of us. That and then the weekend, uncharted territory both. So a few jokes with my pal Jeremy was what I had been hoping for. Just to see me through the next seventy-six hours. Damn it. I'd make some coffee.

When I returned to our office with the two mugs plus a couple of biscuits each Jeremy had quit his desk and was in his at-the-window pose, staring moodily out. Clearing a space, I put the coffee and the biscuits down for him.

The letter that he'd been reading was in the middle of a sea of letters and documents. The other pieces of paper seemed somehow to be buoying it up. One of those manoeuvres gymnasts effect: five standing on the shoulders of four, then three, two and finally the one aloft being carried high. The sight of Jeremy's desk was like that. I bent to cut a hasty look and as I did so some of the coffee from my mug slurped onto the paper.

'Shitamerole!'

Jeremy swung round with a speed I wouldn't have known he was capable of.

'Hands up or else I'll . . .' You know, the Steve McQueen routine.

'What have you done?' His face was thundery.

'It's nothing. Only a drop of coffee.'

He strode back to the desk and we looked at the offending drops together. As we did so the signature of Ruth Flowert loomed large.

'Are you annoyed?'

He sat at his desk and started munching one of the biscuits and blowing on his coffee.

I returned to my part of the room and tried to make myself get through two distinctly depressing-looking manuscripts.

'Time, Josie?'

'What, what's the . . .?'

'Have you got the time, Josie?'

'Yeah, sorry I was deep in this horrible book.'

'If it's horrible why bother with it?'

'But I thought . . .'

'Time's money, Josie. We're trying to make a living here though you might not believe it. You've got to learn not to waste ages over a novel that's a non-starter from the beginning. Which applies to most.' (This under his breath.)

'But you said . . .'

'What did I say?'

'Oh well forget it. I'll just skip through in future, will I?'

'Skip through and bung out a report.'

'You do like my reports?'

44

'They're certainly individual.'

I looked at my watch. 'The time's twelve past one.'

He picked up the internal phone and buzzed through to Sally. I struggled to hold back my tears and cursed myself for being such a baby.

'Put me through to Sylvia,' I heard him say. 'Well put me through to Alan then.' No change. No one in. He banged down the phone. And I willed myself not to look towards his desk and catch his eye. I bent over mine and tried to concentrate on the notes I'd been making.

'Damn,' he said. 'Damn.' He got up and paced up and down the room. 'What are you doing for lunch then?'

'Me?'

'Who else?'

'No plans, why, is there anything I can do for you?'

'I was thinking,' he grinned at me sheepishly, 'we could –' he made a gesture with his thumb in the direction of the door and raised his eyebrows. I'd been there a week and I knew what he meant.

'Fine by me.'

It was in the pub that I got hooked on Jeremy. Though it wasn't then that I recognised what had happened. It was many things. Not least my ability to be able to cheer him up. We talked about nothing. Nothing of importance. About our currently favourite ads, about the test match scores, the other people in the pub, about food, an all-favourite topic for both of us. He was quick and funny, especially egged on by an appreciative audience, and by our second pint we were laughing together like high-school kids. You can take some of the responsibility for that, Josie, I told myself and I felt proud, like I'd done something important.

'Say, I think I might have read some reviews of Ruth Flowert's new book. Raves they were. But is there trouble or what?'

'Trouble.'

'Can I . . . I mean could you . . . I mean I'm a listening ear you know – always.'

'Listen, listening ear, let's pass on to another topic.'

'Sure thing, Jeremy.'

But he was smiling at me and as he crossed the street on our way back to the office he held my wrist. I was kind of pleased.

'That's it for this week.' It was the end of the day. He was collecting documents and stuffing them into his brief-case. I leapt up, stiff from so much sitting on my bum. I stretched, a super gigantic one reaching my arms to the ceiling. I caught him looking at me. And suddenly I regretted my size and awkwardness.

'What are your plans for the weekend, Jeremy?'

'Ugh?'

'Are your family back now?'

'Not till Sunday night,' he said as he shuffled the papers on his desk. 'The house is a pit. I'll have to do something about clearing it up, I suppose. That kind of a weekend.'

'I don't know about my weekend. I don't know what Sylvia's got planned.'

'Enjoy yourself, anyway.'

'Sure thing.'

And so he left and I went upstairs to change for the theatre and felt quite desolate, like I liked to have him around.

But what to wear? There was a teaser. How formal were these guys? I guessed I couldn't make the theatre in my jeans but was it to be the cotton skirt and blouse or the silk cocktail dress that Anna had chosen for me and seemed at least two decades out of date?

I went downstairs again, bumping into Alan in the corridor.

'Oh hi, Alan. You off now?'

'Bit of a rush,' he said. 'Hoping to catch the 6.25 from Waterloo.'

'Going somewhere fun?'

'Isle of Wight. Sailing. See you Monday. Cheers.'

'Cheers.'

I made my way into Sally's office and peered through the inner door into Sylvia's. Sylvia had left her desk. She and Jeremy were standing close together having a heated discussion. I didn't like and tried to ignore the unpleasant feeling it gave me. The stab of exclusion. Just this morning I had my first letter from home, four closely hand-written pages from Dad which ended with:

We're all missing you, darling. The first summer that we haven't been all together at the lodge during August. And I worry naturally – what fond father wouldn't. But as long as you are all right; that of course has always been my main concern. If you are unhappy or uncomfortable, darling, don't hesitate to give me a phone call and we'll book a return flight as quickly as possible. Meanwhile Anna joins me in sending you love and all possible good thoughts and wishes. And the children too. They'll be writing their individual messages on a separate sheet of paper which I shall enclose. P.S. There has been the same constant refrain – 'Wish Josie was here.' So you see how close you are to all our hearts.

I could admit defeat, go back so easily to where I wasn't excluded. Was it sheer inner devilry then that made me grit my teeth and want to stay on. Hit or bust. There were some things I had to find out. At whatever cost. Here. However painful.

In the interval Alison and I looked at the winding snake of people patiently waiting for coffee.

'Do you want a drink that much, Josie?' she asked.

'Chuck it in as an idea, as far as I'm concerned.'

'In that case follow me. I've a treat in store for you.'

She led me up staircases, into lifts, and across an enclosed roof area to an internal space which housed literally hundreds of botanical plants, cactuses, trees, all kinds. It was a place that made you speak in hushed voices, specially at night with the lights so low and being so empty.

'What magnificence! Must have cost millions. Who's it for?'

'That's what continually baffles me, how unused it is.' Her laugh was low and gruff. It came out more of a bark than a bay. It came from some place deep inside.

We squatted on a low retaining wall.

'What do you make of the play, if anything at all?' she asked.

'Yeah, well I mean, I haven't of course . . . Back home . . . Start again. It's kinda different. I think I like it. It's more like music, more a symphony than a play. I mean, the writer, he's hardly an action man, is he?'

'He's certainly not that.'

'Do you know him? I bet you do.'

'We've published one or two of his books, yes.'

'Did he send you the tickets? Is he here tonight? Are we going to meet him?' I was thinking, that would sure be something to write home about.

'No, we're not going to meet him. Hold your horses. Don't get so excited.'

'I'm just culture-crazy. No, really, after the dump I come from, all this,' I spread my arms, 'you know, everything, the excitement in

47

the air, it turns me on.'

'There's a lot of your mother in you.'

'Tell me . . .'

'Josie, that's what you've been saying ever since you arrived.'

'Okay, okay. Tell me instead what you make of the play. Give me the low-down, the background – kinda help me along, will you?'

We were getting along well, great buddies. Then, as we were making our way back towards the lift, she suddenly came out with:

'While you're here, don't probe too deep, Josie. You're young, you don't know pain.'

'To heck!'

'Go gently, Josie.'

'Did she set you up to this?'

'Josie!' She put her arm around my shoulder. Restraining, affectionate; it was meant to be a soothing gesture, I suppose, the kind you might make to a troubled child. I found myself being drawn in, drawn towards her. No, no!

Back in the theatre, while the four seemingly disembodied voices sung their individual stories of anguish and joy and human redemption, I kept thinking, and again later in bed that night, that the arm that had touched me was the same arm that had held my mother, comforted her, brought her a joy that had been so much greater than anything my father could offer. Sufficient to take her away from us, we whom she loved. Sufficient to make her say about Alison as she did that day that Cass was born, 'It's the best thing that's happened to me!' I must not be drawn into her net. I must continue to be wary. Anything else would, after all, be a betrayal to all my lot. And to me. That little me, whom this woman had wrenched out of paradise.

Nevertheless, on a more superficial level I didn't dislike Alison at all. On the contrary. I liked looking into her bright, quick, bird-like eyes. I liked the way she shuffled heavily around the apartment, her glasses askew, the way she ate and drank with relish.

I was always relieved when she was in the apartment. And enjoyed listening to the conversation. It seemed to me that her tastes were broader than my mother's, and that she was more charged, even at the end of a tiring day. It was she who made the running, pushing out further, taking Sylvia with her. Sylvia who was 'her majesty' in the office was no more than the lady-in-waiting – the lady of the bedchamber, I was going to say – when it came to the life of the apartment.

Though the issue of the bedroom, or to cut right down to the nitty gritty, the sex life between them, was hardly at all in evidence. Poor Dad would be relieved to know that. No, sex was not an issue so far. They moved around each other with ease and comfort, but there was no touching, as far as I could observe. At night they went to their separate rooms, whether they joined each other later I don't know. I can only say that I wasn't made aware of it. Of course all this might just be for my benefit. But I don't think so. They were an old married couple, my hunch, no longer a buzz between them, nothing for example like the enduring buzz between Dad and Anna.

Sylvia's thoughts, as always, were impossible yet for me to fathom. I can only say she was different with Alison from how she was in the office, or how she was to me, how she was even when she spoke to her friends on the phone in a trance-like tone. I couldn't put my finger on that quality of difference, not actually pin it down yet. But a buzz, a buzz such as there must have been once, no I didn't think that was there now, even for Sylvia. They were just an old married couple, perfectly harmless, the juices having run out long ago. Is that what it was?

It was an odd night to think about 'juices'; or perhaps not so odd. For two people had touched me today; to both I had responded. And both those contacts unnerved me. For I too have been dormant this last year.

*

'Hi, Dave.'

'Hi, Josie. Hardly a red Porsche. But it will do, eh, for what I have in mind?'

'What have you in mind?'

'Jump in and find out.'

We were in the parking lot once more. End of a day's school. Mid-October. Snows hadn't fallen yet. And although the air was crisp, the sun was bright and the sky a vibrant blue. The kind of day we mostly liked to make the most of, stay outside late as we could, knowing what was in store. For months and bloody months.

'Why weren't you at school today?'

'Had to help my old man in the store.'

'You'll get it for that.'

'The deliveries came today and they had to be unpacked. Couldn't just be left hanging around, Josie. He's done some injury to his back so I had no choice. Anyway I'm free now. You coming?'

'Got a nerve coming up here on a day you've bunked off. What if old Ellison sees. Kinda risky isn't it?'

'You could be worth it.'

'Dunno about that.'

'C'mon, jump.'

I turned to my mate Carol, who'd hugged her books and not said a word during all of this. She was pretty, Carol, perky with red hair, small pointed chin and light slim figure. But she reckoned little to boys. That's, I suppose, how we'd become mates the year before. She had a drunken dad and two elder bullying brothers and a mother who was always being torn between so many male demands and she reckoned she wanted none of that herself. She was bright, a good scholar, already a junior league astronomist; we were going to do great things, she and I. The others could have boyfriends if that's what they wanted.

That was until I began to notice Dave. 'As long as you get the right guy, I'm reckoning,' I told her, 'why can't you have both? Why does it have to be either or?'

'It just does, you'll see.'

So she didn't approve of me going with Dave and the friendship took a downgrader. And Dave, knowing it, had not a word to say to her.

Now I turned to look at her, 'What'll I do?'

'Your life. I don't mind taking the bus by myself if that's what you're on about.'

'She says she doesn't mind, Josie. C'mon, I've come up specially.'

'So who's the lucky one!' Carol under her breath. Which goaded me on. That and the thought somehow of Dave's Dad's back.

'Okay, Carol, if you're sure you don't mind . . .'

I was in the car and Dave had slammed the door and we were off. I waved to Carol but she had turned away.

'Where to, driver?'

'Just sit back and enjoy it, man.'

He whipped the old Chevrolet (69 model) to a hell of a lick. There was a rattling where something was loose above the back nearside window frame. And a kind of groaning from the engine, more of a juddering, as if it didn't want to be pushed to these feats. But that was all part of the fun. The front windows were opened. I leant into the back and opened those as well.

'What's up?' he asked.

'Let's have as much wind as possible.'

'You can't hear the music then.'

'Just turn it up louder.'

And so he did and so we drove. Great like that; great for both of us. We had on some weirdo Kitaro, his latest tape, kind of spooky music, full of waterfalls and eerie sounds and freaky wood instruments. Doleful and joyous all in one. I turned it up so loud it was pretty much deafening us. That's how we liked it.

We were driving out of Edmonton onto the prairie. Flat land. Wheat fields as far as the eye could see; the motorway cutting a straight path down the middle of them.

I sat back on the seat and half closed my eyes against the light. 'The world is flat,' I said. 'Go on driving. On on, drive us over the edge.'

He took my hand. And it lay there inside his. Making me uneasy.

'So what's this?'

'My uncle's farm.'

'This a social call?'

'You bet! Come on!'

A boy appeared out of a shed. About a year younger than Dave and myself.

'Hi,' Dave said. 'Where are the others?'

' 'S only me here just now. Others are out.'

'Give me a hand with the stuff then.'

The boy slowly wandered over to the car. Dave opened the boot, which was packed tightly with cartons of a whole range of provisions. Tins, soap, cigarettes, oil, matches, you name it. A crate of coca-cola.

Between the three of us we carried the stuff into the house.

'D'y'all want a coke?' the boy asked, when we'd finished unloading.

'Please,' I said, 'It's hot work.'

We sat in the kitchen. I tried to chat to the boy. Didn't know his name; Dave never introduced us. While Dave drummed his fingers on the kitchen table and looked moody. 'You're a slow drinker, Josie,' he said. So I slung my coke down and got up. Dave grabbed my wrist, the smile restored to his face. 'Ta, cheers mate. I'll just show Josie over the farm before we set off back.'

The boy shrugged his shoulders. We all left the house together. He turned his back on us and ambled back to the shed.

'Jesus,' said Dave, 'I thought you were going to take for ever.'

51

'What's the big rush?'

'Soon they'll be back, stupid. We've got to make the most of the time.' I walked along beside him.

'How?'

'You know.'

I said nothing. Just kept my eye on the wheat.

'Christ, Josie, we've been together for weeks now.'

'So?'

'Well, you must know how one gets to feel. Don't you feel anything? Physical, I mean.'

'Course I do, Dave.'

'After that dance last week I thought . . . ?'

'I do really like you, Dave. Honest.'

'That's what I thought. Well come on, girl, this is our opportunity.'

Aren't there likes and likes, I thought, but there didn't seem much point saying anything. So I let myself be dragged towards a shed which smelt of hay and horse manure and the grease of old tools.

'Won't anyone come?'

'There's no one here. You heard him say so.'

He pushed me against the wall and started to kiss me.

At first I pulled away.

'Christ, Josie, what is it? You liked it enough the other times.'

'Yes, I know, but . . .'

How could I begin to express to him that that had been kinda contained. The last kiss at the front door, kind of thing, or outside the youth hall where everyone was kissing in the bushes and you knew it couldn't go far – not all the way because at any moment the beam from the flashlight would be directed on us. There'd be that booming voice from old Beacon Face, 'Right, kids, that's enough, eleven o'clock, pack it in. I'm not going home till the last one of you is off the premises and I want to go home *RIGHT NOW*.' So you'd emerge from the bushes mock shame-faced and everyone would look to see who everyone else had got off with. And yes, after a slow start I quite liked being found with Dave. I quite liked kissing Dave. I even quite liked Dave. But I just wasn't ready to go the whole way. And yet how could I explain it? Or why kissing him now was different, just because we could go the whole way?

'I don't understand you, Josie. You're an odd one, like they say at school.'

'Who says?'

'Well, Chris and Darwin for starters.'

'They're lying.'

I pulled his face down to mine and started to kiss him, earnestly, seriously, forcing my tongue into his mouth and wiggling it around. I felt a hardening of muscle in his hip and groin. He joined his arms in the small of my back and pulled me towards him in a tight clinch. Both our knees began to crumble as he drew me down onto the floor. I prayed, draw me in, make me want to, make me take risks, make me be ordinary. But by the time I'd stopped praying he had his hand on my breast and it felt heavy and clammy and my flesh was a mass of goose-flesh pimples. I opened my eyes and looked at him.

'What is it?'

'I just can't do it.'

'Jesus Christ!'

We got up awkwardly. I did up my bra clip and the buttons of my shirt while he combed his hair and stooped to tie up a lace that had come undone.

'Jesus Christ, Josie,' he said again.

'Well you bloody brought me here, didn't you.' Suddenly I was angry. 'I didn't notice you asking me what *I* wanted.'

'With anyone else it'd be straightforward.'

'Like with Pru, you mean.' Pru had been his girlfriend before me. 'I don't know why you ever gave her up, Dave Austin. 'S matter of fact I don't know why you don't just pick it up where you left off. If it's all so much more straightforward.'

'Maybe I just will. You're something else, Josie.' He was striding back towards the car with large angry steps, holding my wrist tight so that when he let it go and I jumped into the seat beside him, there was a large red mark.

We drove in silence. We didn't even bother with the tapes. The sun was setting over the prairie. It looked so still and great.

We'd pulled up outside my house.

'Right then.'

I shifted on my seat.

'What you waiting for?' He bent over and opened the door for me.

'Dave?'

'Mmm.'

'Dave, you're not going to really start again with Pru. I was just joking.' (It sounded weak.)

53

'I dunno. You certainly don't want me. And she's still keen.'

'How do you know?'

'She told me.'

It was a stab.

'When?' I heard myself saying.

Then he said nothing but turned to look at me and for a moment our eyes held each other's.

'I do like you, Dave,' I whispered.

'You sure don't know how to show it.'

He had his foot on the accelerator.

I jumped out of the car.

'Hope your Dad's back gets better.'

'Send my love to that mate of yours, Carol. You and she sure will have something to laugh over.'

'Dave! Dave,' I said in desperation, coming near to the car and putting my face through the opened window. 'Dave,' I whispered, my face burning with the embarrassment, 'I did, I do like kissing you, and if you hung on a bit I'm sure . . .'

But the car was already moving.

'Better luck next time,' he said.

One of those mornings when everything got kinda jumpy and out of place. Woke not to the sound of Anna in the kitchen but in the bathroom vomiting. Lots of us, most of us, it seemed, didn't want any breakfast. Cass played with her egg, somehow managing to send bits of watery yolk flying onto the table.

'Stop that will you. Anna, will you stop Cass doing that.' William looked furiously at his sister.

'Cass, eat your egg,' Anna's voice was weary.

'You make it too soft. I won't eat it.'

'You will eat it up this minute.'

'You can't make me.' She pushed her chair back and ran from the table out of the room.

'What a temper she's got,' said Angus, all of fifteen and a half, stubble beginning to show on his chin, his limbs filling out, half boy half man now. 'She could use more controlling. That's what I reckon.'

'Shut up, you!' Karen had always been especially fond of her younger sister and traditionally the girls tended to band together against the older boys.

'Why don't you eat your toast, Josie?' Anna to me.

'I'm not really hungry.'

'Besides, who likes it when it's always burnt!' William.

'You could always get up and do your own, William.' Anna.

'Yes, you could do more to help, William,' Angus loudly from the door.

Just as William was about to retort Angus departed.

Anna collected a few dishes and started to load them into the washing machine. I found myself doing nothing much more than staring at the jello pot and thinking again of what had occurred with Dave. Unnerving to face school today and I doubted that his Dad would need him for a second day in a row to help with the unloading. I was toying with the idea of pretending to be ill when Angus strode back into the kitchen with face purple with anger.

'Who's been mucking around with my bike?'

No one said a word.

'Anna, I demand an explanation from this lot.'

'I leave it to you to work out.' She moved to the kitchen door, more slowly than with her usual dance-like steps, to the tune of Angus's 'That's not bloody fair.'

By the time she got as far as the door everyone at the table but me seemed to be shouting.

'Children!' she expostulated with an unheard of impatience, as she left the room.

Soon afterwards I left the table myself. I went into Dad's study and closed the door behind me. I sat down at his desk where in front of me neatly written into a ledger book were the household accounts. For a time I looked at the sums, rather shocked by how much it all cost. And then hearing the shouting of my brothers and sisters outside I cradled my hands over my ears and bowing my head deep over the desk, I relived again yesterday's episode at the farm, turning it this way and that. Meanwhile I waited for the noise outside the room to abate. A number of times the front door opened and banged closed. Eventually all was quiet. I stayed on for a few minutes to be sure and then I went in search of Anna.

She was in the basement, in battle with a sheet that refused to release itself from the washing machine.

'You want help with that?'

'Shouldn't you be at school?'

'I've nothing on till the second lesson. Are you taking them out to the line?'

'I was going to, yes.'

'I'll give you some help.'

'I think you should be making your way to school, Josie.'

I said nothing but followed her out into the yard. I took a bunch of pegs and began to help her.

'Anna, I've got something I kinda wanted to ask you.'

'What about this evening?'

'No, now.'

'Your father . . .'

'It's nothing to do with Dad.'

'Josie, not this morning.'

'But it's got to be this morning!'

'Hang on a moment . . .'

She went into the house and I went on pegging up the laundry.

When I went back in she was sitting at the breakfast table, her face a whitish green colour.

'Are you okay?'

'Yes, I'm pregnant, that's all. Much better now that I've been sick.'

'Actually, it's that kind of thing that I wanted to talk to you about.' With all the saner part of me I knew it wasn't the moment, but my need was so pressing, it was usually so impossibly difficult to get her by herself and then today I would have to face him, so I hurtled on after only the most perfunctory congratulations, 'Oh goodness, now that is news!', ignoring all the danger signs.

'But Anna, you know Dave who I've been going around with well . . .'

She put her hands into the small of her back and rubbed it. Then got up and collected a second load of washing.

'Here, I'll do that. Anna, I wanted to ask you . . .'

I was still talking when at some point she returned to the house.

'So what do you reckon? Is there something odd about me?'

'Perhaps you're just your mother's daughter, Josie.'

'What do you mean?'

'You know these things have a habit of repeating themselves. Now if you'll excuse me I've got a lot to do. So have you. Going to school for one thing.'

'Josie, are you still awake?'

'Who's that?'

'It's Anna. May I come in?'

56

I said nothing. She opened the door and came into the room in her peacock-patterned housecoat, her hair, unleashed from its usual single plait and freshly brushed, falling heavily round her moonlike face. Like this, I thought, she looks like a kid, like hardly more than my age. And that blessed sense of responsibility – from being the oldest, I guess – plus what had happened, made me feel sorry for her when all I wanted to feel was horribly angry. Nevertheless the anger was balm to the hurt. So I tried to hang onto it for all I was worth. I turned away from her in my bed, my face facing the wall.

'How did school go today?'

Silence.

She sat down heavily on the bottom corner of my bed and touched my shoulder through the duvet.

'Josie. I'm most terribly sorry for this morning. Of course I didn't mean it. I don't know what came over me. It was just that you caught me at such a very bad moment. But you mustn't take it to heart. Or think that I would normally have said it.'

Silence.

'Josie, I'm pregnant, you see.'

'I know.'

'You know. Then you can understand, can't you. I was feeling very sick. And after Cass's scene and William's temper over his bike I'd just about had enough. You were the last straw. You should have chosen a better moment.' She massaged my back. 'You're usually so sensible.'

'It doesn't make any difference.'

'As long as you do know that it is not my true feeling about you, Josie. Lots of girls are shy at first. It is perfectly natural. Why, when I was a young woman back in Norway before I came to England and met your father –' She launched into stories from her far-off Norwegian past. Her voice soothed. She massaged my back all the while. But she had said that other thing. She could never take it away. It would always be there now.

'So we're friends again, eh?'

'I suppose so.'

'And what do you think about another addition to the family?'

'What does Dad think?'

'Your father knew how much I wanted a baby of my own. Not that I don't love you all very much. He's happy for me.'

'I'll be away from home soon. So it won't affect me much.'

'But this will always be your home. And I'll need more help than ever when the new baby's born. You must try and put that other

57

matter out of your mind. There are ever so many other boys around. Dave's just one. Just a beginning.'

The baby was born the following spring, a boy, balancing the numbers. Predictably Angus and William were mildly pleased, the girls at first disappointed but within a month cooing with delight over their little brother and insisting on taking him into school in his carry-cot to show off to their classmates.

I found I could muster little interest in him. Nor in most things else. It was the last term of school, we had already taken our exams and been graded accordingly. So the rest was all downhill, school photos, leaving parties and the like, most of which I managed to get out of, if I could.

I weighed like ten pounds more than I had done the previous year and, having neither the initiative nor the enthusiasm to buy new clothes to fit, looked a sight in Anna's maternity clothes shortened and converted into smocks over jeans done up with safety pins.

Dad's attempts to cheer me up so consistently fell on stony ground that he'd almost stopped trying. And often went around with a doleful face. Everyone wore a doleful face, it seemed to me, and by then I was longing to get out. Though to where, I had no idea. Certainly not UBC for where I was set. But somewhere much much further afield.

Dad's doleful face was due centrally to the financial crisis into which the family had plunged. Believing that his salary wasn't sufficient not only to feed all the mouths but also for so many potential university candidates he'd started dabbling on the Canadian stock market. And no business man he (this from Anna – until then in all the years of our growing-up I had not heard one word of criticism of him from her) had made a number of crucial errors which resulted in us being far worse off than we were before. For a time there was talk of us selling the house and moving somewhere smaller, but Anna was adamant that we stayed put, especially for the moment while she was so preoccupied with a young baby. So we hung on and began for the first time to count the dollars.

Anna had a bad pregnancy. She was thirty-one. It having taken all these years to persuade Dad, no doubt, if he ever was persuaded. She was unwell on and off through most of the nine months. Things went wrong in the eighth month and she spent the whole of it lying on her back in fear of losing the baby. Gran (Dad's mum) came over from Scotland and you could hear her and Anna quarrelling all over the house. The moment Anna came out of the hospital she sent Gran packing back to Scotland a full six weeks before the original plan. Dad was not pleased. He had not been in on that decision. And to Anna's comments, 'I just couldn't stand her here a moment longer; it was that or me going demented,' he turned a stony face. Implying, I thought, that it wasn't clear which was worse.

The birth had been difficult and Anna was in a weak state for some months afterwards. Dad did more around the house and though he didn't complain he just always looked worn down, as if life was defeating him. Which wasn't helped by his financial worries and by having so many broken nights with the baby.

I took over the kitchen department. I began to think that Anna's cooking had been super ordinary. 'Let's put a little imagination into the meals,' was my continual cry. A desire to be ingenious was augmented by a real need to cut down on the housekeeping. I got the idea of holding back on meat and dairy produce and using loads of vegetables and rice and beans and dried peas and lentils and things. And growing a herb garden and getting into spices and presentation. Sometimes in the early days I made a right cock-up. It was all in the presentation and nothing else. Something would turn out to be miles too spicy or only half cooked.

Dad would eat whatever with his now habitual doleful face. Anna would often not be there with us because, every time a meal was about to be served, like clockwork the baby began to cry. But the kids were often outraged. They resented and felt the lack of security in the household at that time – it made me realise, though I think I had all through, just how much Anna had done for us all – and they took it out on the food.

'Can't eat this muck!'

'She's done it again!'

'Why can't we just have normal meals like we used to?'

'If Josie can't cook we should eat out of tins.'

'This is real cooking, not just boring old stuff. And better for you.'

'Uncooked eggplants, like hell!'

'Give me time.'

'But we don't want exciting food. We want the food we've always had.'

'Dad, please –?'

'Josie's in charge till Anna's ready to take back over. If you don't like it you must leave it. Or take some bread and peanut butter. Now could we possibly talk about something else. Let's not make all the meals revolve round squabbles over the food, as they have been lately. Let's all make an effort.'

Gradually my cooking improved. As I increasingly experimented it became easier to find new dishes that everyone liked. And having made my point I could afford to skip back to some of Anna's old regulars without losing face. Sitting in the old rocking chair that we had brought into the kitchen for her, patting Paul's spiny little back, she yielded up her gastronomic secrets readily and I, slipping in a few extra herbs or an ingredient that I reckoned would make the dish just that bit more interesting, would occasionally manage to elicit comments like, 'Almost as good as Anna's.'

In the spring I kitted myself out in clothes a couple of sizes larger. Anyone can wear jeans and shirts in clear bright colours. Some of the lethargy of the winter had worked itself off and I no longer looked gross, just big. In this way, I thought, judging from the few early photos I had found, not at all like my mother who seemed slender and pretty and impressive. Not something I mentioned, however, how unlike her I was, because I was aware of becoming like her in another way that was beginning to play on my mind.

Through all of that year, when not at school, or cooking, or washing, or shopping or involved in any of the household chores that seemed endless, I was reading with total engrossment. I had always been a reader. But never quite like that before. Being outside, larking with the others as I might previously have done, all seemed to take up so much energy. Easier to sit in a chair curled up with a book. I read voraciously. Eating up the English classics at an insatiable rate. Plundering the school library for everything that was available.

'You're going to be a top scholar at university,' said Dad to me, trying to be encouraging. 'One of the youngest ever professors. Aren't I just going to be proud of you.'

'Nope, I don't want that,' I said. For I had already begun to write a diary and that, plus my first small success in the way of two prizes for essay-writing competitions, had sent my thoughts in another direction. 'I want to be around books, and around people who write. Maybe a writer myself. Not stuck in a stuffy university. Nor in a stuffy town like this. It's all so boring. I wish I knew someone, just someone who –'

I realised what I'd said.

'Who what?'

'Who'd done things!' I started to cry, the tears stinging my eyes. I was aware of Dad's pain and the look he gave Anna.

Then with its usual inevitability that even if you've been in Canada all your life you still can't quite believe it will happen until it does, the snows began to melt and the blue skies stretched across the wide horizon and the last term pushed along with ever-quickening speed to its conclusion. Paul stopped crying so much and Anna and Dad went around arm in arm as if they were trying to make up for a hard time, the meals ceased to be a battle ground and the kids became their old perky selves. And as I saw more vividly that in only a few more months the everydayness of my life with my brothers and sisters would be changed irreversibly I began, in a hurry, to make up for the last bad winter. To force myself out, to agree to games of rounders on the lawn, to swims and bike races, even to help the boys build a new shed for our bikes at the back of the yard. I was the child again, almost with a vengeance, nurturing and encouraging every kind of laughter, every kind of fun. This is how I want to remember it, I thought, because when I leave, geeze it's going to be different.

After the incident with Dave and us having the baby and the bad winter and all that I'd become something of a solitary at school. I didn't want to be aligned with Carol. I didn't feel I had much to say to anyone. But now in the last month or two of our school life, Carol and I began to draw close to one another again. We'd sit on the fence after school, or we'd ride our bikes to the river and talk for hours. I wanted her to come to UBC with me but she was set on Toronto, where there was an excellent department for her particular specialty. We hugged a lot and kissed when we said goodbye and vowed to write lots, like always. I told her I reckoned she would have an interesting life and she told me she reckoned the same, 'when I'd settled down'.

'Don't you just sound like a granny.'

'Whatever happened with Dave?' she asked. 'You never said.'

'No, and I don't want to now.'

She looked at me for a long while. 'You know what I think, Josie?'

'You're going to tell me anyway.'

'I think you should make it to England. And see your mother. Have it out with her.'

'Have what out? And besides you've got to be joking. I don't even know where she is. Plus Dad would never let me. Besides, I don't

61

want to. It would be horrible. You're crazy. I've never heard such a crazy scheme.'

'All the same I reckon that's what you're going to have to do.'

*

Saturday morning. Alison had set off for Oxford at the crack of dawn. Sylvia and I were alone and the white blue clouds merged into the blue white sky so that it was hard to see quite where one finished and the other began. This I knew because I had been out early to collect croissants and brioches from the Continental baker along the main shopping street. I saw raspberries outside a greengrocer and on inspiration bought some of them too. Shops open later here than back home. It still surprised me to see so many of them shuttered way after eight.

Returning to the apartment I made a jug of coffee and heated the croissants and put knives and plates on to the table. Then I sat there waiting, reading the paper and thinking that today I would have her all to myself, today maybe I would begin to find out some more things about her.

Eventually she glided in. She allowed herself to be served. She picked at half a brioche and sipped her coffee. She picked up the paper and put it down again. It seemed to weigh heavily on her that something more was required of her. And I think I began to be quite sure that somewhere locked deep inside she had love to give. That it hadn't dried, that it was just encased, so to speak. Perhaps the embarrassment of being so ill at ease held her back. And yet. Whatever she was, whatever she did, and along with the pain and the hurt and all the rest I was ready to love her. Ready to be her slave. Ready to try and attune my ways to hers.

Conversation over breakfast was in snippets. I tried to rein in my usual enthusiasm, to keep my voice to a whisper (we always had to shout so loud to be heard at home), to check my questions. I wanted to know what she thought about each and every client, I wanted a reading list to cover all that was best of our authors, I wanted to know how she did what she did, and what was a come on – apart from Alison. But all this I checked. I think.

I tried not to jump on any opening, feeble as it may be, that she made. I was like a player of Racing Demon ready to slap on the next card the moment my partner delivered one. By dint of eating two croissants and one brioche to her half, by dint of making myself perpetually busy, boiling more water, refilling coffee cups, running for the post the moment I heard it on the mat, I managed, just, not to annoy her at breakfast.

'Well, Josie, what would you like us to do today?'

'Goodness, I'd no idea I had the choice.'

'You do,' there was a faint though distant smile on her face.

'Uh, um, I really don't know.' I wanted to say, 'Something that we'd both enjoy together,' but that seemed presumptuous. I thought of bookshops, of ambling through the city, of country pub lunches.

'Would you like to come shopping with me in Harrods? There are one or two things I could usefully pick up. And we might find something for you, who knows.'

'Suit me fine.'

So it was to Harrods that we went. She was a good shopper, a deft one, making quick decisions, seeing what she needed and ferreting it out with a speed that filled me with awe. Of course she loved gorgeous things.

'What a lot of parcels,' I laughed, as we sat on toad-like seats round a low table taking an early lunch and as far as I was concerned a welcome breather. Her energy was total. I don't believe she was tired one bit. I guess she only suggested a rest as courtesy to me. I had the sense she could go on choosing and buying until the shop closed.

'Here, can you manage them all? Pass some over to me. Are you sure that's all you want? It seems a rather meagre lunch for you. What about a cream cake to follow?'

'No, honestly, this is just great.'

She ate more heartily than she had done at breakfast. Her eyes twinkled. She watched other people, their appearance and their actions, with a sharp eye. Made comments about this hairstyle, or that earring, or about anyone she thought particularly well dressed. And anyone she did not. On this neutral ground I guessed she felt safe. No hostility in her tone. Could she even be enjoying it? I hoped so.

'Well, time to get back to the main object of the exercise,' she said almost as soon as my last mouthful had been consumed.

'What's on the agenda then?' I tried to be an eager ally.

She ticked off her list. 'Before anything else, let's find something for you.'

'But what?'

'What are you wanting?'

I didn't know.

'Come on,' she said. 'This is going to be fun. She led the way, the already numerous Harrods bags banging against one another.

When she had thought of fun she hadn't reckoned on my figure. With her trim one which fitted perfectly into a size ten and everything looked good on, the fun was in simply deciding which out of so many should be chosen. Not so with me. She suggested various items and I knew with a sinking feeling from the very first moment that the result would be failure. But she was not to be dissuaded.

'You must at least try. Trust me,' she said, winking at an adoring elderly Harrods retainer who clearly thought my mother with her elegance and sophistication just the sort of client you longed to serve. 'Aren't I right?' She would turn to the assistant for confirmation.

'Of course, Madam, if the young lady would just like to . . .'

And so over and over again I tried on outfits, of all shapes and sizes and colours and descriptions, each one of which looked as disappointingly awful as I had foreseen.

'Honestly, Sylvia,' I said after the ninth or tenth time, 'we seem to have spent more time in this department than all the rest together.' I was aware of the afternoon going by. Not to mention the excessive heat, lack of ventilation and rising sense of claustrophobia. 'I don't mind at all not having anything today. Let's stop this, please, and move on.'

'One last attempt.' She plunged into an over-crowded railing, pulling out a dark brown dress which had little to recommend it except a low V at the back.

I tried it on.

'There, that's better,' said the assistant and my mother in unison.

'Lovely,' I agreed meekly.

'I knew we'd find something. Wrap it up, will you. And thank you so much for your time.' She was all brisk efficiency. Difficult to tell who was more relieved, she or I.

I might have been a downer after that. I was longing to finish and get back to the apartment. I followed her limply, more and more like a gasping goldfish, trying to hold onto the good things that were me, Josie, as well as trying to keep hold of our multifarious parcels.

She counted them in the taxi in which we had chosen to return, public transport being out of the question now with fourteen large carrier bags between us.

'Fourteen,' she said, sitting far back in her seat and smiling her gently vague smile. 'Now that's what I call a successful day.'

'You do love shopping, don't you?'

'Certainly. Why, don't you?'

'Yes, I suppose. I don't know. It's not something I've ever done much of. There's never been that much money around with so many of us. And then,' I rushed on not wanting this to become too personal, 'there isn't much you kinda want to buy back home.'

'I suppose not.'

She was thoughtful for a while.

'Spending your father's money, that was something different. That was never much fun. It's not the spending itself, you know, Josie. It's the pleasure, I suppose, of thinking that you have earned it by your own hard work. And that therefore you deserve to spend it. I hope you've dropped this silly nonsense about not liking that university of yours. I wish I'd had a university education. It would have made such a difference.'

'In what kind of way?' I asked.

'Many ways. For example . . .'

But the taxi cab drew up in front of our house and the conversation was cut short.

After the parcels had been taken in and unpacked she went to her room. I made a pot of tea, poured myself a mugful, and took up the book I was at present engrossed in, *Playful Pyramids*, by one of Jeremy's clients, Ruth Flowert. Not her latest, which recently had been so spectacularly reviewed in the papers, but the one before, published two years ago, a copy of which, with a beautiful inscription to Jeremy, I found on the shelf above his desk.

Kicking off my shoes, I tucked up in an armchair in the sitting-room and listened to Segovia on the stereo while I read and, at the same time, waited for her door to open and for her to sail forth. That was the nearest thing we'd got to a conversation in the taxi cab and I was eagerly hoping to continue it.

The phone went. She didn't answer, so I did. It was her lawyer and I was to fetch her as it was something urgent. I knocked on her door, it turned out she'd fallen asleep but she woke up fast enough when I said who it was. She picked up the phone and I went out again but didn't shut the door, just in case she needed me or something. Then there were angry scenes. I heard the names 'Alison' and also to my surprise 'Ruth Flowert'. I heard the slamming down of the phone, then the picking it up and dialling again. A lot more talk. I'm not sure if it was the same person or someone else. Three phone calls. Sylvia very angry, very distressed.

Then after what seemed like a long, long time, it was finished. There was silence.

I knocked on the door. She was lying on her bed smoking. The first time I'd seen her smoke.

'Is there anything I can get you?'

'Oh you. Look, I'll just have a quiet evening in here, if you don't mind.'

'Can I cook you anything?'

'No, nothing at the moment, thank you. I might make myself a tray later. You go on and take what you want. You can amuse yourself, can't you?'

'Of course.'

And so it was.

I wasn't really hungry. But I heated myself some tomato soup and made a slice of toast and read *Playful Pyramids*, wondering about Ruth Flowert. Wondering too about the enigma of my mother. And wishing I could be some help. Wishing someone would tell me something; that I wouldn't be such an outsider.

At one point she swept through the sitting room in a silk dressing gown in search of a cigarette. She was about to move on out of the room without a word when her eyes rested on the cover of the book.

'Really, Josie. How predictably unfortunate. Of all the books in the agency from which you could take your pick. Well really!' This was said while she was contemplating the picture of the naked man, knees crooked, in the bath. Then she swept out of the sitting room and shut her own door with an angry sound. The sound that says let no one else bother me tonight.

I watched the late-night movie and then retired to bed. Better day tomorrow.

But the following morning, when at ten I awoke from a deep sleep, there was a note waiting for me on the kitchen table.

Have matters to attend to. Be a good girl and amuse yourself best you can. Don't wait for me; I might be rather late tonight. Sylvia.

P.S. I did, you might remember, suggest that it wasn't a wise idea of yours to come over. Not at present. But you were determined. So, dear girl, as we all have to in life you must learn to take the consequences. It must seem abundantly evident to you that I have little time to offer you at present. Other matters weigh and press, as no doubt you have surmised. For you are no fool. Messy, impatient and young, very young. But in some ways, even ways I admit to finding aggravating, very much my daughter. So I

66

give you the credit to recognise that other lives and troubles are going on, of which you can know nothing. Nor should. I trust you therefore to make your own way while here.

Find your own amusement. Keep your own company. Bother not Alison, please. Jeremy, I understand, is quite happy with your contribution in the office. So if you put your mind to it no doubt you can learn something over these months that will be useful experience for your work after university. And I advise a full exploration of London during the weekends. Visit the many galleries and museums.

It will be lonely but I cannot, dear girl, be my daughter's keeper. There are things we can do and things we cannot. As we become older, this becomes more and more clear. And I will tell you frankly, as I may well never write again to you in this vein, that those things we cannot do, particularly if it relates to not facing one's responsibilities, are the most painful. And pain, as you have no doubt already observed, is close to anger. I tell you all this so that you do not mistakenly take my necessary distance too personally.

You seem, as I say and despite your faults, basically a good child. It even sometimes makes me mildly curious to see the others. Maybe you and I in another decade or two will talk. But not now. You have hit a time in my life, of all times, when my mind is much on other matters, troubles of which you can have only the most fleeting idea. And troubles into which I have no desire, none whatsoever, to draw you.

I should really not have let you come. More than ever that occurs to me. Or I should send you back. But you have done nothing wrong and I feel that may now be the worst of two evils and be even more hurtful to you. So try to keep occupied, try not to be too much of a bother. Show that independence and spirit which in your letters I recognised so very much as my own. And time will pass.

Tomorrow is Monday and we will start a second week of your visit in the ordinary way. I will trust you to not refer to this letter.

She had called me 'Dear girl!' Perhaps that more than anything else is what struck me.

The second was that I had twelve hours to kill and the thought of my own solitariness appalled me.

The third was that she had said some nice things. That she had tried. That there was hope. If only I could hang on. If only I could hold on to my independence like she said.

The fourth was that in the end, who knows, I might have something to offer.

The fifth was that somewhere in the office must be Jeremy's home number.

Part II

JEREMY

Josie. She was all right, I suppose. A brave kid. What surprised was when Sylvia first suggested that she was going to have her over.

'Thought you had severed all connection.'

'Does anyone ever,' she snapped.

'Don't get me wrong. I was there, darling, remember?'

'How could one ever forget.'

I adore Sylvia. Always have. And of course one can rely on her. Which is such a support with so much at present in rather a nasty state of shift. Temporary hitches. The very words I used to Sylvia. Not about Josie's appearance: that was something else; something it was easy to be supportive over.

'Well, it's certainly a turn up for the books. Pity Daniel's away and the twins are that bit too young. It would have been useful if there had been someone around of her age; especially with the hours you work. Whatever will you do with her, darling?'

'What everyone else does with their children, no doubt, Jeremy. The worst is that she insists on working in the agency.'

'Curious child.'

'Jeremy, be helpful, will you. How can we occupy her in the

office?'

'I could always use her, I suppose. And I don't mean that to sound how it rather does sound.'

'You had absolutely better not.'

'Steady on, darling, steady on.'

As it turned out, it was difficult to be exactly sure who used whom. So much more comfortable like that. 'Though for goodness sake don't tell your mother,' I told her. 'There you go again,' she said, and laughed.

She laughed a lot. That is when she wasn't in a tangle and crying. Like the first time she came to the house to help me give it what she termed 'a proper Canadian Spring clean' — I don't know what she thought we English weren't capable of. That day when after the exertion of the hoovering, dusting, polishing, collecting rubbish and I don't know what, I fixed us both a large scotch — she said she didn't like the stuff but I fixed her one anyway, said she'd have to start some day.

'Why, why should anyone ever start?'

'Just the way it goes, Josie.'

After she'd finished her whisky she became unusually silent, for that kid who was always larking on. She sat there curled up in Helen's chair her face crinkled up and I couldn't help feeling sorry for the kid.

'Come on, tell me, tell uncle Jeremy. I've got children of my own, you know. I do know about these things.'

'You couldn't imagine my "things" as you call them. Nobody could.'

'We all know that everyone's story is absolutely individual. But there are certain similarities. Two months of reading the manuscripts at Fisk, Farmer and you'll get a pretty clear idea of that.'

She looked unconvinced.

'Don't you like your job?'

'I love it, darling, though it's not what you call an easy patch. I'm physically, morally and spiritually tired.'

She looked at me. Her big brown eyes alarmingly earnest.

I laughed. 'Don't take me so seriously. Now back to you.'

'I don't know where to start. I don't know if I should.'

'Course you should.'

'Could I have some more whisky, then?' she held out her glass.

But she didn't drink the good stuff I'd poured into her glass. Instead she crinkled up her eyes some more and then she was crying, whopping great tears wrenching out of her body like a five-year-old.

'Josie, Josie. C'mon it can't be all that bad. And nothing is bad that isn't better shared.' (Liar, Jeremy. But I reckoned this was the stuff she needed.)

'It's all so confusing,' she sobbed, 'and I don't know what to tell you.'

'Well for starters, Sylvia's a doll and my ever-loving partner and I'm not saying a word against her. But it can't exactly be easy for you rediscovering her as a mother. Do you want to talk about that?'

She shook her head.

'What then?'

'I'm so fat.'

'C'mon!' I laughed out aloud. 'That's hardly a major problem. C'mon then, where's all that perky Josie pride I've been hearing all week.'

'No but . . .' And she howled louder. 'Where shall I begin?' she sobbed, as the noise subsided.

'Just begin anywhere. It doesn't really matter where. Have you ever had a boyfriend, Josie?' I suppose it was what her being fat made me think of. In a flash of intuition which these days seem precious few around my own daughters.

So Josie started talking and between talking and drinking whisky and bouts of crying we spent what could not be termed as a merry but definitely a useful and even necessary evening, I reckoned. For Josie.

At some point she asked me about Helen. 'She's left me,' I told her. 'She's taken the kids and gone down to her mother for the moment. Left me high and dry. If I wasn't such an old warrior, Josie, I'd have something to cry about myself tonight. I need you, as a matter of fact, to cheer me up, just as much as you need me.'

That appeared to make her feel better. And naturally there's no point in crying unless you've got a pair of arms to hug you; that's what I've always said.

But God damn it, if she wasn't round at my house the following evening. Ringing on the doorbell shortly after eight.

'Have you eaten?'

'No, but I'm not offering to take you out. What do they do; starve you in that flat?'

'Actually I was thinking of cooking for you. You must be awfully lonely with Helen away.'

'Can you cook? I'm fussy, mind.'

'You just try me; I'm great.'

She looked such a lost soul at the door. I didn't want to, but I had to ask her in. Though had I known how untruthful she was being about the cooking I might have had second thoughts.

'The kitchen's over there.'

'It was meant to be broccoli omelettes,' she lamented. 'It's turned out more like scrambled eggs. See, I was nervous. There was something I wanted to ask you. Will you seduce me?'

I burst out laughing.

'No, don't laugh. That's hurtful. I really mean it. I want to feel I'm a woman, to feel normal. And I figured with you –'

'But Josie, I'm far too old, as well as being married, and having a hellishly chequered past, one which seems finally to have caught up with me with one almighty bang. You don't want to get muddled up with me.'

'Not muddled up, no. Just,' she breathed deeply and grinned, 'just screwed. Just sort of started off.'

'Why not pick someone more your age?'

'They're too – fumbly.'

She had a point there.

'What do you say? You'd be doing me a favour. I feel so muddled up about my sexuality. Please. Just once. No one need know. It'll just be between you and me. Don't say no.'

And still I hesitated, thinking of many things.

'Unless of course you don't fancy me. I know I'm not a patch on my moth –'

'Come here.'

I'd like to say it was the look on her face when she said this that finally swayed me. But no doubt the wine, the lateness of the hour, my year's celibacy, all played their part.

Later, slipping into the taxi she insisted she'd pay for ('There's nothing at all else for me to spend my salary on'), she turned to me,

'Say, shall I come again tomorrow?'

'I thought once was what we agreed.'

'But wouldn't twice be better?'

That's when I first cautioned, 'Don't tell your mother. And Josie, remember, pals we've said and pals it is; nothing more.'

'It's what I want,' she promised from the open window of the taxi, 'Believe you me. You can trust a Canadian.'

So pals we became, and lovers.

After that there was no more nonsense about crying. It was mostly laughter when she came to the house. She was a perky kid. And good in bed. Can't think what she was worrying about. Just the old story, 'Start with a middle-aged man not a high school kid,' I told her.

'There, what did I tell you, that's just what I've done,' said she, looking extremely pleased with herself.

'But whatever you do, don't tell Sylvia.'

And she laughed because this wasn't the first time I'd said it and a kind of refrain had grown up between us that meant a lot to her. 'Don't tell your mother.' / 'Then tell me about my mother.' That was the refrain. Though for some time I resisted.

To be fair to the girl she was not totally without diversity. She didn't have one question, but two. The second being, 'Tell me about Ruth Flowert, what is all this going on? Oh, Jeremy, be a sport and deliver the goods, please do.' There was no way I was going to. She had little idea of my involvement. This, no doubt, helped to while away time in a rather difficult patch. She could have been finding me something of a hero. And however often that happens it does add a shot of the old something-or-other to one's veins.

But she was wily too. If she'd been any more fragile I wouldn't have touched her, naturally. I do have some scruples. But I knew from my first encounters with Josie that she was the born survivor. Had to be with Sylvia's blood in her arteries. I knew that there was nothing to worry about.

So you could say I wasn't surprised that eventually she got her way. With regards to the question of Sylvia that is.

'If I answer one question will you leave me alone on the other, you little horror?'

'Little me!' She flung her arms back on the top of the double bed (with delicacy I had taken Helen's side), where we were both lying nude and warm after a particularly energetic session, and roared with laughter.

I squeezed her waist and then moved my hands down her hips and up her rib cage.

'My God, it's terrible. Who's responsible for this damage? Who's to blame?'

'What are you talking about?' She turned over quickly and bent up on her knees.

'You are getting littler by the day. You're fading away.'

'Don't you like it?'

'There was something so comfortable about two equal amounts of flesh.'

'Really, do you mind?'

'Not as long as you don't suggest running together on the playing fields, and never mention diets.'

'I never will, I promise,' she announced, now sitting astride me and moving her mouth in long diagonal strokes across the hairs on my chest.

'Besides I'm not dieting,' she whispered into a place well below my chin.

'I know,' I pulled her head up to mine, 'you're just losing your puppy fat.' We laughed comfortably and I manoeuvred myself into her as she sat astride and we came in a rush, her little cries, I hope, not disturbing the neighbours. Ten to six on a Sunday evening. When I was a kid we would have been making our way to Evensong.

'How many times do you think you can come in one sitting, Josie? I use the word sitting of course as a general term.'

'You newt. I've no idea. I've no experience. I was a virgin, remember, ten days ago.'

'You poor old thing.'

'Oh he does think highly of himself!'

She began to tickle me and a scuffle evolved in which we both fell off the bed, I on top of her.

'Let's see how many times,' I urged, through clenched teeth, feeling myself rising.

'I'm game,' she responded. And she was. By far the most noticeable thing about Josie.

I told her to tell Sylvia that she was helping me paint the house.

'For if Helen really is deserting me, we'll have to sell up. On the other hand if she's not it would no doubt seem logical, especially to Sylvia's mind, to present my wife with a newly painted house when she does return.'

'Come clean,' she demanded. 'What is the situation?'

I looked at her cautiously. After my recent experiences I was all too aware that you've got to be hellishly careful who you hang

74

around with.

'Josie, you're not going to get ideas, are you? We're just helping each other out of a spot. Right?'

'We're just mates,' she agreed with what appeared at the time to be far more sophistication than other people, who will for the present be nameless and ought to have known better, ever showed.

'But mates ought to be honest with one another.'

Her youth. Honesty. Mmm.

'But ought lovers?' I tousled her hair.

'No, go on, Jeremy, stop kidding around.'

'Ask one question.'

'Three.'

'Two.'

We looked at each other. It had been a particularly tiring day and I was rather hoping that she would cook me a meal while I put my feet up and watched the Channel Four news. Not to mention enjoying an undisturbed whisky.

'Get on with it then. Quick, quick.'

'Is she coming back?'

'She might.'

'Do you want her back?'

'I might.'

'You're not sure?'

'Not allowed. Only two questions, remember.'

'But this is a definition of number two. Come on, Jeremy.'

Her eyes had a straightforwardness which in time, though not this summer, was going to cause some chap a great deal of trouble.

'Let me see. I've never believed in divorce and all that kind of thing. Too much of it around. Bad for the children. Bad for everyone as well as being, frankly, financially disastrous.'

'But do you love her?'

'Now that really is too many questions. Tell you what. Why not make up for your badness, eh, by rustling up some kind of supper for us both. Since I'm your boss I think I can comment with some authority that your day has been not half as exhausting as mine.'

With good grace she moved into the kitchen. But later as we were eating a dubious bean stew with a raw spinach doused in a dressing the like of which I'd never tasted before and wasn't at all sure I wanted to again, she came at me with the following.

'Can I make a suggestion, boss?'

'Mmm.'

'Does that mean yes?'

'While I'm eating your bean stew – however awful – I rather feel I'm in your hands.'

'It's not awful, is it? Listen I was thinking. Why don't we paint the house? Frankly I've never seen such a dump. And if you do want her back, well you'd have done something. I suppose I can't ask you why she ever left?'

'You cannot.'

'No, I somehow reckoned that wouldn't be on. Pity. But something you've got to tell me. Doesn't it make it worse, I mean it can't be actually helping any me being around like this?'

'Don't be a chicken. She's in Dorset. She'll never know. Besides it keeps me cheerful and well fed. I take that back. Fed. And more or less satisfied in other departments.'

'Thanks a bundle.'

'So you see when she does turn up, if she does, I won't be such a grouse. After all it was she who deserted, taking all my children with her.' I beat my chest. 'It's criminal.'

'I think I see. Well what about painting the house? I'd like to feel I was doing something.'

'Oh you, you're always doing something.'

'You're just bone idle, Jeremy Farmer.'

'Careful, we don't want to sound like our mother, do we?'

'Oh and as to my mother that reminds me . . .'

And so we were back to where we started and I had a nasty idea that more than some of Josie's questions were going to have to be answered. Judging by this evening's performance. Still the bean stew was amply made up for by a smashing apple and cinnamon pie.

'Anna's recipe,' she claimed.

'Good for Anna.'

And somehow I found that I had bought litres of white paint at vast expense and brand new roller brushes at even greater expense and the next evening found me half way up a distinctly unstable ladder while my far too eager right-hand mate urged and encouraged, held tins and fetched rags and white spirits and other necessaries, and swore she was keeping a steadying hand on the ladder. But I had my doubts.

Clear it was to me that she was much more 'in love' with her mother, than she was ever in love with me. That's why I was fairly certain that I was doing the child no harm.

She talked much about the agency. Inevitable it was that when she became too serious, I fobbed her off.

'Relief, Josie, some relief, please, girl. It is after working hours, remember.'

'I don't think there is any such thing for Sylvia, do you?'

'Maybe not.'

'She says being an agent is a twenty-four-hour job that's why . . .'

'Yes, yes, but we're not built the same.'

'Tell me how you got into being an agent. I mean did you always want to be one? Did you decide at university, or what? How does that kind of thing occur to you, that's what I mean. Did you know anyone who was, for example, anyone in the family? I don't think Sylvia knew anyone. She must have just . . .'

I knew we were on dangerous ground. She loved to talk about the agency; of course she wanted to enter her mother's world to the full, that I appreciated. And I was a possible vehicle if you like. Or so she thought. And then she was interested in the whole business of it anyway. She had read widely and, except for one or two strait-laced teachers in that school of hers, in isolation. But had dreamt of being in a world of writers, of hobnobbing with the great. Could that have been my dream too, once? I very much doubt it. If anything, I simply thought there would be good money to make out of the whole process. And found myself grossly disillusioned.

She was a romantic. Full of old-world idealism. She was also bright and a good grafter and a fast reader. Though I wasn't too keen on most of the comments she made about the manuscripts she did read.

'Stop comparing them with the greats, Josie. You've got to become a little more sophisticated if your comments are to be worth something.'

'Sophisticated. But it's so much crap.'

'Not a very pleasant way to speak of our potential clients, darling.'

'But really, Jeremy, why . . .'

'It's all a matter of economy. Read the market. Give up your greats for a bit; probably do you good. Your head is stuffed full of so much nonsense. Get an idea of what is selling and why. Of what will sell. Do some homework, if you're seriously interested in this game.'

'I thought you liked my reader's reports.'

'For a college kid.'

'Damn you, Jeremy.'

At one point she really made me laugh. 'I think being an agent is partly learning the art of distinguishing one bad book from another.'

But this was later. For a time Fisk, Farmer, intrigued her to a degree that I had never seen in anyone. She was everywhere at once. A ball of energy around the place. And there was a way in which I wasn't adverse to her presence.

'Thank you for occupying my daughter so well.' Sylvia. I wasn't sure if she was being sincere or not.

'We all do what we can. According to our lights. You know that, darling.'

I didn't like the look she gave me.

'And how is the painting coming along?'

'We've managed the sitting room, plus two of the children's bedrooms. The hall and staircase is the next project. Josie thinks pale grey with a white border.'

'She does? And when did you say Helen and the kids are returning?'

'Ought to be the end of next week. I'm waiting to hear actually at this very moment.' She looked over my shoulder. We had both become such adept liars over the many years at this business that we let each other out easily. She knew of my problems and the cause. She knew too that I was reluctant to discuss Helen at present. I knew that she was reluctant to discuss the latest developments on that other matter. We were, you could say, trying to keep out of each other's hair.

'As to Josie, such a shame one doesn't know anyone of her own age.'

'I must be a very poor alternative.'

'It's something, I suppose. Painting your house must be better than hours by herself in the apartment. I just don't have time to take her out and around. Maybe when Helen gets back she'll know of someone – with all those relatives of hers.'

'Perhaps so.'

Sylvia is a poppet but, as with all people one has worked with for very many years, one learns the necessity of skirting round issues as much as possible.

Skirting was not something which Josie had begun to learn the importance of. In some ways despite great physical dissimilarity she

78

reminded me urgently of her mother when I had first known her, when she wasn't much older than Josie now. The young Sylvia. The Sylvia with fire and passion and determination for life. And it made me only too aware that I had been young then too.

Sometimes with Josie in bed, sometimes when she said something that particularly reminded me of her mother I was acutely aware of all our lives passing, of middle age and compromise and dreams unfulfilled: Sylvia's, Helen's, my own.

'What are your dreams, Josie?'

We were lying on the carpet in the sitting room, looking up at the expertly painted ceiling, our bodies warm from the aftermath of prolonged physical exertion. Her hair was in my mouth and with my last bout of energy I lifted a hand to remove it. Our legs comfortably entwined, she itched her little toe with mine while she thought.

'Sylvia: to make her love me. Or at the very least notice me. And to do something great, I suppose. I don't know what. Though I keep coming back to Lowry. I will not go back to university. I don't even think I want to go back to Canada. So I'll have to make a living here. Books, editorial assistant. What do you reckon?'

'Not easy. Even if you are Sylvia's daughter.'

'And almost Alison's.'

'I suppose there is that too. How do you get on with her, incidentally?'

'Not badly. I think I'd like her in other circumstances, you know what I mean. Actually I think I do like her. How about you?'

'I've known her for a very long time.'

'What's that meant to mean?'

'Means I might feel like qualifying whatever I might say.'

'Oh you,' she tickled my ribs till I caught her hand and stopped her. Tickling was not one of Josie's more sexy points. She did it rigorously, as I imagined she might her brothers and sisters when she was losing in some debate. Or just wishing to tease. Not to be encouraged. On the other hand for the most part it was pleasing to see her hesitant virginal body grow in sexual awareness and confidence. To see something flourishing under my tutorage. Made the depressing summer marginally more attractive.

'What I'd really like to do is write.'

'Oh God!'

'What's the matter?'

'That's what they all say.'

'Who?'

'All my women.'

'All? Not Helen surely. She doesn't sound the type.'

'No, thank God. Not her.'

'Well who then?'

'All the rest.'

'Jeremy, are you being serious. Have you had *many* women?'

'You're the youngest and the best.'

'Bet I'm not. You're just kidding me along. Anyway now I can see why Helen . . .'

'No, you can't see anything.'

One was rather cross. And of course one was aware of her youth at times like that. Of course one didn't mind mildly playing the older experienced man, the surrogate father/advisor kind of figure. But one wasn't having her playing the amateur psychologist. That was absolutely out.

But sometimes with her freshness and her clarity she had a way of cutting through all our pretensions in a way that made me reluctantly acknowledge there was something quite substantial about young Josie.

She was quick in the office and after a month I had to agree with Alan's summing up, that she was potentially a 'good thing'. She was typing both our letters now. The filing had been taken in hand and new systems instituted with neatly worded notices urging us to adhere to them. She told us she'd taken a Systems course as one of her general first-year courses. Along with typing and speed-reading and astrology and Italian and I don't know what. We were naturally suspect of anything learnt in a university, in a no doubt half-baked course.

But there she was with her systems and her filing and her little lists. And gradually letters became easier to find. Manuscripts were housed alphabetically. Phone messages were properly recorded and letters, I noticed, received subtle adjustments. Which I didn't comment on; if the girl wanted to use a token of her dormant literary talent, tightening up the syntax in my letters, let her. I was intrigued to know if she did the same for Alan's but didn't ask him. It's an old joke that my grammar isn't what it might be.

She was genuinely eager. One has to say that for Josie. There she was every morning dressed always in jeans and some kind of shirt or sweater. I never saw her in anything but jeans. But the ones she wore now looked more becoming. She wore coloured belts as the summer wore on. She let some of her hair out of its plait and looped it up in a ribbon or a slide. She washed her hair more frequently and it looked more glossy and smelt of lemon. Her movements became faster, more defined.

She was quieter now, no longer asking questions all the time. She would bring coffee or tea or letters to be signed without the wheedling, 'Shall I bring them now? Would you like coffee now, Jeremy?' She guessed my needs, or worked them out. Alan's too, I gather. We were both pleased with her.

'There's nothing between you, is there?' he asked me one Friday when he was speaking of her contribution to our set-up. 'That would really be . . .'

'You've nothing to worry about; you can't think I'd be such a damn fool.'

'No, I didn't think so. It's just some of the looks she gives you. And then I've noticed such a change in her.'

'She's settling down, I suppose. Finding a niche. Can't have been easy in the circumstances. As time goes by she's gaining confidence, no doubt.'

'She really is only a kid, Jeremy. As well as being Sylvia's kid.'

I put my arm on his shoulder. 'I know, old mate, I know. Believe me, there's nothing to worry about.'

The world divides, one finds, into the physical types and the non-physical. Those kind of non-physical buggers have simply no idea. But Josie and I understood one another. And I had absolutely no intention of allowing it to become a repeat of that other terribly messy business. That was all most unfortunate. But one learns. This was altogether something different. And infinitely more straightforward. And after all it would be over in a few weeks when Helen did eventually decide to return to the old homestead. Josie knew that. Nothing for Alan or anyone for that matter to start worrying about.

Meanwhile the office looked and felt a better brighter place. She seemed to have circumvented our muddle. Not cleared the books and the piles of paper exactly, I'd have murdered her if she'd tried to recreate the neatness of her mother's office. No, just made the mess that bit more ordered. And introduced one or two plants, some roses from the garden, iced tea in the kitchen, a tin of home-made biscuits, even an ash-tray secreted from Sylvia's flat.

'Isn't that going a wee bit too far?'

'She doesn't use it. Nobody does. I found it at the back of a cupboard.'

'Better ask your mother.'

Sylvia came to look at the minor transformations we were undergoing. Josie, hands on hips and proud, for she had just re-arranged the pin-boards, demanded:

'What do you think then, Sylvia? Is it an improvement?'

'I dare say it is.'

If the kid sought affirmation from some other source, who is to wonder.

'She's a mystery to me,' Josie frequently asserted. 'I wish you could help, Jeremy.'

'What would you have me do?'

'Tell me about her. Tell me all you know.'

And some evenings, those when I had particularly enjoyed her easily opened legs, her young quick juices, her mating cries with that tang of Canadian, louder, it seemed to me, than the entire dawn chorus, times when I had risen easily and ridden her hard, coming with that conclusiveness which makes the world for a time feel a sweeter place, those times I could foresee that I might, just might, tell her what I knew of Sylvia.

As it turned out it was more to distract myself than to cheer up Josie that I eventually gave way to telling her what I knew of that early period in Sylvia's life – and my own – that period when she made the momentous decision to leave Patrick and the children, a time which could not fail but to blow breezily with all the happiness and promise of my early years with Helen. Particularly painful just at this immediate present, for yesterday Helen and I had met in an olde worlde tea house on the edge of Salisbury Plain and there over a full cream tea, which sadly I was unable to eat, she outlined her ultimatum. She would not come back. She could never forgive me for this last final tangle, for the pending court case which would inevitably bring us some sort of notoriety throughout the publishing world and no doubt even a few unpleasant digs in the national papers. For no longer being able to believe my promises that I would change my ways. For much hurt over the years at all the other affairs she'd turned a blind eye to.

'Come on, Helen,' I tried to reason. 'Other aspects of our relationship have been substantial enough. And the other you never much wanted. I thought at one time you said you welcomed the respite, isn't that how you put it?'

'Yes, but that was only to keep up face. And look now at the trouble it's got us into; on top of everything you've been so very unwise, Jeremy, in the way you've handled things.'

'Listen, old thing, easy to say that after the event.'

'Don't call me old thing. I'm not that old and now I want some peace before it's too late. Peace from all these unpleasant emotions.'

'I don't know what you're talking about, for years you don't seem to have had many emotions.'

'Jealousy, Jeremy, is a deadly disease.'

'But, darling, you never said, you never let on.'

'Don't tell me it would have changed anything.'

'But of course it would have!'

'I don't believe you any more. That's almost the saddest part.'
And she began to cry, horribly painfully, silently.

Soon after that she'd dabbed her eyes with her napkin, picked up her bag and walked shakily out of the café. And I'd driven back to London. Josie was helping Sylvia and Alison prepare for a dinner party. The house seemed unbearably empty. I shut the door quickly on the newly painted children's rooms. Again and again Helen's bitter accusing expression came to me. I had let her down, caused her pain, and I cursed myself. Damn Ruth Flowert. With the others it had never been a problem. I should have chosen my women more carefully, been more circumspect, never a writer, that was the big mistake. I cursed myself for my folly. And wondered vaguely and more than vaguely, indeed long into the night, whether the damage was irreparable, as Helen insisted that it was.

I did not believe there would be a court case. I put full trust in Sylvia. She's a wily devil that woman. It might go far, but I did not believe it would go to court. A lot of it bluff. And that latest report from Jeffrey looked pretty good for us. No, of course it wouldn't get to the courts. Still, a nasty time for Helen with her kind of disposition. I can see that. Shouldn't have done it to her. Hell, but could one have known . . .

The following week I had little to say to Josie during office hours, little to say to anyone so that each telephone call was a pain in the neck. And as far as the evenings were concerned Josie's enthusiasm for the painting seemed to have waned or her mother had cottoned on to something and was putting up barriers. I can't say. But what was noticeable was that arrangements were made each evening which necessitated Josie remaining at the apartment.

On Saturday, however, by telling a lie, that having lost weight she wished to return to Harrods' 'Way In' for a more successful shopping spree, she managed to cut loose and come over for the day.

'Hello, stranger.'

'Crumbs you do look morose. We've all been talking about it.'

'All?' I didn't like this at all.

'Sal, Alan, and me for starters. Rumours are beginning to buzz round but I don't understand a word of them. Besides everyone hints but no one comes straight out and says. And I used to imagine that was what was so enchanting about you English!'

'Now listen, Josie, if you want to bring office nonsense round here you can just hop on the next bus to Knightsbridge, or how about a trip out to Woolwich to enjoy sherry and gossip with Alan and his girl-friend – if you haven't already.'

'All right, all right, Jeremy, you great big bear.' She came over to hug me. 'I don't know what's happened exactly but I'm on your side. Honest. What about bed? Will that cheer you up?'

'Do you know, I don't think it will.'

She laughed. 'Things *are* changing. What then?'

'It's so hot.'

'Perfect sunbathing weather.'

So we found ourselves on a rug in the garden and later that Saturday, as a distraction more for myself than for the redoubtable Josie, I began to tell her the story of Sylvia's transformation.

'Start at the beginning. When did you first meet her? How long have you known her?'

'Sylvia's story starts way way back. It was her brother whom I first knew. Two pimply boys finding ourselves in neighbouring beds in our first term at public school. Swapping ghastly schoolboy jokes, sharing fagging tasks, and trying to eat packets of crisps after "lights out", without being detected by the prefect's quick ear. We were not close friends but rather for years we were pals in a comfortable kind of way. Timmy had the eagerness, the desire to succeed of his race. I was naturally lethargic; except when it came to rugger and cricket.'

There were a number of Jewish boys at our school. Most of them set apart by missing Saturday morning prep in order to go to synagogue, and missing Sunday chapel in order to enjoy themselves (the general consensus). Timmy didn't go to synagogue, and did attend chapel. But naturally enough at a place like an English public school in the 50s where prejudice was rife, it took more than going to chapel to be able to join in fully. And Timmy, despite his vigorous good looks and quick mind, was always just somehow on the outskirts of what was really going on.

I had my cronies. Rugger playing, beer drinking, always doing the minimum amount of work and being satisfied that by dint of yet another lucky stroke to have just scraped through another exam. Timmy's distinctions, his desire to be at the top of every class, amused us all. And irritated some. But I don't remember him as being aggressive, or anything other than modest over his achievements; and far from being irritated myself I was faintly respectful, even drawn towards him, though not sufficiently to entice me to step outside the group in which, by the third year, I was comfortably ensconced.

When Timmy was in the fifth form, his younger brother Edward started at school. I was struck by how forthright Timmy was in demonstrating his brotherly affection for his sibling, however much it was against the pervading mores of the majority of nasty little public school boys that we were. But Timmy was unrepentant. He did what he believed to be right. Not exactly flamboyant, but certainly at the risk of jeers. Which duly came his way, so surprised were we to see him standing openly in the corridor with his arm round the younger boy. Or talking with obvious pleasure together in a male environment where this kind of show of affection, in general, and perhaps particularly between siblings, was much frowned on.

Not having siblings – my parents were in India and I spent the holidays with an elderly couple in Purley (my second cousins on my father's side) whose own two children had long since grown up and flown the nest – I was intrigued by this kind of so obviously close bonding. And from time to time I found myself wondering about Timmy's home life, these so-called English Jews with their strange quiet pride. And on an Exeat when Timmy mentioned that his parents were up to take him out and would be at the chapel service beforehand, I made a mental note to myself to see if I could identify them amongst the crowd in the top gallery.

That was the first time I saw Sylvia sitting between them in a yellow cotton dress and enormous straw hat shading her face.

That spring we had a burst of unusually hot weather. When Timmy mentioned that his family were planning a canoeing picnic on the next Exeat and would I by any chance be interested in joining them, I accepted with alacrity.

Some twenty miles north of the school the river Ouse meandered its way pleasantly through rolling countryside. We made our way to a village off the beaten track where Timmy's family the year before had happened on a riverside inn whose landlord had bought half a dozen flat-bottomed canoes and rented them out at five shillings a go.

Owing to the heat his parents chose to remain sitting in the shady garden drinking tea whilst Timmy, Edward, Sylvia and myself took a boat and worked our way up to the waterfall.

All four of us rowed. Their intense — not exactly competitive — earnestness about whatever it was that they were doing at the time drove them, even on that hot day, to canoe the river with more speed and vigour than I would have opted for, or anyone else on the river that afternoon, judging by the other boats we sped past on our way.

I was amused. Once or twice I even remonstrated and stopping, insisted that I needed to trail my fingers in the ice-cold stream water in order to cool off. At these moments they teased me for my idleness. And in all these years, things in that direction have little changed.

Timmy and Sylvia sat next to one another, Edward was on his knees in the front, myself at the back. Sylvia was wearing the same yellow dress I had seen her in the first time in chapel. She was almost as tall as her brother. Both were dark and had tanned quickly in the preceding days of sunshine. Edward was fairer and not as stunningly good-looking. Both the others had brown limbs, ruddy faces, red apple cheeks and wide sensual lips of a deep dusky red. Reminding me of gypsy children. I had never before made this analogy when thinking of Timmy, but now with his heightened colouring, emphasised by the counterpoint of his sister, it came to me markedly.

Sylvia must have been fourteen and a half. Half way between girl and woman. She was careless with her dress, allowing the hem to lie muddy at the bottom of the boat and at one point nonchalantly wiping the handle of the oar on the left-hand pocket in a way which made me wonder if she remembered that she had worn this dress last time she came to the school. Or was it only I who had that kind of eye for detail then? She seemed oblivious of her beauty, careless of whom she attracted with it. And it seemed to me, perhaps romantically, that even then, perhaps particularly then, she had them all ensnared. She could have ensnared anyone she looked at. It was as simple as that.

Because she was still oblivious, pre-aware, just a child, she wasn't shy. Nor at all self-conscious. While she rowed, plunging the oar in and out with a swiftness and dexterity that well kept up with Timmy's, she chatted to him and to me with frank interest and friendliness. I was at first disconcerted by how much she knew of our school life, how much of its nasty schoolboy secrets had been shared with her in the holidays, and in the term-time correspondence between them which loomed large in their conversation.

On that first occasion it was generally I who was disconcerted, not she. For I was no longer a child. My taste for the female sex already developed and, at our monastic boarding school starved, I was eager and lusting. If only my energy, as opposed to my idleness, had been more evenly distributed to the other aspects of my life!

At the waterfall, hot and exhausted, we tethered the boat. Shoes were taken off. We ran through the clear, icy water looking down with wonder at the turbulence below. Then, climbing over a stile, we made for the shade of a tree, for a five-minute breather before starting our return journey; which was no doubt to be as arduous as the one out.

'But worth it now we've got here,' Sylvia laughed at me from her position on her back in the purple green grass. 'Don't you think so, Jeremy?'

'Don't bother with him,' Timmy told his sister. 'He'd never admit it, whatever he thinks.'

As we returned to the boat, I climbed the stile before her and put out my hand to help her down. But she jumped wide and ran past me back across the river above the waterfall, a spray of water in her wake.

After the aforementioned picnic Timmy and I unwittingly drew closer. As if we had experienced together something private and special. And consequently when we entered the sixth form, I wasn't surprised at his suggestion that we share a study. Nor at my own easy acquiescence.

Timmy's conversation in the privacy of our study was frequently peppered by references to his family, interspersed with all that otherwise engages the minds of sixth-formers: a combination of work, sport and sex; the latter more often in the head than in the reality. Though in my case the unusual flavour of my home life in

87

Purley compounded by the freedom that it allowed (as long as I was in to meals and retained a healthy appetite my uncle and aunt asked no questions) meant that there was scope to develop my tastes and natural bent earlier than might have happened in other circumstances. Since starting to share a study with Timmy I had already been 'in love' three times, as he pointed out to me.

'And what about you?'

'I'm waiting.'

'For what?'

'Oh for the Grand Passion,' he joked. 'Meanwhile there are "A" levels and Oxbridge entrance.'

'Bugger all that!'

But although I continued to make a pretence that I didn't care a horse's fart, I too was finally beginning to pull my weight academically.

'I might read History at Cambridge,' I suggested one day. 'What do you think?'

'Are you planning to take over from old Rodgers here?' He started to laugh.

'Cut it out, will you, Fisk. What about you?'

'I'm going to do something brilliant, naturally. I'm not sure what yet. Plenty of time.'

'And Sylvia?'

'I expect she'll marry Tony who'll eventually take over from the old man in the business. He'll end up chairman, and she chairman's wife. She'll have a lot of babies. All of them beautiful. Anyway that's the plan for now. Look, why all this talk of the future? Let's see if we can rustle up a game of poker. There's just about time before Evensong.'

Though when I asked questions about his family, particularly Sylvia, he would respond directly, yet I noticed a certain barrier, a privacy about those things close to his heart which made me wonder. It was as if good manners, his natural urbanity, prompted his answer. His inclination would have been to protect her, protect them all. From what, I wondered? From attacks on all Jews down the ages? Or something more particular? Or some sense of family being holy in a way it was difficult for me to get a handle on?

As we roamed the rabbit-warren corridors in search of poker companions, my mind remained with what he'd said. That Tony had apparently already been chosen for Sylvia. By whom, by everyone? That her children would be beautiful. His awareness then of her beauty. Though it was there for all the world to see, the open acknowledgement of it by her brother I found arresting. And though I had eagerly looked to the gallery many times (every time indeed that Timmy's parents were due to come up for an Exeat) in the hope that she would be there, though I was as utterly taken by her early beauty as anyone else around, I was aware too of other feelings; of concern, even of pity, of wondering what that kind of beauty would do to a life.

In the summer of our sixth-form year Timmy invited me to Hove to spend a week with them. As eighteen months ago but more definitely now I leapt at the opportunity. Frankly I was waiting to be asked. My current love, sweet, wonderfully curvacious Brigitta, an 'au pair' with a Purley family, was to be away on holiday with her family for the entirety of August, and the Cosmo coffee bar and other Purley delights were beginning to pall.

I had no doubt that a week with the Fisks would be an interesting experience. Something about them intrigued me as much as ever.

They lived on the divide between Brighton and Hove. The house was large, sprawling, low; built of red brick, in the first decade of this century. The inside was sumptuous, but ugly. Heavy chunky furniture, deep red carpets, heavy green velvet curtains, a hint of brocade. I remember a ridiculously fluffy long-haired rug by the fire. Of the type that you sit on, only to be embarrassed by finding all the hairs on your backside when you stand up. I remember chunky furniture. Much dark wood. Cushions so puffed up that one was reluctant to sit down and lean against them.

My first impression of the ornately furnished, scrupulously clean interior was that it was too formal for these young people, not at all the setting I'd expected to find them in. No, they and the house didn't seem to go together. It was only when later they took me to explore the full extent of their terrain that I became aware of an area quite separate from the house which bore their mark: a walled rose garden in the middle of which there was a summer-house, to which a second floor had been added. Downstairs a ping-pong room, upstairs their space.

It was five o'clock in the evening when I entered the house for the first time. Mid-August. A balmy evening, but overcast. A mist blowing off the sea giving strange definition to the outline of the buildings. I was aware of the width of the street, the solidity of the houses, the kind of silence that comes when sound is cushioned by the sumptuousness of the surroundings.

I rang the doorbell and was let in by a matronly woman in overalls.

'Is this Mr Fisk's residence?'

'It is.'

'I'm expected. At least I hope I am. Jeremy Farmer – school friend of Timmy's.'

'Ah, Master Timmy.' It was a long drawn-out sigh and I wondered what it meant. 'Mr Fisk is in the drawing room. I don't know about the others. You'd better go in. If you'd like to leave your case with me, I'll see it's taken to your room.'

She pointed to the closed drawing room door and having left my case with her I moved across the square hall and entered the door she had indicated. The furniture was pushed to the walls and windows and on the pool of carpet making up the entire centre of the room, were piles of coins, pennies, ha'pennies, sixpences, shillings, halfcrowns, ten shilling notes.

A voice booming and rich.

'Ah Jeremy, old chap, delighted to see you. Just in time to help me count these.' A head appeared from behind the sofa. 'We're nearly there. Nearly through. Now if you could bring over all the sixpenny piles that would be a help.'

Literally in his counting house, counting out his money? It seemed too preposterous to be true. My mind toppled over with disgraceful amusement at the idea, coming as I did from the kind of family where money, like politics, religion, even love, was kept out of sight if at all possible. But only for a moment was I allowed to hold on to this delicious fantasy. For no, the Fisks had opened their garden to charity – The Benevolent Society for the Blind – had had their annual fête in the grounds. 'Timmy and Sylvia ran some kind of water gag, entirely their own show. Very popular. You should have seen the queue building up to pay to have Sylvia throw a wet sponge.' (Yes, I could imagine it.) 'Don't know where they are now, by the way. Everyone seems to have disappeared. Now if you could just pass over the penny piles, we'll soon get the thing under control.'

'Two hundred and fifty pounds, we made,' he told them over dinner. 'Quite a killing.'

'Seventy pounds up on last year, Dad,' Timmy declared. 'It was

Sylvia's water show that did it.'

'All the stands were better organised this time. It was fun,' she laughed. 'We should have invited you earlier, Jeremy, but Timmy thought you'd find it a drag.'

Of course she'd outgrown the yellow dress. How silly of me to think otherwise. She was sixteen now. Much the young lady. Blossoming and proud of it. Natural. Knowing her beauty now but unaffected by it. Taking it as a right.

How proud both parents seemed of their children, enjoying the knowledge that they had benefited from advantages which they themselves had been denied. Timmy and Sylvia were of a piece, Edward the odd one out: his tastes more eccentric, also more solitary. He and Timmy had less now to say to one another, although a bond of affection still held them together. But he was no longer the young boy I had first noted eagerly talking with his older brother in the corridor. He seemed already to convey a sense that his manhood was going to be of a different nature to Timmy's.

Sylvia, on the other hand, was actively engaged with everyone. Timmy still obviously adored her. They appeared inseparable. And Edward still brought her his treasures and his discoveries. She listened to both her brothers with her easy unaffected openness and her smile, as if the world was such a very pleasant place.

Where was Tony, I asked Timmy that night as we lay in twin beds in his clean anonymous bedroom. The room gave the impression that a bevvy of maids had been through it each term when he was away at school, cleaning, tidying, spring-cleaning, endlessly re-papering so that it should bear not the slightest hint, smell, clue of boyhood life. Strange. If he'd told me it was the guest room I would have been less surprised. Tony was with his family in the South of France but would be returning in a few days.

The next morning a letter arrived from the very person in question and I admired Sylvia's quiet confidence and good grace as everyone pored over it and asked questions as if she and her affair of the heart was public business. I, I knew, would have been far more churlish had any of Brigitta's wonderfully passionate epistles been up for scrutiny.

The holiday was a long time ago and my memory is hazardous and often nowadays sadly vague. My children, especially Rebecca, berate me. But what do I recollect? The sun throughout a hazy light. Warm, but much sea mist. The winds when the sun wasn't shining, bracing, and gusty in the garden and in the house. A sense of being exposed, physically, I mean, to the weather conditions. And a sense that the Fisks liked this, that they wished to be more hardy, more physical than their ancestors.

Memories of swimming on the beaches, running on the hard pebbles and pretending not to mind. Of playing deck quoits. Of long fast walks on the Downs. The wind always blowing. Of political discussions, of chewing over world affairs, their affairs, Brighton's affairs, all of the world's problems in earnest breathy voices as we strode the Downs with their three spaniels and their long-haired giant poodle – Sylvia's favourite. Of riding bareback along Devil's Dyke on ponies rented from a local stable, of evenings in the summer-house. That most of all. For jiving was just coming into fashion, as were flared skirts and many-layered petticoats, and Sylvia, dressed accordingly, was eager to teach her brother and myself the latest steps.

Sometimes I sat sprawled on the Dunlopillo cushions edging the wall watching them dance, the two of them so physically similar that the cliché readily came to mind: two peas in one pod. Dancing for hours, it seemed, with myself dizzy and tired from the very act of watching them swirl. Then it would be my turn. I wasn't as good a dancer as either of them.

'Get the rhythm into your body, Farmer,' Timmy would say.

'Don't tease him,' his sister would object.

She was easy and pliant and I would feel myself succumbing. And Timmy impatient, never a watcher he, it didn't suit his nature, would roam out to smell the evening roses or return with comments on the stars or tomorrow's possible weather condition, or he would return to the house and leave us two to our own devices.

And I would treasure those times, not for the physical contact, since I always held myself aloof, knowing Sylvia wasn't for me. Nor for what she had to say which – as tends to be the case with beautiful people – is difficult to remember. But mostly because she gave the air of having life and life's richness in her hands and it was heady to be with her then. Making of Brigitta and my Purley life tawdry stuff indeed.

This was true in its entirety of life with the Fisks for me. It seemed to be composed of something other. Other than my experience so far. I found it heady.

Tony duly returned. With a sister (of this I'd had no forewarning) who had set her sights on Timmy. A sister only a month or two younger than Timmy and myself, Tony being two years older, already a year out of school and working in his father's firm.

I have a vague recollection of Tony. It was years ago and besides I think I was reluctant to take him into my consciousness. His sister I was more curious about. She was after all the opposite sex. And I was secretly interested in any young woman other than his sister who might form a place in Timmy's affections. Soon I realised that Gillian would not do. She had auburn hair, a heart-shaped face and green eyes. She could jive to perfection. But for the most part she was lethargic where the Fisks were energetic, she would come to the beach only to lie and sunbathe, her prettiness demanded continual attention and grooming, and much of what she said was trite.

Timmy put up with her with his usual urbanity, he even humoured her, but one look between brother and sister was enough to let me know what he was thinking. Perhaps he put up with her so continuously because it allowed the four of them to become a pleasant and neat foursome. It seemed to me that Sylvia always enjoyed her brother's presence, even when with Tony, and possibly intuiting this, Timmy fostered this dual relationship. Or perhaps he just let it happen, as he did much else. If life offered anything approximating good fortune his tendency was to grasp it and refrain from difficulties unless they were virtually pushed in his face.

I remember Tony as red-haired: not his sister's deep auburn, rather a sandy crinkly hair. A freckled face. A square jaw. Sensual thick lips. Of medium height. A thick heavily built body. As with Gillian, a sense of someone who was happier indoors than out. Later Sylvia said to me of him, 'He was a good orthodox Jew, kindly but tough in business, good to his own, caring in his community, bound to fulfil all his Barmitzvah promise. But without imagination.'

That was of course much later.

Sylvia and he had been 'going out' almost since that boating trip on the Ouse. Though I found that a sacrilege. As if it couldn't have been anything of her doing. She with the dirty yellow dress of which she was so unaware.

Tony carried with him the air of getting the best, whatever the best was deemed to be. And as far as girlfriends went, who better than Sylvia Fisk. He gave me the impression of not really understanding her. Of seeing that she would grace his table, and his bed – though he didn't strike me as a chap who'd have much imagination in that direction – and bear him fine children, as everyone had said.

There she was, holding his hand, and talking to him with the same sweet partiality she used for everyone. No sparkle, is what I thought. And I already knew that she had sparkle. She'd be throwing herself away, I was sure. But any such sentiment could be considered biased and when I tried to raise the topic with Timmy he quickly let me know – with all his usual courtesy – that it was a closed shop, not open to discussion.

I suspected that Edward, perhaps the most original of the Fisks' children, was the least influenced by his parents. He resisted their subtle yet ever-present drive. He stuck to his guns, and though perplexed by him they were prepared – perhaps had no alternative – but to allow him to become the kind of person he was destined to be.

Whereas with the older two there was a noticeable malleability, a softness that went with their charm. And both parents recognised that and intended to play a large part in moulding their children. For Timmy that naturally meant a career, the university education that the parents had not had the opportunity to enjoy. For Sylvia an excellent marriage, financial stability, queening it in the Jewish community. They wished for them both, though in different ways, to move as far from the mid-European ghettos of their ancestors, as would be possible. And seeing that both had so many of the natural attributes that would enable them to do just that, they were bent on helping them, urging them, to make the most of their advantages.

Father Fisk was tall, thin, dynamic, a face like a jagged rock with an enormous nose which took over as being the only feature of note: eyes, lips, etc. dwindled in comparison. He was not good-looking. But he had a rugged enthusiastic charm and struck me as a highly intelligent man.

Mother Fisk was more of an enigma. I never got to know her well. She was almost as tall as her husband and he must have been near on six foot. She was quieter. I was aware of a good intelligence at work when she did speak, but in her husband's presence she let him do almost all the talking. I imagined, however, that in the privacy of their bedroom she had much to say and was sure that she was a vital, if less easy to define, force in family affairs. She ran a home for cancer sufferers in the locality and this, plus a number of committees and her work as J.P., kept her fully occupied. She had, if I could describe it as such, a kind of queenliness which was untouchable. I never had a sense of what she thought of me. Not then. She let her husband make the advances.

I surmised, and again I may well be wrong, that Sylvia felt that she had a lot to live up to. She was pretty, beautiful in a way that her mother never had been, but her mother had a stern, strong, queenly pride which made the rest of us feel horribly mortal. And I wonder how that defined Sylvia's view of her own life and opportunities.

It niggled me that such different futures were being mapped out for the two of them. Was it because I didn't feel Tony worthy of her? Was I jealous? No, I think neither of these, though an outsider might well have pointed a finger in that direction. I remember being conscious of thinking 'such a waste'. Of being aware of untapped energies, of wanting, even, to tap them.

But Sylvia herself that holiday seemed blissfully happy and at ease. Creating her own magic wherever she went and binding us all to her. Making of all those truly innocent and pleasurable escapades on beach and Downs and over at the summer-house in those long evening hours of dancing and the endless games of croquet on their manicured lawns, occasions that as I said to myself, when ten days later I took the train back to Purley, were memories that dreams are made of.

But Sylvia didn't marry Tony. It was Patrick she became engaged to. A chap from Timmy's college whom he hardly knew before that fatal event — except as nodding acquaintances — and had no opportunity to afterwards.

It was our last year. Two months to finals. Late March. Crisp, cold. Breath frozen in early morning walks, gas fires which required sixpenny pieces and on which crumpets were toasted on long forks. The season of punishing hard work to make up for three years' excesses and recurring lapses.

Timmy and I had retained our friendship as the shift was made from school to university. We were both at Oxford, I following in my father's footsteps at Worcester, he breaking new ground at Balliol. One need hardly mention his parents' pleasure.

Timmy had an extensive circle of friends. He was reading PPE, which suited his talents well. Was rowing, acting at OUDS and becoming prominent (tipped for president in his second year — though he didn't get it) in the Debating Union.

I was reading History, a choice I had regretted half way through, not so much because of my lack of interest in the subject but because the future seemed as unclear as ever. Of course I worked — though no more than strictly necessary — and expected a reasonable degree. Unlike Timmy I had no thought of making a mark at Oxford, which would be left much as I found it.

My goal, if any, was to make a mark on Somerville College. The delights of which were there to be enjoyed and most undergraduates seemed too uninterested, too inexperienced, or too pimply to offer much competition.

So our energies were being occupied variously. Timmy's number of friends and contacts covering an ever wider field. New names on his lips every occasion we met. But he was also careful to remain constant to his old friends, and often, returning to Somerville at some late hour having helped my latest girlfriend over the wall in good undergraduate fashion, I would find him sitting in my room browsing through my books, eager for a chat.

So it was one Friday in late March.

'Well who was it tonight?' he greeted me.

'Kathy.'

'Again? You're in danger of constancy. Better watch out!'

'Nothing like that.'

He looked at me sideways, then laughed. 'You wait till I tell Sylvia that our old friend Jeremy has been seen around with the same girl for a full six months. Could it possibly be true love?' This he trilled with enjoyment as he sat sprawled out on my own comfortable armchair.

'Knock it off, Fisk. Know any new jokes?'

'Listen, the reason for my late visit . . .'

'Reason – what's that got to do with anything?'

'. . . since you look as if you can't keep your eyes open a second longer than you have to – is that Sylvia is coming up tomorrow. Staying over the weekend. I've got myself involved in a rather crazy scheme which could be fun.' He outlined his proposal.

'What a bore. I'm off with Kathy to her folks' place. Otherwise I'd have jumped at it.'

'You want to watch it,' he said, referring to Kathy. The last words he ever spoke to me.

There was a friend of his who had the idea of buying a disused castle in Wales, but who had no car. There was Timmy's glossy black mini – a twentieth birthday present. There was Sylvia for whom Timmy, when approached, thought it would make an amusing trip into the countryside. There was an empty seat and a friend of the man who had his eye on the Welsh castle, who Timmy knew by sight but not to speak to – a medical student – who Timmy agreed might as well come along if he so wished. He did; a day's jaunt being just the thing to blow anatomy or physiology from the brain, and the sweet Welsh air certain to send one back to Oxford to attack textbooks with renewed vigour. Or maybe he had simply heard of the beauty of Timmy's sister. Something impossible to hide, ever. But where more so than amongst the undergraduates of Oxford.

There was the castle beside which a cement works had been built. The castle, which was little more than a number of stone walls, like a half finished game of boxes. There was the disappointment. The long journey there and back. A certain and unusual tiredness in Timmy. He had mentioned this before they started their return journey. And the offer was made by both the others that either of them would drive. There was the matter of the insurance which made such a simple alternative impossible.

There was the approaching dusk, that time of day when headlights are not yet effective but the sun is low and shadows make pools on the road. Half light. The long, not particularly wide, straight road. Timmy with his foot down hard saying, 'With this kind of weight in the car, sixty is the limit, you can hear it groaning.' A number of rowdy songs. The thought that they might later stop somewhere for dinner. A van ahead, but at sixty it was easy to pass it. So Timmy swung out. At which moment the driver of the van noticed the pub on the right and decided to turn into its car park. Only he crashed into the overtaking mini instead.

Now, out of control, it was the mini, not the van, that raced towards the car park. Which was packed with cars whose owners were enjoying a Saturday evening out at this country inn – the kind that might have gone in for dinner dances; music indeed, the tune of the foxtrot, Sylvia later remembered, issuing forth.

On through an arch at the far end Timmy and his passenger-laden mini belted. Belted because the brakes seemed to have been affected by the first jolt and were no longer operational. The inner courtyard was walled like the disappointing castle they had so recently left. They were still travelling at a considerable speed. Timmy's passengers spontaneously moved from seats to the floor. Where they crouched as low as was possible. The moment of impact. The glass, the metal and all the bits that were the mini cascading into the air as if they were being expelled from a volcano.

Then silence. And not many minutes later the screech of ambulance and fire engines.

In a local hospital Sylvia and the recently potential owner of the Welsh castle lay in a critical condition; and the young medical student, who had not expected so soon to be experiencing the other side of his chosen profession, with two broken legs and one broken arm, writhed in excruciating pain.

There was a coffin and in it Timmy's unrecognisable body, soon to be lowered into the earth.

Then followed the long slow months of the aftermath in which one life had been lost and others were changed irredeemably. The monstrosity of it all, and the waste. Leaving – as with all lives young and full of promise – those who remained with the desire to cry out, in crowded rooms and lonely graveyards, why him, why her, why, why?

'Geeze,' she interrupted.

With effort I returned from that terrible time: from the moment of my first knowledge of what had transpired; my own frantic efforts to borrow a car; my meeting with the Fisks at the small and hurried funeral at a nearby country church. 'Well, what is it?'

'You're a story-teller, Jeremy!'

I turned my head to observe her. Not for the first time her youth struck me as distinctly unappealing. The crude linear lines of understanding. Middle-aged men and young women should fuck noisily but eat in silence. Nothing else is possible.

I wanted her out of my house quickly. Wanted to enjoy the rest of the evening (for the day had passed and the sun had already set) sitting watching the moon come up over the terrace of houses that backs my garden, breathing in the full fruitful air of real, unusual English summer, listening to the birds singing their song, so much more true than anything I might say to her. Remembering.

'Sure, it's gripping, the way you tell it. You should be a writer yourself. Perhaps you are, in secret. But it wasn't quite like that, not exactly. For example, you aren't going to lay all the rest on the door of uncle Timmy's death, are you? She is my mother, remember. I do know some things. Besides the way you talk about her, when she was young and beautiful, it's as if you were in love with her yourself, it's spooky.'

'Josie, it was years ago. Years and years ago. I wasn't in love with her, no. There are some people, you'll find it yourself, few, but for everyone some, at least one, rarely more than three or four, whose lives run into one's being. The tracks can go right through the middle, or simply skirt the side. Whatever, it's there, of importance, something one lives with. At the beginning one hopes and imagines, if one imagines anything, that one is going to be a benefit in those people's lives.'

Let her go. Let her by divine providence get up and go.

'Are you going on, then? Next instalment? The grand passion of Patrick and Sylvia perhaps? The brilliant young medical student who with such prescience found himself a seat in the car heading for a Welsh castle. A terrible crash followed by a crashing love. Ha! Ha! I've never quite seen Dad in that light, Jeremy.'

'Bugger off, will you now. Nothing against you, honest. Honest,' I repeated, touching her arm to reassure. 'Just not the time, Josie. Just not the time.'

She got up uncertainly.

'I'll phone you tomorrow then?'

'Good girl.'

Damn! Damn!

It was the following weekend. Sunday morning. Noon. Weather still exceptionally hot and the house stuffy. I knew I ought to make the effort to open a few windows, but most had stuck, due to Josie's extra enthusiasm with the paint brush. With my nerves more than usually ragged and a number of disturbed nights trailing me like a kite string, I didn't have the energy to make any such vigorous effort until after at least two cups of coffee, a bowl of cereal, and some hot buttered toast and marmalade.

So I was at the kitchen table sometime in the middle of a very hot Sunday when Josie peered in through the garden window. I went to open the back door.

'I've been ringing the front door for ages. Couldn't you hear? Why didn't you answer?'

'Bell must be broken.'

'Really!' she laughed. 'Jeremy, you're not even dressed yet.'

'No.'

'It looks as if you've just got out of bed.'

'More or less.'

'Shall we just go back there then?'

'No.'

'Jeremy, you're going off me. All week.'

'All week what?'

'You haven't said a word to me.'

I raised an eyebrow.

'Except bare essentials. Boss-to-secretary stuff. Listen,' she said, are you down in the dumps, as my father would say? Me too. It's

99

rotten in the apartment. They put up such a wall, both of them. I can't tell what the hell is happening. And then I thought at least you and me were pals. I sort of reckoned on that. Look, I know you've got troubles. And I know they're nothing to do with me. But wouldn't it ease it some to tell me?'

'You're too nosy by half. I think I've told you that before.'

'What about Sylvia then? Will you go on with her story? Please, Jeremy.'

She put a hand on her side to flick away a fly that had settled on her and her T-shirt came up from her jeans leaving a slit of bare midrift. She walked towards me swaying her hips ever so slightly. Sensing that it would charm, newly proud of her body. Its poignancy defeated me.

'Jeremy,' she said sometime later into the hairs on my chest, 'when you were talking about Sylvia that other time, I said some pretty dumb things like I wasn't on your wave length or something. But it was only because the whole thing makes me jumpy.' She teased the hairs into straight lines.

'I know that.' I stroked her back. She was only two years older than my Rebecca. In two years time would Rebecca –? And would I be around to comfort her?

'So would you go on? It would be a tease to stop now.'

I sighed. 'I can only tell what I know. Not the whole story, you understand. If there ever is such a thing, which I doubt. After all I've only been on the sidelines. And then I'm not sure if it's what you want to hear.'

'I want to hear whatever you've got to tell me, Jeremy, honestly. Honestly.'

'Too many honestlys, you silly girl.'

'Well?'

'Maybe. Sometime. Not today. It's too hot and I'm not ebullient enough.'

'But it's the perfect day. And who needs ebullience? Geeze, I haven't got all the time in the world. I'll be back in Canada soon. Maybe by next weekend Helen will have softened and returned from Dorset, or wherever she is. Have you told her, incidentally, about the newly painted house? Here, if she did decide to come back I could cook a few hotpots and cookies and things and leave them in the fridge, and you could pretend you've learnt to cook some, all in honour of her.'

'No thanks, Josie.' But despite myself I laughed.

I went for a pee and sometime during its impressive duration I made a decision. A phrase came to me from a book I'd once read – and I hoped to hell it wasn't one of Ruth's, 'A man of desires, not choices'. It depressed me inordinately.

When I went back into the bedroom she was sitting in the same position she'd been in when I left her, with a bright eager look on her face. I sat on the edge of the bed and putting my right arm round her shoulders drew her to me.

'Listen, Josie. I'll make a deal with you. I will tell you about Sylvia, that is, as much as I know. And heaven knows how much good it'll do you. What you don't like you'll simply have to take with a pinch of salt, or say, "That's just Jeremy's way of seeing it, the old bugger." And there's always Josie's way of seeing later. You must never forget that. When you are your mother's age, certain things that seem impossible for you to imagine now, about which you're bound to feel harsh and judgemental, will fit into place through your own life's experience. You'll find yourself thinking, yes, I know why she did this or that, I feel why she did this or that, out of my own experience. Not in *that* way, Josie. You've proved that to yourself, if nothing else. But in other ways. After all, all life's experience is surprisingly alike. There is far more sameness than difference. It just comes in different guises, that's all. But Josie, in future, no more sex between us. That's the bargain.'

'Why?'

I got off the bed and walked towards the window. Saying 'No' to naked young women in my bedroom was not an art that I had had much opportunity to perfect. I looked out of the window at the watery blue sky and the tops of oaks and poplars and the one giant silver beech and thought of another garden and another silver beech. Thought of other times when I should have said no but had said yes. Thought of Helen, Sylvia, thought of Timmy. Of Ruth. Of Josie's youth. Enough was enough.

She was dressing. The sun streaking through the branches of the silver beech and into the bedroom, making patterns on her jeans and shirt.

'I'm not used to saying "no" to sexy young things.'

'Now you're mocking.'

'When you stand like that, I most certainly am not.'

'Well then?'

'Listen, can you just trust old Jeremy in this? For both our sakes it's the wisest thing we can do. In future, just pals.' I put my hand on her chin, drawing her up to my level so that I could see her eyes. 'Don't be hurt. I rely on you not to be. You've had enough of that anyway. Just say to yourself that I have sufficient affection for you not to want to draw you further into my muddles.'

'What we have isn't a muddle.'

'But other things are.'

'Is it because of my mother?'

I said nothing.

'Holy shitameroles, it's because of my mother!'

'No, Josie, it isn't.'

She was horribly silent.

'Geeze!' And then after a few minutes in a small voice. 'We'll still be pals?'

'Yes. Pals.'

I left her then and went out into the garden.

Later, in a mood which fitted well with the sombrely overcast but stiflingly hot afternoon, I took Josie and a bottle of wine to Kew gardens.

There was no reason to go on seeing Sylvia. I had always been a friend of her brother's, nothing more. I expected therefore that the Fisks would disappear from my life; far more painfully than they had ever shaded into it.

I took a not entirely disreputable degree. Then found myself chief messenger-boy and stooge for Charlie Wharton in his increasingly notable and noteworthy publishing house. And naturally enough moved to London. Sharing a flat with two Oxford friends. At the same time my parents whom I had only seen for two short spells since my school days finally returned from India and bought a modest retirement home on the Isle of Wight.

Rather inevitably we found that so many years of living different lives had hastened the process of becoming aware that we had little in common. But common decency was a term that got a certain amount of usage in those days, doing the decent thing by your parents was something that most of us very much took for granted. And doing the decent thing in my case meant aiming to spend what time I had off from Charlie Wharton's exacting demands, down with them, however excruciatingly bored I might be.

Life was not altogether unpleasant. I was enjoying the freedom of London and the wider opportunities and variety than had been possible in Oxford. I was finding publishing not a totally impossible way to spend the days. The small annuity left by my grandfather was more than a little handy in supplementing a meagre income, as well as being an extra help in opening certain doors and charming my way around London.

But the death of a dear friend – and Timmy had been that – shifted my entire perspective. In childhood, youth, one takes everything so much for granted. Everyone one likes will always be there: the others will go away. Why should one think otherwise. All happiness is possible. And I repeat all happiness. So that death first and foremost speaks to one's frailty. One's lack of being on top of events, lack of being able to control them. The lack too of anything ever again being totally perfect such as those days with Sylvia and Timmy had been when we'd swum and walked the Downs. Or the long evenings of bonhomie in our study at school.

When I thought of the many many conversations we had had late into the night, I was acutely aware, in what otherwise might have been an exciting first year in London, that whatever happened to me, whatever I made of it all, Timmy would not be there to laugh over it with me, to encourage or cajole. It left a shade of grey where before a blue sky had spread. You had that childhood sky taken away when you were far far younger, I know. I can only tell you what it felt like for me. The loss. The constant reminder that Timmy was never to experience adulthood, was no more, would never fulfil that so much promise: 'there's so much time,' he'd said at school.

There was a loneliness, a lack of something that crept into my life and left me periodically depressed and wretched. In London going about my business I was usually too actively engaged – Charlie had a reputation of keeping his workers with their noses to the grindstone – to allow time for too much cognisance with my state of being. But in the long solitary patches in the house on Brading beach when my elderly parents slept in the afternoons, or watched television, or played scrabble in the evening I felt filled with restlessness and even anger.

I went for long walks on the beach, majestically deserted in winter, and there, looking at the sky and pondering the curious mystery of existence, I found myself on several occasions thinking of Sylvia and wondering if she had recovered, if she was out of hospital, what kind of a family Christmas would she be having with that tragedy between them. Or weren't the Fisks the kind who adopted their host country's festivities and, if so, perhaps that would be as well. Once or twice I even thought about making a contact with her. But rejected such a notion. The pain that would necessarily be involved. Diffidence. A hundred reasons.

The following summer one or two of my pals were sailing on the Island and I managed to persuade my parents to let them use their house as a base. The holiday was certainly jollier. But Christmas was the bugger and it was with no relish that on the afternoon of Christmas Eve, for the second year running, I made my way by crowded train from Waterloo, and even more crowded ferry, to Brading Sound.

On the deck we were cheek by jowl. Next to me two girls who had been at school with each other on the Island were swapping experiences of their time in London. Mandy, fair and bubbly, a student nurse at St Thomas's: the other, whose name I hadn't yet caught, at Imperial College, London, studying Geography. It was easier to pick up Mandy's name for her conversation was liberally interspersed with, 'So he said to me, Mandy, I wouldn't believe it' or 'I said to myself, Mandy, you've got to go after him if he's the one you really . . .'

She talked fast, her voice rising and falling, vital parts of the endless string of anecdotes of life as a student nurse getting exasperatingly blown away by the wind so that I was left only with tantalising titbits and a sense that she was a good-time girl, a go-getter. 'Life's there for the asking, that's my philosophy. What do you reckon?' she asked her companion. Who wasn't to be drawn. Preferring to ask questions and continue to draw Mandy out.

It was obvious why. She made the journey pass more quickly for all of us. I had my work cut out though in attempting to appear not to be listening. Mandy herself was delightfully oblivious, her companion less so. Once or twice I felt a glance in my direction and an attempt to shift position slightly so that Mandy's indiscretions with a preposterously large number of young doctors (if she was to be believed her record would come near to beating my own) were intercepted before hitting their goal (me, I liked to think) in full force.

When the boat docked I found I had donned more of the cheer appropriate to the beginning of this festive period. The Isle of Wight community was after all a comparatively small one. A raver like this was not likely to disappear into some fortress for ever. She was bound to show up somewhere if I kept my eyes open. Doctors sounded a pretty unimaginative lot, I thought, with some satisfaction. The ten days stretching ahead could be quite interesting after all, if my luck was in.

It was not however Mandy who showed up but the girl to whom she'd been talking, at my parents' Christmas Day sherry party, after church and before the obligatory turkey and Christmas pud. She turned out to be the daughter of near neighbours, Col. and Mrs Tomlinson. There must have been something in the look we gave one another that prompted my father's reaction:

'So you two know one another, do you?'

'Not exactly,' she replied carefully. 'We travelled over on the same ferry. I think your son was rather taken with my friend.'

'Oh dear,' said my father vaguely and drifted away.

'Can I fetch you some more sherry?'

'Please.' She handed me her empty glass.

Half an hour later I was saying:

'Stay to lunch.'

'What about my family? It's Christmas Day not just any . . .'

'Please.'

'There's your parents . . .'

'Please.'

Afterwards we went down to the sea front. It was a cold day but clear with a blistering wind. We wore scarves and held hands through thick woollen gloves. The tide was going out and we leapt from rock to rock, examining rock pools and the fish life therein. Her knowledge of fauna and flora was extensive. I was overwhelmed and enchanted under her tutelage.

The holiday, far from being spent in a series of bedroom scenes fit for any 'B' movie, as I had foreseen on the ferry, was spent trudging for miles and miles, in rain, hail and even snow showers, over beaches, hills, woods and farmland, hand in hand, and for hours on end in deep thoughtful conversation with this dark-haired, serious, knowledgeable young woman.

Helen was unlike any girl who had previously attracted me. She was small but stocky, with little to excite by way of waist or hips. Her clothes gave not the slightest hint of recognition of a concern for fashion or style. Her straight brown hair was scraped back from her pale oval face in a pony-tail. Her nose was just that bit too small in proportion to the other features of her face. But when I walked with her up dell down knoll, the rain splattering on our sou'westers, her small legs vigorously keeping pace with mine – and often outstripping them in her eagerness to show me some sight, some relic that she treasured (she had lived on the Island all her life and loved its streams and woods and cliffs and coves with a passion) I felt no more desire to go chasing for Mandy than to return to Charlie Wharton's sweat shop – the latter a fate regretfully only fifty-six hours away.

'But we'll both be back in London, that's the joy of it,' Helen reasoned. 'Now that we've found each other, why, with nothing standing in our way there's no earthly reason why we shouldn't go on seeing each other as much and as often as we like. Or is there?'

'No reason at all.'

London life, however, from the start – or rather, London life with Helen – seemed fraught with small difficulties. Nothing I could put my finger on. Hard even now to remember. Bouts of influenza. Anxieties with Helen's flatmates which made for tedious tales of Sue who had stolen the kettle and kept it for a week in her room, and Claire whose undies were for ever soaking in the basin or littering the bath. There was the feverish need for her to study (she was always a serious student) and the lack of privacy. There was nerves ragged, jagged; often the calm of our early walks seemed far away.

Nor was she comfortable with my flatmates. Alistair Whitehead particularly annoyed her and in response I thought I saw in Helen hints of schoolmarmishness and superiority which were off-putting. Alistair at the time was going out with Olivia Cavendish, a wonderfully glamorous creature whom Helen accused me of flirting with. There would be tears and more messy evenings. And sometimes a Sunday concert at the Festival Hall or a cheap meal in an Indian restaurant to make up.

Helen preferred what she called 'these simple pleasures' to the smarter life that I had until then previously dabbled in. Which was certainly a relief on my purse. Some nights – rather against her will, I always felt – I would entice her back to the flat, assuring her that the others were out (often the case at the weekend) cook her a splendid meal (I was a dab hand at steak and omelettes) and then to bed.

'We're perfectly fine together when it's just us,' she'd say. 'It's all the strains, of flat-sharing and London living. Now if we were married, don't you think . . . if it was like this every evening . . .' And so some of the money I was saving as a result of our more simple lifestyle I began to put aside towards a down-payment on a flat of our own.

Relying on Helen for the weekends at the very least, I ceased to chase every bit of skirt, every new adventure, across the length and breadth of London and found that I was working longer hours, taking on more responsibility and actually enjoying it. Found that work engrossed many of my free evenings and the glamour of the famous and wealthy even at one remove made up a little for the somewhat puritanical domesticity of my personal life. Helen encouraged me to go to these numerous 'do's' by myself. Which I was half relieved to do. We both agreed they weren't anyway for her.

But it was impossible for me not to recognise – my parents and Charlie himself alluded to it – that Helen seemed to have brought some stability into my life. 'Made of the right stuff that girl. Quiet. But still waters run deep,' Charlie. 'Salt of the earth. You're a lucky man. Her mother's a wonderful woman. Helen'll be the same. Hope you're going to be worthy of her,' my father. 'You know, I think she really loves you,' my mother. 'What are you going to do? You mustn't be keeping her hanging around for ever, Jeremy.' I think that they suspected that we were sleeping together and this was still frowned upon on the Island.

When Charlie gave me a rise and greater responsibilities in the firm ('You're turning out less of an amiable waster than I would have guessed') I proposed to Helen but suggested a year's engagement 'to get our affairs in order'. She was over the moon, sure 'all our little difficulties', as she put it, would work out, just as soon as we were living together in our own place, preferably some way out of the heart of London. 'Let it be a leafy road,' she begged. 'Your heart is in the Isle of Wight,' I teased her. 'Well we've got a year to look. Let's see what comes, see what we can afford.'

It was a gusty day – was it always gusty in Hove, I wondered? Colours were clear and sharp. February. A late snow fall had recently melted but now temperatures had turned to freezing and the remnants were cakes of black ice making the roads prone to skidding and the pavements treacherous for walking. The one or two people out with their dogs were going at a snail's pace. As was I: twenty miles an hour in my second-hand Morris Minor was as much as I dared to. The road was interminable. I kept looking at the numbers and thinking that I hadn't remembered it this far into town.

Finally after many false stops I turned into the driveway. Sylvia was at the window and hurried out, a thick grey cardigan over her narrow shoulders. She put out both hands to take my own, 'Jeremy, I knew you'd come. It's good to see you. Do I need a friend!'

107

'I'm sure you have more friends than anyone has a right to.'

She looked at me sideways. A look I found hard to interpret. Then picked up my overnight bag and hurried me into the house. She led the way up the wide staircase and along the first-floor landing.

'Same room.'

'Do you mind?'

I shook my head.

'Just time to wash and spruce up. You'll hear the bell for dinner in about ten minutes.' She walked over to the window and opened it. Pivoting on her heel and standing facing me, the vibrant light streaking in behind and around her. More beautiful than ever.

'Are you looking for signs of the accident?' A little laugh.

Perhaps I was.

'Why did you open the window; it's absolutely freezing in here.'

'Thought you'd want to blow some of the London cobwebs away.'

'Bloody cheek!'

She took a few steps towards me, 'Oh it is good to see you.'

'The same.'

'We've lots and lots to talk about.'

'Yes.'

'Well I'll see you downstairs then.'

Despite her 'lots and lots' dinner was a mostly silent affair. Fisks père and mère had visibly aged in the last four years or so. They seemed to have shrunk and were huddled in towards one another. Edward was at the University of Michigan, I gathered, and Sylvia had recently returned home after three years on the continent. There was a noticeable unease between daughter and parents.

Sylvia's presence then, perhaps more than ever then, demanded that one looked at it. But something inside her had turned, changed, making her more complex, depths that nobody, I guessed, could read, giving her beauty a more tantalising quality that would, I felt sure, draw many men on – with the promise that they alone would be the one to discover her mystery. Yet I felt immeasurably sorry for her. Perhaps I always had. At that moment too, I thanked my lucky stars for Helen. Sitting eating my sole and glazed carrots in stately silence, though I was aware of Sylvia through every pore. Was aware too of Timmy, as if around her he would always be a shadow, a shade, such their physical similarity. And this awakened anguish which oddly made me angry. She was there; he was not. It was as simple as that. Then I looked at her parents and suspected that something of the same reaction must be in them.

'You've changed,' she said. We were sitting having coffee on the floor in her room.

'What do you expect. I was a gauche undergraduate when we last met. You didn't imagine I'd remain like that for ever, did you? And then, you've changed yourself, from a pretty, suburban Jewish girl — if you'll forgive me — to an (I spread my arms wide in a dramatic gesture) — exotic creature.'

'Ha,' she laughed. It seemed to please her.

'I had to do something,' she said after a minute.

'Of course you did.'

She looked at me gravely. 'It was your college, you know, who gave me your address.' She said nothing more.

The room was small and square. Her bed was a mattress on the floor, over which was thrown a brick-coloured drape of some shiny material. A great quantity of green and blue cushions were thrown seemingly at random on the floor and over the bed, which was pushed against the wall. Rugs, one or two masks and a series of pencil drawings covered the walls. Heavy jewellery hung from nails in the wall. By the hearth on a brightly woven rug were bowls of pot pourri, a mysteriously musky smelling incense, two glass jars of polished shells. The room was the first of many that have held Sylvia's distinctive mark, being as out of place in that perfumeless house, of thick walls, heavy, dark-coloured materials and chunky turn-of-the-century furniture, as one could imagine. And amongst these objects, reclining on the floor, one elbow on a battered leather pouffe, was she herself in gypsy skirt, scarlet with black border, black tights and shoes, black sweater whose simple low round neckline allowed her long white neck to swoop out dramatically, making me marvel that its length and slenderness was the pedestal for so fine a head. She wore no necklace, which seemed at once absolutely right, but large looped red earrings and a number of bangles at her wrist.

She was taller, more willowy. Waist, bust and thighs all more obviously accentuated in the way she walked, with a lazy consciousness where before there had been none at all.

She told me now that after she had recovered from the accident and most of her scars had healed her parents had packed her off to Geneva to do a year's bi-lingual secretarial course. From there to Paris to the Cordon Bleu. She'd enjoyed the new found liberty that this stretch in Europe offered her and had been reluctant to come home. Her parents tried to put pressure on. Tony too. Certain letters passed between various members of the two families. Meanwhile, Tony was not the only one who'd been pursuing Sylvia as far as Paris. There was Patrick. Cycling over for sweating weekends when he could squeeze the time off from his medical studies.

'Two men in love with you, eh?'

She looked both serious and distant.

'Sylvia, you don't have anything – you know, to drink. A drop of port?'

'I'll go and see.'

She returned shortly bearing a round tray on which was a bottle and two glasses.

'No port. Will brandy do?'

I looked at the label. 'Admirably.'

She turned off the wall lights leaving one Chinese lantern with a square paper shade glowing on the sanded floor between us.

'But you were finally persuaded back?'

She spread her arms in a gesture it was hard to read.

'And what have you been doing since you returned?'

'First task to make this room somewhere I could feel comfortable in.'

I smiled. There on the floor, she did look comfortable. She and the room seemed to go together. On the other hand I'd never been a man for floors myself.

'Do you mind if I sprawl on the bed?'

'Not at all.'

I cleared a space amongst newspapers, books, and a number of large and precious-looking beads, in the process of being strung.

'And second task?'

'But what about you, Jeremy. Tell me all your news. So much more important.'

I told her about Jong & Wharton, about Helen, about my parents on the Isle of Wight and the anxiety being caused by a tremor in my mother's heart.

She drew me out. She was a good listener. I closed my eyes and talked monstrously. It was in the early hours that I took leave of her. Returning to the room that once had been Timmy's.

At her door I kissed her nose.

'It's lovely that you don't lust after me,' she said lightly. 'It makes such a welcome change. I think that's why I asked you down.'

110

It was the following day. The wind had not abated and the clouds were becoming blacker by the minute. After an ample breakfast of freshly squeezed orange juice, porridge, kippers, deliciously thick wedges of hot toast and tangy homemade marmalade, she suggested that we walk, between rain showers.

'I wouldn't go far,' her mother advised. 'Looks to me as if a storm might be brewing. I would have thought it a day to stay inside, myself.'

'Jeremy?' Sylvia looked at me in concern.

'I'm game if you are.' It was worth it to see her smile.

Our luck held. The clouds, contrary to expectation, blew away and the sun came out, weak and watery, but sun nevertheless. We had not ventured as far as the exposed Downs but had taken a more local walk, on the edge of the town through a beech wood, planted in commemoration of Elizabeth II's coronation. The wood was in an enclave; below the trees, stretches of grass, then houses, then the sea, shrouded in mist today but visible nevertheless if one strained one's eyes.

Sylvia, clothed in elegant slacks and jacket, white wellington boots and a small white hat perched on her dark hair, walked through the beeches in silence. As we came out into the open and felt the first rays of sun on our faces she took my arm and steered me towards a bench.

'I only brought you out to talk.'

'I guessed as much.'

'Wise man,' she laughed.

'Is it your two men?' I hazarded.

'In a way, yes.'

'Only in a way?'

'Oh Jeremy, what *shall* I do?'

She talked earnestly, your young mother, for a long time. With many promptings from me of course. She wasn't someone who naturally expected to hold the stage by talking. She once told me that the kind of beauty that she then had negates talk, for it has its own presence so that people uncannily connect with it, not the person inside, listening for only minutes and then sloping off into their own thoughts. More frequently, then, it was her role to listen and just be. And it was an irony I did feel then, at the height of my sexual powers, I like to think, randy still with any vaguely attractive girl that came along (though at the time I was doing nothing about it owing to a certain loyalty to Helen) that it was I whom she felt could hear her, could cut through the monstrous power of her beauty and whom she honoured with the secrets of her heart.

I can't remember all our conversation. Only snippets. It was a long time ago and much water has passed under the bridge since.

There was pushing to a head the issue of marriage. Two men loved her and wanted her. There was her parents' belief that a Jewish girl must marry a Jewish man, preferably a wealthy one, and their horror at her so fracturing a course that seemed to have been set so very long ago, a course whose fruition had consequences already taken for granted by any number of distant relatives and friends. There was Tony himself, kind, sane and unimaginative, who had waited, whose behaviour was unimpeachable, whom she had known and all but been engaged to for years and years. 'And yet somehow,' she said.

'Isn't that "yet somehow" saying it all?' I said.

'But doesn't everyone live with their "yet somehows"? Isn't it just a question of when it hits one? The most romantic taking the longest to learn that lesson?'

'You're very worldly-wise.' But there was something else. Something else that I couldn't reach at then. 'And Patrick?'

'Romance,' she said. 'It's terribly moving, his passion and vigour. That he saves pennies, that he rushes over, that he says I am his life, that he says he'll pine for ever if I don't marry him.'

'That doesn't sound right.'

'But he's so fine, so honourable. He's full of the most wonderful stories. And he's doing something in the world, service, making people better. It does move me. Perhaps as a wife to a doctor one would be mildly fulfilling some useful role oneself,' she said wistfully. 'It seems less dead somehow than a wife of a business-man. Can you understand that? Mummy and Daddy can't.'

'But what about for yourself?' I asked. Heavens, you would have thought I was the first women's libber; it was a ridiculous role for me to be playing. But at this she shrugged her shoulders and became impatient. She got up from the bench and put out a hand to pull me up too.

'Let's walk some more. It's not really hot enough to stay still for too long, don't you find? Let's make our way down to the sea front. After Paris I still relish the tang of salt and the crunch of the pebbles under my feet.'

'Fine by me.'

Her energy always drew me along, whereas with Helen mine drew her. Even on this day when moods were dark and troubling the wind in her sails blew strong.

As we made our path through Sussex 'twittens', short cuts, narrow roads, cutting a zig-zag path towards the coast, we were mostly silent. Timmy again was much in my mind, in both of our minds no doubt. No male camaraderie had so far taken the place of Timmy. I doubted if it ever would. I wondered whether we would mention him, whether she would find that too hard, whether she would want to.

On the beach I sensed that we would not, not yet, but that he lay across and between all our conversations that weekend. I sensed too that that was why she had so surprisingly sought me out, her brother's friend.

Marriage, I wondered, what would he have thought about it? On the beach the sun was again gracing us. It had taken us a long while to reach it and now we sat huddled together against a breakwater which protected us to a certain extent from the wind. Marriage, she said, really she had never thought in terms of there being anything else; not for a person like her. What did she mean? I asked. 'A conventional girl,' she laughed and blushed. I sensed she was mocking herself. No, clear it was to her that she was going to marry someone. And everything else would, as she put it, flow round that. It was just a matter of who.

'Difficult for you to see it, from where you stand, Jeremy, your male position. Isn't it, for all her degree and hope of a career, true of Helen too? Be truthful.'

'To some extent, maybe yes.' I was thinking of the incessant theme of our conversations before we settled to become engaged. 'There is a difference though. To Helen *whom* she marries is important. To you, in some curious way, it doesn't seem to be important at all.'

She pushed at pebbles with her Wellington boot. Her face dark with unhappiness. This time it was I who got up first, pulling her up after me. The tide was out leaving a wide expanse of sand. 'C'mon, race you.' We held hands and raced across the beach, the wind behind us. Then she let go of me and put her arms out as if she was a plane, veering to right and left, scooping and dipping, the wind blowing her hair into her eyes and across her face.

'God,' she said, taking my arm as we set off again to make our journey back to her home, 'life's too short to spend it in this kind of youthful misery. And to waste your weekend when I should be giving you a lovely time. I'm sorry, Jeremy.'

I squeezed her arm. 'I want you to feel you can always talk to me.' It sounded pompous, but I meant it.

She squeezed my arm back, 'Thank you.'

The conversation drifted to things less personal, less troubling. I remember little else of note. Except that Patrick weaved himself back into the conversation on more than one occasion so that I began to form the opinion that if it was to be one of these men that she would marry then I would lay my bets on the impoverished medical student. Perhaps that was as far as she could go at the time to breaking convention; and that in itself had some satisfaction.

There was a story that he'd told her that she recounted to me on the walk. I've remembered it always. My kids grew up thinking of it as Patrick's story. I remember thinking from this and much else that he must be a very nice man, your father – though not necessarily the man for Sylvia. Of course I had no idea at that stage that no man was to be for Sylvia. My intuitions were miles and miles from that particular understanding. I felt that something wasn't in place as it was with myself and Helen. But what it was then I would have been too profoundly shocked to have even begun to contemplate. I have also no way of telling, of knowing, how near she was herself to this knowledge. I would hazard a guess that she was almost as far as I was. But that is only, as I say, a guess. Perhaps one day you will be able to ask her yourself.

Before Patrick started at medical college he had a year in Thailand with the VSO. It's a story one of the Akka tribesmen told him. About the cock. But surely you've heard it. No? Well here goes then. Once upon a time there were ten suns and ten moons. But people found it too hot by day and too bright by night. So they decided to shoot some of the suns down. But they shot all ten by mistake. So they were submerged in darkness. In horror they turned to the animals for help. And a few days later the cock said that one of his hens rooting around had found a sun. The cock put it back up in the sky. The people rejoiced. And so it is that the cock crows each morning to make sure the sun remains up in its place.

Josie was crying, in grief, she said, for her father back in Edmonton, in grief for them all that it didn't work out, in grief even that I now seemed to want to pull away.

'Not that,' I said. 'But . . .'

'That's how it seems.'

'I must, you silly girl,' I said, 'there's so much to untangle. Much you don't understand.'

'All that you are telling me is long in the past.'

'No, there are other matters. And some I haven't been quite honest with you about.'

'Tell me now then, tell me all.'

'All is impossible. I'll tell you about Sylvia, that was our bargain.'

'Bargain,' she said. 'Life's not like that.'

'What's it like?'

'It's a bloody mess!'

I laughed and took her in my arms.

'You're a winner, Josie, with your own life to lead. I can only help you maybe to not be too angry with Sylvia. Nothing more.'

Evening had crept in on us. The gardens were emptying, soon to close; the hot evening air was scented with jasmine, gardenia, the sweet musk of roses.

'Hungry?'

She nodded that she was. I fished in my jacket pocket for a bar of chocolate and broke it into pieces.

'I've talked so long this afternoon. Perhaps we should break now. I could take you out to dinner. Poor thing, you deserve it. Or are you expected back?'

'No, to the first,' she said, 'and to the second, I don't know, nor do I care. Go on talking, Jeremy, I'm listening.'

And so, sustained by chocolate and the last of the white wine, we lay on in the grass with its hint of evening dew, listening to the birds singing their evening song, while I sung mine. Also swiping at the occasional mosquito that attempted to settle – God, it was hot – but missing one or two little buggers who did their worst.

Patrick was marrying Sylvia. His Scottish family were putting down the down-payment on a large house in Chalk Farm, she wrote to tell me.

Meanwhile we too had set a date for our marriage, the 2nd of August that year, after which we would be moving to a small flat we were renting in Wimbledon in a leafy road, Helen having got her way over this one.

We sent Sylvia and Patrick an invitation but they were away on a tour of Patrick's relatives in Scotland, and therefore couldn't make it. So it was months before I saw Sylvia again. At her own wedding, held in grand style towards the end of that year, back in Patrick's old college, Balliol. A formal and mammoth affair at which the Fisks, I thought, looked desperately out of place. I had the impression they looked anxiously towards the groom's side of the aisle for the directions as to when to sing and when to kneel. Though out of their element they managed nevertheless to retain their own grace and air of nobility. Especially Sylvia, who was playing her part as if she was a movie star, with the panache one might have expected of her. As to Patrick's family, they all looked to me rather thin-lipped about the affair, but as if like the Fisks they were bound to make the most of it.

During the reception Sylvia dragged Patrick over and introductions were made. I knew him as a nodding acquaintance from Oxford days but nothing more. Helen immediately took to him and rather to my surprise seemed far from unfriendly to Sylvia. And she it was who pressed them to come to dinner once they had returned from honeymoon and sorted themselves out.

I would never have expected the pleasure of a foursome. Helen up to that point had been worryingly off-putting to most of my friends. So her warmth to Sylvia surprised me. And gave pleasure. Two opposites these; but Helen seemed to see what I saw in Sylvia, not the magnificent display, the rare and beautiful bird of bright plumage, but below to a far deeper place. And Sylvia who told me at one point that on the whole other girls had fought clear of her whilst it was the opposite sex who had been attracted, appeared to bask in the pleasure of our casual domesticity. Patrick too. There was something comfortable between us.

Helen was now a qualified geographer and was looking for a job. At the same time she was eager to start a family soon which tended to dampen the fire of her ambition.

Charlie Wharton, who had from the first taken a shine to her, offered her the opportunity to do the geographical maps for a travel series he was instrumenting, a job that suited her well because she was shy and liked to work at home. And so started a career that has more or less suited her over the last twenty-odd years – and has kept her in tights, as they say, though not contributed substantially to the larger expenses that we've had to shoulder.

The following year Helen, to her delight, was pregnant. Though not unwell she was dreamy and lethargic through much of it, preferring to be in and near her own home than venture out too far. As a result though Sylvia invited us to a number of glamorous affairs given in her Chalk Farm home (she was born to be a hostess and believed that this would help Patrick's career – and maybe it would have done) we more often than not refused, Helen far more preferring them to come to us. What we most enjoyed was the kind of evening when the four of us sat around the kitchen table, or went to a local film, or took a walk together over Barnes Common or on Richmond Common, at the time a place of new delight for us. Now of course we know every inch, every deer, every pond and puddle, after years of family walks and rambles – but that's another story.

After Daniel was born the flat seemed unbearably small. For the first few months he slept in our room, then in the bathroom. Soon it became clear we would have to make other arrangements. Besides Helen was clamouring for a garden, a patch however small in which to put young Daniel outside in his pram. Sylvia, with abundant energy, having done up their Chalk Farm house with a uniqueness and charm and the mark that more and more came to be Sylvia, and having organised a buoyant social life, and now, whilst Patrick worked hard long hours and came back exhausted, found herself often at a loose end, and sad, and a trifle impatient that she too was not pregnant, offered to take over the role of flat hunter on our behalf. Typical it was of Sylvia that after a month or two of tireless searching she found something that was sufficiently appealing for neither Helen nor I to be able to resist taking it, despite some obvious drawbacks.

It was unfurnished, and needed what seemed to us like a horrendously substantial deposit. The capital from my grandfather's small legacy had been dipped into to such an extent during my extravagant bachelor days that what remained was now only bringing in the equivalent of a few hundred pounds a year. We decided on a loan from the bank. Helen, now Daniel was sleeping through the night, could take on some work again. I would teach two evenings a week at the local college of Further Education: the History of the Novel, no less. I would also ask Charlie for a rise. Not easy, for with all his other virtues when it came to money he liked to hold it close to his chest. However, I did manage to wangle a meagre increase out of him, and fix up evening work. On this basis we took a loan and went ahead. My parents, living on a pension, had money worries of their own, exacerbated by continuing expensive medical treatment for my mother – theirs was not a generation that took easily to the National Health. My mother's heart was still giving cause for worry. She had now twice had to undergo minor surgery and the future was unclear.

However, after much adding up and nervous biting of finger nails, we decided we could just about manage. Sylvia, as I say, was madly excited about the new flat. And we ourselves were much drawn. It was enormous. Four good-sized rooms, a huge kitchen/ diner, a bathroom that had once been a bedroom itself, with a bath bang in the middle and immediately suggestive of wonderful future orgies. It was on the ground floor of a pre-war block of mansion flats at Putney, looking right over the Thames, the sitting room which faced south opening up on to the flats' gardens, which were virtually unused as all the other residents appeared to be well over sixty and found it too much trouble to climb down from the higher flats to the garden.

The flat was in the most terrible condition. 'But only decorative-ly,' Sylvia urged, 'nothing serious. It won't fall down or anything, and who minds wonderful neo-Edwardian baths and loos? Look at this chain, it's magnificent. And don't you love the lion's feet on the bath pedestal? You can clean them up and make them a feature. Honestly, it will be superb. You must try and imagine how different it will be with a coat of white paint.' 'Three coats at least,' groaned Helen, looking at the depressing mustard colours of the walls and the brown corridor and bathroom.

We went ahead. Sylvia offered to come over and help paint one Saturday, whilst Patrick was on duty at his hospital. In the week Helen bumped into an old friend whom she talked into coming too. 'Let's make it a working party,' I suggested. 'Invite as many people we can for any part of the weekend they can manage. Try for about ten people. I'm sure that's the way.'

She was in agreement. We had signed the lease but had two weeks before we moved in. The place still looked dauntingly unliveable in and we were both eager for any help we could get. I asked around at work, she asked her contacts, including college friends and one or two mums she had met at the baby clinic. Some professed to having their hands full, but others were more forthcoming, like the jolly Roberta who offered to leave their baby with her husband and pop in for at least some of the time.

Of the fifteen who'd said more or less yes, we reckoned on a fair amount of work being done and went out with confidence to buy paint, rollers, brushes, sand-paper and paint-stripper.

It's so long ago I honestly find it hard to remember how Alison got there.

(It's odd, incidentally, how the Fisks in some curious way always manage to be in the middle of my decorating life. There was your mother galvanising us into action. And now, years later, when I've lost all taste for that kind of thing and reached a point when I'd rather get someone in, even if it means spending my last penny, here have you been stirring me to a final effort.)

Well, Alison . . . let me see. At Jong & Wharton there was a girl, Pam – how awful, I've forgotten her surname now. An Irish girl, from Dublin. Soft spoken. Lanky, face that had too much colour in it, particularly around the nose, eyes too intense, eyes that often looked as if they had been crying. Kept much to herself. Wore glasses on those intense eyes. And when she took them off, there was a permanent bridge on her nose. She was high-minded, given to serious conversation on the world's food shortage, the problems of the third world, human misery in any shape or form. The others found her too serious and she tended to be left out of office lunches and get-togethers. She wasn't the kind who is good in a crowd. But I always held a sneaking respect for her – Pam Tinney – that was her name.

When one was just with her alone, she was good company. She was an excellent listener, she was also a damn good copy-editor. But she was desperately lonely in London, and had no push; the sort who'd be gobbled up at a place like ours, always given the worst jobs, last to go in the evening, always reliable, always see something through in a crisis, a workhorse, you could say. She had, besides, a meticulous eye for detail. The kind that forms the backbone of most publishing houses – there's usually one of them to be found somewhere in a basement or in a dingy room with too little light, because they don't have the nous to demand more.

Once every month or so I tended to have lunch with Pam, or buy her a quick drink after work, because I thought she was in need of companionship and, so as not to paint myself as too altruistic, she was sound about company policy and the soul of discretion.

On the whole Pam, though, wasn't someone I'd have thought of bringing home. For Helen, though reserved herself, was far from tolerant of life's lame ducks, into which category when Pam as much as opened her mouth she easily appeared to fit. Helen believed I was far too indiscriminate with my affection, and being more picky than myself, more a person who guarded her privacy zealously, she took it on herself to guard our joint domestic privacy with something that was becoming a fierce possessive jealousy. So, though I might have fought for Sylvia and Patrick's company – but didn't, as it turned out, have to – there was no way that Pam was going to feature in my life sufficiently for it to be worth the bother of

Helen's likely hostility.

However, as I left work that Friday, greedily counting on my fingers the number of helping hands we had managed to muster, I suddenly looked at Pam and thought, why not? If it was to be one of her lonely weekends she'd no doubt be pleased. And on this occasion Helen was unlikely to object.

As it so happened Pam was going to a concert with a friend that Saturday afternoon, but if we thought we'd still be painting in the evening, she said, they might drop in then, if that would be okay with us.

'It'll be a non-stop marathon,' I promised. 'Feel free to come whenever you can.'

'And my friend?'

'The more the merrier.'

As it happened we were eating when they arrived. Having been going at it hell for leather since mid morning.

'Well this isn't what I expected to find.'

Ten plus of us were sprawled across the floor, empty pots and pans, plates and bowls everywhere you looked, people lying exhausted and replete, either sipping the last of the cheap red wine from the five-litre jar we had brought or lying on their backs and staring at the ceiling. All of us indeed as the door opened trying to decide whether we should stagger on to further effort that evening or – as was my inclination – call it a day and start again early the following morning. In all, the scene that greeted the two newcomers must have looked more like the remains of a debauched Roman feast than anything resembling the working party I had described in the office.

From where I lay on my back I looked up at Pam and her companion at the door. No better looking than herself, I thought sadly. Like with like, I sighed. No doubt she'd be another moany type, if given half a chance. And I resented the still half-open door letting in draughts of cold air and regretted in a vague way that I had invited Pam. The day had gone well, there had been a feeling of camaraderie between us workers which had led to hilarity and high spirits over the evening meal. Something of the school-room came in with Pam, depressing me, and cutting into our jollity like a blunt needle into the flesh.

Helen at the time was in the kitchen breast-feeding Daniel. After a dazed moment when all of us looked towards the door but did nothing about it, Sylvia took charge.

'Come in,' she said, 'and welcome. I'm Sylvia. I'm the one who dragooned them into buying this flat.'

'And quite right you were. Alison's the name.' She put out a hand and shook Sylvia's decisively. 'It's a place with distinction.' Then she laughed, a high girlish laugh, self-mocking, 'In ten years time I'll be looking for a place like this myself. Your friends are mighty lucky.'

'Do you think so?' said Sylvia, her voice less certain than usual, as if mesmerised by the other's conviction.

'Just set me to work, whoever's in charge here.'

'Yes,' echoed Pam, more weakly, 'we have come to work.'

'Some of us,' I said, 'were thinking we'd call it a day for this evening.'

'What, at nine o'clock?'

I looked into Alison's burning cornflower blue eyes and sensed that she was not like Pam at all. Only at first glance had I been taken in. No, she was quite some other manner of creature. With reluctance we found ourselves getting to our feet and shuffling into the kitchen with the remnants of our meal. Before we knew it, newly inspired, we were rollering, painting, filing down doors with more energy than I would have given us credit for at that tail end of the day.

That evening we worked on till past midnight. I can recall, still, the look on Helen's face when she had settled Daniel to sleep (no mean task with so much noise going on around) and came back into the living room to find the place a fervour of activity.

Whereas work during the day had been enthusiastic but un-directed, each now had specific jobs and by the time we finally came to quit huge leaps forward had taken place. How this had happened it was difficult to say. But I suspected that it was not unconnected with the entrance of Pam's friend.

'How early can everyone get here tomorrow?' asked Sylvia as we said goodbye at the door.

'Ten,' someone responded.

'Nine-thirty,' said Alison.

'Okay,' Sylvia looked at me and Helen for approval, 'we'll be here just before nine-thirty and then people can turn up any time after that.'

Patrick was having his alternate weekend on in the hospital so Sylvia stayed the night with us. We were back in the flat the following morning, as promised, just before nine-thirty. And on the doorstep within minutes of our arrival was Alison. Smiling, short thatch of straight light brown hair, glossy as if from a hundred brushes, standing back on the heels of her lace-up shoes, her hands in the pockets of a man's corduroy jacket, her large blue cornflower eyes full of a driving power which made me immediately want to go and make myself a mug of coffee and sit down with the Sunday papers.

'Pam's hay fever's holding her up,' she said. 'She asked me to tell you that she'll be here later. I thought I'd make my own way since I said nine-thirty. Besides I'm raring to go.'

'It's really awfully good of you,' Helen told her, 'to put in so much energy for us, whom you hardly know. We do appreciate it.'

'Any time,' laughed Alison, already bustling about. I don't think she was interested in compliments. Nor in what people thought. Her energies seemed somehow as straight as a dye. As straight as a man's, one might have been tempted to say. Some men's, that is. Or I could say that there was a single-mindedness to her which I thought of then as more usually, in my experience, belonging to men. Subsequently I've met other women like that, but at the time she struck me as a novelty. And as I washed floorboards, indeed whole areas of floors, that morning, I found myself continually looking in Alison's direction. With some admiration. Some interest. And a great deal of curiosity. Nor was I the only one.

By mid morning our numbers had swelled to include most of those who had helped the day before. Pam, still sneezing continuously, but protesting that she couldn't let us down, had joined the throng. By some silent unspoken process Alison and Sylvia had taken over as joint captains, with us as crew. Or was it more Alison captain, Sylvia bosun?

On Saturday, Sylvia's energy, her enthusiasm, her sureness that the flat would be a gorgeous place had led us on. She had sung as she painted, her dark hair tied in a cotton scarf. She had danced as she walked, gliding the floor with graceful steps, she had wielded the paintbrush with flowing graceful strokes, not a great deal of expertise (though more than Helen and myself) but with a great deal of artistry and a natural assurance, so that questions about technique, decisions about what was to be done first, how we might share the five brushes and three rollers, were addressed to her.

Helen, I might say in defence of my wife's seeming passivity over the work on our flat, was deeply involved with her baby son, more concerned over such questions as to whether he had burped sufficiently, whether she should feed him further or whether that would only make him sick again, whether his tears were due to hunger, discomfort or the sudden and unexpected noise, and so on. Daunted by what we had taken on, particularly after three sleepless nights in succession, she was pleased for anyone to take over the task of organising this strange mob of people; anything to facilitate the flat being finished as soon as possible (we hoped to move in the following weekend), the doors once more being closed, and us returning to the sanctity of our close domestic life.

With Alison as well as Sylvia at the helm on Sunday this seemed more likely to be the case than ever I might have hoped for in my wildest dreams when planning this weekend. Alison's energy matched Sylvia's. From sometime that morning I was aware of a growing dynamic between them. Each, I believe, goaded the other. But whereas Sylvia's leadership was general and for want of a better word charismatic, Alison's was, like all of her, directed and ordered. A human cannonball. I had in my living room a real-life example of what this term might mean. She was also a most experienced and practised decorator, having worked during her school and university vacations in her two older brothers' decorating business. In short there was little Alison didn't know about housepainting, and clear it became that the flat could be turned into a place fit to live in virtually with her eyes shut, such were her accomplishments.

Whereas on Saturday all of us were energetically attacking small bits and pieces of the flat, on Sunday under her tutorage we found the whole coming together; energy fanning out from the central conception. Things beginning to fall into place. Suggestions for tasks to be done making good sense. She was not bossy, she was not assertive, quietly she suggested ways of going about things. Quietly she assumed the authority. Quietly she worked, but worked like a trojan. And by the time Helen made us a cup of tea at around four, I could see the end in sight.

Who can say about the dynamic between people, what it is that attracts? Perhaps always it is a mystery. More than ever for a man speaking about two women. They were both women of unusual energy, Sylvia and Alison. And such was the make-up of Sylvia's nature that rather than finding her nose put out of joint by this blunt, ordinary-looking girl whose authority cut through her own, she seemed on the contrary delighted, as if she recognised an equal, a more than equal. And the pleasure with which she responded to Alison, the way she brought not only her own energy but her great

123

charm to bear equally obviously delighted and enchanted. I say obviously. What I mean is that all this was there to be seen by anyone who looked. I doubt that anyone did look, or perhaps notice anything strange. Why should they, after all? Though Helen, who by then knew Sylvia relatively well, at some point directed her gaze at the two girls and raised her eyebrows at me.

But for me what was noticeable and even moving, was that there all of a sudden was the same Sylvia I had seen as a girl. The Sylvia who plunged her paddle in the Ouse carelessly and matched her strokes with her brother's. The Sylvia who had been one hundred percent engaged in what she was doing. The Sylvia who, as she had moved into adulthood, I had thought, and not without some poignance, perhaps lost and gone for ever. And particularly and most obviously in her relations with other people, Patrick, myself, her friends; it was as if she was moving through the world, beautiful, with her easy grace, and yet as though at least some part of her wasn't there.

Those people who knew her more recently, I had thought, must think her to be always like that. I had even wondered about Patrick. But Patrick, of course, and you mustn't take this as a dig against your father, was utterly immersed in his medicine, and deeply in love with Sylvia, of course he was. He had won his prize. And she was there at home for him, when he came home. He would have done anything for her. Anything that was in his power. He considered himself the most blessed young doctor of them all. He had said as much on more than one occasion when the four of us had been together.

My eyes were drawn again and again in the course of that afternoon to the sight of Sylvia painting alongside Alison, dark strands of hair falling out of her scarf and being covered with white paint as she impatiently brushed them away, her eyes alight with the joy of living, her cheeks pink, her whole body taking on a sense of direction, a firmness of movement, as if it had been woken out of years of a somnivolent state.

By evening we had done more than I could have dreamt of. The place was transformed. 'Let me get everyone a drink,' I offered. 'I can't thank you all enough.' We downed tools, washed paint-brushes and ourselves, cleared floors of newspapers and even I looked at our handiwork with some admiration. 'Not bad, eh?' Pam who had found her niche rocking Daniel, and who for the last hours had been acting as surrogate mother in order to enable Helen to do her share of scrubbing and sanding, now handed him back to his mother. He immediately started crying again.

'Sounds like he prefers you to me,' Helen said to Pam.

I got out the crate of beer from under the kitchen table and found the plastic tumblers we had brought from home that morning.

Toasts were made. The sort of hilarity you expect at the end of a day such as ours. Patrick arrived grey-faced from twenty-four hours on call and a terrible coach crash involving o.a.p.s on the way to a day at the sea. Three had died, he said, on their way to the hospital. Others needed plastic surgery. His team had worked straight through the night.

Sylvia was all sympathy. Putting her arm through his she said she was ready to leave immediately, to make him scrambled eggs and cocoa which he could have in bed.

'Not quite *that* bad, darling,' he laughed.

'Come and see the flat then.'

It was the first time he'd been there. Still with her arm looped in his she took him around our new home, proudly pointing out cornices, details of doors and plumbing, oddly shaped windows ('too late to see the magnificent view') as if it were all her own.

'We've transformed it. And all in a weekend. You'd have been horrified if you'd seen it as it was when we started. Truly, Patrick. For you have no imagination for this kind of thing yourself. You'd have thought it was quite an impossible task to take on. But with a little elbow grease. And such a magnificent team.'

Patrick smiled benevolently at us. 'What are you lot doing about something to eat then?'

No one had thought that far. Daniel was now at last fast asleep again in his basket.

'We could perhaps risk the local curry house?' I looked at Helen enquiringly. Suddenly it seemed to everyone, even Helen, a good idea. I found myself ravenously hungry.

'So will you two join us?' I asked Patrick and Sylvia.

'Why not,' he said.

Some of the others thought they'd be going. Pam and Alison opted to come with us, plus another two of our team and one of the other editors from work, Paul Elliott. Nine of us and Daniel in his Moses basket set off for the Indian restaurant.

The conversation revolved mainly round books, a fair amount of shop. Inevitable, with so many of us at the same firm. Alison, it turned out, was junior editor on the Social Science side at Blacketts. Pam and she had met at one of those training weeks the year before. She was as fiery, as energetic (more so perhaps) when she talked about her work, as when her attention had been directed to home-decorating.

It was the late sixties. Feminism was still a word that wasn't regularly bandied about. *The Female Eunuch* had yet to be published. A few student voices were being heard, but mostly in America. Here was this girl then, passionately committed and articulate about her cause in a way that was new and refreshing.

I thought much of what she said overheated. I judged that time would knock off some of the sharp edges and mellow her. On the other hand, lazy bugger that I've always been, I've always admired those caught up with a fire that has never been mine. And Alison was one of those. Moreover, she was no fool, her mind was crystal clear. Had she not decided her future was to be in publishing, she could have become a successful barrister, I felt sure. She was persuasive, logical and highly articulate, though a rough diamond, and her north country accent might then not have been as acceptable at the Bar as in our world. But she had chosen publishing, not by default as I might have said of myself, but with a missionary zeal; she was out, she claimed, to educate women, and to influence them. Had I been a head-hunter, I would have head-hunted Alison there and then. I instinctively knew that she'd do well; that of all of us, as I looked around the table, she was the one who would really get somewhere.

She talked of the work of American writers. Friedan, Alice Rossi, Kate Millet. People who were just names to me. She talked of Margaret Mead and her anthropological assertions. She talked of the Europeans, of the 'structuralists', and of using Marxist inter-pretations to bring to bear on the history of women's affairs. And when we said that was ridiculous and far-fetched she gave an exposition which, although not entirely convincing, was certainly sufficiently well reasoned to give me food for thought. She outlined the direction her department might take when she was commission-ing editor there. When, not if. There or elsewhere.

Whilst I was amused and Helen and Paul and the others uncertain but not uninterested, Sylvia was entranced. The bloom of the day had far from left her. And from our side of the table she seemed to be bending over nearer and nearer to Alison as if to be caught up in her ambit. She, it turned out (I was surprised at this), had read one or two of the books Alison mentioned and admitted now to being intrigued. She tried to express her own concerns and the questions that some of these ideas raised.

Patrick was becoming increasingly restless. He looked at his watch once or twice and drummed his fingers on the table. (We had long since finished eating.) He yawned audibly. And the yawn (or was it only the yawn, was there a jealousy already recognised and accepted between them?) goaded Alison into open irritation.

'I've never had much sympathy,' he said, 'for women who feel they're so badly done by, by men. Maybe it used to be so. But not any more.'

'Not since they got the vote!' Alison flashed at him sarcastically.

'Any woman worth anything has as much chance now of rising to the top as any man. Most of the others, it's my belief, are happy where they are. And don't need to be urged into discontent and an angry sense of injustice by a group of miserable, neurotic women who for the most part couldn't be happy whatever life had given them. And then worst of all those women give the impression that it is the only important thing, the only thing worth fighting for; forgetting the serious ills of the world, sickness, death, terrible poverty, terrible conditions in which most of the world live and work. Now there are things to fight for. If you have to fight for anything. Come on, Sylvia. It's been a long day. A long night too. Jeremy, I think this will cover our food (he thrust some notes towards me). You'll understand if we push off now.'

'Wait a moment,' said Alison, standing up too and coming round the table so that she was facing him. 'You're too self-satisfied for words. Being involved in life and death struggles doesn't automatically give you the right to believe you understand all about the human condition, you know. It takes a lot more imagination than that. Something a lot of you doctors blind yourselves to. For example, lesbianism. Yes, to you it's still a dirty word. I want the time to come, and it will for my generation, when women can stand up and say freely that they are attracted to their own sex, if that be the case – and men too – without having to be ashamed of it, without having people like you curl your lip at people like me. And with so little understanding.'

And then his face became impassive, a mask of polite breeding, as if he wanted no more of this barrage, would hear no more of it. He took Sylvia's arm and started to move as if he would walk away from Alison, whose blue eyes became poker hot.

'Can it be right,' she said, 'for example, that you go home now and expend your lust on your wife, with society's blessing, whereas for me to express the force of my own desire to touch, to kiss, to hug, and the sense that she feels the same way but will have to go on living a lie because she's too afraid . . .'

127

'This is ridiculous. I'm not listening to any more.'

He dragged Sylvia towards the door of the crowded restaurant. From where he stopped and turned towards us.

'Fine company you keep, Jeremy!'

His voice hurtled over the heads of other tables at us. Exciting attention and a hubbub of talk. As to Sylvia she was pale as alabaster, her dark eyes two pulsating points, but as so often I couldn't tell what she was thinking.

That was more or less the end of our friendship with Patrick. I think he in some way held us responsible. Or if not, he didn't want to be reminded of that evening. Attempts on the part of Helen and myself, after we had moved in and were agreeably living in the new flat, to recommence our cosy foursome, with lures to meals or invitations to join us for an outing to theatre, cinema or art gallery (we had found an excellent babysitter in the elderly woman who lived in the adjacent flat) were met with excuses: Patrick thought he'd be on call that weekend, Patrick might be too tired, too busy, they would phone us back. Always something different. Gradually we came very sadly to accept that for Alison's outburst we were not to be forgiven.

We were sad but young, enjoying our own life, making new friends – strange how they all seemed to be couples with young babies. Helen during this phase was eager for the companionship of other women. Which I encouraged. I was in my own way fairly submerged at work. Charlie seemed to be relying on me to a greater and greater degree and I saw the not impossible situation of the role of editorial director being offered to me on Luke Hyams's retirement, if I kept my head down and did nothing silly.

So I thought little about Sylvia. She, despite the rift with Patrick, managed to keep vaguely in touch. Especially with Helen. The following year she herself, to her great delight, was pregnant. With you. Very occasionally on an odd afternoon when Patrick was in hospital she would make her way over to the flat. But always leave long before Patrick was due home. Hence it was that it was more often that Helen saw her and reported news, rather than I. I had the idea that she did not tell Patrick of these visits, that at one point perhaps they had caused some rupture between them. But I may be wrong. Helen was herself the soul of discretion and hated any discussion verging on the personal. So though she and I had wondered over Alison's behaviour for several nights in a row after the famous Indian meal, it was not something that Helen ever out of delicacy would have thought of bringing up with Sylvia. Nor did

Sylvia mention it herself.

The following five years slipped by. As Sylvia had more and more children, her visits to us became increasingly rare, until she was once again almost entirely out of the immediate perimeter of my life. I had no way of knowing if she was happy or no. Though she spoke warmly of her children and Helen gauged that she was enjoying motherhood. Reflecting Helen's own state of mind. She was enormously enjoying our own young family, now enlarged by the birth of the twins, who had made their entrance into the world two years after Daniel.

One day, one very rare day, Sylvia brought the children over to visit us. One Saturday. There were four of you, then. You were there, the oldest of the brood. You must have been about five or thereabouts. A sturdy little thing. Tall too. We both commented how like your mother you were. As far as I recall it was the only time you came to the flat. Do you remember the visit? No? Well I suppose there was nothing about it that would have stuck in your mind. We must have seemed to you just some acquaintances of your mother's. And there must have been many more, more regularly seen at your house. I remember you bringing a skipping-rope. You'd been given it as a birthday present the week or so before, you announced. It was Autumn. All you kids were dressed in dungarees, duffle coats and bright-coloured wellington boots. You wanted to go out in the garden despite the cold and drizzle. I remember how determined you were to work out how to use that rope. The boys kept pulling it from you but you got it back and tried some more. I remember noticing your stuck out little chin and thinking of your determination that it was Sylvia's. Our lot refused to go out in the rain. They stood at the window and watched.

Karen, at the crawling stage, was involved in tearing our daily newspaper into shreds. Sylvia wandered over to her, disengaged her from the paper and set her down in another part of the room. Where she immediately took off to explore the area under the dining room table.

Helen looking towards her, laughed. 'It's the stage where you can't afford to take your eyes off them for a moment. It must have been like this for you continually over the last few years.'

'There was a favour I wanted to ask,' Sylvia said. 'Talking about having one's hands tied. There is a weekend conference at Sussex

129

University next month. I particularly wanted to go. My parents are away in Switzerland but they've offered to loan us the house. Patrick and I were to take the children down. And well' – she smiled ruefully – 'for once he was going to do his fathering bit, while I had two days of intellectual stimulation.' (Even as she said it her self-mockery was evident. As if, I thought, she really had no right to claim anything as much as that for herself.) 'But now as luck would have it, it's a weekend when one of the others on Patrick's team will be away and there's no question of him being free. He wants me to cancel. If it was just one or two children one could leave them with friends or relatives. But four are such a handful and besides most of my relatives are too elderly to be able to cope.'

'Have you ever thought about an "au pair"?'

'Oh, I love being with them. We have lots of fun together. You know I taught Josie to read before she started school. And now I'm starting with Angus. Half an hour every afternoon. We're both getting so much out of it. And as to Karen,' she picked her up, 'eh, my pet. New tricks every day. No it's just that . . .' her voice trailed away. 'Patrick says it's a crazy scheme,' she said again. 'A bee in my bonnet that sounds as if it should be caught in a glass of water and quietly drowned. But sometimes, just sometimes I feel as if I'm being drowned. Heavens, it is only two days. So much fuss with Patrick about it. And I was wondering well just wondering . . . I know it's a terrible cheek . . .'

She looked from one of us to the other.

'Speak up, Sylvia. What the hell were you wondering?'

'If I could tempt you to come down for the weekend with me and sort of, sort of . . .'

'Babysit?' said Helen smiling.

'Yes.'

'I don't know,' Helen looked at me. She was still smiling. Sometimes I thought what a very great deal of affection she had for Sylvia and my own affection and respect for my wife escalated at those moments. Those were times when I felt confirmed in my choice of her, pleased in my marriage, despite certain strains under the surface that were inevitably beginning to show.

'Jeremy what do you think of this unusual request?' The lilt in Helen's voice implying the tease.

'Of course if it's inconvenient . . .'

'We'd make it convenient, you ninny.' I took her in my arms. She hugged me, then releasing herself from my embrace, hugged Helen. 'You're super people!'

I was heartened by how much it obviously meant.

'Jeremy's been to the house before,' Sylvia now said joyously to Helen. 'He came for a holiday, you know, when I was a kid.'

'A kid, is that what you were?'

'I wish you'd known Timmy.'

'I wish I had,' said Helen simply.

As we moved into the kitchen to make high tea for you children there was a familiarity between us and a warmth of a rare quality. I felt Timmy's presence there in the room with us. I felt too that my holiday with them at their home in Hove had only, surely, been yesterday.

At some point either Helen or I must have asked Sylvia what the conference was on.

'Oh, just a number of present-day women writers.' She named a few.

The date was 1971. *The Female Eunuch* had been published six months earlier, Simone de Beauvoir's *The Second Sex* the year before, Betty Friedan was stirring young women to action all over America. The social revolution of the late sixties, the excitement of student riots in Paris and at the LSE and, to a lesser extent, universities all over Britain and Europe, the readings of Che Guevara, the Vietnam marches, the socialist fire and Bader Meinhoff group in Germany, the social revolution for the young, the rich, the professional classes, for everyone young and thinking. And the women who had taken active or not so active parts in all this were now beginning to forge something of their own, to use the same terminology for their revolution, determined no longer to be second-class citizens. Alison at Cambridge, the first of the angry young women and 'bugger to her accent', as she put it, had fought an embittered battle for an equal number of women's colleges, for better representation, for women's rights, up till then unheard of. After one year of PhD (she had switched to Cambridge after a brilliant first degree and a contentious history as leader of the students' union at East Anglia) she had decided to forgo the more reflective and isolated life of academia for something more in the world.

The conference was one of the first in England to address an issue so close to Alison's heart – woman's changing role. She herself was talking on the comparative climate of the women's movement in a variety of European countries.

Did Sylvia know that she was speaking or was it one of those chance happenings? Helen suspected the former, I was more inclined to the latter view.

In the evenings in Brighton, Sylvia returned charged up and restless. 'What can I do from my house in Chalk Farm?' she asked.

'You have a family and a super one,' Helen argued. 'Heavens, you're doing the most essential thing of all. You've got what most of those women talking at your conference would give their eye-teeth for. If the truth be known.'

'Yes but . . .'

In the loft you kids found a dressing-up box that had belonged to Sylvia and Timmy. Once more the summer-house came into its own. Dressing up, acting out well-known nursery rhymes, waltzing in and out in strange costumes that kept us all in fits of laughter. Your mother too.

But her restlessness continued. In Chalk Farm she put notices up on newsagents' boards and in the library and formed a Women's Working Group. She even persuaded Helen to come to the first few meetings from Putney. Though in time the length of the journey and the extreme views of some of the women combined to make her decide to ease herself out.

Not, however, before Alison was invited to speak to the group. Eccentrically dressed in green dungarees and a man's shirt, her mop of thick hair cut like a pudding basin around her palish face, her eyes blazoned and burned with conviction. 'The most stirring thing since Hitler,' Helen commented dryly to me later. Afterwards when it was over Sylvia took Alison out to a pub. Helen somewhat reluctantly got drawn along.

'She's too much,' moaned Helen, when she returned home. 'After five minutes in her company I feel exhausted. Not so Sylvia.'

'She'll mellow,' I responded. 'I like Alison.'

'All the same I'm worried about Sylvia.'

Sylvia was pregnant again. This time she did get an 'au pair'. A number of times in the following months we phoned the house to be told by Patrick or the 'au pair' that Sylvia was away at this meeting or that. Patrick seemingly having forgotten the old antipathy, or perhaps he had forgiven us in view of more recent and far more serious events, sounded chatty and warm on the phone. I sensed his concern, his desire to talk, but his reluctance, due no doubt to loyalty to Sylvia.

'You should suggest meeting him for a drink,' suggested Helen. 'I bet he could do with a man friend. Someone to talk things over with.'

'What things?'

'I'm saying I think he needs help. I've got a feeling things are going badly awry between him and Sylvia. Alison . . .'

'That's ridiculous. You're round the bend. You're surely not suggesting –'

'I am. Think back, Jeremy. Remember what Alison said at the Indian restaurant. She painted her colours pretty clearly.'

'For heaven's sake. She only said that to goad Patrick. Anyone could see that. It's in her nature to play the "enfant terrible".'

'They're seeing an awful lot of one another.'

'Yes, they might be. But I've known Sylvia for years. What you're suggesting is absurd. Why does everything have to come down to sex – that's what beats me.'

'Coming from you!'

'I've never thought Sylvia, despite her looks, a particularly sexual person. And as to Alison, it's the intellectual stimulation, the pleasant relief from all that domesticity. No doubt she is genuinely fired by those ideas of Alison's. And why not? Of course it isn't anything more.'

Helen looked at me levelly as if I was the fool. And I was the fool. I had never known a lesbian. I'm not sure that Helen had. But perhaps with the instinct of her sex she sensed what was going on whilst I refused to recognise it.

Sylvia had for so long been someone special in my life. Someone I thought highly of. And lesbianism, it was a leap of imagination that I was unable to make until it was far too late and it was being pushed in our faces. Mind you all these things have their inevitable progression. I hold no belief that I could have stopped anything. No doubt Sylvia would say it was bound to happen some day, some way. Still, I might perhaps have been there for them to talk to, Patrick or Sylvia, had I not been so blind.

Saturday evening. A wild wet night. Wind howling. Our river frontage making us feel especially exposed. Sound of water dangerously high against the banks. Rain beating on the panes. A week or two from Christmas. Helen, eight months gone, moving clumsily, slowly, around the flat. Daniel and I playing chess. Remains of our supper still on the table. The twins tucked up in bed. Daniel, bothered by a cold, continually wiping at his nose with the sleeve of his dressing-gown, which called for sharp reproof from Helen and whines from him. 'I can't *help* it, Mum.'

'Yes you can, use a handkerchief, for heaven's sake.'

'Oh do leave him alone, Helen, let up nagging him.'

'He's not a baby any more.'

'I thought you were going to try and get the cards finished tonight.'

'What about it being a shared occupation, like in other families?'

We looked at one another, over Daniel's head, and the look had war in it. Then the doorbell rang.

Sylvia's voice on the intercom. Breathless, weird, sounding much unlike herself. Yes, of course she could come up, I told her.

She flung herself into the room scattering rain drops and wet outdoor clothes everywhere. In her tow, Alison. Sylvia's eyes were red, her face pale with arteries and veins exposed as if everything was throbbing near the surface. Her heart was beating noticeably fast. One could see its rise and fall through her blouse. She asked for wine, she moved fast around the flat, not managing to settle in any one place for more than a minute. Her body no longer seemed to belong to herself but flowed outward in every gesture. Towards Alison. Who was the quieter of the two. Almost angry, I thought, with a dark-faced, purple, sombre anger. Alison so implicated and yet implying at the same time, so much fuss, it isn't what I ever imagined, or what I'm cut out for. And yet accepting with resignation that she was in it, she must stand by, must live with whatever it was that was raging and in which she had been and was a prime mover. But also that she wished it didn't have to be like this.

She sat down on a dining room chair, swivelling it away from us towards the window. She drew the curtain back and there with elbows on knees, trousered as always, feet wide apart, a man's stance, she stared out silently at the rain.

Sylvia came towards me and took my hands in hers. 'Jeremy, Alison and I love one another. You can understand, can't you? You and Helen?' she said turning round to include Helen in whatever it was that she wanted to express. 'I can't go on living with Patrick now. Our marriage would simply be a lie, and couldn't do any good to anyone. Patrick, myself, the children. You do see that, don't you?'

'But wait a minute, why can't you go on living with Patrick?'

Sylvia looked towards Alison.

'Isn't it obvious?' said Helen.

'Not to me it isn't. I've known Sylvia for fifteen years. I'm sorry, Sylvia, I find it hard to believe, to take seriously.'

'Nothing could be more serious.'

'God damn it!' I found myself shouting.

She drew a sharp breath. 'This is the 1970s. Sometimes I think we've hardly developed in our understanding since Oscar Wilde's trial. Patrick I can understand. But you, Jeremy. And what about you, Helen, do you feel the same?'

Daniel, still sitting at the table, was staring at the pieces on the chess board.

'Dad, what about our game?'

'Sorry, old thing. We'll have to finish it tomorrow. Go and get into your pyjamas.'

'Daniel, I'm so sorry I've spoilt it,' said Sylvia. 'Look, would you like me to sing you a song when you are in bed?'

'What can you sing?'

'Most anything. You can choose.'

He nodded. 'But I want some hot milk, Mum.'

'Do what your Daddy says. Go and get undressed while I make your milk.'

Daniel and Helen left the room in different directions. Leaving Alison still staring out into the rain, and myself angry, quite extraordinarily aggrieved with the revelation that Helen's premonitions had been along the right lines. I kept looking at Sylvia and thinking, someone so beautiful, so very much of her sex. There seemed something idiotically wasteful about it. That was my first reaction. I was moreover furious with Alison. Refusing in the first heat of the moment to accept that, as Sylvia many times later pronounced, it would have happened anyway. My first reaction was an entirely personal and selfish one. I identified with Patrick, thought it a terrible waste, an affront, that something 'ours' by right (by which I mean man's in general) had been scurrilously taken away.

'I don't know if I want to know anything about it, Sylvia. I'm going to get a drink. Would you and your friend like something? A pint of beer no doubt for her. To celebrate?' Neither said anything.

And I left them and went into the kitchen.

'It's all too much,' I said to Helen. 'I don't think I can take it.' She said nothing. For once I couldn't read my wife's look.

When I returned Alison had swivelled her chair back to face into the room but was otherwise in the same position. Elbows on spread knees, face looking angrily into the world. Angrily and at the same time removed, as if to say, none of the fuss has anything to do with me – that's all your affair.

Sylvia was kneeling on the floor beside her friend, also with her back to the window, looking in towards the room, her arm up and linked through Alison's.

I opened a bottle of red wine, plonk from our local supermarket; an occasion on which anything else would have been wasted.

'Either of you interested?'

'Thank you, Jeremy.'

'And for you, Alison?' I could hardly speak to her.

'No thanks.'

So I poured for Sylvia and myself.

The silence was unutterably heavy. Outside the rain continued to spatter the window and the wind howled around the walls of the 1930s building. I found myself wanting Helen to return and from time to time looking towards the door. Meanwhile I drank fast, hoping the grape would help us all, and was soon pouring myself a second glass. I looked towards Sylvia's. She had hardly touched hers. Now her arm was resting on Alison's trouser leg just above the knee, as she bent towards her. But she looked at me steadily and spoke quietly now and more in control. 'Jeremy, of all people, I thought you were my dear friend.'

'Of course I'm your friend. But this!'

'But isn't this what friendship is about: accepting the unacceptable as well as the acceptable?'

'Puts a high premium on friendship, Sylvia. Could be too much for me.'

'Try.'

I saw, almost felt, Alison's collar bone tighten with rebuff. And at the same time I could feel the electricity in my hair drawing it up towards the ceiling. Two dogs sniffing round one another, dying to attack.

Sylvia sensed it. 'You're both my friends. Please, for my sake, Jeremy, at least try to understand.'

Then Helen did come back. 'He fell asleep as I was reading to him. But thanks anyway for the offer of a song. Maybe some other time.'

'Yes, some other time.' Sylvia sounded as if time no longer had any meaning for her. All was clouded in uncertainty.

Helen flopped into the armchair and I kicked the pouffe towards her. She put her hands to the hollow of her back and groaned gently, reminding us all of other dimensions.

'Patrick is saying,' said Sylvia tremulously, 'that if I persist, there's no way either he or a court would let me keep the children.

136

That's the only thing that makes it so awful – other than hurting Patrick, which truly I hate to do. I have no fight with him, it's just that . . .' She looked towards Helen, 'He can't make me give up the children, can he?'

It was an evening for silences. Helen deep in her armchair pondered, seemingly incapable of offering the advice or solace that Sylvia sought.

'You both think he's right then,' Sylvia cried, off and moving round the room, interlocking her fingers between her two hands and unlocking them again as a child might.

Now it was her turn to leave the room. I poured myself a third glass of wine.

'Sure you don't want one, Alison?'

'Perhaps.'

For two pins I could have turned her out of the flat.

A gasp and a sharp intake of breath from Helen.

'What is it?'

She started to pant, her face turning grey, the colour draining from her lips. Alison and I looked at her transfixed.

'Darling . . ?'

'I think,' she said, 'I might be going into labour. How inconvenient.' She laughed a little hysterically.

'Helen, are you sure? It's awfully early. Don't you think it's just the little bugger shifting position, or doing an almighty kick or something?'

'Could be. I'm not sure. I feel better now.'

Alison passed her glass of wine over to Helen, 'Here have a sip of this.'

Helen shook her head.

'You'd probably prefer a good old cup of tea.'

'I would actually, thanks. Jeremy can show you where everything is.'

'Don't worry, I'll find my way around. Just give me a tick,' and she was off towards the kitchen.

'Sure you're okay?' I asked Helen, apprehensively. She had shut her eyes and seemed to have fallen into a half somnolent state.

'Sure,' she said with her eyes closed.

'I think I'll just go and see where Sylvia's got to.'

I walked out into the corridor and thought I detected the sound of weeping from the bedroom. Sylvia was sitting at the dressing-room table, her head bowed over the brushes and pots of cream.

'Sylvia,' I said, going up to her and putting my hand on her hair, wondering at the same time if even that repulsed.

'If I can't even talk to you, my closest friends,' she whispered.

'Sylvia, there's something funny about Helen.'

She immediately sat up. 'What do you mean, funny?'

'I don't know. She had a kind of turn, just after you left the room. At the time she said she thought it was a contraction.'

'Where is she now?'

'As far as I know, still in the same place. You know about these things. It always makes me uneasy. Have a look just in case –'

Sylvia willingly followed me back into the sitting room, but by the time we got to the door it was obvious to all of us.

'Call a taxi,' said Alison, 'or an ambulance.'

'I suppose I could take her.'

'Yes, you take me, Jeremy. That's fine. Lots of time.'

'I'd prefer it if one of you came too. Just in case.'

'Yes,' said Sylvia. 'Okay. Come on now, Helen, let's get this rug around you.'

'I'll pack up a nightie and things,' said Alison. 'You just tell me where, Jeremy.'

'But quick, quick.'

Helen was groaning again. I calculated the hospital to be twelve minutes by car.

At the door of the flat suddenly it occurred to me, 'But what about the children?'

'That's why I'm staying,' said Alison.

'You are?'

'I am human, you know.'

'Alison, she's not so bad,' I said. I was father of a brand new baby girl, Helen was sleeping, and I could afford to be generous.

We were sipping the most vile black coffee out of paper mugs in the maternity ward lounge.

'Of course she's not so bad. I wouldn't love her unless. She's the finest person I've ever met.'

'Does she think you're beautiful?' God knows what made me ask.

Sylvia blushed, then seemed to reflect. 'You know, I don't know. I don't know whether that really matters to her. It's not about that.'

'No?'

'It's the freedom. She doesn't want to own me, like men have seemed to. She thinks of me as a dynamic force. As someone capable of something quite, quite different. I'm not sure what yet.' (Again that little laugh of self-depreciation.) 'She – we – we're together, we share the same ideas. It's just so different, utterly –'

'Compulsive?'

'No, utterly right. Surely you can see that. It's as if I've found out who I am, Jeremy.'

'And what about your family, your parents?'

Her face darkened. She looked towards her hands. 'All that's a torture. It's not as if I have a choice. I can't go on making love with Patrick after Alison. Now. Any more. It doesn't make any sense.'

'Other people manage, keep up appearances; think of Harold Nicolson and Vita Sackville-West. Surely there can be genuine affection, if not . . .'

'Yes, but Patrick wouldn't want to. He's not like that. I agree the Nicolsons were magnificent. But he must have been more understanding. Then it's not as if I'm a writer or anything magnificent. Wasn't that part of the way it was with Harold and Vita, that he knew he had a most extraordinary wife and wanted her anyway, and accepted her as she was. It isn't at all the case between Patrick and I. He just can't, you see; he just won't. We could only go on if I admitted to it all being a mistake. And that would be a lie to my very being; you must see that. How can I do it, Jeremy? Besides, even then I'm not sure that he'd ever trust me again. He'd always be waiting, watching.'

And I said nothing. For I saw that in that, at least, she was right.

'You don't think it's just lust, do you?'

'No. It's anguish,' she said, 'the either/or. Surely in the long run Patrick can be persuaded to let me have the children?'

'Perhaps.' But neither of us believed it.

Then she cried and I sat there holding her hand.

'Courage,' I said.

'And you have another daughter,' she whispered, trying to smile, trying to control her tears.

'Yes,' I said. 'Yes.'

'It's like peeling an onion,' Josie said. 'Peel one skin, and confront another. I think I understand some things. But not others. Why is she so unhappy now? She got what she wanted, after all.'

'Do any of us?'

'What kind of an answer is that? Please tell me why she is so unhappy. Is it me?'

'Josie,' I said, giving her what I saw as being a last friendly hug, 'not you directly. Though your presence here is bound to make her confront her own feelings of guilt towards you all; or run away from them. But that's only a small part of the whole picture.'

'Then tell me about the rest. Finish off what you've begun. Fit in the other pieces of the jigsaw.'

I shook my head. 'That's as far as our story goes. Besides, it's getting late. I must put you in a taxi.'

'And will I ever see you again?'

'Every day.'

'I didn't mean that.'

'Josie, I've always assumed that I could rely on you to be the sensible one. Can you just believe me that I have my own battles to fight right now?'

For the second time in our brief relationship I wanted her out of the house. I was much relieved when some ten minutes later the taxi arrived and I handed her into it.

'Pals,' I said. 'Remember.' I tried to grin at her, reassuringly.

Then I returned to the sitting room and did some serious thinking. Later, in the middle of the night, I was heading towards the West Country; Josie's visit, it appeared, provoking not only Sylvia to face certain truths.

Part III

ALISON

The girl's letter declaring her intention to stay was a bolt out of the blue; and horrid for Syl. One could not help but be taken by the irony of the situation. That she should want to come at such a time! We talked about it little, as one after another letter passed between them. For communication between us has been at the lowest ebb ever. A state of affairs that doesn't suit. But though I might have rowed when I was younger, I have little taste for it now. Experience has taught me that these crises, whether at work or at home, tend to tide themselves over in the long run. Better if possible to keep one's head down and say little. Besides, Syl has always been a tigress about her clients, about the agency in general. In principle a good thing, but this time it has gone too far for her own good as well as for all others involved. In particular Ruth Flowert.

Damn that Jeremy Farmer. Who but he would make such a cock-up of the whole thing. And cock-up is just about it. If he'd put a little less energy into his cock and a little more into activating his not inconsiderable – though going to seed these last years – brain power, it would have been a darn sight better for him. To say nothing of Syl, Helen, Ruth, all those with whom he is unfortunately involved. And now to cap it all – and almost beyond belief for sheer outright irresponsibility, the girl, Josie, no more than a kid. Moping around as if she's only one step from Waterloo Bridge, though her sense of London's geography is luckily such that I doubt if she'd know where to find it.

Since her arrival she's either been here or at Jeremy's house. Syl has taken her on not one sight-seeing expedition. And I doubt if Jeremy had that in mind when he invited her over, to 'paint his house'. Really, really, as if the girl didn't have enough to contend with, far too much, without having to be drawn into involvement with that old reprobate.

While Syl was indecisive I said nothing but once a decision was made, the girl apparently being so persistent that Syl could not find it in her heart, whatever the circumstances, to let her down, we went out to dinner. No longer the days of cheap Greecos for us. Though it makes me horribly aware of middle age creaking on, I admit to liking the comfort I have earned. And happily one of the joys of Islington is the number of excellent local restaurants.

We have only recently moved here, to the flat above Syl's office; a decision taken after a great deal of heart-searching. And one that has not been without its complications. Previously we kept our life together as a secret: shielded in the top-floor flat of a villa in Clapham, which we implied we shared with one or two others. A situation which never entirely suited either of us and did not come easily to me in the early years.

Having known since I was pre-pubescent that my sexual proclivities were unusual and having torn my hair, beleaguered my poor helpless parents, and ranted at my teachers, having cried for help and found none, I had early on settled down to an acceptance of one of life's little quirks, such it was. I ought to have been born a boy. But I was not. But I would not hide anything, I would not be ashamed. Nor would I let it bugger up my life. And gradually as my teens and early twenties developed I found that this very aspect of my life, far from ruining it, though most forcibly complicating it, could be turned to good by enabling me to understand certain aspects of women's struggle for independence more clearly, just because of my position. I saw how I might have a role in changing and shaping sexual politics.

I'd had a number of affairs before I met Syl. None of them happy. Though all with their own degree of pleasure and fun, intermingled with the pain. Generally the other women were either the older type who wanted to mother – my first affair when I was still at school, with the young biology teacher – or the young diffidents who looked up to me in my university days and afterwards complained of my coldness. 'You're ruthless.' 'You're no better than a man.' 'Your mind is always some place else.' And so on. In response I found most too clingy; most lesbians taking up this stance for lack of something better, because in some way they were half-cocked, half-people, hiding from men and at the same time regretting it. I was disappointed in the general choice of lesbian partner, I suppose. And sensed by the time I met Syl that a solitary life might be mine, with occasional forays into sexual exploits when the old sexual libido got the better of me.

Syl, I hardly need to say now, was something else. Never in all the things I have gone out for in life – and there have been many – will anything ever equal the heady impossible sense of glory and belief in myself, my luck, having the gods on my side, as when I fought and eventually won something I wanted so very much. Though I had to wait. Six and a half years. And there were many times when I saw the day as never coming.

To want something very much and to gain it is to be damned, some jerk has said. I'm not certain about that. But there is always a second side to being the winner, the dark side of the coin, never appreciated at the time. I took Syl with her guilt. She had to leave something enormous. Something to which, on whatever premise, she was previously committed when she came to me. And this to her, whom I thought I could make happy (for what else does one think when one loves someone very much), has had consequences unforetold, which have run like a stream through all of what has followed.

A stream I think describes it nicely. Not a river. Nor a reservoir which has no tides, alters little in different weathers. This stream is capable of many changes. Of being fast and full-flowing. Of being full but calm. For long periods it can be overlooked. Or it can dry up completely in a long hot summer so that one need not be an intrepid explorer at those times to walk across. But then unaccountably and inevitably the rains come again. And it was like that with the events in which Jeremy was so incriminated, that led up to Josie's arrival.

It had been some time since we had chosen to eat out together, since indeed we had passed words that were more than civil. Eating an excellent soupe de poisson, as good as you'll get anywhere in London, Syl told me of her capitulation to energies, she allowed, perhaps stronger than her own.

'You'll help,' she said. 'I can rely upon you for that?' I agreed that

I would. Then we turned to other matters. I did not expect her to say in so many words, 'Don't let her see a coldness between us.' Nor did she. Nor did she say, 'I can never see your point of view over this matter between us; I consider that you have let me down and will continue to do so.' All that was evident. All was apparent. As was my certainty that here for once personal and public lives and conflicting loyalties could not, should not, be allowed to intermingle. In the intervening months she had called me 'pig-headed', I had called her an irrational, over-emotional Jewish tigress. No doubt other terms were bandied about in the privacy of our bedroom which were not nice to hear. And hence the soupe de poisson. She wanted to be sure of a truce.

Syl warned me that she hardly saw herself being able 'in the circumstances' to be a good mother and I had said, 'take it as it comes, darling'. I determined to play a low-key role in this relationship, to keep quiet and give Syl time to get to know her daughter. But it would have been hard to have anticipated, however, quite how difficult it was for Syl, how set she seemed against any communication with the girl. Harder too to have foreseen that Jeremy Farmer would once again put himself in the role of 'coming to the rescue'. Dear God. When would that man ever learn? Or to have foreseen a situation in which Syl would get to the point where she found it in her best interests to scarper for the weekend leaving me face to face with the girl who had to, she insisted, simply had to have someone to talk to.

'It's either going to be you, or Sally, I'm promising you. I'll take her out, get her busted drunk and make her tell. C'mon, Alison, you don't want that, do you? Besides you know it would be better to hear it all from you. You'd be so much more reliable.'

'I'm not sure how much Sally could tell you.'

'There you are! So it's got to be you.'

'It isn't as simple as that. And then there's your mother.'

'Yes, and you can just see her having an intimate conversation with me. I'm in such a mess. So confused, Alison. You've got to help. You're the only one.'

The girl had a kind of persistence that reminded me of myself. This was Saturday morning; there were chores to be done, shopping, clothes to be collected from the cleaners. I had an appointment to have my hair cut. Disagreeable but necessary.

'Perhaps later in the day, Josie.'

'Let me cut your hair,' she said. 'I promise I'm a dab hand at it – save your money – meanwhile you tell me the stark truth about what J.F.'s been up to. C'mon, Alison, what do you say?'

'Well . . .'

'Cut the English diffidence bit, please.'

If her haircuts were anything like her cooking, I was thinking, it would be an extremely bad bargain indeed.

Later, in the sitting room, I was squatting in undignified stance on the Business Section of last week's *Sunday Times*, whilst Josie wielded the kitchen scissors dangerously close to my left ear. I wondered whether on any level at all, this was a wise move.

'I've had a kind of affair with him,' she announced. 'I imagine you both guessed. I kept thinking you'd say something. Or Sylvia would. But I've come to the conclusion there's no point expecting anything so ordinary from you lot. At home Dad and Anna would have been on to me at the first sniff of any such thing.'

'No doubt that's why you waited till you got here.'

'Ha! Still, did you guess, I sometimes saw you looking at me?'

'I certainly wondered. I didn't believe, though, that Jeremy could be quite that irresponsible.'

'Was it irresponsible? He took me under his wing. I was bloody unhappy, you know. With you and Sylvia acting like you never wanted me in the flat.'

'Your mother . . .'

'She's had a hard time. Having one. I know, I know. As a matter of fact I do know a bit more about that than I did before.'

'Courtesy of Jeremy Farmer?'

'Yeah, he told me all about you and Syl at the beginning, you know, that kind of stuff. He's been a real friend. It's just that now I think he must have gone off to try and sort it out with Helen. I've phoned lots of times. I think he really loves her and . . .' She burst into tears. 'The truth is I don't understand what the hell is going on. Is it something to do with Ruth Flowert? I guess it is. But why is Sylvia so annoyed, why won't she talk to me? And what has that got to do with Jeremy and Helen? You're the only one who can explain it. The more adult I try to behave, the more like a little girl I feel, being kept out of the really important things. Know what I mean? And tell me something else. Are all you English so complex?'

I laughed. I've known more intelligent young women, more witty and decidedly many more mature. But there was something likeable about Sylvia's daughter, something open. I admired her spirit in the face of adversity. And perhaps it was this quality, more than anything else, which finally persuaded me.

Meanwhile talking was not to be encouraged while she snipped.

Far too hazardous with someone so emotional. For a time she bit her lip and concentrated ferociously. And the effect, half an hour later, was far from displeasing.

'As good as a hairdresser, you've got to admit, Alison.'

'Not bad, I grant you.'

'Not bad! Oh come on, they'll all be asking who cut your hair so stylishly at Harper & Wiskert on Monday.'

'Few people comment on my appearance, Josie.'

'What about Sylvia?'

Our eyes met.

'When it's not like now, when she's not . . . What *is* it all about? Oh come on, Alison, spill the beans now. I know it's not just me being around. Jeremy taught me that much.'

'What Sylvia has on her hands, Josie, is a legal battle which, if it comes to court – the hearing is set for one week from Monday – will throw the future of Fisk, Farmer into jeopardy, possibly for many years. Now you know of course that your mother's work is of prime importance in her life. Perhaps the one most single thread. No doubt if Jeremy explained anything to you, he explained that. He didn't? Ah, such our Jeremy. No, don't defend.'

'A court case! I suspected something, but not that. Tell me about it. Please, Alison. I can't go on being here like this not knowing.'

Eventually I agreed to give her an overview of the state of affairs, hoping it would go at least some way towards helping her to understand her mother's present state of mind, and some of Jeremy's actions.

'But you must remember,' I told her, 'that I too am involved. How will become clear as the story progresses. So you must take that on board and eventually make up your own mind about what I tell you. Meanwhile I shall be as succinct as possible, but I want no interruptions. Your own opinions I am not interested in. I am satisfied that I see the matter straight. Nor do I wish it to eat up this productive period of my life, whatever it is doing to others. Therefore I have had to distance myself. Do we understand one another?'

She nodded.

'Let me see, then. Background. Do you know who Tickle is? No. Ah. Well, when Sylvia first left your father and she and I started to live together, she wanted to enter what I might broadly call "the literary world", but she had no qualifications beyond those of a bilingual secretary. So taking the best available to her she went to work as personal assistant for a literary agent with the unlikely

146

name of Gideon Tickle. Gideon Tickle had worked for many years in one of the large agencies, then he decided to set up on his own: the path taken by so many of that tribe. He took a number of established writers with him when he left and during the first years that Sylvia worked for him, his was, I understand, a thriving business. Then for reasons never clear to Sylvia, nor to his wife, he had a nervous breakdown.'

For a matter of a half a year Sylvia ran the firm single-handed. Work was curtailed. Many of the better authors left. Sylvia, good and efficient as she was, was young to the business and neither had the stature nor the contacts that Gideon did. On the other hand she put prodigious energy into stemming the flow of departing writers, working long hours, evenings and weekends. I like to think that I was some support during this period.

Towards the end of the six-month period, at a point when Gideon was over a second breakdown and returning from his 'rest-home' with the optimistic conviction that all that was behind him, Sylvia was just beginning to see results from her hard work and drive. The agency was more stable than it had looked at any time during the first half of that year. Understandably she was proud of her record, and looking forward to sharing with Gideon her modest success. So it was a bombshell to her when he returned only to announce that he planned to close the agency.

'Damn it, woman,' I said to her. 'Here's your chance. Take over the whole show yourself. Think what that would mean. You can take on authors you choose. Run it the way you want – one of the advantages after all of being a literary agent rather than a publisher.' At the time I was myself exasperated by the far from satisfactory process of corporate decision-making.

We discussed the matter at length. And finally she decided, bank willing, to buy Gideon Tickle out. Persuading the bank, however, turned out to be no mean feat. To their eternal discredit. Syl was faced with a regressive male chauvinist bank manager of the type not naturally prone to facilitate possibilities for single go-ahead women. The kind with the little wifey at home, doing nothing all day but wait for husband to reappear so that she could serve his supper; a state of affairs he was worried would come to an end if too many women like Syl were facilitated in their business aspirations by loans from banks such as his. He reminded her that a woman who left husband and children was not likely to be a stable bet. He had the cheek even to mention that there might well be a pattern of quitting things.

I suggested further attempts at reconciliation with her monied parents. But Syl was reluctant, believing them to be too beaten by life to be faced with more complications. As it was, convinced as they were that Syl's liaison with me was a second major tragedy that had befallen the family, they had retreated further and further into themselves, resisting all attempts on Sylvia's part to stay in communication.

Eventually a number of our friends intervened with the bank. One even offered a partial collateral, and to our great joy the loan finally came through.

After months of the thing hanging on irritatingly like a loose tooth, the agency was Syl's. I saw myself, of course, as heavily if invisibly involved. The first year, when money was tight, accounts were pored over by us in the evening. Decisions discussed together.

At that time a number of authors, particularly with a first or second book, did not see the need of an agent. And many could manage adequately without them, expecting the same service from a publisher with or without. But even then the situation was beginning to change. I was in touch with a number of bright young authors whose books I was publishing who were beginning to feel that they would benefit from having an agent. Maybe the contracts were becoming too complex or there was a question of conflicting interests, overseas sales, etc. These authors I was able in a number of cases to pass on to Syl.

I've satisfied myself that there was nothing unethical about this. Sometimes, indeed more often than not, it happened in a casual kind of way. An author whom one was publishing might become something of a friend. Friendships tend to spring up between writers and their publishers. If I was eating out on such an occasion, Syl might often join us. It was known that she was an agent. Introductions were made, etc. It was always up to the writer. I never directly pushed business Sylvia's way. But in a number of cases I was able to make an introduction that Sylvia found useful. Amongst the bright young writers who were introduced to Syl in this way was Ruth Flowert.

Sylvia must have been operating for just about three and a half years when Jeremy left the firm of Jong & Wharton under a cloud. There was a cluster of incidents there, the sequence of which now escapes me. I know that when Luke Hyams retired Jeremy did not get the advancement he was hoping for and was furious when Charlie Wharton brought in an outsider; particularly as this was an outsider Jeremy could never see eye to eye with. Someone who had made his name in one of the large paperback houses and had ideas of a new broom sweeping Jong & Wharton, which Jeremy was suspicious of. Nor was he happy at the way Charlie changed allegiance and began to block Jeremy's every turn – 'treating him like a school boy' was the way he put it to Helen. Who put it to Syl. Who tut-tutted for her brother's erstwhile friend.

I never had much sympathy with this association. Nothing against Helen, except for believing her a ninny for being so prepared to be put upon and for overlooking the increasing lapses of marital fidelity (publishing is a small world, gossip rife, nothing goes undetected unless one is most particularly cautious, as Syl and I were committed to being while we were both building our careers) which Jeremy was none too secretly indulging in.

Helen is a woman whose desire to ameliorate has ended up by making her bitter. But I have nothing against her. It was with Jeremy from the first that I felt impatient, Jeremy who has rested on his public school upbringing and Oxford contacts. Born with a silver spoon. Affable because he could afford to be. 'He has always been so understanding – you've no idea,' Syl defended him once when I first tried to influence her view of him. 'No mettle,' I snapped. And have not had reason to change my opinion. Quite the contrary.

I don't know how and if mettle came into the débâcle at Jong & Wharton. But no doubt it underpinned the odd quirkiness of behaviour he exhibited. The business of Jeremy's dismissal was curious, to say the least. He'd had a certain amount of influence with Charlie Wharton. At last he was in the position of having a free hand to buy for the firm outright; to be able to say 'yes' to this one, 'no' to that. And publishers, Josie, like that power. Become addicted to it. I myself am no exception. Simply judicious in having waited till it was placed firmly in my hands. And luckier perhaps in whom I worked for in the early years.

Charlie – always a changeable old devil, rumour has it – tended to play hot and cold with his staff. And this recent appointment of his quickly became the new favourite. Jeremy was out of favour. But he didn't take well to having his say with his authors vetoed. So he became secretive, buying books off his own bat for increasingly large amounts and keeping these deals close to his chest. Some apparently involved Charlie in enormous capital outlay. Eventually there was a show-down and he was out on his ear.

'They've behaved terribly to him,' Syl reported to me one night. 'Out just like that, no reasons, no loyalty. And after he's worked for

Charlie Wharton like a slave for years. On a pittance of a salary too. It's a disgrace. I feel so sorry for Helen. After all they've four children to support now. Oh it's hateful, it really is.'

She must have seen my look. I moved fast from sitting room to kitchen to avoid saying just what I thought of Jeremy Farmer. But she was on my tail. Grabbing my hands across the kitchen table, 'Alison, for Christ's sake be human.' This was never a good approach with me. It had been used once too often by the time I was in my mid-thirties – though not usually by Syl – and generally left me cold. Why after all should anyone suspect that I was not human. Just able to see things for what they were. No shields over my eyes.

'Alison, you must see how awful it is for him. Come on, he's never done anything to hurt you. He's always in fact been the soul of goodness to me – to us too. And you've got a heart as generous as anyone when you want to. We've got to do something.'

'Something?'

'You must see it; we've got to help him.'

Then I exploded.

In what followed, which was brief but more angry and bitter than we had till then ever been with one another, I saw the tigress in Syl. I had noted it before, with amusement and pleasure, in the way she would go hell for leather for her clients. The maternal instinct diverted from her children would make her, I suspected, an excellent agent. But the same trait to less effect was here being used to defend Jeremy. She was unable to listen to the draught of cold reason I attempted to bring to bear on her wild plans. Though we made up and made love with the renewed passion that is one of the great pleasures of reconciliation, though I agreed to consider her plan with an open mind, I knew from the beginning that we were in an area of unsoundness that was going to have repercussions in our relationship and on much else besides.

Syl up to this point had rarely talked about her children and the terrible loss it was to her. No doubt she deemed this something that might hurt, and wished to protect me. Or so I thought. Maybe simply she couldn't cope with it. Whatever, it appeared locked up in a secret part of herself. For a time I wondered jealously if she talked to others about it, other women, or Jeremy perhaps; what was this hold over her that he had, what part of her did she wish to share with him that she didn't share with me? Or was it simply that she could feel maternal towards him and needed to?

Of one thing I was certain. That was no good basis to start a partnership. For such was the plan.

'I want a partner, Alison. It's not just Jeremy being available and that it would be a solution for him. I'm not that soft. It would benefit us both. I'm not the sort to soldier on alone. I want someone to share the day-to-day business of the agency.'

'You've got me.'

'It's not the same. You know it isn't. I've been thinking this way for some time now. So that it really seems to suit both of us.'

'Jeremy and you?'

'That's right. It's got nothing to do with you and me. It won't interfere in any way. I know Jeremy through and through – it's not like choosing any other kind of partner – and because he knows about you and me it will be one person I don't have to dissemble with. He's like a brother. He'd never do anything to let me down. We've got too much behind us – too many memories that bind us together. I have a confidence with him that I might not have in taking on someone I know less well. I'm sure, for example, that he would never try to usurp my place in the firm.'

'Too lazy for that.'

'Alison!'

'All right, all right, I'll say no more. Besides, I suppose it's all decided?'

'He does seem to think it would work. And would give him the independence he wants. Actually I think he'd make a rather good agent. Come on, Alison,' she said, slipping her arm through mine, 'looking at it impartially for one minute you must admit he's got some of the right qualities, and his strong publishing background will stand him in excellent stead.'

Any further doubts I had I kept to myself. When one is going to be over-ridden there is no point expending unnecessary breath.

Your mother was like a child with a new toy. For weeks while the transition of Jeremy was in the pipeline, she was a fountainhead of vitality, exhausting even me. She had recently become seriously interested in Indian cookery and the larder shelves were now full of jars of spices, poppy seeds, ground ginger, tumeric, cardamons, coriander, red chilli powder, etc., etc. In a local market she had picked up some glorious Indian material and was busy sewing cushions and curtains for Jeremy's office to be. This started a market craze and for some months we would forage in the London street markets on Sundays, Syl swooping with delight on china vases, plates, drawings, etchings, paintings on glass, till the flat could barely hold more. Then a room would be transformed, be it our bedroom, or sitting room, or the kitchen, and come to life with

151

an entirely new flavour.

Syl loved to create a space, and although I'm aesthetically blind in that particular way, I nevertheless enjoyed the ambience she could so easily create and the fun she had in doing it.

I began to see too how great a relief it was to her to contemplate a working partnership, how she was indeed not someone to go it alone, as I might have been. And not able to regret her good spirits and the personal benefit that accrued, I ceased to be so grudging about the idea of taking in someone new. I was aware too that with my fiercely possessive nature I would have perhaps had other reasons for anxiety had her choice fallen on a woman. So my antipathy to Jeremy eased, though never disappeared.

Jeremy was to be a director with some shares in the company but to be paid a working salary. Gideon Tickle had remained a director though he paid no active part in the company. He also retained a minority shareholding, the rest being held by Syl. There was talk of this situation changing if and as the company grew and Jeremy's role in it developed. Jeremy's contacts at Long & Wharton, a number of authors whom he had worked with at some stage or another, either came his way themselves or introduced other authors to him. At the same time Syl handed him over a number of clients with a generosity and warmth of spirit that left me cold.

'Let him rattle up his own list, for God's sake, Syl.'

'One has to give him a starting point. Besides he's an excellent editor and can often help in a way I'm not able. And then some of the women actually like having a man agent. Especially the single ones.'

'You bet. Well for goodness sake go carefully. See how he gets on with one or two first.'

'Oh I am, I am.'

Ruth Flowert was not one of the clients whom Sylvia was considering transferring to Jeremy's tender care. Nor was she one of the single ones.

She was married to an architect who worked for Hackney council. She herself had read law at university and was working part-time in the Islington Law Centre, charged with left-wing idealism which seemed to come more from the mind than the heart. Nevertheless I had a considerable soft spot for her first novel, which we had published in 1972 to some critical acclaim, and was waiting with interest for her second. Which was a long time in coming. Subsequently she had published articles and half a dozen quite fine short stories, but was having trouble with the sustained concentration necessary for a second novel. I also suspected that she was one of those whose early critical acclaim worked as a barrier, making further attempts unnerving: a fear that new work will not be as good. Some authors are like that, Josie, and if you stay long enough in the business you will learn to pick them out.

Ruth has a striking individuality and from the time she and her young husband first walked into my office – they had married only a couple of weeks before and were on their way back from honeymoon, a fact with which she immediately acquainted me in her breathless eager voice, maybe as an explanation for why they were holding hands – I was attracted to her.

Don't look like that, Josie. No one, of whatever sexual proclivity, remains faithful in mind and imagination to the one person they are partnered to. Simply do not believe it. Morality and social taboos have opted for monogamy. But mother nature knows nothing of that. A normally sexual male or female will be attracted to many people in a lifetime. Whether or not one does anything about it, is another matter.

For myself I have up till this point been faithful to your mother. But the experience of finding another woman attractive, that has sometimes been there. Often inappropriately in my own case, which might on those occasions have made it easier to hold back. A woman with lesbian tendencies becomes used to treading with care. Not always inappropriately, however. Sometimes one can feel certain that if one made a move it would be reciprocated. But my loyalty and bond to Syl go beyond that.

I can see that you are thinking, 'I should hope so too.' Fierce in your judgements, Josie. The right of youth. But it might be well worth asking yourself why you allow a different code of honour to Jeremy Farmer.

In my work life I have always had to be particularly careful, and have long exercised a self-discipline which by the time Ruth entered my office had become second nature to me. She would have seen me then, and still does, I believe, as nothing more than a caring and thoughtful editor.

But there she was hovering, holding hands with her bearded, skinny, vibrant husband, whose wiry red hairs mingled with the brown in beard and eyebrows. He had intense eyes, a Yorkshire accent, a need to make jokes and to look at her to make sure she was laughing at them. A keen mountaineer, he had taken her to the Alps, she said, for their honeymoon, but she could only manage the lower reaches, finding herself terrified of anything higher.

'She wants me to give it up; and settle for beer brewing or photography. I can see the quarrels we're going to have ahead.'

'Oh nonsense,' she pulled at his arm, embarrassed by the amount of their personal life he was injecting into the office.

She was in her late twenties, medium height and build, an oval face with a mole just under her right cheek bone. Fine brown hair straight but flicked up at the bottom – I imagine with some effort. Her large brown eyes, flecked with gold, were continually changing in as fine a range of expressions as I have ever seen. She was wearing a denim skirt and jacket, a bright red sweater and red woollen scarf around her neck. She could almost have been plain, until she started talking and then immediately one thought of her as beautiful.

She had corrected the proofs on honeymoon, she said, 'so soothing'. And here they were. I imagined that she was one of those for whom life was experienced at too fast a rate. And that soothing was most important.

She and her husband became acquaintances I sometimes social-ised with. They were delighted with the way we handled the book. And then distressed about the 'block' that followed. Once or twice she came into the office to chat about her frustration at getting nowhere with the second. There was little I could do except listen.

I could never imagine her in that law centre of hers. About which she talked much. She seemed far from soothed but rather angry and endlessly bubbling over at a large number of social injustices. Though she herself lived with Ted complacently enough. They were busy doing up a terraced house in Tufnell Park. 'Ted says all part of the gentrification process,' she sighed. 'But what can one do? At least I do put in time trying, you know, to help those worse off than myself. Better than masses of others who simply aren't even aware.'

I thought of her as naive; a young woman whom life had hardly touched. But then, thinking of my own childhood and background, it was all too easy to be critical. There was something messy about Ruth. I could never imagine her with sufficient efficiency to run any kind of an office. Messy, but heart in the right place, at least asking questions. And perceptive about human emotions. And wonderful when writing about Norfolk where she grew up – the subject, not surprisingly, of her first novel.

She fretted also about her part-time job. She only worked three days a week. And there was pressure on her to work full-time, both from the centre, and financially while they were paying off the mortgage. 'Ted never actually pushes,' she said, 'but I can sometimes see what he is thinking – or believe I can. Not much sense having this time if I don't do anything with it. Might as well chuck in trying for a bit. What do you think?'

This wasn't my realm. Actually, I have little patience for it. Give me a good book and I love to do something with it. Give me an outline or an idea and I enjoy shaping it. I'll do any amount of editing or working for a book once we have it in house. But too much chest beating – no, that isn't my style at all.

That was when I introduced her to Syl. The two took to one another and Syl was able, with far more patience than I could ever muster, to bring her motherly instincts to bear on Ruth Flowert and to encourage the short stories which helped her to regain self-confidence. Then she got her going on a second novel.

It was encouraging how much Ruth flourished under Syl's tender ministrations. The second novel was far more wide-ranging in scope. Some of the critics thought she hadn't quite managed to bring it off. But then you can expect a more hostile reception to a second novel. Flawed but interesting, my judgement when Syl first passed over the manuscript to me. We were in complete agreement over this one.

'She'll be bloody good in the end,' Syl pronounced.

But the third novel, delivered fast, only some eighteen months later, was so dense as to be almost impenetrable. She was developing a mythological poetic language which one suspected, for all its flights of imagination and at times sheer brilliance of imagery, would have a limited readership. We printed in small numbers. She was disappointed. The reception of the critics was mixed. Her fourth followed the same pattern. Both Syl and Ruth were disappointed at the small print run, the only moderate interest here, and the lack of interest amongst American publishers.

'She needs a boost.' One of our bedroom conversations. 'She's beginning to lose faith in herself.'

'Isn't she always about to do that. A writer's preoccupation, I would have thought. Don't be so soft, Syl. Come on, I've heard enough about authors' fragile egos already today.'

Nevertheless I determined to find time for a talk with Ruth, at least to probe her future plans.

She was in the early stages of pregnancy by the time we fixed up a meeting. Now in her mid-thirties. No spring chicken. Her emotional and overwrought nature would not, I suspected, make childbearing easy. But contrary to her own expectations, she claimed, when she stepped into my office, she had never felt better in her life. 'Early morning sickness, of course,' she confided, 'but nothing more than that. Generally it's a lovely experience. Something every woman should go through.' She stopped short, looking at me. But I was able to reassure.

'Some of us aren't built that way. It has never been on my list of priorities.'

'Oh I guess so. I just can't imagine it at the moment.'

'Of course not.'

I sent my assistant out for sandwiches and winkled a bottle of passable Riesling from the wine cellar. She passed over the wine, however, and hardly touched the sandwiches.

Talking at double the speed of most ordinary mortals, using her eyes, mouth, eyebrows, nose, in all manner of gestures as she did so, she was amusing and vibrant company. Full of anecdotes of her life with Ted. She had become interested in Eastern meditation and a wide area of related fields. She and Ted had become practising vegetarians. They had planned for a walking holiday in the foothills of the Andes, but this pregnancy had scuppered all that. He'd been so disappointed. So she was forced to relent, what else could she do, and he was back to his old tricks, climbing in Scotland with a couple of his pals.

She was full of plans: for moving out of London, for keeping bees, for natural childbirth, for learning more about foot massage, based on the principles of acupuncture. In the end it seemed both churlish, and I judged it unnecessary, to discuss in any detail the direction of her writing. I was comfortably convinced that this change in her lifestyle and the advent of the baby would bring their own changes. All of which were likely to have a more than odds on chance of affecting her writing and hopefully bringing it out of the tight corner into which it had dug itself.

She left my office an hour or two later, leaving me pleasantly exhausted and reflecting as I drained the last of my wine that bees and foot massage might be on, but that if I were her doctor she was not one of those I would have given a more than one in a hundred chance of natural childbirth. Too tense by half, I concluded to myself, complications are bound to set in.

But life rapped Ruth over the knuckles in quite a different way from anything I could have expected.

Ted was in poor shape when he returned from mountaineering, and complained of pain along his left side. He lost appetite and as she put on weight his already skinny figure dwindled to nothing. Cancer in the liver was diagnosed, already rapidly spreading to other parts of his body. For the last three months of her pregnancy he was in hospital. And a mere matter of days before the baby was delivered he was dead. I was right about the natural childbirth but it was cold comfort before such grotesque suffering.

Syl of course kept in constant touch, and kept me posted. After the baby was born, Ruth went to live for a time with her parents in Leatherhead but eventually returned to her Tufnell Park home where both Syl and I on separate occasions visited her and her skinny, red-haired, screaming son. Towards whom, in all natural gestures of motherhood she seemed, even to my mind, embarrassingly awkward and unschooled.

But a writer, a serious one, isn't to be kept down, as you will come to find out in time, Josie, if you stay in this game. True to form a year later she was round at Percy Street, as anguished as ever, perhaps more so, and with good reason, complaining about her writer's block. On one of the occasions when she was sitting in Syl's office Jeremy came into the room and to Syl's amusement, as she reported it to me, failed to remember that it was only to find a file he had mislaid. Imagine it like this . . .

On went the story. For a time Josie sat on the floor, transfixed, listening to Alison's voice.

*

It is a fortnight later. Ruth is back in the office. She is just passing by. She is just wondering . . . There was something mentioned that last long meeting on which she'd like elaboration. She just wondered did either Jeremy, standing hovering at the reception desk, where she had caught him, 'did he –' she raises and flutters her eyelids a little, modestly but implying how much it would mean to her, implying too how valuable she knows his time is, 'if he or Sylvia –' here she looks towards Sylvia's door. She utters a little sigh, is it relief because Syl's door is closed and there are voices issuing from inside, 'if either himself or Sylvia – of course it was an awful lot to ask, and just on spec too – would have the time for perhaps just a further half an hour?'

Jeremy looks at his watch. 'What we need is a drink.'

'A drink. Now?' She waves her thin delicate hands with the blunt finger tips uncertainly into the air. 'Isn't it awfully early?' she says. He frowns in case it be so; but on looking at his watch his face spreads a warm slow smile. To which she responds, feeling warmth as if she has been hugged. And taking her immediately back to her anguish.

But he is saying, 'Twenty-nine minutes past exactly. If we spring up the road we may well have the pleasure of being the first ones in.'

Rather clumsily he reaches over Liz, the assistant, who cannot quite hide her smirk, and fiddles with a minute key in the keyhole of an old, ill-fitting drawer.

'Can I help you, Jeremy?' she asks. After the jiggling has gone on for some minutes and her arm has been bumped in the process unceremoniously against her chair more than once. Besides he is too near. His maleness too aggressive, too pervasive. Which she feels while he feels nothing. She is invisible to him. The assistant. That irritates. So now for her tiny quota of power. 'Can I help?' knowing he is helpless.

He curses, 'This goddamn drawer.'

'Were you wanting anything?'

'Petty cash,' he mumbles, his right hand and his newly growing moustache helping to hide his mouth. He resents having to say the words.

Liz glows with her little pleasure. Meanwhile Ruth Flowert stands all of a whirl looking at Syl's shut door. Not knowing what to think. Not wanting to think. Telling herself that if it will help her writing. Ah, the voracious appetite of the muse!

In the pub (they are not the first, one small elderly man in cloth jacket and cap darts close to Jeremy's legs and in through the door before them). Fit, thinks Jeremy. I hope I, at his age . . . time pressing on relentlessly. And then with the one well-tried and most often used of man's tricks for kidding himself, at least temporarily, that he is stopping the tide, or at least halting it at this given moment for just a little longer, he turns to his companion. 'What will you have? You must be looked after.' With all its implications. Only he, only she. 'Pineapple juice,' she breathes, and wonders whether to confide that since the, since the . . . since that terrible time, her doctor has been prescribing Valium regularly, rather too complacently, she suspects.

How much she would like to ask, all of a sudden, what he thinks to all of this; is the doctor being too irresponsible, too relaxed in the question of this prescribing? She has heard of over-prescribing, of addictions. And no fool. She a writer. But over-sensitive – yes. What does Jeremy think, she would like to ask; his shoulders she now perceives as being pleasingly broad. What does he think of this whole matter; you are someone I can rely on. But meanwhile she doesn't. Doesn't offer the explanation that on Valium it is better to keep off alcohol.

'Pineapple juice,' she says, waving her hands dismissively. And then her mouth clamps shut. But trembles a little at the corners. She is not used to keeping it shut. Indeed she recognises at that moment the touch of upper lip on lower with surprise. Almost as if, she thinks, her lips are making acquaintance. It was, she supposed, the charge in the atmosphere, the newness all around. No, not in the pub, where she looked at the other people now crowding in, smoking, talking, drinking, relaxing after the day; but in the ridge of space between herself and Jeremy as they sat on their high stools at the bar.

Both were quiet. He was busy paying for the drinks, her pineapple juice, his beer. She was worried: though only in part it seemed something to worry about; more like something pleasant to ponder over, of the sort one stores up for one's first waking moments, before the inevitable foot on the carpet – or the floorboards if one is not so lucky. She herself had only recently, only last year when Ted . . . Ted. Again she looked at Jeremy, again not at his face, nor this time at his broad shoulders, but at the dip of his back, the swoop of his spine as it was presented to her from the lie of his jacket. A part of her mind – a fragment now – was still in the outer office of Fisk, Farmer & Tickle, her eyes going through Sylvia's shut door and hearing the fresh mint colours of her voice. But who wants a mother, when she can have a father? So spoke the little girl in Ruth Flowert, investing in Jeremy Farmer attributes which he has as much claim to as most. But how imperfect and fleeting, to say nothing of how unreliable. However, for the moment –

As the remembered cadence of Sylvia's behind-the-door voice became loosened in her mind and eventually floated quite free, like a stamp that has been soaking for a long time in tepid water and now finally, its last bit of gum dissolved, curls satisfactorily at the edges and rises to the surface, she acknowledged with a little sigh (which Jeremy, his ears intensely acute at that moment, noticed and stored to ask her about if the conversation after a few more drinks ever became as intimate as he hoped it would) that drinking now here in the bar with Jeremy was not an idle and inconsequential action but was indicative of a shift of loyalties – no surely, she corrected herself, that was putting it a trifle too strongly – from one to the other. The safety of Sylvia, who would always of course remain a friend, for the excitement of . . .

For one moment she had an intense vision of leaving her mother in the kitchen, steaming handkerchieves, a floral apron round her waist, whilst she opted for the greater but more terrifying pleasure of going to the swings with her father. Would he push her too high, would he forget all about her? No, this was ridiculous, she thought as she shifted on her stool, the leather making a purring noise as she did so; she was a woman now. A mother. A widow. Ted, Ted. But he would have wanted, had said over and over again towards the end – what? That she was not to shut herself away. Even that she was a woman who liked men and must. But Jeremy of course was married. Was he? She knew nothing about him. It was just that the relationship between agent and client was a special one, a close one; and with a man perhaps one could lean on him a little bit more, share certain things that she never felt she could talk about with Sylvia. For example, how inadequate she felt as a mother. Of course Sylvia had never had children herself. But was that why? She didn't know. It was just that she suspected with Jeremy – Well, he seemed so extraordinarily human, approachable. Quite apart from the writing business. Quite apart! She laughed at herself. Everything is the writing business. Yet again, still not quite comfortably convinced.

He had been looking at her. In no rush. The headiness of knowing that something is going to play into one's hands. As one gets older one recognises the art of it, to play it slowly, taking all the time in the world. No need to rush. All too soon. So now he was drinking through the froth of his beer into the cool clear substance below. In a number of unhurried rhythmical intakes. Each leaving a little bit more foam on his newly growing beard. Meanwhile as he drank, he observed his companion. Not her body (bottom and bust, generally for him equal favourites: nonsense he thought it to talk about men being divided into one of two camps over their preference in this matter) – having been sized up in a time now which already seemed long in the past; but her face, which he looked down on from his height on the bar stool.

He took pleasure in the wide lips (room for manoeuvre, he liked that) her small pointed teeth (the rim of her glass brushing her top ones), her high cheek bones, on the right side of which rose the snail shape of her pale brown mole, her speckled almond-shaped eyes, her smooth white brow, the way her hair fell in wads to the sides of her ears. He even took pleasure in the deep dark circles that shadowed her eyes, leaving a hollowed darker area which extended

160

as far as her cheek bones. For it spoke to him of a fragility which made him feel more a man of the earth than he was wont to do most of the time these days.

'Tell me, how is it,' he said to her, quietly, gently. 'How are you? It can't be easy. I can imagine, myself.'

Her eyes clouded. Tears gathered in the corners, but remained there. So nice of him to ask. Most people after the first month or two. Well, people are on the whole awfully callous. She'd always known, laugh and the world laughs with you. Mustn't go on crying. It's only that –

'It is sometimes most painfully lonely,' she told him. 'Ted and I . . .'

'Sylvia mentioned how very close you seemed to be.'

She said nothing. Hanging her head. Willing no more tears to come and surprised too that they still did come so easily. After all this time. You would have thought there simply weren't any more to shed. And yet.

'I want to cheer you up. Not make you cry.' For the briefest of seconds he rested his hand on her lap.

'I know,' she said, 'forgive me.' Taking a paper handkerchief out of her bag and dabbing at the corners of her eyes.

And then there she was telling him not about her writing, not about those extra matters that their conversation a fortnight before had given rise to, which had stimulated her that very day to get dressed up in high heels and some gesture towards make-up, into tights and out of jeans, and determine that yes it would be all right to leave Toby with the neighbour just once more – three times already this week but surely she would soon have things under control.

She had told herself it was of the utmost importance to get herself along to the office of Fisk & Farmer and ask for further elucidation about some of the remarks Sylvia and Jeremy (perhaps especially Jeremy) had made. For if she was sure, it would doubtless be so much easier to find the flow once again, the flow of her writing. Whereas now with all these doubts. So of course poor Toby too would benefit in the end – after all she'd have to support him somehow for years and years. Ted had hardly anything of a pension, having only worked with his firm for three years and three days. And then if they were to stay in the house there was the pressing matter of the mortgage. So it was for Toby's benefit, she assured herself, as she slipped on her tights, found that a ladder was creeping upwards from the heel, cursed and scrabbled through her drawer for another pair, that she leave him with kindly Susan across the way and step off briskly in the direction of Fisk, Farmer, to settle in her mind what it was they'd really been driving at.

But now it wasn't about her work, a pub anyway seemed almost too brusque and manly a place for Ruth Flowert's sensitive writing, that she talked on her high stool to Jeremy Farmer. It was about Toby.

An hour or more later the two, still talking, left the pub. She was heading, she told him, in the direction of the tube station. He back to the office. However, still in intense conversation as they were, his steps remained apace with hers.

'Of course I mean it,' he was saying. 'I admire you greatly for the kind of honesty, the sheer mettle that allows you to say the things you have. To see so much more clearly than other women, who often feel just as you do, I believe, but don't dare to let themselves contemplate such a position. And, as I was saying, if you can bring such a relevant subject out for exposure, if in your new book you can . . .'

'Yes, yes,' she said hurriedly, for they were fast approaching the ticket desk. 'Well here we are. Jeremy, you have been such a help. I simply can't tell you, can't begin to, how much better you've made me feel. How much more confident too. Ridiculous how much confidence-boosting we all seem to need, eh? I wouldn't have your job!'

'It's been nothing but pleasure this afternoon.'

She wanted to believe him. She cocked her head, angling it as a robin might. And blinked at him out of her speckled eyes. Was there more she wanted to say? What was it? Or just a desire to keep him there, fuelling her grate. Afterwards the wet autumn evening would begin to close in on her. Her uncomfortable high-heeled shoes would step on sodden yellow leaves as she made her way up the street from the train to her home. The trees plump with rain water would no doubt shower her. And while she struggled for her key her son would cry and wriggle. Inside, she'd have to make supper. Just she and he. And then later, much much later, that half of the large bed unbearably empty. The hours and hours of wakefulness. She'd always been a light sleeper. But now. And no one to make her a cup of Ovaltine. So she stood, her ticket in her hand, her head quaintly tilted, searching her mind for something she still had to stay to him.

And so he stood, smiling at her with good intention, showing no impatience to be getting back to the office and perhaps other pressing matters he had promised himself he would have in hand by the end of the day. To hell with them all.

But she could think of nothing else.

'I'll bear in mind,' she started, 'I'll bear in mind then, all that you have said. Such a help.'

'Deadlines,' he said.

'Pardon?'

'Deadlines are always a good thing.'

'Oh I've never thought. I've never been the kind of person.'

'You've got to become absolutely professional. I want that now of all my clients.'

My clients. She wasn't at all offended. On the contrary, inside her a further spurt of pleasure. Almost sexual.

'Professional?' she said mildly. 'Aren't we all in our own ways. Any writer whose . . .'

'Of course,' he cut her short. 'But I want something more than that.'

'Oh.' It was a small gasp.

'Too much emotionalism in this game,' he said. 'I want my authors, each and every one of them, to toughen up, to be exacting on themselves. For their own sakes, of course. And deadline is part of that. It sounds as if Sylvia hasn't been pushing you hard enough.'

'No, she hasn't been pushing me,' said Ruth wonderingly.

'For example, if I were to say I want to see the completed first half, even in draft form, in, let me see,' he looked at the date on his watch, 'on the first of December, that gives you exactly two months, what would you say?'

'I could try.'

'Good. Good. I'll see you then.'

And so it seemed it was settled. Quite a lot was settled.

Hastening down the crowded escalator Ruth's heart was thumping not at all unpleasantly.

Meanwhile Jeremy returned to the office. Liz had long since departed and Sylvia's door was open.

'Hello, Jeremy,' she called.

'What a day! Have a drink.' She moved over to the cupboard from which she took out two elegant glasses and a bottle of whisky and Perrier. 'Your usual?'

'I'd better go slowly. I've started drinking early tonight, with Ruth at the pub.'

'Yes, I thought I heard her earlier. Have you ever noticed her voice, Jeremy? That odd combination of softness and deep croak. One of the most unusual voices I know.'

Jeremy does not know about Ruth's voice. Her figure, yes, the imaginative range of her writing, her domestic situation (after this evening) and even, he believes, he has gleaned the beginning of acquaintanceship with what at his most romantic moments he might call her soul. But her voice, no.

'What will it be? A weak whisky, mostly Perrier? Or something different?'

'No, that will be fine.'

As she pours, her movements as deft and precise as his are often clumsy, he flicks through the papers on her desk, now at the end of the day piled in four neat piles. This flicking through, this reading anything and everything that might occasionally look interesting, this disrupting a natural sequence, continuously shuffling the pack, irritates his partner and confederate. He has worked in the firm for fifteen months now. A whole host of irritating attributes, which Sylvia at night swears to Alison she could never have imagined of her brother's friend, make Sylvia grind her teeth and hold her peace, sometimes only with a steely determination.

'How quickly other people's habits grate,' Syl would occasionally complain. 'Really, Alison, awful as one gets older to find how shockingly intolerant one becomes.' However, fifteen months after Jeremy's arrival these conversations were still rare. At the same time there were certain gifts of Jeremy's she had great respect for. And such was her character that it was her natural instinct to foster talent where she saw it, both in her clients, and, it appeared, in her colleague.

His wide range of acquaintances, his natural gregariousness (her own always curtailed by her domestic circumstances), his strong editorial skills, his ability on top form, or with one or two drinks inside him, to make the client feel like the most important person and the most brilliant creator, all these were valued. So the other was what she called 'the far more unimportant side'. Though from the first I doubted it, for in the little gestures, I believe, we see the man.

But latterly, indeed in the few weeks directly preceding the occasion on which Sylvia was ministering a weak whisky drowned in much Perrier to Jeremy, aspects from the unimportant side had pressed a little too closely onto her notice. Only that morning there had been a letter on her desk from one of the clients whom she had

164

early passed on to Jeremy, complaining that his last two letters had not been answered. Twice in the last couple of weeks clients had been left waiting long hours in the office. Inevitably ultimately Sylvia herself had had to break off from what she was doing to dispel the anger that was noticeably mounting in the reception room. And on both occasions one thing had led to another so that it was only an hour or so later that Sylvia had managed to pull back to her own affairs, while Jeremy was meanwhile conducting long and boozy lunches with publishers on what Sylvia anxiously worried he saw to be an unlimited expense account.

'One must think big, Sylvia. Not count the pennies.' She wasn't so sure.

He was all right when he wasn't drinking. That is what she concluded. But he was drinking increasingly. There were rows apparently and strains between Helen and Jeremy. And Sylvia neither knew nor liked to ask what was at the bottom of it. But when he drank he was unreliable. And Sylvia had not bargained for all the little ways in which at these times it would be she who picked up the pieces.

So it was that when on this evening he approached her on the subject of Ruth Flowert she was far far more hesitant of passing his way a good client (to say nothing of a good friend and someone for whom she felt some considerable degree of responsibility) than she might have been some half a year earlier. And no fool, Jeremy, for all his vagaries, was aware that this conversation with Sylvia might not go as well as many earlier ones had done.

This little matter of the client whose letters he was not replying to. She had it in mind to mention it to him.

But instead with affection she put her hand lightly on his stomach.

'The beginning of a paunch, Jeremy?'

He gave a half yawn, twisted the sides of his growing moustache.

'Just middle age colliding with a naturally good appetite and a healthy enjoyment of beer.'

'You were so long and lanky, you and Timmy — as boys,' she said.

'Wonder if he'd have put on weight. No, he wasn't the type.'

She liked it that after all these years they could now talk about him like this.

'He would have said you were out of shape,' she said. 'He would have ragged you no end. And I feel in his place . . .'

'You're just as lovely as ever. But of course, harder.' He smiled at her.

'At least exercise ten minutes in the morning, as I do, or run or something.'

'Run!'

'Cut down on your drink. You mustn't, you know, begin to let yourself go to seed.'

'Darling, you're sounding much too much like Helen. Talking of which, she's out tonight, and the children catered for, come on let me take you to a film and to eat somewhere afterwards. It's ages since we've had a night out, just you and I. I'd really like it. Phone and tell Alison we've got business to talk over.'

'Talking of business . . .'

'Later, later. While we're eating.'

So it was that the two of them went into Islington to the Screen on the Green and watched a film that they had both seen a number of times but enjoyed as much as ever. Relaxed and close, having shared the emotional impulse that drove the film to its cathartic ending they walked out onto the Green and watched two punks having a fight. As they looked up together at the indigo red of the sky, where one of the punks had thrown up something small that fluttered, for an instant holding its own against gravity then fell like a bullet, it seemed to them that their own lives, past, present, future, were indeed satisfactory.

In the Italian restaurant of Jeremy's choice they ordered a light meal. For it was now late. Both of them had had a long day. Jeremy talked of Helen and domestic problems. Sylvia listened, soothed, felt for him. She who had not looked for sexual and intellectual compatibility, but had, she said later to me in bed, found it, how could she not feel sorry for him when he talked of the pockets and gaps in his own and Helen's relationship, the deep discontent marking itself like an accusation permanently on Helen's face. And yet, urged Syl to Jeremy, 'You and Helen have a lot. And I'm not only talking about the children.'

'I know, I know.'

'Life's a funny business,' she took his hand with great care and affection.

Then returned her hands to her cutlery. 'But Jeremy, I too have my worries.'

'You?'

'In the office.'

He yawned, a trifle impatiently.

'No, Jeremy, hear me out.'

She told him of the client who had complained to her about the unanswered letters, about the other small indiscretions. She said that of course he was brilliant and it was lovely having him around. But perhaps he wasn't quite, here she took his hand again to soften the blow, pulling his weight in the way she needed. One had to be, in whatever one did, so she judged, 'absolutely on the ball, absolutely all the time'.

'You Fisks,' he said, 'so ambitious.' He laughed at her.

For one moment she flushed dark, not pleased. This was the first moment ever she thought that he had made any direct and unfavourable comment on her Jewishness.

'No. Not that. Alison agrees.'

'Darling, surely you haven't been muttering about these minor details with Alison?'

This calling her darling. She had noticed it recently. What was it, middle age too? She had noticed the term slipping in in direct reverse to the real warmth and closeness of their relationship. Or was it since he had become an agent? A new role he was putting on. She shrugged. Whatever it was, it seemed uncomfortably distant from the clarity and honesty they had shared in their youth.

'Alison,' he was saying. 'Now if you'd wanted a business partner like her, you should never have chosen me, darling. I have great respect for your Alison, as you know. But I'm simply not the same kind of person. And luckily there's room for all sorts. I thought you of all people believed that.'

Now he looked at her with some kind of appeal and she felt again how hurtful things must at present be for him at home. How somehow their long friendship must be hitched to a more secure harmony in the agency, how being the forerunner, and having made the decision to take him in, she must find ways of making it work.

Only fifteen months, she was saying to herself, there are bound to be discrepancies at the beginning. She sought a way to find in herself the affinity she had experienced on leaving the cinema.

Meanwhile suddenly he needed to pee, so badly that it couldn't wait, and rather roughly apologising to her as he pushed back the wooden table, he stood up and made for the Gents. When he returned the two men sitting at the neighbouring table were trying to engage Sylvia in conversation. She looked pleased to see him, tired; still, for all her new, more tailored clothes and air of quiet efficiency which she had adopted over the years since leaving Patrick, hiding as far as possible her passionate nature, as well as the unusual nature of her private life. She still, at a moment like this, and it struck him anew, struck him with poignancy, looked tremendously vulnerable. So often she came over as not so in the office. And in a sense her being the boss was not always easy. Timmy's little sister had sure as hell turned into something else. So that he didn't always remember her as that.

But now just seeing her sitting there, her beauty aglow as she defended herself from the approaches of the men, he felt towards her – curious indeed coming so soon after the bar experience of Ruth Flowert – the consequences of which he must speak to Sylvia before the evening was out – the old stirring sexual attraction which flowed over, as it had done from early days, into a need to protect, to help her, a need not to impose on her. He felt indeed how horrible it was for her, more horrible than for other women, these men's advances. And he himself was above that, with his own sexual desire for her (how could it not be so with such a beautiful woman) well under control. Friendship. Now at the end of the evening, he felt less selfish, less shut in his own world than when he had walked into her office. Of course he must think of her, support her, have fewer long lunches. From tomorrow he would get up when the alarm clock rang. No more ten-thirty starts.

So when he had brushed off the other men's attempts at conversation and he and she were drinking their coffee, he leaned forward over the table and smiled at her, his lazy warming smile – but less lazy than usual at this very minute. And breathed confidence into her, in a way that only Jeremy knows how. These little matters, he implied, forgive. Minor boyish transgressions. But she was right. Of course they were inconvenient to her. Perhaps he hadn't thought about it sufficiently. And then there were difficulties too for him making the adjustment. Never having had a woman boss.

'Oh I'm not a boss,' she laughed. He was teasing her. It was not disagreeable.

'No more late lunches,' he said. She was inclined, desired to believe him. 'And as to that client, it wasn't strictly slackness, you know. You mustn't always think the worst of me. No, on the contrary, I deemed it politic . . .'

He acquitted himself not badly. 'When he wants he can make out a very good case for himself,' she said to me later. And he did want.

So Jeremy worked his Jeremy charm and she slipped into a more and more relaxed state. Wanting to believe him. Able to believe him. Some of her own worries about her clients came out then. Now it was his turn to listen. And happy he was to advise. Before they knew it they were making plans for a bumper year to come. All sorts

168

of Jeremy plans were under way. He was reminding her how solid the agency's growth had been and was now. Creating a picture of success – in which he loomed large – in a way he was so good at.

'You have, you know, a basically sunny, optimistic temperament,' she told him.

'Most of the time,' he purred, ordering for both a second cup of coffee, and damn the consequences.

'Ruth Flowert,' he suddenly said. 'She is going to be one of the great clients, the kind that having one or two of will make an agency in the end.'

'Ruth, but goodness knows what will happen to her after this tragedy.'

'That's just it, Sylvia. She's got to use the tragedy, make it work for her. And she can. She and I were speaking at the pub. I made some suggestions, you know, following on from the conversation when she was last in. She seemed terribly excited. It's going to be a breakthrough, this new novel.'

'If she can concentrate sufficiently. At the moment I have my doubts.'

'I've demanded a deadline by Christmas. First half sent in a draft form then. That's the kind of treatment a writer like her needs. And I know what you're thinking. Especially in these circumstances. Believe me, Sylvia, I've known women not totally dissimilar from her before.'

Sylvia looked worried. 'So how did you leave it?'

'She'll be sending me the . . .'

Sylvia's eyes stopped him. For the second time he lent close over the table. Lowering his voice putting more urgency into the tone.

'I believe I could help her, Sylvia. I really do. We'd all benefit. You know that. We could share her. I don't want to take her away from you or anything like that. It doesn't have to be a case of yours or mine, after all. I just would like to put in some input. What do you think?' He looked at her boyishly. 'And Ruth herself seemed awfully pleased.'

Sylvia was silent. Jeremy called for the bill. He knew there was nothing more to be said. He knew he'd won. 'Bless you, Sylvia,' he said. 'See you tomorrow at nine-thirty prompt then.' He brushed her on the cheek. 'Send my regards to Alison.'

They waited for a taxi. He saw her into it.

'Life's good,' he said to her through the last crack before the door closed. 'Remember that. And it is going to get better and better.'

Of course Jeremy will not have an affair with Ruth. Somewhere in the back of his mind he stores this decision. There is Sylvia, whom he will not let down. There is the fact that though he has had numerous affairs, of both long and short duration, with a wide assortment of women, including air-hostesses, waitresses, women met at parties and through friends, girls of all sorts and varieties, in the publishing profession he has never yet done anything as foolish as to sleep with one of his authors; nor does he intend to. One must draw the line somewhere, he comfortably tells himself. Of course not from any moral standpoint, but just that it wouldn't do; it could create the kind of muddle that could well become nasty. On top of which his whole extra-marital love life was up for scrutiny now more than ever before. Helen was creating. She was more strained, more belligerent than ever before. And so his mind wandered away and on to far more pleasant things.

Meanwhile Ruth Flowert worked doggedly during the autumn months. Fired as she was by the conversation she and Jeremy had shared. The evenings and nights continued wretched, the afternoons with Toby just about bearable, but the early mornings – she woke at four-thirty and wrote through till nine, with Toby shut in his cot and not allowed to stir until that time, however much he screamed – were powerful, potent and worth, she thought, everything. She would have a second period of work in the evenings after Toby had been put to bed. These were far more grind and less productive. But nevertheless, she reckoned, all helped. While she wrote, or rather in the other periods of the day when her writing life was sifting through her mind, she thought often of Jeremy and of his reaction to what she was writing. One could say in a way that she wrote it for him, even to make him fall in love with her, though she would have never been able to recognise anything so startling.

She was determined she would keep to the deadline. She often thought about the clothes she would wear on the very day when next she would walk into the office, December 1st. So the two months passed. She resisted invitations to go out with old friends of hers and Ted's, pleading babysitting problems and money worries, and, huddled in on herself with Toby, lived a strange half-life, breathing what she could into her writing.

She is again in the office, in Jeremy's room. Jeremy is moving piles of books so that she can find room on the leather sofa to sit down. It is again late afternoon. This is the time she finds it easiest to get away. She is working in the law centre mornings now while Toby is in part-time day-care. The afternoons she walks as much of London as she has energy for, pushing the pushchair that is beginning to look worn and battered. She does not like the Heath or any green spaces, but on the contrary is more soothed by hard London pavements, by the variety of houses, architecture, shop windows, noise, dirt, all the clamour of the streets. She likes to look into the windows of houses and will make up stories for Toby, which he is beginning to listen to (though his attention span is still short) of the people that live inside those they stop to peer at.

This afternoon Toby is with the mother of one of the other children they have met through the day-care. Ruth has a cold. In the end she did not dress up, though she would not for the world have given up her fantasies of new and snazzy outfits that had sustained her over the ensuing time. Meanwhile in jeans (all her tights had runs and even to buy a new pair at the local newsagents struck her that day as too much hassle) and a navy fisherman's jersey that had been Ted's, she wanders round the room saying, 'Ah it is the first time I have been into this part of the office. A very different kettle of fish.'

Jeremy's thick white hair falls forward over his eyes as he leans to move books, files, newspapers in order to make space for Ruth to sit. His glasses too come forward over and along his nose and need re-adjusting. She is surprised, as she had been last time, at the pureness of the white. His moustache now fully grown in not so pure in colour. A speckled grey and white effect. But the crop of hair on his head seems powder soft and newly washed. He wears it long, the last wisps touching his shirt collar. From the moment she walks in she is aware of the physicality of Jeremy – that his hair for example smells good, the smell of washing on a line, clean and sweet. It is his close maleness, after such an eternity since Ted, that threatens, but does not then sweep her off her feet.

'I wonder what you'll think,' she says, hugging the manuscript to her, not giving it up. 'It's quite different. I have a sense of it being good, myself. And I think by this stage one knows, really. Still your opinion –'

She looks at him. She is very bunged up, she feels. Her cold now in its fifth day. Past the sneezing stage, past the rasping sore throat but still dry and uncomfortable. A tightness too in the chest. Blocked sinuses which make her voice sound thicker and mean that she has to take continual little pauses in order to breathe through her mouth.

Her lips too are dry and chapped. On the way out, she thinks, she will buy Lypsyl.

She has hoped for a further encounter which would again bring out the woman in her, something that she could store up over all the miseries of the prolonged festive season. But today she could simply give out no buzz to Jeremy or anyone. Cruel the turn of fate. So best, she thinks, to leave the manuscript and hurry out. What more after all to say, until he and Sylvia have read it. (He has said that he will pass it on to Sylvia; that she happens to be in Birmingham this afternoon but sends love and will call very shortly – thus letting Ruth off the hook.)

So now no sooner almost than Jeremy has cleared the sofa sufficiently to allow Ruth to sit down, and before even he has taken a chair adjacent to her himself – whilst he is still in the process of clearing books from that chair, she gets up and pulls the cape which she has taken off but is still holding, close round her, as she does so leaving the manuscript gently on the near corner of his desk.

'Ah, you're in a hurry.'

'Yes. No.' She flushes. 'I'm just not particularly sociable any more.'

'You ought to,' he says. He gets up too. And sprawls a leg across the chair with the books on it. Half kneeling, half standing, resting against the chair's back he looks hard at her.

Too hard, she thinks.

Resting along the chair as he is, he seems to be arresting her movement towards the door. But she won't sit down again. Inside her cape she gives a little shrug of her shoulders.

'Tonight, for example, good friends of mine, very old friends, are having a party; of course they've been urging me to go but there's just no way, with Toby.'

Now why did she say it, she wonders. For the last thing in the world she wants to do, is to go to a party. But the pleasure of a moan. Or is it that despite all indications to the contrary, her dress, her cold, her general demeanour, what she has just said about not any longer being sociable, she would like him to think of her nevertheless as a popular woman, someone others wanted?

'I will babysit,' says Jeremy, it seems to her quite magnificently.

She stands blinking her eyes, looking at the jackets of her own and other authors' books which line the walls, trying to imagine Jeremy in the neglected narrow terraced house. So much that Ted had been going to do had been left undone, the upstairs bathroom only half-plumbed, the kitchen range half-finished – the fate of architects always working on other people's houses. And then her own lowering of standards since Ted's death. She, never very domestic, never enjoying cleaning, housekeeping, had previously forced herself to think about these things, even to the extent of orderly division of labour. And then Ted had always done more than his share. But now there no longer seems any point. And whatever she attempted was anyway messed up two minutes later by Toby. There was a smell of urine, she suspects, dust, garbage, toys and those odd bits of household jetsam, which were so much more alluring to an infant than toys, scattered everywhere on every floor space. The windows were so dirty it was impossible any longer to see out.

And yet, she thinks, looking round the book-littered room, it is not difficult to see Jeremy in her house. Indeed of all the people she has come across in the last year, old friends, who saw her no doubt as dreadfully going down in the world – losing her grip – those at the law centre, parents of other children she has bumped into on her walks, or at the nursery, of all these Jeremy is the one she feels most comfortable about bringing into her home environment. It is all too easy, all too agreeable to see him there. And yet professionally. Why after all should he do that for her?

She puts it to him. But he, now tipping the chair toward her as stretching along it he talks, is bland and easy. Why, it would be easy, no problem at all, he himself has nothing on for that evening. Besides it would do her good, he smiles at her.

'I don't know,' she hesitates.

Didn't she deserve, he asks, to give herself a treat after such a period of intense work? He points at the manuscript.

She is aware, all too aware, that if treat she is giving herself it is not by going to the party. In fact she wonders for how long she will manage, coldified, bunged up, tingling with temperature perhaps, to stand on two legs (which she experiences even now as heavy as pillars), holding forth in a bright social voice to people she does not know, nor care about. She hates, and always has, party conversation. But he is saying, 'What time shall we say? About eight-thirty? That will give you a chance to get young Toby ready for bed.'

Still uncertain, she looks perhaps for security, perhaps to remind herself of the purpose of her visit, towards her manuscript now on Jeremy's desk.

He sees her look and has a happy idea. 'Tell you what, I'll bring the manuscript over and read it while I babysit. The perfect opportunity. There, what more speedy service could you have from an agent? Then Sylvia will be able to take it home for the weekend

So you see you've nothing to fear, it's a work evening after all, just in other surroundings.'

'Really, I'm not imposing?' It did indeed sound more acceptable the way he'd put it now.

'Ruth,' he says, at last sliding off the chair and making a move towards her, 'it was my idea. You totter off home now and get out the old glad rags.'

'Glad rags,' she laughs to herself as she makes her way out of the office of Fisk, Farmer and out into the bite of cold air that greets her. Snow, she guesses, will fall early this year.

It is Sunday the week before Christmas. Snow has indeed fallen for the past two and half days and is lying three to four feet deep in many parts of the country. This Sunday, so cold that Ruth's breath hurts her even inside the terraced house, is gloriously bright, the sun pushing strong rays against the dirty panes. Toby, on tiptoe, peers out. He notices the strange shapes made by his breath on the cold pane and laughs. The preceding couple of days sitting in his pushchair he has been enchanted with the snow, holding raw red fingers (Ruth rarely remembers mittens), the same blunt tips as his mother, out to catch snow flakes, and whooping with delight as they brush through his fingers or melt on his nose.

'Out, out,' he is saying in the hope of more such pleasure. He does not see as Ruth does, that the snow has settled.

'Soon,' she calls to him, 'soon. Try to be patient, Toby.'

Grown-up words that mean nothing. Meanwhile he bangs against the pane.

Just when the noise is getting to be more than she can bear the doorbell goes, and Toby momentarily distracted takes his hands from the pane.

Ruth is a little breathless at the door. She wears Ted's fisherman's sweater, under which a pale blue linen shirt (also Ted's) and a clean pair of jeans, newly washed and tight enough to mould well the shape of her hips and legs.

All of which, and much more, Jeremy takes in as he stands at the door being greeted by her. Under his arm a carrier bag, from inside which, when he puts it down on the kitchen work top, he pulls out freshly ground Columbian coffee, wholewheat muffins, a pound of satsumas.

'Have you had breakfast?'

174

She cannot remember whether she has eaten or not. So many hours she seems to have been awake. But she is pleased. This little celebration. She puts a pan on the stove to heat water. Jeremy meanwhile steps between the many sundry items on the littered floor, the downstairs space is open-plan kitchen, living-room, playroom, all, as if it is second nature to him.

Toby has picked up a wooden spoon. And now, still at the window, he shakes it at him. In a few strides Jeremy is over the room and whooping him up on his shoulders. Ruth with her back to them hears the sounds of their male voices, the games of man and boychild that fate has deprived her son of, leaving her so utterly inadequate to perform anything of a substitute, and wills the tears forming not to flow freely. She busies herself finding a taper from which to light the grill for the muffins.

Over breakfast Jeremy is promising Toby that indeed they will go out in the snow, all three of them. They'll walk on the Heath and take the remains of the muffins to feed the ducks – 'I don't think they like the snow, like you do, you know' – providing Toby hasn't been so greedy as to finish all the muffins himself. 'But first,' says Jeremy to Toby, 'I must take a look at the washing machine to see if we can work out what's jamming it. Are you going to help me, eh?'

Toby puts out his hand to Jeremy who with infinite care and patience waits for him to take each gigantic step up the stairs.

'Got a screwdriver, Ruth?' he calls from the head of the stairs. When Ruth arrives, bearing Ted's tool box, she finds both Jeremy and Toby squatting on their haunches contemplating the inside of the washing machine, which now has its back off, Jeremy with his jacket off and sweater sleeves rolled up to his elbows.

Jeremy, who has not mended a thing in his own homes if he can get away with it, always giving in gracefully to Helen who is the more practical of the pair, or to the expertise and expense of professionals when Helen deems it absolutely necessary, now grapples with the problem of the blockage. For such he has found himself promising, when in chance discussion on the night of the first (and so far only) babysitting, the trials of broken machinery somehow managed to get into the conversation. Now, looking back on it, neither of them can remember how. And quickly he had offered – when she said how hard it would be to get a plumber in these weeks before Christmas – that he himself might pop over sometime and have a look. 'Oh you mustn't,' she thought of saying, but had neither the heart, nor the desire.

In the weeks that followed she wondered whether after all to attempt, however hopeless a quest it might seem, to find an obliging plumber. Or to ask the husband of her neighbour. But meanwhile she did neither, trudging with Toby to the launderette and cursing her cold which refused quite to release its grip, now manifesting itself in a hacking cough, which made her even more tired than usual.

Then there was the problem over the novel. Jeremy had expressed difficulties he had experienced over the middle section. This in a telephone conversation a few days after the babysit. He used many expressions of praise about the sum experience that it was. But felt that the middle section needed more work. Should he give it to Sylvia, he asked, for a second opinion? 'Or of course we could send it straight to Alison?' But Ruth wanted none of that. She cursed herself that sticking to his deadline she had let herself down. She herself, she declared, was more unsatisfied even than he. He was to send it back immediately. 'Or drop it round,' he suggested. 'Whatever,' she said, she knew what she must do.

On the phone her cheeks were flaming red: that she herself, at this point in her career, had not been her own careful watchdog, but had impulsively let out of her sight this not quite sufficiently strengthened novel. She poured on the middle section far more damning criticism than he would have been capable of. And yet still not damning enough, she felt. No, she must scrap the middle section entirely, she told him, start it again.

In the event, she was not quite as extreme.

A week later, the manuscript came back to her. By post.

And so she plodded to the launderette, and brooded on the changes she would make and the cold became a cough and got rooted deep in her chest.

Then with the fall of the snow these last two days, it at last appeared to her that she was truly on the mend. And today when she woke up, watching the dawn break and knowing that the snow having ceased to fall, the world would be aglow, she felt for a brief but important time a surge of life, brighter, more gleaming than that she was by now habitually experiencing. She thought it must be to do with the fact that today she saw how the middle section of the novel must go.

At nine Jeremy had phoned. Was the washing machine mended, or this morning would it suit her if he appeared, had a go at it? He was promising nothing, however. Whatever his promises, it suited her well, she said. Very well, she said. 'It seems to me the perfect morning to mend a washing machine.' He laughed. He would be right over, he told her. 'I'll heat some water for coffee,' she declared. But forgot to. Until she saw him, his presence, the reality of it at her front door.

Later, after Jeremy has applied himself with considerable effect to the blocked washing machine, they do indeed walk on the Heath, just as he has promised Toby. The clarity of the day, the breathtaking warm sunshine on so much glistening snow has brought out all of North London.

Toby soon gets bored with his pushchair. Encouraged by Jeremy and less impatient with her son than usual Ruth stops at intervals to let him out to explore; running short distances from the chair, he burrows his hands (this time warmly clad) into the glistening snow, laughing with delight. Jeremy shows him how to shape a snowball and eventually, very gently throws one at him and encourages him to throw some back. All this watched in amusement by Ruth.

On the path the crowd is thick. They are making their way up to the top of Parliament Hill Fields. On the way they jostle past neighbours of Ruth's who look at them enquiringly. Ruth considers introducing Jeremy as 'my agent' but decides it too silly so nods and passes by.

From the top they watch the toboggans. Toby is fascinated by the noise, the activity. So many other children whooshing and shrieking as the toboggans gather speed. But the crush is considerable. Jeremy picks Toby up and sets him on his shoulders. Ruth remembering being at the top here another year another time with Ted, feels a desire to loop her arm through Jeremy's. But restrains herself. Instead she looks down towards the three ponds, still and glistening, having taken up the colour of the sky and the surrounding expanse of so much snow, at the throng of people in brightly coloured scarves and boots, and thinks the whole is like a Bruegel painting.

Then Toby from on top of Jeremy starts flapping his arms and pointing. Ruth and Jeremy follow his arm. He has seen Katy from day-care, with older brothers and parents, ascending the hill dragging a bright orange toboggan. While the father takes the boys down the mother stops at the top with Katy, and Toby wriggling to be let down runs over to his playmate. Eventually after the toboggan has descended and returned to the top of the hill three times Ruth and the mother move towards one another. This time

Ruth does introduce Jeremy, albeit reluctantly. 'My agent,' she says.

'Oh I see,' says the mother, looking him up and down.

No, she doesn't at all, thinks Ruth. The father returns to the top with the boys. Katy now embravened by the example of her older siblings demands to have a go. She pulls at Toby. Toby takes her hand and looks at his mother enquiringly. Ruth is amused.

'If you're sure it's okay with you,' she says to the father.

Ruth and Jeremy stand watching Toby disappear into the distance.

'Enough for the moment,' says the father when he returns. 'You have a go.'

'Not me,' responds his wife.

So he turns to Ruth and Jeremy, 'What about you two?'

'Your boys?' enquires Ruth. They are engrossed in a snow fight.

'Right then,' says Jeremy. 'You game, Ruth?'

On the toboggan Jeremy draws his legs wide apart and pulls Ruth close to him – on her lap the two small children.

'More, more,' they shout, wanting a second, third and fourth ride.

'What about your brothers?' Ruth says to Katy and her parents when yet again they attain the top of the hill. But the boys have now found a friend with a toboggan and are enjoying making the run without adult supervision.

'You go on till you're exhausted,' says the father to Ruth and Jeremy. 'In truth I prefer to watch.'

'What about coming back to cocoa and crumpets?' later the parents suggest, when the toboggan is finally returned.

'Oh no, no thank you,' says Ruth hurriedly, 'for Jeremy, you know, he's only dropped in for – a short visit this morning – just to pick up a manuscript.'

Jeremy is amused. He shakes the others' hands warmly and thanks them for the use of the toboggan.

Toby and Katy are now playing in the snow and have to be prised apart. They both cry. And Toby is angry this time when once again Jeremy puts him on his shoulders. He doesn't want to go home. He probably hasn't had such a good morning in all of his little life, poor little sucker, thinks Ruth.

Jeremy tries to distract him by telling him a story but that doesn't work. Then he invents an orchestra, making the noise of each separate instrument, and Toby quietens down and tries a few of the noises himself. He also tries pulling Jeremy's thick white hair – just for fun.

'My ears are damned cold,' says Jeremy, wanting to rub them but not able to take his hands off Toby's little legs. He is regretting not having worn a hat.

Again Ruth has the temptation to slip her arm through Jeremy's; again she resists. All three are cold now. They begin to move faster in a burst of desire to be back inside, to be by a fire, to be drinking a hot drink.

Inside the house Ruth takes Toby from Jeremy's shoulders and puts him on the floor. Then she takes Jeremy's sheepskin jacket from him and shakes out the snow in the hall. She notices with the intensity with which one locates small details in emotional moments, how wet the hairs are at the nape of his neck.

Toby on the floor is whimpering. His socks are wet. And much else besides. She picks him up and carries him upstairs. Taking his clothes off and towelling him down. In his cot he falls asleep the moment his head touches the pillow.

Downstairs Jeremy is cleaning the grate that looks (rightly) as if it hasn't been used in a long while. There are a number of logs which Ted had brought back from the country two years ago, and now have a thick layer of dust covering them.

'Cocoa seems a good idea,' she says gently, 'don't you think?'

He nods.

For a long time, it seems, she sits watching him make up the fire while she sips at her cocoa. He has difficulty getting the fire to take.

There is a silence between them. She thinks about putting on some music but decides against, preferring the silence. Eventually the fire takes and he comes to sit beside her on the bare floorboards. She reaches for a cushion and passes it to him. He puts it under him, stretching his long legs towards the fire's warmth. He takes up his mug of cocoa.

'It must be cold by now. Shall I heat it up?'

He shakes his head, 'No really, don't bother.'

They sit staring into the fire.

He knew that she was there for him, to be touched, cuddled, comforted. There for the asking. What was it then that made him hold back? The canny part of him accepted that this would be no light affair. Too much would be invested. Messy is the word that came to mind, and for the present helped him to resist.

And then, because there was no fight, because she was so completely vulnerable, he could be his most responsible self, the caring father that she, in part, wished him to be. So, he would hold

179

back, he decided. He would take care in nurturing her talent. He would be agent and friend. Nothing more. Somewhere in his thoughts Helen and Sylvia were located. Helen for whom he sensed an affair with Ruth would escalate home tensions to danger level – and this he turned aside from – and Sylvia to whom he had made a silent promise. Over this, Ruth Flowert, he would not let her down. So he sat on with his luke-warm cocoa letting the moments pass.

Ruth was less resolved. Passive, waiting. She felt the space between them as no longer the ravine of the pub bar stools. But instead as if the two were swimming in a warm sea (the Adriatic: this the result, though not entirely, of the cocoa and the fire) and that either by the smallest shift of direction they could find themselves touching, closing in on one another, becoming entangled, or if even that much energy was deemed not worth it, it would make no difference for all they had to do was to go on swimming as now, in the course already set, and fate, the tides, the casual sway and swerve of the waves would simply bring the necessary result. They had to do nothing about it. So she sat, blinking her speckled eyes on the bright patterns of the fire, one ear to the sounds from upstairs. Soon Toby would be waking.

She considered asking Jeremy about his marriage. But thought it unnecessary. Though curious, more than curious, she viewed all that outside life that he lived, whatever it was, as unnecessary, as a thick tangle of seaweed floating along in the sea at some indefinable distance from them that, were it to come nearer, were it for example to brush against her body as she swam, might simply touch her gently, albeit slimily, and then float away, or might mass and grow into an inexhaustible amount, twining round and round her legs and the rest of her body, clinging to her, pulling her down. So for now the unknown, the seaweed out there, in sight but not in focus, was preferable.

Instead they talked about art, they talked about tennis, in which it turned out they both shared a passionate spectator interest, they talked about cricket, which he still played when the occasion arose (he was a fine left-handed bowler) and she enjoyed watching, about children, education, the state of the world, about the bomb and possibility of a nuclear holocaust. Thinking about those things, what would happen afterwards, would there be an afterwards, and if there was would they want to be part of it, was one of those ripples of Ruth's warm sea which shifted their paths drawing them ever so slightly closer together.

Into the silence that descended on them again, calm and close, crashed the noise of Toby's tears. He had had a nightmare? He had fallen out of his cot? Ruth rushed up the stairs to see.

And shortly afterwards Jeremy took his leave, for he must go home for lunch.

Christmas came and went. It was lonely for Ruth. Back in Leatherhead with her parents it was as if Ted had never been, and she was still the little girl: their little girl. Toby enjoyed playing with his cousins and his grandparents. As a result he was off her back for a number of hours each day.

Still she breathed a sigh of relief when she entered the cold empty house in Tufnell Park once more and shut the door behind her. With renewed energy she was working on the middle section of her novel. She was obsessed, often working right through the nights for two or three in a row. Besides there was no point not, since she could hardly sleep at all. At any one time two hours would be enough. Then she would wake with a start; wide awake, her heart beating fast, the commotion of her inside frightened her. She ate little, felt much nausea, pecked at food, the left-overs that Toby turned down or lost patience with on his plate.

She bothered hardly at all about herself. Except for the novel, except for keeping going. Toby and the law centre both dislodged to the back of her mind, where Toby, in particular, suffered. She bought cheap wine and drank a glass before she started her nightly stint. The middle of the novel formed and reformed. She wrote in bursts and then cut rigorously; and then wrote again. Sometimes as she walked the pavements in January with a cold, often whimpering Toby in his pushchair, she had long conversations in her mind with Jeremy and these conversations, she discovered, were becoming the subtext of what she was writing.

By the end of January and the beginning of February she felt – particularly in one nasty incident at the law centre – that real life for her was receding fast. The realisation scared her. Friends, old friends, called, but she gave them short shrift. She must finish, finish what she was writing, nothing must interrupt. For longer and longer spells she took the phone off the hook.

Then one of the times when the phone was not off the hook Sylvia phoned. Calm and caring. Just wanting to know. 'Yes,' breathed Ruth down the phone. 'Yes, everything is fine. As a matter of fact I might have something to show you soon, something I believe to be

181

really good.'

There, now she had said it. She was driven into a panic by the words. Their promise. She would have taken it back.

'I was thinking of coming over perhaps next weekend to see how you and Toby are getting on,' Sylvia's kindly voice was saying.

'No, no.' It was a gulp. Great whirls of emotion in Ruth's voice.

'Oh,' said Sylvia, expressing surprise. At being for a moment at a loss, while she took in what this might mean. 'Well never mind,' she followed lightly – she in the business of dealing diplomatically with her clients, 'you just come in to the office when you're ready. Don't forget we're always here. And if there is anything, you know, that you do find I can do . . .' her voice trailed away.

March, the weather as cold as the period directly preceding Christmas. Ruth is now more or less satisfied with the middle section of her novel. And is working in a slower fashion on the last re-workings of the final section. Now her typewriter breaks down, her typewriter on which she has been banging restlessly and consumingly for many months. Putting Toby in the pushchair she wedges a brown wooden board across the arms over his lap, on top of which the typewriter. Making him promise to keep his arms tightly around it she sets out for Kentish Town High Street.

The typewriter will be away for a full week. She uses her pencil, shifting words this way and that. Cutting and tightening sentences. Pruning, pruning. But the week without the typewriter is not a good one. She feels as if a limb has been lost. She cannot settle. She is aware more than she usually is of Toby, of his ceaseless demands. Now without the typewriter they penetrate further. And anger rises from gut to head on more than one occasion.

And yet sometimes she looks at him, feeling the impossible unfairness for him. It is just tiredness she tells herself, all will be better soon. And then the thought occurs to her, why not take one or two days' holiday? No writing at all. Abandon days just to pleasure, herself and her son.

'What would you like to do?' she asks him. But this is outside the vocabulary of his knowledge. He just smiles at her. At this age, she thinks, so totally forgiving, accepting. She vows for the time being to let tyranny of the book loose its hold and to concentrate on her son.

'Well, it will be the zoo this afternoon,' she tells him. 'How about that Toby? Elephants and kangaroos, lions and bears, monkeys, giraffes – the whole lot. It will be so exciting.'

Toby enjoyed it, whether his mother's attention or the animals more it was hard to say. Afterwards back home, she lit a fire and cooked fish and chips which they smothered with ketchup. She made herself eat. I've got to look after myself, she heard herself say, for Toby's sake. She read him animal stories which impressed him greatly. 'Like the zoo,' he kept on saying. Then she played patiently with him in the bath and sang to him in his cot. When she kissed him goodnight he put his arms close around her neck and hugged her tight, 'Nice nice mummy,' he crooned.

Was she? she wondered.

The following day was a bank holiday. A whole long day stretching ahead. What now? she considered, staring out of the windows at bare trees and grey sky through which a glint of sunshine suggested a tentative presence. She ran through in her mind a list of possible options.

'What would you like to do?' for the second time she asked Toby. But this time he was more ready.

'Go on chuff chuff train,' he replied.

'A train,' she laughed. 'Well let's see. Breakfast first, young man, then decisions.'

She herself forced down cereal, brown toast, fruit. Hoping that with the sugar intake her energy level would rise. Journeys, but to where . . . ? She idly considered: Brighton, Southend, Bournemouth, Oxford. But no, not with a small child, just she and it. Trains? Then it came to her, of course, the small overground train to Kew.

'Okay, Toby, she told him, 'a train ride it will be.'

It was a blustery cold day. The streaks of silver sunlight, gleaming down ruefully through shifting levels of cloud, brought almost no warmth. But lit the gardens, cruelly emphasising their March starkness, the barrenness of earth, the destitution of bough. The enormous clumps of crocuses were pleasing but it was too cold to do anything more than nod and pass on.

Despite it being a bank holiday Kew was noticeably empty. And most of the people who had made their way there on this particular day were cloistered inside the two giant greenhouses, sighing with relief for the warmth they found inside and determined to linger lovingly over every cactus and plant until it was time to go home.

Toby does not like the crush (Ruth unwisely has not brought his pushchair this time) and Ruth feels at a loss as she holds his hand tight and attempts to whisper soothing words to him. But suddenly it is too much for him; he starts to bawl as loudly as his lungs will allow.

'Hey, what kind of a racket is that, Toby?'

Ruth swings round and there, about four behind on the narrow overcrowded path, is Jeremy thronged by a bevy of teenage children, boys and girls; Ruth's speckled eyes do not take in details at this stage. She holds Toby back and lets the other three people pass.

'Jeremy.'

'Ruth, a long way from home, aren't you?'

'Have train; do travel,' she laughs.

Toby, initially silenced by the surprise of it all, starts to bawl again.

'He's got a point, you know,' says Jeremy. 'Who'd want to spend the afternoon amongst this immense crowd? Come on,' he touches her hand through her gloved fingers, 'home to tea and a game of scrabble.'

'Yeah,' chorus the bevy of teenagers. 'Let's get out of this place.'

'Excuse me, excuse me.' Jeremy is trying to retreat, holding on to Ruth and Toby as he does so. The teenagers have no compunction in flaying a path in front, like so many scythes flattening the grass (or rather the people in the way) wherever it seems appropriate. Eventually they are outside the pavilion.

'So?' Ruth with Toby now in her arms looks at Jeremy surrounded as he is by the very real parts of his life, those she has shut out.

'Well, come home. Why not? Helen'd love to meet you, I'm sure. She had a rush on with some work and we promised to leave the house quiet for her.'

'We'd no idea it would be this much purgatory,' said one of the kids, 'or we'd never have agreed.'

'She won't want more to tea then. And Toby's not likely to be any mouse.'

'Nonsense,' says Jeremy, pulling at her again. 'Come on, stop dithering, woman. It's far too cold for that.'

It seemed to Ruth that he was still pulling at her as they entered the comfortable sprawling 1940s house that was Jeremy's home. The drive was a long one. He marched up it in giant strides. All the while his hand on the sleeve of Ruth's coat slowed down the pace. But Jeremy was impatient. 'Helen, Helen,' he called loudly, standing in the porch and divesting himself and her of their coats. 'Helen' again, more impatient.

184

Eventually she appeared, calm, stately. She observed them from the first-floor landing. A smile on her face but wrinkles on her brow. 'Look who it is,' he said. It could have been Father Christmas. Helen tilted her head as if to say, who is it?

'Ruth Flowert,' he replied with boyish delight. 'I've brought Ruth Flowert. Rescued her from the crowds and the cactuses,' he sounded positively delighted with himself. 'Now what about some tea? My God, we're cold all of us. That was a mission and a half you sent us out on today, darling.'

On the hawthorn table rigged up by Jeremy's eldest son in woodwork classes at school, family and friends competed at scrabble. Around the triangular-shaped table they sat on a collection of low chairs, pouffes, cushions, stools. A coal fire burned invitingly. The large light room with its blue paint just beginning to peel, its walls massed with an eclectic collection of art and mementoes, its well-worn carpet on which stood piles of books and many suggestions of a busy active household, had something of the informality of Jeremy's office, thought Ruth, but far more love and care. A woman's hand behind, guiding, making a home. A room in which to read the Sunday papers, or a good book.

A strong person, Helen, Ruth assessed as she looked at her smiling and sneakily attempting to seek advice from her daughter over the difficult combination of letters on her rack. Tea had been bustled up without fuss. Unhurried, giving Ruth the sense of a boat sailing on a fair wind. Tea, hot water jug, a wonderful collection of delicately painted china cups and saucers, no one cup and saucer matching another, homemade scones, and a coffee cake, all just waiting there, all brought in by Helen and her children as if this kind of amply stocked larder was nothing, was merely to be taken for granted. A bib was even found for Toby. Their youngest daughter Alice obligingly found old toys, a wooden rocking horse, a train, a teddy bear with only one eye, and the best of all a post box with large wooden shapes to be posted into it. What with the scones, the post box and the attention, Toby was in heaven.

There was something about their warmth, their familiness, that drew delight. Ruth saw not strains and disintegration but on the contrary something solid, vibrant, something built on sound foundations; something like her own love had been for Ted, but which in this case (their tremendous luck, no cruel God having intervened) had had the chance to go on growing and growing. Creating a family life like this. This she might, she thought wistfully, have established with Ted. It was the opposite of the tight, narrow, confining life she had lived with her parents: relaxed, casual, open; each doing their own thing and yet drawn together for moments like this. So she fantasised. Wanting to draw closer to Helen, to know her better. So she complimented and so Helen after the first uncertain start smiled down on her.

Tea had been cleared and Alice, not so interested in scrabble, had offered to wash-up. Now back joining the throng around the table she was content to squat on her haunches and play with Toby. The competitors then were Jeremy, Helen, Ruth, Daniel, Rebecca, Hugh, and Chris and Nicco, next-door neighbours.

The game worked its way through an hour or so of darts and forays into increasing ingenuity with the English language. Ruth had not played since as a teenager herself on holiday with cousins; hers not the most literate of homes. At university long games of poker is what Ruth remembered. Ted enjoyed chess, Ruth likewise. But on the whole she wasn't a games person.

There was a way, she thought, that the whole ethos of games went with large families, families in which normal friendly competition could be brought out into the open. Here the Farmers sparred with relish. The children were bright, and at the age when individually and collectively they were determined to bring their parents down. Minor tensions came out into the open. The oldest son was irritated with his father for keeping them all waiting for ages while he contemplated the best move. Helen suggested words that others denied were in the dictionary, which as a result had to be frequently consulted. Hugh was found swapping a letter with his twin behind everyone's back.

Gradually the number of letters left was reduced to a handful; one by one they played their last words. Greater ingenuity was needed now than ever. More concentration. With the heat from the fire and the competition, the room grew quieter. The angles of bodies, Ruth noticed, became more rigid, more tense. All of them like so many anglepoise lamps over the hawthorn table. Even Toby feeling the moment for, if not what it was, then for something special, climbed into his mother's lap and stayed quietly there, hugging the one-eyed bear.

Ruth was juggling with the last letter in her hand, determined for a final coup. In scores half self-consciously she had been competing with Jeremy (what else can a writer do with his/her agent in a situation such as this?) and now she prayed silently for a last stroke of intellectual ingenuity, preferably nothing short of genius. She moved the letters round and round on her rack. Then became aware that faces were upon hers. She was keeping them waiting this time. But she was the guest. They were too polite to say so.

Then she had it. 'What about this?' she picked up the letters and placed them on the board.

'I don't believe it!' Daniel, Chris, Hugh.

Rebecca was already counting, 'Thirty-eight and seven, forty-five. Another thirty for the tripled 'q'. And then double the whole thing. That's unbelievable. A hundred and fifty points. What a way to finish!'

'And I've been eyeing that spot for the last six rounds!' Nicco.

Ruth laughed. She was flushed. 'Sorry, folks.'

'Nothing to be sorry about,' said Jeremy standing up and yawning. 'Does them the world of good. They just don't like to be beaten, these young people, and certainly not by someone of our age.'

'It was luck,' said Ruth.

'I thought you played a very good game,' said Helen quietly.

'Yes, you did,' said Daniel. 'You're clever at it, Ruth. It was fun. Come again.'

'The greatest praise,' laughed Jeremy. He started to put some more coal on the fire and people began to disperse from the table. The scrabble board was packed up. Rebecca went over to her father where he bent over the fire and from behind put her arms around him.

'Poor old Dad, you usually win, don't you?'

'Does he?' Ruth asked.

'Actually he always considered himself the ace of all times at this game until you arrived on the scene,' Jeremy's children told her.

'Poor, poor old Dad,' crooned Rebecca still with her arms around him, mocking him.

Helen looked on smiling.

And Ruth the outsider felt the first whiff of a chill wind. She must think about going.

'Well,' Ruth got up herself, shaking Toby free of her lap as she did so, 'I must be thinking of wending my way back to Tufnell Park. It's been lovely. So much better than a freezing afternoon at Kew. Thank you very much, Helen, for all your hospitality.'

'Come again,' said Helen, it tripping off her tongue, Ruth thought, with non-directional ease, as if she'd said in response to a question 'I'm fine, how are you?' Now Ruth considered. How was she to get back to the railway station? 'Is there a bus?' she asked Jeremy.

'I'll give you a lift.'

'No, honestly, you mustn't. So warm in here, so cold out there.'

'All the more reason. Besides it'll only take a jiff.'

'Don't want to go home. Don't want to go on a chuff chuff train,' cried Toby, 'I want to go to bed here.'

'Poor little thing, he's tired,' said Alice.

'Dad, why don't you drive them all the way home,' Rebecca suggested. 'I'll come too, if you like, for company on the way back.'

'Oh no no no,' said Ruth horrified, 'far too much trouble.'

'Nonsense,' insisted Jeremy. 'It will take no time at all. Rebecca's right. Now I come to think of it, I insist on delivering you to your door. Besides Toby can sleep in the car; a much better plan.'

And so they put on their coats.

But then there took place some conversation between the twins and the boys from next door. So that at the last moment Rebecca pulled out. She hadn't realised that the others were going to . . . would Dad really mind?

There they are on the front seat of Jeremy's spacious if scruffy, elderly Vauxhall. Toby sprawling out on the back seat with a rug over him is trying bravely but unsuccessfully to resist the sleep that is closing in on him.

From inside the car the silence is as blanketing as snow. Ruth feels with her thumb the slight hardness on the second finger of her right hand where she has pushed away at the typewriter keys so mercilessly.

Jeremy puts out his hand to turn on the radio and as he does so a small gasp escapes from Ruth. The chasm of bar stools, the warm air between them as they sat by the fire, and now this. She is as aware of the thin thread of a divide between two separate beings, the way that flesh might touch flesh, the way they might merge, might break through her insupportable loneliness once and for all. So aware. As alert as a warrior. Every sense straining with expectancy, her ears, her nose, toes, knees, thighs, lips, eyelashes, the roots of her hair. And he, she can feel as if it was her own flesh, the blond hairs along his arm shoot upright in attendance, so many soldiers. On the radio Brahms's violin concerto.

'Do you think it will disturb him?' Jeremy's voice is normal but quiet.

'Not if you turn it down low.' She makes her voice match his.

The two listen to the music. In the back of the car Toby stirs then settles.

Ruth wonders what Jeremy is thinking about, his home, his family, what he will do with the rest of the Sunday evening.

Is it this, the unbearable gap between their two lives, that causes her to ask him in? And him to accept. Because he feels safe, because he is ringed by a family Sunday, because there has been less strain with Helen of late and a certain amount of increased efficiency in the office (he has kept his promise to himself and Sylvia, his hours have been more regular, he has taken more responsibility, Sylvia has been talking more happily about the 'team' they were) he feels he can afford to relax a little the barrier, be generous to Ruth, poor woman.

So now Ruth, voice level, struggling for a casualness she does not feel, asks him if he would like a drink before his return journey. 'The least I can do after you've been so generous,' she says.

He looks at his watch. 'A quick one would be most welcome.'

So he carries in the sleeping Toby and together the two adults make their way up to the child's narrow bedroom, where Jeremy lays him in his cot and Ruth, taking off his shoes but not undressing him, arranges the cot blankets around him. 'Shame to disturb him,' she says to Jeremy. What she means is that she doesn't want to risk it.

And so downstairs where from a low oak cupboard Ruth takes out fine tulip-shape glasses with dust on them and exclaims with despair that all that the cupboard holds is a bottle of vermouth. She had thought there would be gin, Dubonnet, at least sherry. 'So long since someone has come for drinks.' She feels an anguish at this inadequacy. 'Doesn't matter, doesn't matter,' Jeremy soothes. 'Vermouth will be fine.' With a tea towel Ruth wipes the glasses then pours the vermouth.

'Ice? Or is it too cold a night?'

'Ice would be lovely.'

'I don't even have a lemon,' she says sadly.

'Really, no matter, Ruth.'

Jeremy sits on the one comfortable armchair. Ruth on a cushion, her back to the fire, which they do not light. Jeremy looking at the clock above the mantelpiece makes a mental note that he must leave when he has downed his vermouth.

Meanwhile Ruth talks about his house and his family, complimenting him on the easy informal yet warm relationship she has perceived between his children and himself – not easy these days.

Responding to all she gives credit for, he feels more solid every moment, more durable, more able to take risks. And, yes, he will have another glass of vermouth.

There is a moment, the inevitable moment, when they move towards one another. He sitting in the only comfortable armchair. She on the floor, nearer and nearer to his feet, as they talk about whatever it is they are talking about, his children, her writing, the broken typewriter, the crowds in the greenhouse. There is a moment when he takes one of her gesticulating hands. When he takes both. When he bends over her there and she sits on the floor below him (so easy, so impossible to resist). A moment when warm cheeks touching cheeks but not yet lips to lips, she whispers, 'Stop, what about Helen, should we?' and he answers, lying dramatically to give Ruth credit, 'Helen and I haven't slept together for ten years. You can't imagine, Ruth, what that means, the frustration, the pain of it.'

And she answers, as she finds his jaw bone, the corner of his mouth, 'I think I can after what I've experienced these last two years without Ted.'

Afterwards, in the bed she has shared happily with Ted she is smiling up at him and he is looking at her contemplating the glory of it.

'The first time I've seen you smile,' he says, 'really smile.' She smiles some more.

He has given her a present, he thinks. This man who loves women. And somehow surely he can wangle it. Negotiate Helen, Sylvia. Of course it will take a bit of attention, of care. But then what in life that's worth anything doesn't take just that. He has given her a present, he is persuaded. This man who loves women.

Jealousy, guilt, complications, the waiting waiting for the doorbell to ring, for the voice one wants to hear at the other end of a telephone, all this, as well as the other side of the coin, the great ecstasy of any circumscribed relationship, the terrifying poignancy of stolen moments (this thing is not for keeps, therefore we owe it to ourselves to live more vividly in the here and now than ever before), in short the lack of a clear passage, slows Ruth's writing and clouds her mind. Her nights are awash with dreams of semen and vaginal fluids rather than the words that make up complex passages in the final pages of her novel.

Meanwhile Jeremy, handling the situation best he can, as he believes himself capable, lets it be known that he is seeing Ruth, just very occasionally, just extremely casually of course. Just popping in on her one or two Sunday afternoons. To give her, as he puts it, 'help and encouragement with her novel which she needs enormously, poor thing, just the odd boost, she's been so lacking in confidence, you know, since Ted died.'

'I'm surprised she even lets you in,' Sylvia told him. 'Judging from the way she spoke to me on the phone, she sounds in a terrible state. As a matter of fact I am quite worried about her.'

'Oh no,' said Jeremy hurriedly, 'it's nothing as bad as that. And incidentally from what I have read of this recent book of hers I believe it is going to be super. Quite a breakthrough.'

Sylvia sighed but said nothing.

She smiled at him. 'You know, you have lost weight, Jeremy, that paunch has almost gone.'

He changed the subject, 'What did you think of that meeting with Mick Chadwick yesterday?'

'Well,' she said, 'let's look over the papers today. On the whole yes.' But the phone as ever rang at this point, breaking into one of their endlessly fragmented, but not, thought Sylvia, totally unsatisfactory, conversations these days. There was something more directed, more alive about Jeremy. He had more energy, more vitality. Perhaps things were after all better with Helen. She sighed. Yes, touch wood all was going well. The agency was making real headway. People who had at first been dubious were beginning to accept the partnership between herself and Jeremy. Even Alison had recently stopped expressing her doubts. Though Sylvia doubted whether she'd ever wipe them away. But that was all more a personality conflict than anything else.

And as to Ruth, well, though a doubt, a hidden anxiety itched away at the back of her mind, the unerring instinct of mother hen with her surrogate children, still she was content to let it rest at that for the present. There were more pressing problems. And no doubt Ruth herself would sort it all out, would come through, she had the grit of all true writers, Sylvia believed. And not the suicide type, not with that son of hers. But perhaps, she made a mental note, if she was anywhere near Tufnell Park in the next month or two, and if she'd heard nothing from Ruth meanwhile, perhaps she would drop in unannounced for, as Jeremy had proved, that seemed at present to be the best way with Ruth.

Meanwhile with this comparatively quiet and buoyant period at the office she could turn her mind again to that which was presently most close to her heart: the issue of whether they should buy the long lease on the top-floor flat. A matter which for weeks had been under discussion.

*

There was a hiatus. Alison had suddenly noticed the time (it was by now late on Saturday afternoon) and expressed an imperative need to take herself off to the local supermarket in order to do the week's food shop – the fridge and larder being virtually bare. Whilst she was gone Josie washed out her jeans and a couple of shirts and then lay on her bed wondering, wondering.

It was not until Sunday morning that Alison recommenced; first, digressing in order to say something about her and Sylvia's move, which was far from insignificant, she assured, in its connection.

'There was the flat,' she explained, 'vacant, wonderfully convenient and at the same time, by the quirks of the situation, an extremely good buy. Syl was fiercely attracted to its possibilities. And though I was content to leave all that side to her, I could see that with little effort of the imagination it would make an extremely stylish home. However, it was far from an easy decision to make, because it involved opening our life to public exposure.

When we had first come together I had had the idealism of youth. In those early years I had tried to persuade Syl to live more openly. But she was adamant about secrecy. Insecure, intent on building up her own professional life and anxious to a point about how that might be obscured if her lesbianism was public knowledge. When I pushed, she wept. 'Haven't I done enough?' she would say, or imply. And about that I felt there was no argument. 'You must compromise over this,' she insisted. After a few years I stopped nagging.

Then, when I was a junior editor, by pronouncing my colours I would have had nothing to lose. Besides, a junior editor's personal life is more or less his or her own business. But far less so the editorial director of a large publishing firm. And I disliked myself for having any moments of doubt because of my career.

A lover of beauty Syl, I think the very spaces, the floors, the ceilings, the proportions of the flat, to say nothing of its views and the convenience, drew her. She said she felt it would be a home, not just a way of running away from the world, as she had been doing since she'd left Patrick. She claimed the journeys tired her. And the thought of walking up merely two flights of stairs after a long day's work was heaven. But I believe it to be more: that she, a natural home bird to a far greater extent than I, wished to unite her home and work life in a way that other agents did and in a way that would come naturally to her. Entertaining, going with clients to theatres and parties, the mingling of the personal with the business, using those magnificent hostess talents she had to make others feel at home, to cook, to serve, to create a good environment, all that had been put into abeyance. She had worked for ten long years to create a viable and indeed successful agency, worked long hours and often weekends in the office, without using this bit of herself which would in other circumstances stand her in such good stead.

And now, entering her fifth decade, already into it by one year, for she was two years older than I, I believe she felt the need and the ability to consolidate. She was convinced that her little world was secure. Her clients, she felt sure, would not leave. She had earned that reward, to prove that she was well liked and respected sufficiently to be able to show her colours openly and to be no worse off for it. Her little treat to herself for brownie marks accrued.

Though I was far less proselytising than when I was a young woman, I still had a hovering sense that it would be 'good for the cause' if we could get away with it. However, there was a part of me that now enjoyed being something of a public figure and found distasteful the thought of the possible comments, particularly from a scandal-hungry media. Had I been the sole instigator I might not have made the move at this stage in our lives. But taking into account the pleasures of the flat itself, Syl's conviction and enthusiasm, my own theoretical position, I was reluctant to see myself as the one to put a veto on the plan.

So we moved. So we exposed ourselves. And it was in this new period of change and risk that Jeremy, bless his school-boy well-worn socks, played his Sir Walter Raleigh act once too often, and never more unsuitably, taking off his now faded brown corduroy jacket and equally worn (I've often wondered if it is the same one I first saw him in near on twenty years ago) and throwing it down, never more unsuitably than for Ruth Flowert.

And then, almost as inevitably, picking it up again and leaving her bespattered in the mud.

*

Cold March blossomed into warmer than average April and by early May people were pronouncing it to be one of the most lovely springs in living memory. Alison and Sylvia proceeded to move house: Sylvia was joyous to be using her home-making techniques once again and to such effect; at the same time gradually, bit by bit, the nature of the relationship between them became known to a wider circle of people.

Alison found that it made little difference to her. Apart from one or two guarded comments in *Private Eye* and a salacious article in *Publishing News*, which she had no trouble at all in over-riding, for after all everything was fair game, the issue of her lesbianism of no more import than Hugo Marks's double wart or Stefan Bridinski's legendary stinginess, there was little public exposure. And as far as her publishing life went, what did it matter the nature of her sexual choices? She was, as it turned out, in too strong a position, too invulnerable to be too severely persecuted. Many articles about her at the time of her promotion to editorial director (which happened a mere six weeks before the move) made no mention of this fact at all. She had, she believed, skated round the issue of her personal life cleverly. And later in the summer she was no longer newsworthy except to the small clique of literati. Something she felt she could easily weather.

For Sylvia things were not going quite as smoothly. As the word began to get round to a number of her clients they responded with a mixed reaction: surprise, anger, a sense of being cheated. A woman agent needs to be invisible, to keep her persona at a distance: Goddess, mother figure, sound and solid helpmate, with no problems, almost no life of her own. Each of her clients wanted to believe that she was there for them, for feeding their needs, for playing into their fantasies, whatever those fantasies might be. Writers are meant to have all the problems. Not agents. And this vulnerability, this apparent confusion in Sylvia's life, did not altogether go down well.

After the first shock at the hostile reaction, and some stock-taking with Alison, she eventually came to accept that it might be necessary after all to compromise. So far they had only told a limited number of people. In future they would say that it was Sylvia's flat. And that Alison, old friend, who had recently bought a share in a cottage in the Cotswolds (true), would for convenience, for the time being, be staying with Sylvia during the week. Two friends. Convenience. The closeness of their association would become more obvious; but for the rest, people would be left to decide for themselves.

Sylvia claimed that if directly asked she would give an honest answer. But the times when she did so continued to have such a bad effect that she increasingly decided it was unwise. Of the clients who already knew, one or two left, others found reasons to pick arguments or query the efficiency of work. Sylvia went through a harder time than Alison. It was not the one or two aspersions in the literary press that bothered her; rather the way personal friends and long-term clients still, in the 1980s, found the central fact about her antipathetic.

And with this she became bitter, momentarily disillusioned with the agency, found it harder to accept the central division between human sociability and the blight of her own secret which must now to all intent and purposes be hidden. Found that people on the whole were no more understanding than her parents. Felt the world a sad place, wished to turn her head from it, suffered depressions and headaches. Was quicker to anger. Something of her cheerful giving spirit, her belief, faded now at this 'second rejection'. She thought daily, as she hadn't so consistently for years, of her absent children; of the loss that life had required of her. She assailed Alison angrily, 'It isn't the same for you, it just isn't the same for you. You just bounce through.'

'I've never had much time for tragedy queens,' said Alison. At some point, at the end of her tether. And so they pulled back into themselves, coping as best they could with the shifts and changes.

Sylvia experienced rocky days, irascible days, days when she was hard put to give what she had always given so unstintingly to her clients. Then there were days when she managed to pull herself together. When she looked the old sunny Sylvia. But it all took a great deal of time, trouble, attention and make-up.

Meanwhile the agency had been increasingly beginning to attract important clients. There were moments of fun, moments when power and money seemed almost enough. Whatever else, Sylvia determined, she would be professional, keep everything going, keep the agency buoyant. If her life was not to be successful on a personal level, it was even more important, of the utmost importance, that it was successful on the professional. She would have that. No one could take that away from her.

She continued daily to arrive in the office before her secretaries, working if possible even more unstintingly than before: making deals that were tougher; fetching sums for her clients that caused the breath to be drawn in; causing comment in trade papers and around the literary world. But for all that there were aggravations at work of a kind she'd never experienced before. Knots of contention one after another. When a client left the agency she would not know if the word had got round to him on the grapevine, or why. Was it that she couldn't hold her clients any more? The summer, apart from the large amount of energy that inevitably went into the move itself, was a period of difficulty. The successes equally matched the failures. 'Ride it through,' said Alison, 'that's all you can do.'

Over those months, meanwhile, the sexual relationship between Jeremy and Ruth blossomed into something which was, he thought, quite different from anything he had ever known with another woman.

Was it his age where potency and experience finally met at such a peak? Was it her mercurial and passionate nature? Was it the complex nature of their connection, agent/writer, that drew him so, drew him in? He found that he was falling in love with Ruth Flowert, wanting as he'd never wanted in all his extra-marital adventures ever before, to be with her, increasingly obsessed, increasingly wanting and needing to cross the barriers between what was possible and what was not. And gradually, as the warm spring opened into a flowery beautiful early summer, the apple, the almond and the cherry flowering earlier than he ever remembered – or she – he became more casual, more lazy in his attempt to hide the force and direction of his affections. No longer was his mind on covering his tracks. Rather, it was almost as if he was laying a trail.

Because their life was so simple, so insulated, just Ruth and he and the boy, every detail of its domesticity was luminous for Ruth. The imagery of her days were the small details of domesticity and love-making with Jeremy. Later she would think back, for example, on the scrambled egg made with the parsley that he had brought and they had nurtured in a pot outside her back door until at last it sprouted, delighting them both. Neither had ever before managed to keep it alive, they claimed; mint of course, chervil, dill, thyme, no problem, but parsley, oh dear no. Now here was she snipping at last the tops of a number of healthy shoots and chopping it into the scrambled egg, their small London produce, their attempt at culling the earth, their demonstration of a life together on however small a scale.

She would think of the teddy with one eye that Rebecca had sent to Toby when once Jeremy had risked saying openly at home that that was whom he was visiting: 'just to pick up part of a manuscript'. The teddy who became part of so many of the

196

triangular conversations, she, him, Toby. She would think of the vermouth, their drink, never would they have any other they now declared though neither had had any taste for it before that March evening. She would think of certain books, certain radio programmes, of a rug always used when they made love in front of the fire, of the way the small house had shifted and adjusted to Jeremy's constant visits.

And always between visits she and the child were waiting waiting. It was as if all of time stood still, as if nothing was of importance, except for the times they were gloriously together. She would go to work, she would write, she was on the last section now, on the final editing, beyond the typewriter almost. With a fine pencil (pea-green, a gift from Jeremy) drawing fine lines through individual words, transposing, fining down. Slowly slowly. For days hardly at all. But as if she had not the willpower to bring this thing to its conclusion. Or the energy. For so much energy, more ever than with Ted who had slept with her every night in the same bed, was being spent on the sobbing, poignant, passionate intensity of their love-making, as if each time was a goodbye, and at the same time a re-verification of life, so intense so complete that it seemed quite impossible to let go. As each time drew them together, made them more vulnerable before one another. More tremblingly naked. More in need. She would look after and feed Toby but all the time she was waiting, waiting for his arrival.

And he would admit to the same when she claimed this power he had over her life. He would say it was the same, swear to it, that he wanted nothing more than to be in her arms, to be here as now, to be existing thus for all time, thus thus. He would claim that work was intolerable, that each day the hours and hours without her were almost suicidally hard to get through. He would claim that home was worse, and to her questions (now becoming more jealous, more persistent about Helen, about the family) he would claim, to please her, to cheer her, to collude with her, to bring her the happiness he so wished to impart, that evenings at home were long and drear, a necessity because of the children, nothing more, that he and Helen had nothing whatsoever to say to one another, had lost contact with each other's lives years before. That in bed they were as if strangers. It was a torture, a duty, he was simply counting the hours until he was with her again.

'Are you sure?' asked Ruth, winding her arms around him.

'Yes, sure, I give you my promise.'

And then she would smile as he had first seen her smile after they had first gone to bed together. But no, it wasn't quite the same smile. It was as if she was trying for a replica without success. Trying to stem the tide of her need, her dependency, of all the ways this having half (or less than) of a married man's attention was not satisfactory, of all the ways the pain increasingly was flooding the pleasure, trying trying to stem the tide, to be pleased with what is, trying to return to the open innocence of that first smile with all its hope, belief, all its blind sweetness.

Now Jeremy, colluding with Ruth, and coming again and again in her arms on the rug in front of the fire in her narrow house, while upstairs Toby, only weeks from his third birthday slept soundly in his cot, night-light sufficient to chase away night fears, increasingly lost the centre of his energy. He began to get dark lines under his eyes, his hair had a new electricity and refused to fall meekly in any kind of acceptable shape round his head. At home he couldn't sleep. He was sometimes in the office before Sylvia, to her surprise. He was working harder than ever, doing much initially to stem the tide at Fisk, Farmer; he was like an engine driven.

He would prefer to be on the move than to sit at his desk. He had always been someone who walked around the office. Now he often worked standing at his desk. He was forever picking up parcels and surprising the secretary by delivering them himself. He would make appointments out of the office that involved any and every part of London. He was here, he was there, he was everywhere. And everywhere he drank black coffee, food ceased to interest, he wanted to be hungry, to be lean and then to be filled by Ruth and to fill her over and over again.

Meanwhile at home his excuses for his increasingly frequent departures no longer, even to the most benign of wives, seemed to make any attempt to add up. He would contradict himself. He would forget what he had said earlier. He would become completely unpredictable, saying he would be in at one time and coming in at another. Saying he would be going in one direction which involved the tube and then proceeding to the garage and making no secret of revving up the car.

Helen was frightened. Helen was angry, though her anger was muffled by her fear. It had never been like this, never in all the years that she had known him and in all the later years in which he had been idly, casually, selfishly (she thought) unfaithful to her. Never had it been like this. She knew as a wife must that her husband was out of control, that he was a man driven. It could be work, as he claimed when she had asked; the need to support Sylvia at such a difficult time, the extra demands, it could be his health: he was not eating, he was losing weight, looking far from well.

Did he have cancer, she wondered, was it that, and was he unable to share it with her? Or *was* it the other? Was it as she increasingly, with a feeling of sinking hysteria, suspected, was it love? And would it destroy, and what was she to do? Hang on, say nothing, hope it would go away? And then when he was around, he was so tender, so kind to her, so supportive over the various problems of teenage children and ageing parents. Often they were companionable in bed as they hadn't been for a good long time. And he still seemed to want her. In fact their love-making had been better, less mechanical, more various and affectionate than she had known for a number of years. So she hung on to a hope, despite all the messages her brain gave her; no, it couldn't be love.

And then there was the morning – it was a particularly good morning – when she was standing in their bedroom, a Monday morning, she would settle down to work after a number of household chores, including clean sheets on their bed and a Monday morning wash. The sun was streaming through the bay window. She took up a pile of books littering the chaise-longue that was placed in the bay and picking up a letter from an old friend now living in Australia, whom she hadn't seen for years, and who wrote enjoyably, wittily about husband and family, she permitted herself, ten o'clock Monday morning when all the rest of the world she felt sure was at work, to sit on the chaise-longue in the sun re-reading the letter. It was a good morning, one of those when everything for no reason at all seemed to come together. She had slept well, woken refreshed. Jeremy had said he would be home for supper. Daniel had worked solidly every evening for the last fortnight so that she began to think there might still be hope for his 'A' levels. Rebecca had announced over breakfast that she wanted to grow up to be 'just like Mum'. Idiotic. Of course she'd change her tune in a year or two. But still heart-warming. Work was coming in more steadily than ever – the age of the freelancer, she thought, was truly under way. With encouragement from Jeremy she had just raised her fees colossally – by almost twenty percent – and no one had raised more than an eyebrow. Yes, a good morning.

She allowed herself two last minutes in the sun. Then stripped the bed. Took off the pillowcases. As she bundled sheets and pillow-cases into her arms, a small inoffensive white square, miniature version of a sheet, fell onto the carpet. One of Jeremy's damned handkerchieves. Tissues, she thought, are so much more hygienic.

She stopped to pick it up, uncovering a hint of red. She let her bundle fall on the mattress and observed the handkerchief more closely. The red writing script was a nametape, left over from school days, the name distinguishing it from any others, so that no other school boy or matron sorting the laundry would misappropriate it into some other pile; Edward Flowert.

It was drawing towards the close of July. A magnificent spring and early summer had given way to three weeks of almost continuous rain in July. Rain, grey skies. The wind and driving rain continually seemed to be pushing at the copper beech outside Ruth Flowert's window. And its seemingly ducking, sagging attempt to escape the strength of its assailant reminded her of the paths a hairdryer makes across a head of hair. Or of herself. Resisting, or trying to, the daily bouts of longing, of loss. For Jeremy, early in the month, had gone to America, and Helen had gone with him, ten days in New York on business (that had been long planned) but then a further week and a half's holiday in Washington. A decision that followed the revelation, the tears, the anger, the telegrams and bouts of hostile jealous rage that followed Helen's discovery of Jeremy's affair with his client. So they would go away together. It was the least he could do. He would be in anguish all the time, he told Ruth, but . . .

So Ruth stayed behind and suffered and wondered. And what of the future and how could something like this end? That he chose to go away with his wife suggested something, some durable loyalty to something else. Suggested, thought Ruth, the way the future would be shaped and the kind of further pain she was due to suffer before the end, whatever the end would be. What would Jeremy decide after America? What would Ruth herself decide? But she knew herself to be too weak, too dependent when it came to Jeremy to make any decisions, certainly and particularly the decision not to see him. Besides she trusted him; he had said that he loved her, that in the long term it would all work out. She trusted him, she could not do otherwise.

Meanwhile there was one decision that she could make and that was to bring her novel to a state where she could see it float free of her. And this in the rainy and bleakly lonely month of July was what she attempted to do. Her energy no longer focusing on Jeremy, on their exhausting, passionate and totally absorbing love-making, she now threw herself back into the book. Returning to the typewriter with what she thought of as a final bout of vigour. Again she was working through the night, again she was eating little, again she was obsessed with words, new ones, streaming out of her, and a new lucidity which made her want, need, to tap every moment of creative energy, as if it might never be like this again. During the weeks of Jeremy's departure she wrote as one possessed.

August. Still rainy though more intermittently. Jeremy on return had told Ruth that he had promised Helen that he would not see Ruth for the month after their return, that Helen (Helen!) was extremely vulnerable and such a promise was necessary for her state of health and peace of mind. But in early September when Helen was stronger they would get together once more. Meanwhile he thought it perhaps better all round. Meanwhile good luck in her writing. All this in a letter.

Again she was pulling back, pruning now, seeing how the ending would be. If only she could make it, if only her health wouldn't give way (unlike Helen's). Toby whined often, often for Jeremy. She tried to block out the sound, working solidly in the early morning hours and again in the evenings.

End of August. She wrote a note to Jeremy then on second thoughts phoned him at the office. It was a Thursday afternoon. Jeremy's secretary (a new girl, a voice Ruth had never heard before, and was not sure that she liked), crisp and efficient to the point of stand-offishness, said 'What a shame' with a laugh as if it wasn't a shame at all. Ruth has just missed him; he had gone with family to spend a long weekend in Dorset. Ruth must have missed him by about half an hour. Was it something urgent? He wouldn't be back till about Monday midday they imagined. Could she help with anything?

'Is Sylvia busy?'

'I could see.'

'Yes, put me through to Sylvia, if you will.'

'Who shall I say is calling? Can you give me the name again?'

'Ruth. Ruth Flowert.'

Onto the phone came a voice that she knew well and the moment she heard recognised how much she had missed. The soothing, caring tones of her old friend and agent.

'Ruth, how lovely to hear from you. How are you?'

'Well, thank you. Fine, Sylvia. I've actually finished that novel of mine.'

'That's wonderful news. I am delighted. I suppose you'll want to let Jeremy have the first look at it. He said he'll be back midday Monday but of course one never knows. What about leaving it till

Tuesday? Why not come in around lunchtime. We could all have a bite together. How is Toby?'

'Sylvia,' said Ruth. 'You know you mentioned coming round to Tufnell Park. What about this weekend?'

'This weekend?'

'Say Saturday afternoon. Unless you're busy?'

Sylvia thought regretfully of all the things she meant to do in the flat, still in its early state of transformation. But knew too that she couldn't refuse her client, knew or rather sensed that this was not any old light-hearted request.

And she was right. Ruth having put down the phone heaved a sigh of relief; with the uncertainty, the pain over Jeremy, she needed Sylvia. She began to sense with the canniness with which every successful writer nurtures his/her work that the agency's role in her life had its own and vital place and somehow she had to find the way to begin to detach that from too close a bondage with her emotional life. Somehow she had to find a way of involving Sylvia, of drawing her back into connection. She had to make sure that as far as her writing life went she was 'safe'. The book, this book in particular, demanded that. Demanded, she felt, even ruthlessness, even unscrupulousness. Though if you'd asked her, challenged her to tell you what 'safe' was, she most probably couldn't have done. She only knew that when Jeremy's new secretary answered the phone, when she had to give her name, in its full solemn entirety, as if she was starting at the beginning again, as if once more she was a stranger, she had felt far from 'safe'.

Sylvia had been looking forward to a weekend of quiet. Which is to say without interaction with other human beings. Migraines had pressed all week. But no one in the office, she hoped and believed, would have guessed.

Alison was presently in the Cotswolds. Sylvia had foreseen the weekend as being one of hunting down a particular fabric she required for bathroom blinds. Of framing some old prints, a hobby she had recently acquired and gained pleasure from, of getting through a number of manuscripts in the pile that never seemed to diminish in size however much she read.

But now there was the promised visit to Ruth Flowert.

It is wet underfoot, the sun by mid-afternoon is palely shining from behind a thin gauze of clouds. The morning has been taken up with shopping and sundry Saturday tasks. The material has not been tracked down, but the necessary equipment for the framing has been, plus a number of bits and bobs that Sylvia has managed to pick up in a hurry in the early afternoon: a wooden mug holder and towel rail, a number of sample tiles, hooks for bedroom doors, etc. All are in the car, as she makes her way, after stopping a last time in order to purchase a chocolate cake, towards Tufnell Park.

Sylvia enters brightly dressed in scarlet woollen suit, a scarlet scarf tying up her dark hair. She hands the cake to a tired and transparently pale Ruth. Toby grabs at the box. Ruth doesn't have it securely in her hands. The box falls to the floor. Ruth curses, Toby cries.

Tea is like that. The house is cold. Sylvia noticeably shivers. Ruth asks repeatedly if Sylvia is cold. Expresses anxiety but is incapable of doing anything about it, or perhaps wanting to. Toby either cries or makes a nuisance of himself throughout. Ruth gives him rough treatment. The kitchen is uncomfortable. The cake, with its icing still on the floor, is cut into pieces unceremoniously and put onto plates which look to Sylvia's eyes far from clean.

To all Sylvia's questions Ruth replies in monosyllables. She will say nothing about the book except 'Read it, read it'.

Unlike Jeremy, Sylvia has now become unused to children (it seems so many years ago) and, besides, the memories she has are not easy ones, this year more than usual. So she prefers to try to ignore Toby's existence, which is firstly patently impossible to do, and secondly only makes things worse.

After a tea which has many silences, and which no one enjoys (no one, thinks Sylvia, can cope with Ruth in this mood) Sylvia brings out of her bag the gift of a story-book for Toby. Toby insists that it be read.

'Not now, not now,' Ruth exclaims, resentful of her child.

'I don't mind,' asserts Sylvia. For what else is there to do. The boy insists on scrambling onto her lap, creasing as he does so the skirt of her suit and kicking against her shins with his shoes. Sylvia's shoulders are still hunched. The two cups of strong (too strong) tea have done little to warm her. Her bottom is uncomfortable against the wooden boards of the kitchen chair. The mess on the table (which has not been cleared before tea began) disturbs. How much easier to see clients in the office, she thinks.

But she reads to Toby, who quietens, enjoying as always the tiny fillips of attention that so rarely come his way. The central character in the children's book is a peacock and after the story has been finished Sylvia talks about peacocks, about their colours, about the fun it might be to draw one. He likes their tails, he says, 'all the pretty colours'.

'I have some peacock feathers at home,' she tells him. 'Next time I come I shall bring you one.'

'Now, now,' insists Toby.

'Well I haven't got them with me,' she laughs.

And Toby dissolves into tears. And this time the tears go on and on, seemingly for ever. And Ruth is beside herself.

'Sadly he is too old for a cot death,' she says through tight lips.

Sylvia sits on her uncomfortable chair the small boy on her lap, stroking his hair, trying to soothe him, looking from one to the other. She senses that the two are too desperate to leave them alone together. And yet she has a longing to be out of the miserable environment they inhabit.

'I've just bought the flat on the top floor above the office,' she says to Ruth, 'and am in the process, the long process, of decorating it. There are some ideas I have that it would be good to talk over. Perhaps you and Toby would like to come back and see it? The car is outside. Then Toby could get the . . . Besides, I'd like to see what you think of it.'

'Yes, yes,' cries Toby.

Anything that will reduce the hours alone, just she and him, thinks Ruth. So she agrees. She goes to look for outdoor clothes for her son. And for her manuscript which she hands to Sylvia, who hugs it to her.

'I'm looking forward to reading this.'

In Sylvia's own flat the atmosphere improves. Ruth loves the space Sylvia is creating; she exclaims, compliments, asks questions. Toby is given the peacock feathers (by which time he has lost much of his interest in them). Then Sylvia finds her large collection of old beads, which delight him. He sits on the thickly carpeted floor playing with the cats and the beads. Both women relax. Sylvia tells Ruth that Alison will be sharing the flat during weekdays for the present and Ruth seems more interested than before in Sylvia's personal life. Sylvia says that some years ago she left her husband whom she hadn't got on with, and since then the agency has become her life. Now it was good to have Alison's company.

'I always knew you two were good friends,' Ruth tosses off. Turning back in her mind to her own loneliness, her own much more unsatisfactory, she feels, ways of coping. And hence back to Jeremy. Sylvia says nothing to Ruth now, or to anyone, about her children. No one in the world into which she'd moved knew, no one but Alison and Jeremy.

Again the conversation lapses and the sad look on Ruth's face returns.

'You seem so down,' says the older woman. 'Of course to a certain point one always feels like that on finishing a book, I do appreciate that. And the circumstances have been so difficult. But I was wondering if it was any more than that?'

'It's nothing more than meets the eye,' says Ruth, 'the predominant loneliness which I'm not very good at coping with, I'm afraid, and even worse, as you can see, at coping with him. Mind you, marriage itself is so often not a bed of roses. It's just that I was so lucky the first time. And then it seemed so utterly unfair . . .' She cries a bit, feeling it might bring relief. Having dried her tears she goes on, 'And then so many marriages don't work out; I'm aware of that. Yours, from what you say. And Jeremy is obviously having a hard patch in his at the moment.'

'Oh he'll muddle through,' says Sylvia.

Soon after this Ruth, clutching her little boy's hand, leaves the flat.

Sylvia phoned Ruth from the office on Monday to say that she had read Ruth's novel the preceding evening and thought it magnificent. 'Very strong, quite a breakthrough,' as Jeremy had predicted it would be. In short she was delighted with it. Jeremy would be reading it the moment he got back and then later in the week it would be going on to Alison.

'No need to send manuscripts any longer by post,' Ruth quipped. To hide her overwhelming sense of relief. It was, as she thought, good. She hugged herself when she got off the phone. Then out of character, she hugged Toby. 'This book's a really good 'un,' she told him.

On Sunday by coincidence while Sylvia had been reading the book Ruth had been attempting to take herself to task. Urged on by the cold winds of Sylvia's comment about Jeremy's marriage. And by the fortification of the two months they had not seen each other. She herself would have the strength to bring it to an end, if it wasn't already at an end. She would see him, she would not weaken. Now fortified by this, the best of her books to date, she would try and be more positive about her life. Take herself in hand. Maybe sufficient money would come in to afford more help with Toby. Maybe, maybe. So she reasoned as she pushed Toby on a swing in the bleak wilderness of an early Sunday afternoon in Tufnell Park's adventure playground.

Jeremy was returning to London from his father-in-law's hospital bedside. It was only a minor coronary luckily; tomorrow he'd be going home – still he'd need to be careful in future. Jeremy was fond of the old man. And all brushes with death remind one of one's own mortality. Driving back beside a serious mournful Helen he had promised her. Never again would he see Ruth. He'd put an end to it. Once too often. This time almost out of his control.

'Such a force, that woman,' he told his wife. 'I never really wanted to, but she, she just drove me straight into it. But this is an end. An end for ever. Believe me, darling,' so he'd promised.

So now in the office, staying late – he deemed it sensible not to take this particular manuscript home, but warned his wife that work (and only work) was keeping him late. So he read. So he knew they had a winner on their hands. 'A contender for the Booker,' he burst into Sylvia's office and announced to her. 'Quite possibly,' she concurred.

'See, I knew we could do it,' he hugged her. And though she pulled away and said to him, 'Don't jump your horses,' she too felt a surge of excitement. 'Let's drink to it,' he said. As they drank it was for all the world as if it was nothing to do with Ruth Flowert.

His own emotions now were more complex than Ruth's. He had made up his mind to bring the affair to an end, though dreaded the complications of getting out of it, sure of (relying on, could one say?) the fact that Ruth would make it difficult for him. But determined – for her sake, he would say to her. But he would mean for his own, for his marriage's, for the main chance. At the same time the book was flattering to him, and Helen was no longer ever flattering. On a level he couldn't touch, or recognise until he was with her again, he was still, in some ways more than ever since reading the book, in Ruth Flowert's thrall.

So he would go and see her, have it out with her. So he phoned; her voice was shaky but quiet and steady. It was marvellous, he said. How was she?

206

How did he expect? she said.

He would come and see her after work on Friday, he said. Would that be all right? And incidentally, Sylvia was saying did she have a second copy he could pick up?

'Yes,' she said.

And would it be all right for him to come?

She expected it would.

She is in jeans and Ted's fisherman's sweater. The mole on her cheek more noticeable than ever in her pale face. She stands at the door submissive as a child. It is later than she expected (eight o'clock) and for once she has got Toby to sleep, telling him nothing of Jeremy's expected visit. She has lost weight, Jeremy notices. The jeans look too roomy around her legs. She seems altogether smaller than he remembers.

He does not know what kind of a connection to make. In the end with some awkwardness he puts his hand on her shoulder. She steps backward and they walk through into the kitchen. Which is clear of all debris. There are sweet peas in a small pewter vase on the middle of the table, smelling sweetly. They sit opposite each other at one end of the table. On the other end of the table lies the second copy of *Wasted* which Ruth has put out for Sylvia.

Jeremy catches sight of it.

'Ah, the second copy. Good. Yes, I must try not to forget it when I go.'

'And why should you?'

He is more nervous with her than she with him. For the urge now he is with her to take her in his arms is almost, but not quite, overwhelming.

'The book, as I said on the phone, is a masterpiece.'

It seems to him that she is looking at him cynically. Scenes like this, words like this, thinks Jeremy who has always been a man of his senses, should not be spoken like this, coldly, in restraint, across a table. It isn't right, isn't how nature made it to be. They should be said warmly, with passion. In bed. Still he withheld. Thinking of his promise to Helen. And no doubt it would be better for them all.

'Well,' says Ruth, 'would you like something to drink?'

Her hands with nervous blunt fingers are crossed on the table.

'Not particularly.'

Silence.

'How have you been?' Jeremy asks. As he has on the phone.

Ruth spreads her arms. Expressing what? That she did not wish to vocalise how she had been, that he should know perhaps?

'Whatever, it is in the past now,' she says low.

'Ah Ruth, don't be angry.'

'Angry is not what I am.'

'What then?'

Her shoulders go up in a strange gesture of despair. 'Exhausted.' Again silence.

'How was America?' Her voice she finds is more controlled than she could have hoped. So he talks about America and she listens. Questions. And some time later they open the bottle of wine that he has in his briefcase for her but has thought would perhaps have to be taken away again unopened. Now she prises open the cork, old-fashioned method, bottle between her thin, jeaned knees, and he pours into the two tulip-shaped glasses. The same glasses.

He asks her about Toby. But she is reluctant to talk about her own news. To let him in. Finding it easier to talk about things outside herself.

'And your father-in-law?'

He wonders if this is dangerous ground but tells her what she wishes to know. Praying that she will not ask about Helen. She does not.

So now, playing the agent, he says to her, well into his second glass of wine, 'Let me tell you what kind of a deal Sylvia and I hope for on *Wasted*. It will have to be handled differently from earlier books, Ruth. With luck we can make you a fair sum of money on this one, enough to change your lifestyle, eh. Maybe you'll be able to give up the law centre and put in central heating,' he smiles at her. He maps out their plans.

Ruth listens calmly. It all seems beyond her somehow. She knows that she has to let Jeremy as lover go. She wills him to become for her again agent and friend (if friend is ever what he was) but senses that the process will be impossibly hard. And yet what choice does she have. The talk of money, the talk of deals, the talk of a possible film, the talk of tactics and auctions, all seem somewhere over her head. As if she is a grown woman in the world making business arrangements which she is not fool enough to not know will benefit others as well as herself. And yet wanting to be the little girl comforted and caressed.

She is blown wide open by the months and months of concentrated work and by the physical passion re-ignited, though she

208

fights it painfully, by seeing Jeremy again. She hears his words but she thinks of him in bed, inside her. At the same time. She has made up her mind that now she can end it – and apparently he has come to the same decision though neither has said so in so many words. But it is for the best, of that she is convinced.

And now while she has pride, has some modicum of determination. Now while there is still a chance that friendly relationships with Fisk, Farmer can go on as before. Now while she is on a high. What an odd thought. She laughs to herself, hardly listening to Jeremy's words about facts and figures. She simply prays for strength (not sure to who), strength to get through this meeting, to keep her dignity, her resolve. She knows that next time they meet, in the office, it will be easier. And the next time easier than that. And Jeremy (is he being understanding, she wonders, or just saving his own skin?) is talking about the extent to which Sylvia will handle the negotiations. All that will make it easier.

And Jeremy talks on, painting a bright future. But he is unnerved. The speeches he had planned about why the affair must come to an end, have in some way he can't quite fathom become redundant. It is as if it is all decided and yet nothing has been said. He is relieved. Just what he wants, with his conscious mind, is happening, quietly, without tears, without dramatics, with Ruth's concurrence, apparently. Even by Ruth's desire. And she so quiet, so pale. Is she angry with him? he wonders. And that troubles him, that a woman, any woman should have a bad opinion of him. It makes it harder and harder for him to leave. For him not to desire a shift, a sign from her that all is forgiven, all is understood. He cannot bear, he thinks, to leave it with this coldness.

But it seems that he must. 'I must go now,' he says.

'Yes.'

They both push back chairs and stand up.

'I'll just take a pee,' he says.

'You know where to go.'

He climbs the stairs. She waits in agony in the kitchen, looking out of blurred speckled eyes at the pink and lilac of the sweet pea petals. Now he has left, though he is only upstairs. She can imagine the desolation after the front door has closed. Without conscious thought she climbs the stairs. To be nearer him. On the landing, half pretending to herself that she is looking in on Toby, she is waiting outside the loo, nestling against the wall for support. Jeremy, opening the loo door, finds her opposite and slightly to the left, in shadow. Above the noise of water re-filling the cistern he hears the

209

unmistakable sound of her pain. When he is not expecting it. When he is no longer schooled to withstand it. When perhaps he has even begun to hope for it.

Jeremy the comforter. In a minute he has his arms around her. He is drying her tears. And creating more. As he leaves her bedroom some hours later he is promising her that he will be back the following Saturday in time to fly a kite on Parliament Hill with Toby and that somehow he will wangle it to stay to dinner.

'We'll have a feast,' says Ruth. 'I'll cook something splendiferous.'

Jeremy half way to the bedroom door walks back to the bed and kisses Ruth tenderly on the lips, on the cheeks, on the eyelids. Then he lets himself out of the room and out of the house.

Alison's views on *Wasted* more or less concur with Sylvia's and Jeremy's: Ruth's most impressive novel it was to date, no doubt about it. In her elevated position she was on the other hand no longer Ruth's editor, so she passed it on to the bright young man the firm had recently head-hunted to take major responsibility for the fiction list.

She was interested to see how he would respond. He had only been in his new position for a matter of weeks, and trust and new lines of communication were in the early stages of being fostered. Alison would have taken the book on by this stage, whatever; for she was more than convinced that it would be a winner. And besides Ruth was already an established name though in a minor way, so the book would have had to have been virtually unsaleable for her to have turned it down at this point in Ruth's career. And it was far from that. On the other hand whether she passed Ruth over to this new chap or to someone else, that depended on how he responded. Meanwhile she would wait. If he liked the book, he could negotiate the contract.

Sylvia and Alison had always been aware of the pitfalls, the complexity of their particular position. And to this end they had early on laid down ground rules, determined that they would not be guilty of partiality. Each fiercely put the interests of business or client before their personal relations. Alison would take a new client of Sylvia's, or Jeremy's, where she could, but often it did not suit her list; it was as simple as that. Besides for many years her interest in fiction had been a side line. Though she had always had fiction authors, her large feminist and social science list was her main and steady love, and this is where she had most specifically built her reputation. When Sylvia sent books either to Alison or to others in her firm and they were turned down, it was the rule between them that this was accepted without demur. Otherwise, they quickly saw, it would make for an untenable position. As to negotiations, each would fight toughly, enjoying the battle.

As far as Sylvia was concerned she would pride herself that her clients must come first. If it seemed better for a client to send him/her to another firm this would dictate her action. Till this point no more partiality had been shown, Alison and Sylvia would have argued, than in the many situations where a publisher and agent are particularly friendly and want to do business if it is at all possible. All publishers prefer working with some particular agents. And vice versa. The advantages Sylvia would have reckoned to have been two-fold: the early introductions to a number of agentless clients, and the reduced cost of postage that Ruth had so aptly tumbled on. But no more than this, and no less.

Business talks were mainly kept to business hours. To give room for the other side of their relationship. And particularly because Sylvia, until recently passionate and vulnerable in bed, did not feel she was in the right frame of mind to argue toughly for her clients. For that she needed her tailored clothes, her wall of make-up, her office, her secretary, her desk, her new rose cut freshly every morning from the wild entangled garden. The rose. One of the bonuses of the move. From which apparently it still looked as if there were many disadvantages.

However, the shock and dislocations of the late spring and early summer were settling, and though far from settled or happy she was more philosophical.

A mere ten days after the meeting between Jeremy and Ruth, dynamic Mark Riding had read *Wasted* and expressed himself one hundred percent behind it. He had also used the ubiquitous term on everyone in publishing's lips, a Booker contender. So negotiations were in progress.

Sylvia was delighted that she would not be dealing with Alison over this, for in new bearish mood, brought on by the year's events and underpinned in this case by her belief in the book's worth, she was determined to play very tough indeed. To make *Publishing*

News once again by the sums fetched. She and Mark had crossed swords earlier that year (in his former job) and each knew the other's methods. Now Sylvia was going to enjoy the fight. It would take her mind off personal problems: the fact that she was dreaming of her children nightly, and knew not the reason, nightly when after the first few years of anguish they had become more or less dormant in her mind for so long; that she had less heart for sex with Alison, owing to Alison's apparent coldness and lack of sympathy over the consequences of the move; that it seemed months since she had had a non-disturbed night of sleep, owing to the fact that she had begun to wonder increasingly, however hard she wrestled with these thoughts and tried to keep them from her, had it been worth it. Had it?

So she welcomed this challenge over a bloody good book, over a client who would benefit enormously from substantial sums of money. There would then be the possibility for the little boy to have a nanny and private schooling, and a mother more relaxed, more time for him, many things to help buffer against the loss of father – she could do all this at last. And the particular pleasure of helping someone for whom, amongst all her clients, she had always had a great affection and warm sense of maternal caring. And then the money and the prestige for Fisk, Farmer, they too were considered. She swiftly promised herself an antique sideboard that she had her eye on, if she fetched the price she had in mind. So negotiations started. *Wasted*, meanwhile, was being read in a hurry by a number of paperback houses. At Alison's firm the number of manuscript copies had multiplied to four times their original number.

So there were phone calls between Mark Riding and Sylvia at Fisk, Farmer. Telephone calls all through the following week. The fun had begun.

By the following Wednesday after one particularly heated morning call Sylvia felt the need to cool her head and think about further tactics out of the office. Sometimes in these circumstances she would walk on the Green if the weather was clement or (in the new situation) go up to the flat, recline on the sofa, listen to music for a half an hour or so, before returning to the fray. But this particular day she was restless. She missed the old companionability with Alison, she felt the flat was still far from being a home and she had yet again dreamt of her children. Of them needing her: crying for her. It was absurd.

She knew, that Wednesday, that she was far from her best, most centred self. Many agents in those circumstances take to drink. A great temptation. Not Sylvia, whose life had been based so largely on self-discipline, on which she prided herself. She sipped at wine, pecked at food, did not believe in indulgence. She did exercises for ten minutes every morning before she showered and dressed. Occasionally on a Sunday morning she swam lengths at a local pool. She still rode well when offered the opportunity. Still having a beautiful body, she was not for committing crimes against it; she believed it was hers to be looked after, to be preserved.

So now she resisted seeking relief in an early repair to the drinks cabinet. In the flat she took a tomato juice out of the fridge, sat on the sofa in the sitting room, and sipping it, admiring still – the novelty had not worn off – the expanse of sky, she wondered how she was to get herself back into kilter for the rest of the day. Feeling, unusual for her, insufferably isolated, she experienced the need to talk; to someone, not Alison, someone with children. And so she thought of Helen, who, owing to busy lives, mostly her own, she had not seen for some time now. She picked up the phone and dialled her number.

'I need to get out of the office,' she said. 'Suddenly have a great desire to see you. Are you going to be at home? May I come over? Just bread and cheese. Don't bother with anything more. Will that be okay, I won't be disturbing anything?' She assumed always Helen, mother, patient wife, freelancer sitting there waiting, waiting always for things to happen.

Helen said that she could come. She sounded neither overjoyed nor displeased over such a suggestion.

It was early September the day when Sylvia left the office, got into her white Mini Metro and went to visit Helen in her pleasant rambling home in Kew. Helen and Jeremy's children were still on holiday from school, or waiting to go up to university. The twins were around when Sylvia arrived and they greeted her with affection. They were having a hurried sandwich lunch in the kitchen before rushing off to do this or that. With mouths full they greeted Sylvia and told her snippets of their news that they felt suitable for adult consumption.

Meanwhile Helen, looking, thought Sylvia, more strained, with new tight crow's lines appearing round her temples, bustled at the stove saying little while she heated soup. She prepared a tray with bread and cheese, and when the soup was steaming poured it into two large earthenware bowls.

'Come on, Sylvia, we'll take it through into the sitting room.'

Sylvia reluctantly left the pleasantness of family life and the talk of these young people, which cheered her because it was so far from her own life and troubles.

Carrying the tray Helen moved into the sitting-room. And behind her, bearing the pepper mill in one hand and a jug of water in the other, Sylvia followed. Into the sun-filled room where Sylvia, taking off high-heeled shoes and slipping slim elegant legs underneath her, as she made herself comfortable on the flower-patterned sofa, ground the mill of the pepper thoughtfully over her soup whilst wondering if she would confide in Helen how frequently and disturbingly she was dreaming about her children. But it was Helen, that lunchtime, not Sylvia who did the confiding.

'Jeremy,' said Sylvia to Sally, on returning to the office, 'can you buzz him for me, or better still pop in and tell him I want a word.'

'Jeremy went out at lunchtime saying he wouldn't be back till three, Sylvia,' Sally told her.

Sylvia looked at her watch. 'It's three-fifteen now,' she growled. Despite herself Sally smiled, when had Jeremy been known or been expected to keep time so precisely.

'Buzz me the moment he comes in.'

Sylvia went into her room and shut the door firmly.

Anger fuelled her fire. She had no trouble phoning Mark Riding and dealing a tough and dextrous hand. With skill she exacted the promises she wanted, taking the many moves of contract negotiation slowly, enjoying each, knowing she had him where she wanted him, knowing before they talked how it would fall out.

When she returned to the outer office she was in better humour. Seeing a rosy future for Ruth, whatever Jeremy's present idiocies. And for herself the sweets of success. She knew she'd done a damn good deal, some aspects of which, she told Sally with a smile, now all pleasantness and light, some aspects of which, had she been Mark Riding she would certainly not have agreed to. 'Still it's a large firm, they'll weather it; this and a lot more.' She wondered fleetingly what Alison might have to say to the new terms. Meanwhile.

'Jeremy still not in yet?'

'No sound of him. What a silly thing to say!' Sally laughed at

214

herself, endearing her to Sylvia.

'I think I deserve a cup of tea after that.'

'I'll make you one,' Sally was immediately up from her chair.

'No, you stay put. Would you like one while I'm at it?'

Sally would; she smiled at her boss, thinking how erratic and at times downright difficult she found her changes of mood. How cold she could be at times. Although the outgoing assistant when she took the job had stayed for two and a half years and spoke glowingly of Sylvia. Sally was finding it a harder ride. And wondering why.

Still she nodded about the tea. Odd how a small gesture like that, just once to have tea made for one, not always to be treated as the paid skivvy (she with her university degree) helped enormously.

So Sylvia made the tea, chatted for a few minutes with Sally, then returned to her office to attack some paperwork until the arrival of her next client. As he entered her office, charming, balding Max Winton, who treated her always like a long-lost favourite daughter, often bringing her roses or chocolates, she thought she heard Jeremy's voice in the outer office. But Max was kissing her on both cheeks, and telling her how well she looked. And she in turn told him how well he looked, which he liked and which he should do – for he had just returned from a holiday in Greece – but which in fact was only half true. Max had worries. All Sylvia's clients had worries. Or did they, she sometimes wondered, simply dredge them up on the day they came to see her? A few minutes later, like the good professional woman she was, she had forgotten about Jeremy and was giving one hundred percent of her attention to Max and the problems of keeping up with a young, energetic – to say nothing of ambitious – third wife.

When Max went, the phone rang. Over and over again. As Sylvia talked into the receiver she signed letters and waved goodbye to Sally who was in her coat and eager now to take off.

Finally there is peace in the office; it is well after six. Sylvia thinks again of Jeremy and leaves her desk to go and find him in his lair; the word comes to mind, making her smile.

'Oh there you are.'

'Here I am!'

He waves a script at her. 'Colin Hardcastle's film treatment; it's come in at last, damned good, I reckon it to be. Have you the time to have a look at it this evening?'

'Jeremy?'

'Sylvia?' He smiles at her, all boyish charm.

'Come into the garden.'

'The garden? What kind of proposal is that, my old mate?'

'Come,' she says. 'I want to talk to you.' She slips her arm through his.

He looks at her quizzically, scanning her face. Which gives him no clues. So he follows her out of the office, out of the front door of the building and round the side entrance into the overgrown, for many years unloved, garden which has nevertheless been doing famously on its own. Now on this balmy early September evening the scent of hundreds of wild roses and of honeysuckle climbing prodigiously along the entire south-facing wall of the garden strikes them both so that they gasp with the pleasure of it. In the honeysuckle the bees are busy. The mating sound of birds is everywhere to be heard. The paths are overgrown. It is difficult to traverse the length of the garden. Sylvia in her high-heeled shoes, her light delicate feet and ankles, again slips an equally light arm through Jeremy's. 'It's another world out here,' she breathes.

'Now you own the flat as well, we should really try and speak to the landlord about gaining more control of the garden; it's criminal to let it go to waste like this.'

'Oh I do agree.'

'Are you imagining the same as I am?' he asks her.

'What is that?'

'Summer cocktail parties out here.'

'Elegant champagne lunches,' she laughs at him.

'Well you know,' says Jeremy, still with her arm through his, 'you have to admit things are going famously well. Sylvia, you've become rather ominously silent. Has anything happened this afternoon? Come on, don't hold me in suspense. Why have you brought me out here?'

'Jeremy, I needed a break at lunchtime. I rang Helen and went over.'

'Yes?'

'Do you have anything to tell me? Anything that perhaps you should confide?'

'I can't think what you're talking about.'

'Can't you? Ruth Flowert, perhaps?'

To the side of his left eye a muscle twitches convulsively. 'Oh that.' His face is impassive.

'Jeremy,' she has never raised her voice to him before. 'For goodness sake don't "oh that" me. How could you be such a fool and so utterly irresponsible? I can't expect you to have thought of the effect on Helen, after all you haven't for years . . .'

'Now that's a bit steep . . .'

'But what about Ruth? You damn well know how vulnerable she is, how stretched.'

'That's just the point . . .'

'That it would be a madness. Christ almighty, Jeremy, I would have thought that even you would have stopped at something.'

'I might stop at something, yes.'

'At this, Jeremy, at this!' She is shouting at him. As Helen has not yet done; though she has wept and wept the preceding Friday evening when he had come home late and she had known that he had gone back on his promise.

Now all Sylvia's anger, her pent-up rage, went into her attack on her partner.

Near the patch that had been a vegetable garden they find a low stone wall and squat on it. Both look away out of the garden at the glow of pink sky as the sun sets.

'Good weather tomorrow,' Jeremy mutters.

It was over, her rage. 'Don't you care for the agency at all?' she asks sadly. 'Even if you can't think of Helen, of your responsibility to Ruth, to me. Couldn't you have thought of the agency?'

He looks at her, thinking of the gulf between men and women. 'It's an impossible situation. Of course I care. It wouldn't have happened unless I cared.'

'What a wretched mess.' Heartbroken she turns away from him, watching the sun go down below the horizon and the sky dramatically darken.

For a long time neither says anything more.

Then out of the dusky and eerie light that is drenching the garden, his voice floats over her shoulder where she has her back to him.

'It's not going to be a mess any more.'

'I doubt if it can ever now be anything else.'

'Yes it can. Christ, people are having affairs all the time and pulling out of them. Where have you been, Sylvia? Not in the literary world surely for the last decade or so.'

'I know, I know, but this is different.'

'That's what they always say.'

'And with your client! And, Jeremy, a client so vulnerable.'

'I know, I know. It's just because of that.'

'What?'

'I doubt you'll understand.'

'I doubt I will.'

There seems as if there is nothing more to say.

So Sylvia wonders why she has started talking about her recent dreams. About her recent insufferable yearning for her children. In the early hours. About early days, days she was still with Patrick, days when she walked with the children on the Heath and through the parks, days when she had brought them all to visit Jeremy and Helen in the flat that was for so many years their home. Jeremy lets Sylvia talk, lets her relieve as best she can these burdens, these topics of conversations that she can never share with Alison.

Instinct has served Sylvia well once again. She had not planned it this way. But the effect on Jeremy is better than any further attacking could have been. They are bound. Bound by the past, by his stake in her future. When she is bossy in the agency he feels the right to be irresponsible, when she is vulnerable, the need to protect. As now. He experiences his own strength coming back by just this admission of Sylvia's own present state of mind. In direct proportion. Swings and roundabouts. And Sylvia almost always for the majority of her life has had the unerring instinct for making people comfortable.

So when an hour later they leave the garden, peace of sorts has been established between them. She sees him to his car.

'So you think you can handle it,' she asks, 'bring it to a close, before there is irreparable damage?'

'That's what I anyway had in mind,' says Jeremy as they step out of the garden and onto the gravel driveway.

The following morning Sylvia phoned Ruth to tell her about the terms that had been agreed on for *Wasted*. It was Toby who answered the phone: a silence first, then childish breathing, then a squeaky voice saying 'Hello, hello,' a voice overtaken by the awe of handling such a grown-up instrument. Sylvia patiently asked the little boy if she may speak with his mummy.

Ruth, taking over the phone, sounded a different person from the one who had entertained Sylvia to such a miserable tea recently. Her voice was strong and musical. Sylvia could hear that she was playing with Toby while talking to Sylvia. Sylvia had an image of Toby sitting on his mother's lap being tickled. She heard his squeals of laughter and his 'Mummy, stop, stop.'

'Well, you sound in a good mood this morning,' observed Sylvia, 'and before I've even given you the news too.'

'I am in a good mood. I never want to write another word,' sang Ruth. 'I've been dreaming up the most delicious meals all day.'

'For whom?'

'For Toby and myself,' lied Ruth.

'Oh well,' said Sylvia, 'every writer deserves a rest between books.'

'No, this is the end, really. It is such a trap, such a snare. I'm absolutely through.'

'That's what they all say.'

'Do they, so?'

The two women laughed.

'Besides a little bird tells me that the sums that *Wasted* is going to fetch, if nothing else will go towards changing your mind. Though one would have to say, you won't *have* to write ever again.'

'It can't be as good as that.'

'No, but it's pretty good.' Sylvia savouring the moment, quoted figures. As she did so hoping that they would serve against the rainy day of Jeremy's retreat.

'Marvellous, Sylvia,' sang Ruth. 'I always knew that you were the best of agents, the best.'

'You can go away for a holiday now. You deserve it. Take Toby and go to the sun for a few weeks. Go to Greece.'

'Who wants a holiday when London's so gorgeous at present,' sang Ruth.

Ruth is singing when Jeremy arrives at the door that Saturday. Toby with his kite firmly between his knees, every few minutes he just puts a hand to it to check that it is still there, is in his favourite position, perusing the street from the front window. At Jeremy's entrance he and the kite are in his arms in an instant.

The house is aglow with flowers, carnations, freesias, wallflowers, at least half a dozen pewter and pottery jars full of anemones. The sun streams in, lighting up the yellow walls of the living room and the pine floorboards, which shine as if they have just been freshly sealed. In the far corner of the living room above the low table at which Toby plays, Ruth, in bold colours and with bold strokes, has painted and decorated for him the letters of the alphabet.

'That's new,' says Jeremy.

'Yes, I did it last night after he'd gone to bed.'

'Straight onto the wall.'

'Why ever not?' she laughs at him. 'Oh Jeremy, we should all take more RISKS.' Toby has already struggled down and now it is Ruth's turn. She comes up to Jeremy and takes his two hands in hers. Beaming with pleasure – and with love – she starts to waltz with him around the empty spaces of the sitting room. Toby, onlooker, makes his own contribution by banging his kite on the floor in what he no doubt believes to be an attempt to keep time with the music.

'What is that smell?' Jeremy suddenly asks.

'My God, the fudge, the fudge.'

'Fud, fud,' Toby repeats after her.

All three make for the kitchen where the fudge is just saved from burning.

'Chocolate fudge,' says Jeremy. 'It's ages since . . .'

'Here try some,' she hands him the first piece.

'Me, me,' demands her son.

Was it yummie, quite the yummiest fudge in the world, or so she felt. Or was it the sun, the yellow walls, the prospect of putting in a bag that which they didn't eat now – her two males were at present making such pigs of themselves – and spending the whole delicious late summer afternoon – blue sky, a gentle breeze, a soft but radiant sun – what more could anyone want? – wandering over Parliament Hill, flying the kite (she had absolute faith in Jeremy's ability to achieve what she never had, actually get the thing to fly), occasionally sneaking a hand into the bag of yummie chocolate fudge, occasionally sneaking a hand into Jeremy's own. And to hell with the world. She felt so safe when he was here. Even with the anticipation of him coming, for days before everything somehow fell into its right place.

She begins to sing again.

'I've never known you so happy.'

'Oh I am, I am happy,' she laughs into his eyes.

'You're going to be a rich lady now.'

'Yes, that too. What do you think of the flowers?' she sweeps her arms out, taking in the surfaces on which they are perched and clustered.

'They're magnificent.'

'They're a celebration,' she sings.

'Of the book?'

'Of us.' She goes up to him a second time and this time taking his arms and twining them behind her back she moves her lips closer and closer to his, whispering, 'I love you, I love you.'

'Scandalous woman,' says Jeremy. 'Hadn't we better be thinking, young man, of dispatching that kite of yours high into the sky?'

'I'll fetch sweaters,' sings Ruth. 'You'll need a sweater, Toby, it'll be cold at the top.'

Nothing could shift and threaten her mood today. Even Toby's remonstration that he didn't, wouldn't want a sweater, and Jeremy's assertion that she was fussing over her son like an old mother hen.

'You be careful, my man,' she laughs at him, 'or I'll start fussing over you!'

Jeremy flew the kite with dexterity but he was in a state close to torment. Sylvia's anger had fired Helen's own; had given her courage.

'Have you and Sylvia spoken?' she demanded to know when Jeremy had arrived home that Wednesday evening.

'Yes, Helen, we talked.' His face was wooden.

'Well then, isn't it more to the point to talk to me. ME. YOUR WIFE,' she shouted at him.

'Quiet, the kids will hear.'

'Perhaps they should hear.'

He managed to quieten her, but only for the hours when the family were together. The night was a torment of no sleep, of tears, angry recriminations, all the unfairnesses of their marriage, as Helen saw it, being brought into the open and looked on by both as two opposing players might.

Jeremy was weary, he did not really wish to discuss it at all with his wife, who was so beside herself as to make no sense at all, so he told her. Besides he had already made up his mind once and for all to bring the affair with Ruth to a close.

'How can I believe you?'

'I really don't mind if you believe it or not.'

That was unwise. And untrue. Spoken at the height of feeling so got at. Damn women, damn them all, thought Jeremy. His unwise comment, however, negated further sleep for most of the hours of the night. Helen's tears and anger coming in gusts like a storm that refused to die down.

By the morning they were both shattered.

221

'I'm hardly capable of going to work,' said Jeremy. 'I feel like a pillow with all the stuffing pulled out.'

'Whose fault is that?' she wanted to know.

'Helen, don't start on that again.'

So she went to fetch him a cup of coffee and relented to the extent of bringing him toast and marmalade in bed.

Thursday night they had said little to one another. Made love silently but with some attempt at warmth, and slept early. Then both woke in the night, troubled and restless.

Friday was a difficult day at work and Jeremy arrived home grey with exhaustion, tension, lack of sleep. Jeremy had told Helen that he would see Ruth on Saturday and bring the affair to a close. 'I'll have to handle it very carefully, you know, there is Sylvia too to consider.'

'Damn Sylvia!' This from Helen was rare.

'And she is one of our best clients. And terribly unstable. There's a lot to consider. I've got to do it gently, I don't want to hurt her too much if possible. Still I've an idea how I'll play it, but it might take some hours, Helen. You'll have to accept that. In cases like this it's important to talk it right through.'

'You should know!'

'If possible it's best if both sides are in agreement about what they're doing.'

'Jeremy, Jeremy,' Helen moaned. 'If you talk about it, you'll be right in there deeper than ever. I'm sure about it. She's just that sort of woman.'

This conversation from the early hours of Thursday morning was in both their minds as they sat down 'en famille' to Friday supper. Jeremy took his to the coffee table and turned on the television to watch the news; he couldn't bear to talk to any of them.

All day as Helen had worked on her maps in her sewing room on the second floor of the house she had felt her anxiety and her anger rising again to boiling point. And now again looking at Jeremy's face as he sat watching television and feeling the gulf between them. What *was* he thinking? They were no more than strangers – the pain of the situation struck her as if a long sharp needle was piercing into her.

Without wanting to she was like a fishwife that night in their bedroom. Later she would hardly believe of herself the things she'd said, the anger, even, that dredged from somewhere deep in her childhood, that part that had nothing to do with Jeremy whatsoever, for so long repressed. She lashed out at him over and over again for (she claimed) making her a martyr. Hating him more for being the cause of so much anger – and so much unseemly behaviour. For she hated to see herself behave this way. She wouldn't have known she had it in her. And she felt at that moment that she would never forgive him, for causing this to happen, for bringing her to this.

Jeremy tried to comfort, but comfort was not what Helen wanted that night. And eventually in self-defence, and because he was so tired, and because he had tried everything else, he started bitterly to attack her – for everything, even for trapping him into a marriage he'd never wanted, he suggested, in the first place.

'How, trapping!'

And so they fought and tussled. Both saying things they regretted only hours later. Both trying to hurt. Both succeeding in wounding.

And then it was Jeremy crying, for he felt somehow Helen's strength, felt despite all he'd said, that she was a better person than he, felt she was his conscience, to some extent his alter ego, as well as the mother of his children, the woman who had kept house for him, offered him her body, though erratically, but still consistently, along with all other types of sustenance, for nineteen years. He felt towards her abjectly guilty, wishing, wishing in one self-pitying minute that he had not been born so blessedly prey to those emotions which had made a situation such as the one with Ruth not only possible, but all too likely. I just like women, he said to himself, but they don't understand that, none of them do.

So, in guilt, and not because he couldn't take any more of Helen's abuse, but because he could not continue the role of attacking her, he started to cry himself, huge heaving tears, laying as he did so his head on her lap, where she was sitting, upright, angry in the bed. And as he cried and the tears trickled onto her nightie and down onto her inner thighs, she found herself – though she cursed herself at the very same time, for her weakness – she found herself stroking his soft, wild white hair, she found herself drawing him to her, as if he was indeed her baby.

So, as the afternoon wore on, the fudge, so yummie at first, was now making them all feel slightly sick and wish that they hadn't eaten so much, as the wind picked up, catching at all the kites on the top of Parliament Hill Fields – and there were many. As Toby's own kite, doing so nicely in the blue sky, scooped and whirled and dived above their heads, as Ruth put her hand in his pocket (signifying possession) and he let it stay there, he wondered with anguish how he was ever going to begin the task of becoming untangled. It seemed almost as impossible a task as to separate the two kites, the red and the black skull-and-cross-bones, which having become entwined in each other's strings were now lying in a life and death embrace in one of the giant oaks while a group of sad-looking children and their parents looked up helplessly, and equally helplessly shook the tree.

While he, Jeremy, had been laying the groundwork for what he saw as being the outcome of this meeting, Ruth's thoughts had apparently been going in quite another direction. And why shouldn't they, that was the devil of it. How could he possibly blame her? He didn't. On the contrary, now with her he felt impossibly sorry for her: for her widowhood, for her gigantic overwhelming need for a substitute father for Toby, for her anguishing vulnerability, her need to be protected, her sensitivity, the way she was almost too frail for this life: for her imaginative powers which made all ordinary daily experiences so impossibly difficult for her, but which made her such a good writer – and lover. And, too, for what he was going to do to her by deserting her, when she, as she confided in him while the kite danced above them, had finally after their last meeting come to terms with the role of mistress, of having only half a man, if that man was one whom she loved as much as she did Jeremy. Yes, she'd become wonderfully philosophical about it, she told him: she would put on no more pressure, happy with knowing that he would be round once or twice a week. And that that would be, even for Toby – look at him now – so much better than nothing. And now with the money from the book, of course it would make many aspects of their lives easier – make her *feel* easier, no doubt. For the first time since Ted died, she was telling him with her sparkling speckled eyes, she felt life was worth living. Really worth living.

They walked home, swinging Toby, playing hide-and-seek with him, telling him a story in which both took alternate turns to tell a part. And all the while Ruth's hand was in his pocket.

Back in the house Jeremy found it easiest to concentrate his energies on Toby. While he built Lego garages and tower blocks, while he piggybacked the child round the small house, while he bathed, dried, talked to the boy, while he ate his supper, read to him at his bedside when, clean, fed, tired and content he snuggled under his duvet cover, Ruth sang, hovered, looked on with such a glow on her face. There was such soft moistness in her eyes that Jeremy found it almost more than he could bear, to look at her.

Then Toby was finally bidden goodnight. The parent and surrogate parent left the room. At a loss momentarily, having to make the adjustment to being without the child's continual demanding presence.

'How hungry do you feel?' Ruth asks in the corridor.

'I'm still suffering from too much fudge.'

'Me too. Here I want to show you something.' Ruth suddenly has an idea. Jeremy follows her into her bedroom. There is nowhere to sit but the double bed and so on it he sprawls. She meanwhile stands on a chair to reach a high shelf above her wardrobe. Turning round he sees that she has in her arms photo albums. Not her and Ted, he prays, he couldn't stand that.

No, it is photos of her as a child, photos of her growing up, photos of the countryside that she has captured so well in her books, photos of old friends and relatives. She comes to be close to him on the bed and as they turn the pages she tells him the history of the people or landscapes which feature.

She is in fine form, an expert story-teller always, and now knowing that she has a more than approving audience, she takes her time, spinning stories, swapping from this to that, one long digression after another, taking Jeremy deliciously, fascinatingly through her childhood, about which he realises he still knows so little, despite her books. And wants to know more. She has a way of hooking him in.

So they talk, so the sun sets outside the window, so Toby next door sleeps peaceably. So time goes by. So Ruth takes Jeremy's hands and puts them provocatively on her breasts, slipping them easily inside her cotton shirt. So Jeremy thinks, of course I must talk to her, of course, but meanwhile, just one more time, one more time. What can it hurt? And maybe later, maybe over dinner, somehow an opening will occur, the opportunity to explain in a way she can understand, but it is all a question of finding the right opening. It is all a question of timing, he tells himself. Finding himself sliding her jeans off, finding himself sliding inside her. Finding himself crying out to her how much he loves her at the moment of his ejaculation.

The sun was going down and the sky darkening as they lay on the bed in the curtainless room, watching the night begin to seep in

225

through the window; listening to a cock crow in Tufnell Park, somehow confused into thinking it was morning; listening to summer night noises, birds, the occasional car, the clinking of glasses at a nearby pub, people laughing in the neighbouring garden, people chatting in the street, a clarinet being practised by an open window. She lay on her back. He too. He could not look at her. She was talking about the future they would share; the part-future. He could not disabuse her. He was agreeing with each and every one of her plans, telling her that he thought like she did, that they were made for one another. 'And even,' she assured him, 'if I have to wait till all your children have left home to have you entirely to myself, I'm happy to wait, indeed believe that's, the right thing to do.' So she glowed. 'I can wait.' Meanwhile she touched him tenderly. 'Are you ready to come again?'

But a second time, no. Jeremy's anguish was increasing by the moment. He wanted to talk, to share with her the impossible situation he was in: he wanted to share with her that he was far from the man she thought him, that he was idle, a philanderer, that he'd never mended a washing machine in his life before he came to her house, and if it hadn't been for her inadequacy, her vulnerability, he wouldn't have offered to do hers; he wanted to tell her how he felt that he had often failed to get home to bath and play with his own children when they'd been young, despite all Helen's continual pleading – nagging, he'd have said at the time – because he had been engaged in building up his career, which he'd thought more important; he wanted to tell her how he hadn't, it seemed, slept for nights; how Helen was in such pain; how he did love Ruth yes, but had lied to her about many things, most importantly about Helen. For if there was one thing he was absolutely clear about after these last days, he was not indeed sure that he had never not been clear about it, it was that he loved Helen too: always had. That she was his wife, had borne him children, had stuck with him, and that he couldn't leave her, cause her that kind of unhappiness, could not build with any success a new happiness on top of that wrench. He wanted to tell Ruth that he'd only been trying to protect her, to nurture her, she who needed these things from a man so much. He hadn't wished to hurt her. He hadn't foreseen – and this is where he would have liked to have her hug him, cheer him, tell him it wasn't quite his fault, quite so utterly black – he hadn't foreseen that it would end like this, that it would be like this.

But he could say none of these things. For Ruth with love's blindness, love's total conviction, could not by now have had her mind on anything further away than endings. And for want of finding a way of even beginning to approach the kind of dialogue that Jeremy, whilst driving to the house that day imagined having, he found himself saying the direct opposite, firing and echoing Ruth's own conviction, so that when she later said he misled her, he deliberately lied to her, when she claimed that he was guilty of a hundred and one crimes of deception in what took place between them that day, Jeremy did not believe her to be entirely unjustified. And so his agony grew. It was a nightmare. He began to find it harder and harder to see a way out. A way to approach her.

And so it was that when sometime after ten she slipped downstairs to put into the oven the smoked haddock Koulibiac and the stuffed vegetables that she had spent all morning preparing, and take the summer pudding out of the fridge (the night before she and Toby had lovingly washed, stoned, prepared each individual redcurrant, blackcurrant, strawberry, raspberry, cherry, blackberry that had gone to make up the rich mélange), telling him, 'Have a snooze before supper, you look tired', Jeremy lay still in the upstairs room in a greater personal turmoil than perhaps he'd ever been in his life. He simply could not face her with what he had to say. So she laid the table and sang to herself and tossed the salad dressing, also made the night before, over the salad, now washed and waiting in the colander.

So Jeremy came down the stairs with a heavy stride.

'You didn't manage to sleep then?' she called.

'No, but I shut my eyes for a few minutes. It was as good as,' he lied. 'Just going out to the car. I've my own contribution,' he told her.

So he closed the front door carefully. With his hand still on the door handle he drew three or four heavy breaths which came rattling up from somewhere deep in his lungs, hurting him. Then he walked to the car, got inside, and drove away. And Ruth inside the house for many more minutes went on singing and preparing the table so that it should be just exactly right.

*

The rest you can guess at, I think, I said to the girl, who was sitting opposite me, her face pale and an expression in her eyes almost as hostile as her mother's had been when I confirmed to her, despite all remonstrations and pleadings and arguments, that I had determined after careful consideration though with much reluctance to assuage Ruth's wish to cut Fisk, Farmer right out of the contract.

A year ago. Almost to the day. And from thence, need I say, the emotional life of Syl and myself has suffered quite considerable – sometimes I wonder if they are quite unconquerable, though I hope not – setbacks. I have always been blessed with clear sight, Josie, I told her, unlike the many muddlers I have been surrounded by. It was as clear as daylight what I had to do. And I have never for a moment felt a twinge of doubt that in the most unfortunate circumstances it was the right decision.

'Why did you tell me all this?' Her North American voice was choked with emotion.

'A little story of human folly.'

Sitting on the carpeted floor as she now was, her long gangling limbs still carrying with them traces, though faint, of adolescent life, folded over one another, leaning on her elbows, fingers crossed in an arc in front of her face, her thumbs, unnervingly close facsimiles of thumbs I have loved, pressed furiously against her lips, she breathed long heaving breaths in and out, in and out, shattering the afternoon calm with their noisiness. They had all the power of a car revving up in the road outside one's bedroom in the early hours of morning, or of the soaring path to climax.

'Damn you, Alison,' she said. 'Geeze! Oh Geeze!'

She was holding her head and rocking from side to side. I wasn't entirely sure whether she was trying to keep in the knowledge I had imparted to her, or to defend herself against more. Or to defend herself against screaming out.

In the role of the story-teller which, for the first time in my life, I had assumed, I had to admit to being faintly piqued that the extremity of Josie's reaction would deprive me, I now foresaw, of recounting to her the last scene. That in Mark Riding's office.

On the following Monday morning Ruth had come to our offices and introduced herself to Mark, who was naturally delighted to meet her.

'I don't want the contract to go through Fisk, Farmer & Tickle,' she said flatly. 'But instead to be directly between your firm and myself.'

'But come, come,' said Mark Riding pleasantly enough, trying to humour her, trying to gain time, to gain clues. 'You're their client. Anyone who has Sylvia Fisk on their side should count themselves lucky indeed. After this last demonstration of her talents I rather think I should go down on bended knees and get her to be my agent, should I ever write a book myself. Which of course is highly unlikely.'

He was rather supercilious, Ruth thought.

'That may be so. But I mean what I say.'

Mark might be new to this particular job but he'd already had much experience of emotional writers over-reacting to minor slights.

'May I ask why?'

'You may, but I have no intention of confiding to you my reasons. Let me just say my decision on this point is final.'

Mark Riding looked at his watch. 'Come on,' he said to her, 'it's such a lovely day; how lucky we're being to have one after another like this. A real Indian summer. Too good to waste in a dark office. Tell you what, let me take you to an early lunch. I was planning to invite you, you've just made it happen all the sooner by popping into the office so unexpectedly. If we leave now we'll beat all those other sods and hopefully be able to find ourselves an outside table at Luigi's; then we can talk over whatever is troubling you, and I'm sure I can help sort it out.'

'No to Luigi, no to any kind of lunch. And very sadly, Mr Riding, there is no possibility at all of you being able to sort out what is troubling me. I've been wounded in such way that nobody, as you put it, can possibly "sort it out". Most especially not a man. And now, before I leave your office do I have it agreed between us that you will draw up a contract which will be directly between your firm and myself? Though that won't help me with my long-term problems it will certainly go some way to relieving my today's worries. Which, incidentally, I appreciate you being concerned about. So then, is it agreed?'

Mark was silent for a moment or two.

'Mr Riding?'

'Take a chair. Don't stay standing like that.'

Ruth remained where she was. Waiting. Mark sighed. He would really have preferred not to cross her.

'It simply wouldn't be technically correct. You know as well as I. A professional writer such as yourself. They are your agents. They have negotiated the contract. We can't just cut them out.'

'Why not if the facts justify it?'

'Whatever the facts. Unless of course they've done something legally criminal. Have they?'

He didn't believe for a moment that they had.

'No.'

'Well you see, if it's just a whim . . .'

'It's far more than a whim.'

'Sorry, can't do it. There is our reputation,' he told her, becoming more supercilious by the moment, she thought. What he actually was becoming was more anxious by the moment, which made him expose his 'all women are idiots' attitude; something which, unless under stress, he tried carefully to cover.

It was the expression on his face as he explained to her about 'their' reputation which drove her resolve to a steel edge.

'I'm not haggling, Mr Riding. Perhaps you think I am. Either I have an assurance from you that the contract will not be handled through Fisk, Farmer, but instead directly with myself, or I take *Wasted* away from your firm and offer it elsewhere.'

'Oh you wouldn't do that. And with the terms you've got!'

Ruth could see that he thought the terms too generous.

'Try me. Besides I know enough to know that terms like that create other similar terms. I might do even better in the long run. It's what you call the beginning of a hype, isn't it? And imagine the publicity.'

Mark could imagine it.

'Don't you think tomorrow you'll have calmed down? Changed your mind?' He was making some effort to sound more con-ciliatory, more pleading.

'I won't have changed my mind in a year's time. Let alone tomorrow. So have I your promise?'

'It really is enormously difficult. It's not a decision I could make by myself.'

'I thought as much. Let me see Alison.'

'No, wait a moment. I'll get back to you tomorrow.'

'Morning, first thing.'

'Morning, first thing. Now are you sure you won't change your mind and have a little lunch?'

'Quite, quite sure.'

But now I should withhold of course this and further denouements; the two elucidating conversations with a distraught Ruth who felt able to open up to me in a way she had not been able to with Mark; those angry conversations with Sylvia, and the long ones with

Jeremy which were of the kind one tries to forget the moment they have taken place. Then there were Syl's many attempts to speak to Ruth on the phone, Ruth each time hanging up, claiming to me that she could not afford to let Sylvia dissuade her from her course, nor could she bear to talk to Sylvia, imagining her proximity to Jeremy. Finally the one-sided phone calls led to letters, their tone became increasingly bitter, increasingly accusatory. Ruth's anger and sense of betrayal swinging into full kelter in which she imagined the wildest things, even finally turning against poor Syl, her old friend. And finally the decision on Syl's part to sue. A course as treacherous as Ruth's own. A course from which I begged her to desist. For though we had taken the contract from Fisk, Farmer I always imagined (and if the two had not been so intractable, surely it would have been so) that a settlement fair to Sylvia would eventually have been reached in the fullness of time.

But Syl by this time was as I had never known her. 'And I regret to say it, Josie' – this I did say directly to the girl – 'showed a single-minded obtuseness which I hope is not a trait you will develop. Nor the same lack of judgement. And so – very sadly, very stupidly – the court case.'

'Maybe where my mother really showed lack of judgement was in ever ever seeing anything in you!' she fired at me, standing up, walking up and down, wrapping her arms tightly around her body as if to wrap herself in.

I admit to being taken back. This I had not anticipated.

'In the story we have together observed,' I told her, 'I see myself essentially as background material.' I was mild. She was Syl's daughter. But it has never suited to be crossed. I do not take to it well.

'How can you talk of human folly?' said she. 'Your folly is by far the greatest.'

I looked at her, with one eyebrow raised, challenging her to proceed, exerting as best I could the control which the years have taught me. I was reduced, however, to grappling with my famed temper and not at all sure that I would be the winner. For two pins I could have cut the girl down to the midget I felt her to be. Satisfying it would have been to wound her with my words. But I hung on.

'Folly,' she said, 'in daring to be a divine narrator, in ever thinking for a moment that just because every one of them talked to you, that you could know – that you could ever imagine, for one tiny moment, how it really was. How could you presume so? Just because you are good with words. And pride yourself, I suppose, in being clear-sighted. Geeze. You literary women. What a trap. Why did I ever think that life here was better than at home in Edmonton?'

'I wonder why you did.'

She continued to look at me in hatred. Her chest heaving in prelude to more emotional words, no doubt.

'Can't you see, can't you for one moment see, you cold English woman, you who think you're so clever, you who reduced everything to nice equations and look at it all so apparently impartially, so unemotionally – even those bits about my mother – can't you see for example that it's *your* world view that goes into the story. It isn't the truth. God, it's as far from the lousy truth as anything could be: it's all poppycock. You don't know Ruth, you don't know Jeremy, I even doubt if you really know my mother. You're shut in your old cold world, analysing, not feeling *ANYTHING*. That's what the trouble is. No doubt the trouble too between my mother and you . . .'

'No, wait a moment, this is going too far . . .'

'I won't wait a moment,' she rushed on. 'You've done enough talking. For a start, Alison, can't you see you're a man hater? Hasn't that much occurred to you? How could you possibly understand Jeremy? He isn't at all what you think. In part, yes. But he's a lot else. Even I can see that because he was a friend to me, and kind, and in life, while you're just on the sidelines. I saw how he wanted to be kind to me just because you two did nothing, and I bet it was the same with Ruth. It isn't just weakness, you know, to be engaged in life. To make some mistakes, very human mistakes after all, but geeze, to be living; isn't that better?'

'I do hope you are not planning as revenge the length of monologue that I have – apparently misguidedly, though with the best of intentions – and at your behest, I might remind you – indulged in. For you'll forgive me if I say that I don't think I could bear its inelegance, its lack of a mere modicum of articulateness: the standard of English in North American universities must be quite as abysmal as I'd always imagined. A haranguing match I will not have.'

'You will not "have" a lot of things,' she cried. 'Isn't that the trouble?'

'No I won't. And you coming here to make trouble I will not have either.'

'That's a bit much after what you've told me.'

'Further trouble. I will not have further trouble, Josie. If your own view of certain aspects of the story does not tie up with my own, then that is your prerogative. I told you when I started talking, you remember, that in the end, finally one must make up one's own mind. And if the attack on your friend Jeremy is more than you can take, then I apologise. Obviously you are fond of him and it is bound to be hard to accept. But you have wanted the truth and I have tried to deliver it to you. Now I think we should talk about it no further. But try to calm down, both of us, before your mother returns. There is, however, one last point I'd advise you to take away and consider with regard to your friend Jeremy. He caused a very considerable amount of pain. A very considerable amount indeed. And is it sufficient to say his mistakes were "very human"? I think not, Josie. Now we will leave it.'

'No, damn it, we won't. Not just yet. Pain, Alison, and what about the pain you caused? To me, to my brothers and sisters –'

'Ah that.'

'Don't toss it off with an "ah that". If I never say anything else to you ever, you're going to hear me now.' She was sobbing and pointing a finger at me, her eyes wild and dilated, her breath still wheezing through her lungs as if any minute it would give out, the volume of her voice unsteadily shifting as she got her words out in bouts. 'And to my mother by being so bloody bloody cold-hearted and lacking in understanding. If she's become as I see her, an unhappy tortured woman, a mask of what she was, then if you love her I reckon you should take some of the responsibility for it, instead of being so damned self-righteous in all of this business – before you ever mention the word pain again. You have caused pain, to my mother and to me, and I hate you, hate you.'

She ran from the room. I did not follow her. For had I done so I could easily have murdered her. Because it was too horrid for me to acknowledge that though overwrought and childish in her attack as she'd been, what she'd said had any kind of truth in it.

Over the following hours of that Sunday evening I tried to put the whole lugubrious business out of my mind. No more was seen or heard of young Josie. However, I felt more than usually fidgety and while I did the wash, the ironing, a modicum of cleaning, the irritating tasks that had become pushed to the tail-end of the weekend owing to the rather exceptional way in which we had spent it, the girl and myself, I rapped myself over the knuckles more than once for having made the decision to share the knowledge I had of the Sylvia/Jeremy affair with young Josie. Who was, I now saw, far far too young for any such revelations. I regretted, too, having opened myself to any form of attack. Though that business about her own pain, that was bound to come up at some time or another. And perhaps best out in the open. Clear the air. But as to the rest, how dare she imply in any way that I have not supported her mother to the utmost? What reasonable person, I ask myself, could possibly have done more?

I was well satisfied that she had retired to her room, and hoped she would stay there until after Syl's return. For I had no desire to spend any further time in her company this evening. Indeed I was rather hoping for some time alone with Syl, time with her alone was something I was conscious of not having had, nor perhaps making any attempt towards having for far too long now.

But as eleven became eleven-thirty, eleven forty-five, I was conscious of a wearisome tiredness – midnight is, I'm afraid, my limit these days. So giving up on the expectation of a chat, I began to prepare for bed. I was anticipating an extremely full day in the office tomorrow, and I could not afford to be working at less than full par. As I got into bed I did just spend a last final moment thinking of Josie; she had been quite unusually quiet for such a noisy person, nor had she left her room to take a bite of food. I hoped she wasn't starving herself on my account.

In bed I experienced a second uncomfortable, more powerful twinge of conscience. She was only young after all, overwrought and a horribly emotional child. One tends to forget or to be too tough on this new brand of outspoken youth. They rather lose out, I think, in having more of an ability, or rather a lack of restraint in wounding their elders in a way we'd have never dreamed of. It makes it harder to remember the depth of their own rawness.

Cursing myself for any kind of soft-heartedness, but she was after all Sylvia's daughter for whom we were each in our own way responsible – and that is something which I have fully decided to put off no longer discussing with Syl – I put on my dressing gown and went to her door. I knocked. I did not expect an answer. But then I did not expect either what I found.

Part IV

ENSEMBLE

JOSIE

After writing the note that evening I grabbed everything, except my 'friends' – nothing for it, I had to leave them behind this time in that dismal place to which I planned never to return. Between the two of them and the agency and good old Sally, bless her English cotton socks, they could rustle up a number of Jiffy bags and send them on, I reckoned. Actually grabbing everything was kind of metaphorical, I guess, but that is what it felt like.

For a time I ran the dusky evening streets, hot, hell so hot like a stove that's been left on by mistake. Hot, worse than the day. Suffocating. The temperature had been climbing steadily since morning. Inside and out. And now it was as if the buildings and those damn hard streets could contain it no longer. An explosion was likely: inside and out.

A pot on steam, I hardly felt the weight of my case. Swinging it from one arm to the other every few blocks, I hurtled down Upper Street, at the Angel turning right into Pentonville. Sunday night. Not as many geezers on the sidewalks as most other days. Most of them moving out of the way pretty quick. I had to put miles between myself and that cold bitch.

By the time I was alongside King's Cross, I was panting, dripping, a regular melted ice. It was the kind of evening when it would be good to be sitting in someone's backyard, ours for choice, yeah, sitting on our old hammock eating Anna's homemade icecream. Don't I just pity these guys who have to live in this city all the time.

Came a time when I knew I couldn't go on running any more. Even walking seemed like not such a hot-shot idea. So I zipped into King's Cross, and down into the Underground. My case was a zinger on the escalator, but we got there in the end. Eventually a train arrived, God knows how patient they are about waiting, these types. I changed somewhere along the line; it was all pretty much a jumble of screaming noises inside my head. I was trying to ask people where to change but not being able to listen to their answers, not able to hear or something, kept grinning foolishly at faces I didn't want to see, I only wanted to see Jeremy, had to get to him somehow, had to find him.

Then I was there finally beloved old Kew Gardens. I was running again, my case banging against my shins and bruising me through my jeans. But it was only, after all, up this road and down that one, only across the main road at the lights and then on beyond the house with the crazy pixies and only one more turning and. Soon. Soon.

The house is in total darkness. He's got to be there. Maybe they're all back the whole familyload of them; maybe they're all taking an early night. It can't be that late, can it really? Maybe, maybe. Oh, hell! If I throw any larger stones I could crack the window. Why isn't he opening up. Jeremy, you've got to be there, Jeremy –

There is no one there at all. The house is in brutal darkness. I can't take it. There has to be some human contact besides Alison, besides that mother of mine who doesn't seem to care a damn. I'm in a state of mind that night that's hard to describe. Like I've never been before. Like I'm about to blow up, blow away. Like the adult world, if this is what I've been trying to enter, is all too painful. Like I want to retreat to my childhood, not to that interim time in Edmonton, but way way back, like when I was a babe in her arms. When she cared. And want to retreat and yet I don't. I don't know what to do. Stuck. Between going forward and back.

My thoughts outside Jeremy's house that night come every which way. Not logical. Like screaming at me. Like who am I? Where is my place in all this? What is real? Nothing seems real. And through it all I keep hanging on to the thought of Jeremy, whose house I am bombarding with stones. Almost now without thinking like someone who leaves the phone ringing because they've forgotten that that is what they are doing, waiting for it to be answered long after there is any hope that it will be. Because they are desperate, or absent-minded. Or both.

I have crazy thoughts. Difficult to remember this bit. Don't even want to much. But crazy thoughts. Way, way, over the top, like – if he's not there inside, if I can't get to him tonight, then all is lost, I'll kill myself because I can't go on.

In my pocket there is the ticket back home. And from time to time all evening I've been fingering it, scuffing its edges, caressing it; no, something stronger, more like mauling it back and forwards. Brutal. It's that kind of a night. Brutal.

Yeah, I could go home, could phone Dad and say that I was on the next plane. No problem. Back to the calm of Edmonton. The prairie, the wide open blue sky, the kids, the crying baby, Dad's perpetual frown, as if he can't understand life, and Anna's laconic warmth. It's all there for me. Could, but I can't. As if I've set myself some kind of a dare. As if I've come here for something and that something, whatever it is, I haven't accomplished. And if I went back now I'd go round the twist. I couldn't live with it. I might as well die if I can't win through here. That's what I felt that night.

Then I threw a larger stone, and a larger. Like I said I hardly noticed what I was doing. And with more force. Haven't had brothers for nothing. It cracked. Geeze, the noise in the stillness of night. Not to worry; all the geezers around here seemed to have gone to sleep hours ago. But how was I going to get up to it? I was a fool. The gutter was too far away and the tree branches from which I might manage went off round the side of the house.

It was then I realised that I was going to break in. Jeremy was asleep, it was just like him and I was going to break in and surprise him. And – I don't know what all else. But, yeah, I was going to break in. The decision instantly gave energy. So I collected a large sharp stone and moved round to the side of the house where the branches of the wistaria reached nearly to his window. Now if I'd been any burglar I'd have tried the downstairs windows. But you couldn't catch me like that. I'd been in the house too many times. I knew about the burglar device on each of the windows. But downstairs only, that was the trick. Like all things to do with Jeremy it was kind of half done. Half done but with charm, I'll always think of that as an English trait.

I climbed cautiously and with attention. Having first left my case hidden behind a tree. There was a bright moon, only a day or two off full. A clear night. A mass of stars. Gradually I heaved my way nearer and nearer the window. Peering in I knew what I'd known all along, that he wasn't there. But I had to get in. I didn't seem to have a choice. Something would occur to me when I was inside.

It wasn't hard to prise the pane of glass out and then open the window. In a jiffy I was inside, mentally promising Jeremy that I would replace the pane, and that other cracked window, somehow. Tomorrow.

I called his name, Jeremy Jeremy, like a kid, like a child tucked up in bed for the night, who doesn't like the dark and calls for his mother but without any hope of her coming. That kind of a sound. Like a bleat. And with the part of me I could hear myself doing it, almost laughing at myself (but I couldn't quite get that distance) yet with the other part dead earnest. 'Jeremy, Jeremy. Jeremy.' It was useless.

It smelt of him though, all the house had his brand of kind, musty smell and eventually I went back to his bedroom and lay down on his bed, burrowing my face in the smell of his pillows and cried.

'Jeremy,' I cried, 'Jeremy.' And then after a bit I was that child again, after Sylvia had gone, those terrible days when Dad wouldn't talk about it but Anna told us that Sylvia was never coming back. That she'd done something awful, too awful for Daddy to talk about with us, because it hurt him so greatly. And I couldn't believe that she'd done something awful, only that I'd lost her. That she'd left us, that we hadn't been good enough, maybe I shouldn't have been so bad when the new baby was born. And now she'd left us and would never come back. 'Mummy,' I started crying, 'Mummy.' And the tears were an anguish that seemed to have no ceasing.

SYLVIA

Three momentous moments in my life; when Timmy died, the meeting with Alison and tonight, my arrival at the flat, Alison's distraught face and Josie's letter. All my life I've listened to other people talking, I've been a person that other people talked to and while they talked to me they looked at me. It was as simple as that. Perhaps I've never had much to say; though I'm not sure. It was for the most part as if my looks said it for me. They were me. And in my family it was the men who talked.

My mother was a reticent woman. Tall and unusually upright for our race. Statuesque, as if she always rose above the humdrum and the hurly burly. She was intelligent, she was discreet; she had an excellent mind, which those close to her enjoyed, though those not so close knew nothing of. She was not one to sport her talents. She had no need to. Mostly her intense good judgement and quiet wisdom were known in the community through people's presumptions. For it was obvious in the community that my father, who was much about, who was a charismatic figure himself and a leader of men, looked always to my mother. And people knowing him, respecting him, assumed that if he looked to her there must be a reason.

My mother had no need to do more with her talents. She was of the opinion that the way men excelled was different from the way women did. And I, though living in an age where other of my contemporaries were pushing eagerly into avenues where women had never trod before, for some long while took on my mother's mantle, not out of intellectual conviction but because it was the easiest thing to do.

My childhood was blessed with happiness. A quiet easy contentment in our family. We were without troubles financial or emotional, we were leaders of the community, my parents enjoyed a private relationship of exceptional closeness and that seemed to be echoed in the relationship between Timmy and myself. Edward was the odd one out. From the start an eccentric, a loner. But this was of little consequence. We were really two close-knit couples, each communicating almost without words. Or rather the men communicating, the women understanding and responding as if by osmosis. So we were ready for an eccentric and welcomed him easily. A great pet of all of ours was my brother. A great pet for me.

Positioned then between older and younger brother, with agreeable parents giving security but leaving us much to our own devices, just as long as those fitted with their wishes, there was little to complain and be unhappy about for any one of us three. Unless one was a complainer or unhappy by nature. Which none of us seemed to be.

My peers envied us. Many of my girlfriends, as I grew to adolescence, fell in love with Timmy. And Timmy's friends had no difficulty in incorporating me into their arrangements and activities. It was almost as if I didn't have to lift a finger for life to be exceptionally agreeable. As if all of life was one warm afternoon, drifting up the Ouse.

Like all those with happy childhoods, I had no thought that it would ever come to an end. Blessed, one tends to believe that it will always be so. Observing that it is not necessarily the same for others, one puts it down to the particular circumstances of their lot.

I was not even especially grateful for my happiness. Until afterwards, I never even termed it such. But no doubt deeply embedded in this happiness were the seeds of what was to follow. Not Timmy's death, but my dependence on him, the shape and structure of our family, liberal yet taut like the tightest elastic, certain unspoken codes and morality unyielding in my parents, which made for each of the events that affected their children's life: Timmy's death, my sexual deviance and Edward's escape to California and marriage to a half-Indian girl, a certain rigidity, an inability, unlike some others perhaps less fortunate to start with, to cope. Gradually they tunnelled themselves in; making of all our fates an abiding tragedy.

It was as if those five energies harmoniously bound together found no way of reconstructing after Timmy. From almost the moment I came out of hospital and returned home, they and I seemed to be locked in battle. A battle at first without shape, without name.

My early twenties were marked by jabs of extreme behaviour, a belated adolescent rebellion, a dance, or more of a bullfight, in the face of death.

A silent, cold hostility hung in the home air between my parents and myself. The old sense of being blessed gave way to anger at the kind of pressure they were exerting, as well as their lack of understanding of that person who was me; the cry no doubt of every young person down the ages. The gulf became visible only now; for so long, for always, since my earliest days, it had been buffeted by Timmy's close understanding.

Timmy's death, in their view, left the course of my being the good daughter, with all that entailed, all the more imperative. Such was to be the mainstay of their attempts at consolation. But then I began to resist. I was young, perhaps it was in essence as simple as that. I wanted to live through grief, they were old, ready to embrace it.

So the atmosphere of the house changed. And in the period when I lived back at home before my sojourn in Europe, and in the intervals when I returned on holiday, the house was a cold difficult place.

Edward was young too, fighting his own battles. He was still at school. Fond as he was of his older brother, he was the least affected by acute personal loss. He was in a particularly egocentric phase, heavily engaged in his own interests and life, and minded perhaps most that the cataclysmic effect on his family meant that they were no longer interested to share such with him, at a stage which, with hindsight, I see was of fundamental importance to him.

And in this he felt understandably, and I now see that I let him down. Left without Timmy – extraordinary that it has taken me all these years, till tonight, to see some of these things – we let each other down. I Edward in that when he brought home to me his news, his ideas, I had little heart, I was less there for him, less able to listen, to support, to share; less an eager mate, an encouraging older sister than he wanted, no doubt needed. Certainly had habitually expected and had been up to that point a mainstay of his childhood, just as Timmy's interest was to me. Such the links, now the one breakage giving way to the other.

And as if this wasn't enough for poor Edward to cope with, my behaviour, a certain pushing of the boundaries of what was socially acceptable for a nice Jewish girl, a desire for new freedoms, compounded or rather deflected some part of my parents' pain into a series of skirmishes with me, each increasingly more damaging. So that the atmosphere Edward came home to was not just one of grief, but of the three remainers locked in battle. No one of us noticing nor quite having sufficient time for him.

He responded to this by an anger with me, a desire that I would toe the line, behave as my parents wished, marry Tony, cause no trouble, be the acquiescing girl. In this he sided with my parents and against me. And the sweetness that was between us, tagged as it were to the tail-end of Timmy and my closeness, was no more; each feeling let down by the other.

Edward, after school, left England for the United States. He took his first degree at Harvard, did his graduate studies at M.I.T. and now is a full Professor of Bio-Engineering at the University of California. His visits home were at first infrequent and then eventually petered out altogether. His marriage to a girl with Red Indian blood was the final straw.

He has not wanted to see me since I left Patrick for Alison. And since Patrick took the children to Canada I doubt there is contact between them and their uncle, although I'm not sure. Something I might have asked Josie.

It is the waiting for morning that is surely the worst.

241

I wonder now if it has been my lack of willingness to expose myself, lack of ability to see myself in the talking role, that has made each of these crises so cataclysmically difficult to cope with. Had I had another nature would I, I wonder, have been forced out early, so to speak, to communicate, to stretch out into the difficult, depressing waters of our different understandings and made small stabs. Instead, communicating as I did through all the years of my childhood with Timmy, there was no need for anything else, but to listen, to smile, to be easy, the level on which Timmy heard me was sufficient. I had no sense of what others must normally feel from the day they are born: an aloneness with which they wrestle, accepting the knocks, the dissatisfaction.

Perhaps had Timmy lived, I would have remained married to Patrick, who knows, for my role with men would always have been of a certain kind. I would have been happy perhaps to smile and grace; there is no doubt all that gave me pleasure. Being assured of the other. What it would have done to dear Timmy, God knows, but that is a problem that we were just beginning to wrestle with in the intimate exchanges of the long sweet afternoons we spent together in his rooms at Oxford, and was something that was cut off, along with everything else, before it ever became a serious issue.

Had I spent the first twenty years of my life striving towards communication with an outside world, I might have been more adept at it by the time communication became essential.

But cut off from Timmy, there seemed to me nothing else. An outward show of pretty dresses and fashionable make-up and hairdos. The outside being a creation, the inside nothing. Tony, my parents, Edward, all hardly touched me. I seemed to make the motions, of acquiescent girlfriend, of hostile daughter, of impatient, sorrowing older sister. So great was the change between what had gone before and what was then, I hardly knew myself. I was flashes of things, of colour, of sensuality, of developing womanhood. But nothing was sustained, nothing consistent. All was confusion as I tried to shut out the flooding pain and anger that he had been taken from me.

Other girlfriends played a sketchy part in my life. At Varndale I was part of a loosely connected group of girls, with a close ally and humble admirer, Tabitha, with her freckles and her two scruffy ginger plaits. No one tied a messier plait than she, Tabitha, who remained glued to my side from the day I first entered the school at ten to the day we left at eighteen.

We were an oddly assorted couple but content enough. Though

our friendship remained strictly within the bounds of school. For she was a Quaker and outside the school grounds my social life was very much within the Jewish community.

I enjoyed school. But when I began to be too eagerly interested in a topic, my father would caution, 'Careful, we don't want you to become a blue-stocking now, do we?' So that the edge of intellectual excitement was over and over again cut away. In such a way I think that I hardly noticed it, agreeing that no doubt they were right. An intelligent wife, married to one of the leaders of the community, doing her bit in social work and the like, admired and looked up to in her role as wife and mother, that is what was wanted.

It seemed a not disagreeable prospect. Much a continuation of what was then, just so long as there was Timmy to make my private life glow. In my early teens a prospective husband was chosen, in the shape of Tony. Our families knew each other well. I could see even then that within our community one could do no better if my parents' values in this matter were to be handed on to me. And so it seemed settled.

It would be an untruth to say that I didn't enjoy the flowers on Valentine's day, the chocolates, the attentions, the always having someone to ask to the school dance. I did. And no doubt it increased my sense so that it was absolutely taken for granted that I was someone to be admired. I wasn't surprised when in my last year at Varndale I became headgirl and starred in the school play (I had modest acting ability, but sad to say my looks went a long way). Of course my parents were delighted. There, on the first night, parents flanked by Timmy, Tony, Tony's sister Gillian and other well-wishers took up, to a mixture of my chagrin and delight, the entire front row. Afterwards Tabitha, bless her heart, presented me in the dark maze of corridors behind the stage with a rather squashed bunch of roses – I've always loved roses. Reminding me now, as they always will, of our family garden and my father, with me often hanging on his arm, in the early morning when the dew was still on the flowers, helping him choose the perfect one to wear in his button-hole for work.

So much admiration demanded a certain humility. Sometimes other girls complained that it didn't seem fair that I had so much, and I thought it true. But assumed that given what I had (of everything I valued most my family, of whom I was inordinately proud), I should grace it as fittingly as I could. And be generous to everyone who had less. Such my resolve. Such the slant of my relationship with Tabitha.

I had no sense in those days of the nature of my sexuality. I would say that I had none. As if it was on ice. Unlike Alison who tells me that she was rabidly sexual at this early point in her life.

Now, looking back, I see that it was my brother who drew me. As we learnt to dance in our stumbling ballroom class and later taught ourselves to jive in the summer-house – I felt it immeasurably easier, more natural with him than with others. There was a way our limbs seemed to fit together. But I was not aware of problems; I'm not sure how early he was.

Until his Oxford days this went unspoken between us. Even then it was only he who stated his position, having no urge to draw me out or to unruffle the smooth waters of our affection.

So yes, I loved to dance with Timmy, to row side by side, to ride our horses across the crest of the Downs, to lark in the sea, to urge each other to all manner of dares. But it went no further.

Tony was older, not good-looking, but of sterling worth. It was understandable, he told me, for me to feel a certain modesty. But he had time on his side, lots of it, and meanwhile he would lay siege to my heart. Girls, particularly Jewish girls from good families, he assured me, take longer to come to these things than boys. Well he should know, I thought. So be it.

It was only after Timmy's death that I knew I could not make the adjustment to Tony, or not the whole-hearted one that he required. But then the muddles set in. And the confusion. So much grief; how to tell one thing from another.

Tony had the theory that my grief, only natural in a loving nature, coloured all. But that time would change that. I was beginning to doubt it.

Who to turn to, who to ask about the frightening feelings I was experiencing? 'He was only a brother,' both Tony, and later Patrick, would say in their different ways. My parents too were anxious lest I should become a grass widow for Timmy. How much less acceptable than a blue-stocking. 'Marry Tony,' they urged, 'have your own children, your own little Timmy.' I felt it to be the ultimate in disloyalty.

I was sent abroad to do an international secretarial course in Geneva. And from there I moved to Paris where I lost my virginity to the director of an art magazine for whom I worked. 'You're beautiful but a cold fish, Sylvia,' he said. And I wondered.

Then Patrick who had been in the car at the time, with Timmy, started visiting me. The craziness of his love, the valiant all-night rides on his motor-bike from London to Paris, the urgency of his mission, to be a brilliant doctor, to save people, create less pain, all attracted my imagination. Possibly as his helpmate it might be as if I was doing something in memory of Timmy. Maybe it would give point and shape.

We slept together in his seedy hotel bed. Sex was bad. He was skinny and exhausted. Up many nights studying and then these long journeys. But was sex so important? One of the world's more recent myths, he thought. He had other priorities. Which in some ways let me off the hook more than with Tony. Meanwhile my parents fumed and raged and insisted that I come home. Something had to be done. I was in limbo but I couldn't return to my parents' home for long. Something had to be decided.

And yet. I knew that I was in a state of turmoil. But who was there to talk to? My parents were quite written off. Edward was out of the question, and anyway too young, and far too wrapped up in himself. My girlfriends, Tabitha and co., I had left behind at the school gates, their lives seeming to have taken such different directions from my own.

Eventually I thought of Jeremy, cherishing the childishly mystical belief that because of their closeness a bit of Timmy would be there in any communication I might have with his friend. I mentioned the desire to get in touch with him to my mother. She seemed, at first, as in almost all remarks I made at that time, unhelpfully tight-lipped. But the following week surprised me by suggesting that I invite him down to stay.

I was cheerier than for a long time in the days before his visit. Having impossibly high hopes. Of what? Of something that had gone out of life so completely with Timmy's death, the simplest thing in all the world, so that when you have it it never seems a gift: a free and easy communication.

Jeremy's visit was not that. In many ways it was a disappointment, leading me to acknowledge that I had expected too much. But I did feel able to express some part of my confusion; and God knows how little I knew of what was happening inside. The day by the sea with Jeremy, though he'll never know it, was the best I'd spent in the months, years, since the crash. It gave me not peace but the glimmering of hope; it gave me courage too.

Subsequently I threw myself into marriage and motherhood.

Meeting Alison I still find hard to talk about. It was as if a door I'd assumed closed for ever, re-opened. And this time and in a different context, by daring to flout convention and take greedily to myself the full nature of the pleasures offered, I experienced for the first and only time in my life a full sustaining love. Strange, but not wholly inappropriate, to say that Timmy was the forerunner to Alison.

But inevitably there came choices, decisions. And like all fools I thought I could have it all. I imagined that in the end I would not need to compromise, somehow if I stuck out I'd have my children too. Jeremy warned me otherwise, and Helen too, and others. My parents were urgent in their pleadings; not without a certain foresight that I was blind to. The bond between Timmy and me had given me a taste of what I would call a divine state of closeness and now, in the full flood of my life, finding Alison I could not let go. I needed therefore to believe, no doubt, that all would come my way in the end.

At this second juncture again there was a difficulty in expressing myself, except to Alison who was, naturally enough, wholeheartedly and persuasively convinced of the rightness of our action. But outside Alison . . . To Patrick I was an enigma. No, he couldn't understand, couldn't believe that I would . . . and so on. He was angry and very hurt. With my parents it was the same. And after a few stabs at communication I retreated, creating a rift that has never been bridged: 'their final shame', I think they called it.

It was to Jeremy again that I turned. I could not hear his warnings vis-à-vis the children. He could not hear the root of my need, nor understand the nature of my sexual choice. But in that he made more of a brave stab at understanding than anyone else I knew, out of a friendship that stemmed from some now almost forgotten, mythically happy time in the days of the summer-house in the rose garden, I treasured him and felt bound to him and Helen in a friendship which I felt sure nothing could break. Nothing. After Timmy there had to be some things one could hold on to. Alison, Jeremy.

The period after my defection to Alison was sparked by letters to and fro. Patrick, Alison, his solicitors, mine. I lived in hope and on the crest of a wave. It was Alison, I believe, who saw before I that I would not win. Alison with her terrible realism took perhaps six months after my defection to analyse the situation, whereas I hung on with hope for a good few years.

Meanwhile I started to work and a new life opened out. The full and pleasurable communication between Alison and myself, the intellectual stimulus that had been far from the reality of marriage with Patrick, the liberation of sexual needs and hungers I had not known I had. It seemed to me that my body was coming into its own, that it had been made as it was for a purpose more than to be looked at and admired. It was a body to be used, and changed dramatically under Alison's eager and experienced tutorage.

At night I heard the children's cries, but kept this to myself. And kept up too, increasingly by a furious willpower that mocked reality, the belief that eventually by making a stable home with Alison and showing that I could support myself economically, and the children too if it came to it, that Patrick would be persuaded to return them. The children had had all my time, a fraction of his – the hospital taking perhaps eleven-twelfths of his commitment. To him the children were for hugging on Sundays. He hardly remembered a name or a birthdate. Not that within that frame he wasn't devoted. But I could not seriously imagine that that being the case he would deem it right, or society would, to leave them with him rather than with me.

It was not to be. I think it was during the period when Gideon Tickle had his breakdown that I finally came to realise it was not to be; that even my letters to them were being withheld. Alison urged me to consider taking over the agency in my own right. Hoping and imagining, as do we all no doubt, that one's own recipe for happiness will mirror one's loved ones' – the sum total of absorbing work and a good relationship would block out those other cravings.

Make your bed and lie on it, my parents had said. There was nothing else for it.

Life in the decade that followed brought its share of pleasures. As long as I didn't mention the children or, to a lesser extent, Jeremy, life between Alison and me was contented enough, even at times actively, gloriously happy. And the price I tried to grapple with and put behind me.

For a time, indeed, it seemed almost as if I had done so. The agency began to take off in a big way. And I enjoyed the success that it brought, also the sense of partnership with Alison in our joint yet divergent literary endeavours.

Jeremy's coming into the agency was a decision I made myself. Alison was fiercely opposed but would not stand in my way. Being by nature a sharer, a person who needs to be in partnership, I thought this a solution to Jeremy's lack of a job and the future of the agency. I was mindful, too, of how many favours I owed him. At last I was in a position to offer one. Again Alison's sense of reality showed her part at least of the truth whilst my romanticism shrouded me in the ignorance that I required.

And so the years up to Ruth. The move into the flat; becoming more open about our life, at last, when I felt we were established, fortified, successful enough to brave it. But not so. Society's bitterness and repulsion. And on top of that Ruth. Alison in the last analysis letting me down. And into all this the cry of why? why? What is it all for, what have I built to replace what I gave up? The dreams, the early morning wakings, the pills, the pains.

I wanted to put Josie off coming. Indeed I tried on many occasions. Of all times that she should want to come now, when I have nothing to offer, when I am in too much confusion myself to try to help her to understand what has happened in any way that is positive and will be a help. Surely, Oh God, I thought, haven't you given me enough. Let me just fight the court case, keep my marbles, perhaps effect some kind of peace with Alison instead of this separation and hostility. Let me get over the next few years, hopefully into a happier state and then, then I will see my daughter, we will talk. But not now, not now.

But it wasn't to be. Josie's drive reminding me of other members of the family, my brothers, my parents. All these energies that are more powerful than my own. Or perhaps it was that youth wouldn't wait. She had to come now. Now. And so she did.

But I couldn't – I couldn't. And now. And now. Oh God, don't let anything have happened to her, oh God, give me a chance. Despite all the transgressions in my life, the selfishnesses, the what you will, God, if there is a God, you who took Timmy away when he was so young, before his time, give me a chance this time. Don't let anything happen to Josie tonight.

It is the waiting till morning that is the worst.

JOSIE

I thought of her, as she was now, so tied up in her own world, so cold to me, so distant. As if angry with me for being here, imposing. As if she really had left us, as if she'd wanted to leave us. Even as if she didn't like me. And I felt dissolved, as if I wasn't a person, as if I was a river of water with no containment. And the anguish was too unbearable. I wanted to die. Let me die, I thought, I'm not a person, I can never be a real person. Let me die.

But the hours of the night went on and on and somehow I didn't die. I was still there as the first rays of dawn light lit up the sky in the uncurtained bedroom, still there, still with my pain, but still with all of myself, unresolved, real. I put my hands to my sides and started to feel my body. And felt even a slight comfort from its new shape, its slimmer hips, its firm bust. I was all here: Josie. And I thought for a moment what Jeremy had said about my body and smiled.

Then I thought of Sylvia who hadn't even noticed the change that had come over me. Hadn't noticed nothing. Didn't want to know. And I said to her, through the sheets, with clenched teeth, 'You've damaged my life, you know. You're hateful. Not a nice person at all. Dad's right. He is nice, but you are hateful, selfish, hateful.' And I said to her, shocked at the force of my own venom, I, who because she had not been there always held her in some kind of awe, 'You are just a very ordinary woman after all, and a cold one and I hate you. I hate you, do you hear? Hate, hate.'

I was shocked at myself. It seemed, how to explain, a sacrilege to hate Sylvia. Hate was what one felt for those things which were accessible, everyday. Hate suggests some knowledge. Sometimes I'd hated my brothers and sisters when they were a particular pain. I hated Anna the day she said that thing. When I saw Dad's sad face I hated that. But I'd never hated Sylvia because she was sacrosanct. Sylvia untouchable, fragile, other. And now here I was hating her just like all the others.

I waited in the silence of the room wondering if anything would happen to me. Would lightning come in through the open window and strike me down? Nothing.

So I got up and went downstairs, not turning on lights because it was lovely in the pink mauve dawn colours, lovely to see the freshly painted kitchen that Jeremy and I had done with our own hands. I cut myself a thick chunk of bread and rummaged in the larder to see if there was any cocoa or chocolate.

I turned the radio on, that programme tailor-made for insomniacs, and hugged myself, even danced a few steps round the kitchen table in my crumpled jeans and shirt. Must have looked a sight, but who cared.

I felt like – well, I hated her and that's that. I'm still here. She can't diminish me. She can't ruin my life. I won't let her. I've still got it. All of it. I'm Josie and I am something to do with her, and something to do with Dad, and something even in a way to do with Anna. But also to do with none of them. I'm myself.

When Jeremy and when Alison had been talking it occurred to me, all the time it had been growing on me, that it had nothing to do with me. All her life, almost, seemed to have nothing to do with me.

That was the most painful. Though I never let on. Not till the end when I couldn't take it any more. And now I thought, who cares, that's their business. Sod them. Leave them to it. And then I thought maybe I will go back, maybe I will go back home, and I danced some more.

After I'd eaten, I snooped around the house, picking up letters, rifling in books. Just idle like, just curiosity, just getting the feel of Jeremy's house without Jeremy in it. I wasn't looking for anything exactly.

I liked the house, I'd have liked to have met Helen and Jeremy's children. I liked the mess in their rooms, the crazy stuff on the pinboards. I liked the dried ferns and litter of books everywhere and all those old newspapers and old worn cushions and old worn chairs that are comfortable to sit in. And the Jeremy smell.

I stuck in the sitting room, stopped my roaming and curled up in the large armchair by the fireplace with my legs tucked under me. It was still very early. My watch was upstairs but I guessed it to be about six. I wondered about Jeremy. I wished he'd just come breezing in from wherever he was. But less desperately than last night. You and me are chums, Jeremy, I said to myself. 'You don't owe me anything.' I hoped he'd get back with Helen. He should be married, a man like that. Also a man like Dad. And for his children I hoped so too. Maybe he was sorting it out with Helen right now. I thought about that Ruth stuff. I didn't want to feel jealous, I didn't want to believe it all. I tried to put it out of my mind. Probably she'd just been screwy and he'd just been kind like he'd been to me. And Alison made all the rest up to tell me a good story – no doubt to put me off men for ever. Send me her way. Wouldn't be surprised.

Well, I wouldn't be sent her way, sod that for a laugh. That was one thing I had learnt anyway since I'd come to England. Worth coming for. Jeremy, you taught me that. And I had to persuade you, didn't I, you never really wanted to.

You were really very decent. It's just that the way you went was kind of odd and hurtful. Like I didn't count, didn't count to anyone. But no doubt you couldn't help it. I would have liked to talk to you again, just once before I go. Because you are a friend. But I could always write to you, I suppose, or leave you a note.

I went back to the kitchen to cut myself another slice of bread. All this thinking does sure make you hungry.

Then the phone went.

I let it ring for a long time. I shouldn't be here. Should I be answering? And yet it went on and on. Had a kind of urgency to it.

Or was that just how it sounded to me? Sod it, I couldn't let it go on ringing. It sounded to me like me, last night, throwing the stones at the window.

'Hello, hello.'

There was a clicking sound. Then the line went dead. Bugger it all. Who would be phoning them at this time in the morning?

The phone call made me feel jumpy again. But geeze, wasn't it going to be another sizzler of a day! You could feel it in the air already. My shirt was beginning to stick to my ribs. I rolled up the sleeves to the elbow. I'd like to wash my face and brush my hair. I tried to locate in my mind what had happened to my case, then remembered that it was still under that tree in the garden. I opened the back door and raced round to the side. It was still there, looking battered and trustworthy. I heaved it inside. Felt better with cold water on my face.

Some decisions were being called for. To it, Josie. Is it to be London airport and heave onto the next plane home? Somehow I didn't think so. Not quite yet. Not quite this moment.

Monday morning, phew, what a corker of a day it was going to be. Not a day to be on a plane. A day to be by the sea.

Then an idea seemed to be coming to me. Slowly. From a long distance, a sort of shape forming in front of my eyes. Something I could do.

SYLVIA

That night I was awake till near on five. Waiting waiting for time to pass till I could legitimately phone anybody. Long after the dawn chorus had played a far too jubilant tune, and when I was past hoping or even desiring any such thing, sleep eventually came my way.

I woke to the sound of a tea-tray rattling and Alison's presence somewhere near my right shoulder.

'God, you startled me. What time is it?'

'Seven-thirty. Thought you might welcome a cup of tea. Don't expect you slept much.'

'So right. Thanks, Alison.'

She sat down on the bed. The months of our physical estrangement charging the air. Why be churlish and keep up this warfare? I needed Alison as never before. I put out my hand to her.

'Help me through this.'

Whether I moved first or she stretched out her arms to me I'm not sure.

'Your daughter told me I was an obstinate and blind old fool – or words to that effect. She could be right.'

'Did she indeed.'

Our embrace was like stream water after a drought.

I clung to her. 'I'm so anxious, Alison.'

'Yes, yes. First drink your tea.' She pushed it towards me.

'She's most likely to be with Jeremy, I suppose, if what you tell me is correct. Though I can still hardly believe it. I thought about eight would be the earliest –'

'Otherwise the police –'

'She is nineteen. Have you any idea about how much money she had on her?'

'None at all. Of course she might have flown home. She did have an open ticket, didn't she?'

'Then Patrick would know. Perhaps one should contact him. But if she hasn't one doesn't want to throw him into an unnecessary panic. Oh God, she wouldn't have done something silly, do you think?'

'No, of course not.'

'How wrought-up do you say she was?'

'Really, terribly hard to judge.'

We looked at one another. There were things that neither of us could say. Yet. Finally, glumly:

'I think I'll get dressed.'

And then at the door:

'For my part –'

'Don't say it, darling. No need.'

At the kitchen table, waiting for the minute hand to arrive at eight, we went on discussing possibilities. Jeremy first. Then perhaps the police. Though she was nineteen. Independent. No fool either. And if she was somewhere with Jeremy – though I really couldn't believe it – one would want to handle it with care. One doesn't want to make things worse. Drive them to one another, I've seen that happen before. And then there's Helen to consider. I do think, I keep coming back to it, that for the moment one should give Josie the benefit of the doubt. Which it seems to me my parents weren't able to do. We must go carefully, cautiously, step by step, I tell Alison.

On the other hand, it is of course vital to find out that she is all right, not in any kind of trouble, not about to . . . 'You don't think she is pregnant, do you? It is so difficult to tell anything from that note.' And so we mulled.

It was settled that at eight (now five to) I would phone Jeremy and depending on that, decide on the next move, if she were nowhere near him, which I suspected. Here I thought Alison was jumping to conclusions. It seemed she thought there was nothing he would stop at, even with my daughter. I did find that hard to believe. The thing with Ruth was very very silly of him, quite irresponsible, but he did fall deeply in love. Josie, Timmy's niece, no I can't quite – I'm surprised that he even looked at her, but Alison convinces that they were more friendly than I'd assumed. My own blindness, these last months, so bound up. One cannot blame the pills, one should not blame the pills. But all the same I do not think I will take any more.

If Jeremy knows nothing then perhaps I should speak to Patrick, though I dread it. After all this time. But Alison thinks. And one must be responsible. He is her father. And if anything *should* happen.

Josie, I hardly know you. So I cannot imagine where you are, what you are thinking. Only I'm trying to send out messages to you. Don't do it. Don't do anything wild or silly. Life is painful but it is sweet too. You've had a great deal of pain, I know, in your young life, but in time – And perhaps I could help. I'd like to try. Wherever you are, wherever you are, wait. Don't.

*

At three minutes to eight, whilst in Islington Alison and Sylvia were waiting at the scrubbed pine kitchen table for the minute hand of the clock to move onto the hour – such their belief over what seemed a lifetime of working together but was in fact only a decade, that precision meant order – Helen, in olive green candlewick dressing-gown, despite it being August, her once glossy black hair (her only good feature, she had claimed to Jeremy all those years ago on the Isle of Wight when he, charmer always, had said, 'You're such an attractive girl only you don't have a high enough opinion of

253

yourself: we must change all that') now turned prematurely to a thatch of grey, pulling the wrap close around her for it was cold despite the outside temperature, entered the stone-lagged barn of a kitchen of her parents' Dorset house.

Both were elderly now, both were frail. They had had her when they were pulling well on into middle age. An only child, she had brought pleasure and been dutiful. But now on top of other burdens the burden of their joint responsibilities rested on her shoulders. An only child herself she had wanted to spawn a large family. She often wondered if by doing so she had set the marriage on its downward path, becoming, in the course, too obsessional, developing traits that were hard later to throw off. Sending Jeremy perhaps more out into the world for his fun than would have otherwise been the case.

And yet and yet.

When she and Jeremy were at the stage that her parents were at now, their children would not have to shoulder this thing alone. Whether she and Jeremy were together or not, the children would have each other, to telephone, to worry with, to share out duties. She had enjoyed their upbringing. Soon, when the twins were also at university, the house would seem sorrowfully empty. The house, or wherever it was she would be. She was dreading it.

In bare feet, despite the ouch of the cold as the soles of her feet made contact with the stone floor (she rather liked it, it suited her mood, grim survival), she made her way to the Aga to heat up more coffee. It was to be her second breakfast that morning.

In the morning room, small, sun-trapped, taken over by lemon-scented geraniums that saw no sense in not growing in every direction available to them, Jeremy, nursing painful feet, waited.

He was desperate. What more could he do, he wondered, against the bulk of Helen's rejection? Last Sunday he had driven through the night, exhausted, exhausted with talking to Josie. Driven through the night determined somehow to break through his wife's impassiveness as always he had in the past. For what after all was love, what after all was twenty years of being vulnerable to one another, twenty years of crying out to one another at the moment of ejaculation or orgasm, if it could all be thrown to the winds like this. Was it all so tenuous, Jeremy wondered, all of life? Even someone like Helen, a bulwark, until this morning, or should one say, until the night they had both just come through. A night worse even than that prior to his breaking off last year of the affair with Ruth. A night such as a man could only afford to live through once in a lifetime, and preferably not that. At the back of his mind, behind logic, behind questions, he had believed that he could win her back. But now, finally, he wasn't so sure.

Last Sunday driving long hours through the night. Both ways. For, yes, she had shut the door to him, hissed, 'You are not welcome here, Jeremy. Go *away*. I'm so upset as it is and can't afford to make things worse. There are my parents to consider.'

'But making me drive back through the night. Doesn't that seem ridiculous?'

'It was ridiculous to come,' she hissed. And shut the door.

Driving back, half asleep, driving like crazy, making the eleven-year-old Vauxhall rattle till its engine seemed to be groaning 'can't, can't go faster', the window open despite the night air, or because of it, the window open to ward off sleep, the damn radio on the blink again, so nothing even to listen to to distract the mind, despite his fury, his impotence, his having the door shut on him by his own wife, when inside his children slept soundly (he hoped: how else would their mother explain *that* little incident to them in the morning?), despite his grim mood and slack grey jowl, by the time – near on six a.m. – he'd reached the house in Kew, he nevertheless did not feel what he felt now, as he sat and watched the swaying leaves of the lemon-scented geranium.

The plant was far too prolific. He had an urge to find nail-scissors and chop it back. He half thought he would; then changed his mind. Perhaps later, sustained by coffee. What he experienced now was quite different from what he had felt a week ago, despite the night drive and the hissing Helen. Then he was angry, thrusting for what he would next do. Not knowing, helpless, but only, he had been sure, temporarily. Something would come to him, in time. It always had. But now, only eight days later, this horribly hot Monday morning, he felt something quite different. Despair. Cold real despair.

So Jeremy sat waiting for his wife to bring coffee, staring at the geranium, reflected on the state of his affairs and found them grossly unsatisfactory.

The twins were away this weekend camping on Dartmoor. (And a good thing that had been.) Alice in Scotland. His parents-in-law still in bed. It was just he and she.

He tried to work it out, how it had come to this. But found the going hard. That terrible business with Ruth. Of course it had got quite out of hand. Had grabbed him by the throat. But on the whole, over the sum of years hadn't he been as good a husband and father as most?

Last year, yes, was particularly messy. Not a year to be repeated. But since then? He had given up Ruth only to find that Helen had replaced their twenty-year-old bed (a good one, present from the parents-in-law). And yes, it had needed replacing. They'd been talking about it on and off for the last couple of years; though it was far from top of their list of priorities. Still, twenty years is a fair life for a bed, a fair – what would be the equivalent of 'shelf life'? – floor life. The mattress, like them, no doubt, had grown soft to the point of slackness and no longer supported. In the mornings his spine would creak and groan. And many times he would say to her tetchily, 'We ought to change the damn bed; we could do with something firmer.'

But not what he had expected. Two singles. Pushed together, but two singles nevertheless. 'I don't want to make any kind of public statement about it,' she'd said, 'nothing the children will see and be bothered about. But frankly, that's the end as far as I'm concerned. You've lied to me once too often, Jeremy.'

That was of course after the opening of the court case, the details of which, all the grizzly letters back and forth, all the accusations Jeremy, it seemed, was powerless to keep from his wife. Gradually as the story became clearer, Ruth's story, Ruth's grievances, Helen could see – it would not, she acknowledged to herself, have taken a very clever person to see – how far, at one time at least, her husband had betrayed her to his mistress. 'In the height of his passion,' defended Jeremy, 'wasn't that to be forgiven?' But that he had said, so Ruth claimed, that he had not slept with his wife for ten years, this Helen could not forgive. 'Let's make it true then. Single beds. I never wish to sleep with you again. Or rather, it isn't a matter of wishing, I feel too hurt, Jeremy.' He hardly had the desire, or energy to fight her.

That was the beginning of a gloomy year. The two of them trapped together in the house, neither with the impetus to move towards the other. And Helen's threat over his head. 'If the case really goes ahead, then I tell you, Jeremy, that would be the end. It will kill my parents, kill me. You've got to find some way to stop it.'

But stop it he could not. Women. At work there was Sylvia with the bit between her teeth, more stretched, more unreasonable, even, he thought, more unreasonably angry than ever he'd known her.

By this time they'd taken a third person into the firm. Alan Boddington: a part-timer, a critic, a writer of travel books, a dabbler. But genial enough. And hard-working, whilst there. A bachelor with expensive tastes like sailing and horse riding and skiing; all of which had to be paid for somehow. He had, it wasn't to be denied, a way with people. He had a large number of contacts. And he was refreshing. Gave Sylvia someone else to confer with and to charm. Though there had been little charm this year at the office. Jeremy was never quite on the same wave length as Alan. On the other hand he didn't regret his presence, for it made the atmosphere all in all a less tense place. And there was no doubt about it, he was pulling in the work.

Conversations between Jeremy and Sylvia were rarer. Both had retired to their separate camps, both with their own thoughts, certain subjects better not approached. Sometimes there was the old spark, when an aspect of the work engaged the two of them jointly, when the fate of a client was in the balance. Sometimes Sylvia would come and sit in his room and it would be as if the case was forgotten and it was like old times. But never for long.

Not an easy year. Jeremy found he was pushing his way through it. He needed a complete rest, he told himself, a complete holiday. He was, as he'd told Josie, morally and spiritually exhausted. A complete rest was what was needed. But there appeared no way to get it.

The days at the office were long and exhausting. Often he arrived with little energy and seemed literally to be pushing himself through the day. Eating too much, too often the wrong kinds of things; developing a weakness that was new, for cream cakes. Again reverting to his old tendency to long pub lunches and too much beer. He had given up swimming in the local pool and was taking little exercise. Too tired, too little time.

He began to look more shambly than ever. Uncared for, uncaring for himself. The days could only be got through with little treats. And all those damn clients wanting so much out of you, the last drop of blood and then look what happens. You put everything in to help them and then they go and sue you. Ungrateful, ungrateful.

So the days were far from easy. Then back to Helen and a sense of gloom about the house. Both had put off the decorating that badly needed doing. The twins were talking eagerly of leaving, of going to university. The house had a sense of being run down, of its time for them coming to an end. Every day something new broke – a kettle, the toaster – and was not replaced. And when Jeremy mildly complained to Helen she threw herself into an ungovernable rage, out of all proportion. This affair has brought on the early menopause, Jeremy said to himself. Despite all the provocation her behaviour is simply not normal. Not normal, I swear it. And whatever else Helen is, I always thought of her as eminently normal.

So he classified it the early menopause, and held the classification as a secret weapon. It excused everything. It excused him. He made no effort to understand her, no further effort to make up for past sins as she would have wished. He had not the energy, nor the hope.

Both pulled back into different worlds, both let their relationship slip. Helen with anger, Jeremy with apathy and disappointment. What was the point? Helen buffered herself with the children. Who still gave pleasure. But it was all too clear that their thoughts and emotions were otherwise engaged. Poor old parents!

They wanted out, did the children. Daniel was already away. The twins' minds were taken up with such issues as whether their parents would agree to them doing two nights a week at the Spud-U-Like in Barnes. For if so they would be able to afford to go with the rest of the in-crowd to Corsica this summer, after their 'A' levels. And then there was the question of saving somehow for driving lessons, and then there were girl and boyfriend issues, and then somewhere along the line were the 'A' levels themselves.

It was the year of UCCA forms, the year of university choices, of saying 'with two Bs and one C', and holding onto that like a totem. For two Bs and one C as a minimum meant an escape into the next stage of life, a way out of the house in Kew. Where all was not well, but more than that they did not wish to acknowledge to themselves. Not with good old Mum and Dad. There were so many horror stories around. So many of their friends' parents . . . But not good old Mum and Dad, surely?

So the year passed. And imperceptibly, but increasingly, like something gathering momentum as the months passed and the court case grew nearer and nearer, Helen detached herself from Jeremy.

The family holiday in France was a vague attempt on his part, still without too much effort, but relying on a liberal dose of sunshine and good French food and cheap vino to help things along, to bridge the gap. To make things easier between himself and his wife. To remind her, too, how important was family solidarity.

But the attempt was half-hearted in the extreme. He inadvertently left some of his travellers cheques behind, failed to buy a new bathing costume as Helen had requested – 'at least don't make me too ashamed of you' – but instead brought the old off-white one which he'd had for years and which she'd always detested. And overlooked other small courtesies which he knew would have helped, if only he'd cared sufficiently. Somehow he just didn't.

The holiday, then, did nothing at all to improve the situation. If anything it simply confirmed for Helen, being so cooped up the six of them (Daniel had joined them for ten days of the holiday), how hopeless the whole thing was.

And afterwards she made the decision. (Daniel was returning early to Bristol. Alice, luckily, had been invited to Scotland by a school friend's parents.) She would take the twins down to her parents. Where she would sort herself out and gather strength.

Jeremy had had ambivalent feelings towards the intrusion of Josie into his life. When Sylvia had first told him, his view had been that he could do without the hassle of some young thing who would be playing at the game of working when what she really wanted was to be with her mother. Obviously she would make a hopeless secretary. What he could have done with for choice was someone wonderfully efficient and respectful, who sorted him out and never said a word except when spoken to. For Jeremy hardly had, these days, the energy to open his mouth.

So a young, over-bright college kid was the last thing he relished. But he had no option when Sylvia asked him to help her out. He was mildly curious to see Sylvia's daughter and welcomed a bit of drama outside his own. But only mildly. For choice he could have done without it, but there she was; talkative, eager, hopelessly keen to help, keen for knowledge, hopelessly enthusiastic about the whole damn package. The magic of a literary agency, my foot!

Of course it was charming that she obviously leant so heavily on his every word. After all, no one else seemed to at the moment. He did not find her attractive. Indeed he felt sorry for her that physically she had been endowed with so little of her mother's grace and delicacy. But he did come to enjoy larking around with her. And sometimes, just sometimes, for short periods, it had taken his mind off his own problems.

It had been a kindness on his part that he'd invited her to the house. Or looking back, wasn't it she who invited herself? There was no doubt about it, she was in a pickle in the flat with Sylvia and Alison (what else was to be expected?) and needed a friend.

As to the rest. He had promised himself a clean board after Ruth. Though he hadn't bargained on a year without. But had nevertheless been celibate, kept his promise to Helen, despite her obstinacy. Those few days, just a handful of occasions. It had all been so harmless, almost incidental. She'd seemed to know what she wanted and he'd been completely honest with her from the first.

The irony was that it was actually his friendship with the girl that

259

had spurred him on to make one last effort with Helen.

It was the way he had, in his talks with Josie, re-lived the earlier parts of his life, his childhood aspirations, his friendship with Timmy and Sylvia, the beginning and foundation of his marriage to Helen. It was all that which had enabled him to see clearly, even more so than at the time when he had broken off with Ruth, that his marriage must be hung on to, must be made something of. For without it, he saw, he would be a broken man, and others would be broken too. What kind of a future, after all, was there for Helen? She a middle-aged woman, past childbearing. What was all this talk of 'wanting peace', after all.

Fired, he'd determined to go and see Helen, make her hear what he had to say, make her realise that they'd be crazy to –

And so in the middle of the night he rifled the garden of Michaelmas daisies, lupins, wallflowers, anything else he could put his hands on, despite the fact that there were many, many more flowers in his parents-in-law's garden in Dorset; it was the gesture, the gesture that counted, a gesture it was that was needed. Rifling the garden, then, and throwing into the car handfuls of flowers, he'd driven through the night. But when she'd shut the door the flowers had remained in his arms.

'Such a foolish waste,' was all she mourned.

The ensuing week at work had been near insufferable. Arriving back at Kew at six he had slept till noon. To be woken by the phone to be told by an insufferably uppish Sally that there was a client waiting in reception for him, and where was he? Where indeed?

'You apparently know where I am.'

Sally sounded hurt. 'Sylvia asked me to phone through and find out what we should tell Mr Humphries.'

'Tell him to get – Oh hell, tell him I'm really sorry, Sally. Tell him something unfortunate, unavoidable has come up. Look, have you got any lunch plans yourself?'

'Why me?'

'Listen, be a good girl and do me a favour. Take a tenner out of petty cash and go and have a drink or a sandwich or something in the pub with him, will you. You get on with him, don't you? If you can hold the fort, I'll be there by about half past one.' (Two o'clock, Sally said to herself.) 'But it is really quite important that I catch him today. There is something that I need to discuss. Will you do that for me, Sally?'

Sally sighed. She'd been planning to start looking for a present for her boyfriend's birthday this lunch hour. Besides Oliver Humphries was one of those who'd be patting her knee before she knew it. At the same time as boring her head off with talk of his books and successes. She was never sure, she reflected, which was worse. Jeremy was still at the other end of the line.

'Sally?'

There goes her lunch hour. 'Okay then.'

'Thanks, you're a doll, Sally.'

At five to two Jeremy had relieved Sally in the pub. 'Look, let's move on somewhere more comfortable for coffee,' he said to Oliver. To her: 'I suppose you'd better be getting back to the office . . .'

It was after four before he was in the office himself. The coffee had been accompanied by liqueurs. Oliver had quite forgiven him his lapse. On the other hand, that was the day shot.

He rather did not want to see Josie in his room and was relieved when Sylvia and Alan called him into a conference on an American contract that was proving tricky. A conference which mercifully spilled out into other matters (was he himself stretching it out; he heard Sylvia once or twice say, 'Oh Jeremy, come off that old hobby-horse of yours', but he took no notice), and lasted for the rest of the afternoon.

The following days he was morose, monosyllabic, distracted. He even went so far as to invent one or two outings for Josie: a jaunt to the London Library, on behalf of one of his clients, and another to the BBC, in order to have her out of the office. He wanted his room to himself. He wanted to think. Work was an agony. So was her fresh young face. In a way, her hope and his sense of failure. Besides had he got her in too deep? If so, he didn't want to know about it. He'd like to believe he hadn't. She was after all a tough kid. And for the moment, he told himself, Josie, you're on your own. I can't help you now.

Luck was on his side to this extent. Alan had a work rush on and had requested help from Josie. Jeremy had been able to be generous: 'You can have as much of her time as you want this week. We've all got to muck in and help one another, after all. That's what an agency like ours has always believed.'

Josie looked hurt but said nothing.

Thursday, sitting in the office with a bear head, that felt larger than a football, was interminable for Jeremy.

Friday was one of those days when he seemed to be ploughing through the work with always more ahead. By early evening he could take no more; whatever was undone would have to wait till Monday. He went to find Sylvia.

'Are you free, my old mate?'

She looked up from her desk, tired, worn herself, he thought, but with a faint smile.

'Can I pour us both a whisky?'

She gestured for him to do so. Then inevitably the damned phone went. These clients, he thought for a second time this week, is there not ever to be any stopping of it, not even on a hot Friday evening after a week which has seen no letting up? He prayed it wouldn't be for him. It was for her.

The conversation went on and on. He picked up *The Bookseller* and began to read. He could hear even at this distance the anxious high-pitched voice on the other end of the phone, pouring out its troubles. And Sylvia soothing, reasoning, for all the world as if it was the beginning of any bright fresh day and she had all the time in the world.

He could bear it no longer. He scribbled a note – 'Had to leave. Hope the flat isn't too hot this weekend. I don't know how much more we Londoners can take of this. It was nothing important, by the way, nothing that can't easily wait till Monday. See you.'

He left the office and made for Kew, from where he phoned Helen, who agreed to let him take her out to dinner, provided that he stay at The Bull and not at the house.

He managed, he thought, to play it just right. Cool, no nonsense, no pleading, never put yourself in the defensive position. He did not talk about the future; or the possibility of one. Nor of the past. He let her lead the conversation and joined in willingly with talk of the children, her parents, her worry over the upkeep of their house, which the old people were now unable to cope with themselves.

He agreed that in some ways it was fortunate that she had been with them this month. For being at close quarters for such a sustained time had given her far greater insights into their needs than before. He picked up on the village gossip. He offered her snippets (albeit truncated) from his week at the agency.

At first he was the one on edge, expecting more, more emotions no doubt. Waiting for the inevitable turn of events. But nothing happened. He asked no favours, never mentioned coming up to the house. Tried to imply that he wished to be her friend, that was all.

And she had to agree that it was as pleasant an evening out (on the surface) as she'd had with him for a long time. No one could be quite so charming as Jeremy when he put his mind to it, she told herself. 'How long is it,' he asked her as they were drinking coffee and liqueurs, 'how long since we have had a meal together like this, just the two of us? Too long, surely.'

She concurred that it had been too long.

'You'll want to be getting back. Shall I walk you up to the house? Of course I quite understand if you'd prefer to go by yourself.'

She pulled back the curtain from the window and looked out into the dark night, the moon lighting up the church tower but making it look sinister.

'Perhaps you'd better. Thank you.'

They walked alongside. He keeping his distance, resisting a desire to slip an arm through hers or otherwise engage her.

At the gate. 'You'll be okay now?'

It was she who said, 'They'd like to see you. Father keeps asking. You're the only one who can make him laugh.'

'Laugh, eh?'

It was the way his face crumpled. It was the way Helen saw in the collapse of his features, his pain, more clearly than ever before. That caught at her heart. Damn it, damn it.

'Is the bed comfortable down there?'

'I'm sure it will be fine.'

'What are you going to do tomorrow?'

'I hadn't made any plans yet. I'd rather thought the children would be around.'

'No, the twins are camping on Dartmoor and Alice is still in Scotland with the Skeltons.'

'I see, I see.'

He sighed. The moment hung between them.

'Perhaps you'd like to come up for lunch . . . ?'

She was tentative. Wondered what she was doing, why she was doing it.

'I'd like that very much.'

And so it was decided.

Saturday morning he'd taken a large leisurely breakfast in The Bull. Porridge, egg, bacon and mushrooms. Wedges of hot white toast presented in a toast rack. The real thing. He'd asked if by any chance they had a spare newspaper lying around and they'd provided him with the choice of *Telegraph* or *Mail*. He'd taken both. And enjoyed himself.

It was not as hot. The Bull's dining room looked out over the village square. The spire of the church was visible, and behind it a patch of sky, streaked with welcome clouds. The Green itself was in shade, making him feel refreshed, ready for anything.

He was in better spirits; his nerves, he found as he ate his mushrooms, were far less stretched than yesterday. It wouldn't be quite true to say that he sensed that he was winning, only that a crack of hope, eggshell thin, but a crack all the same had appeared on the horizon of his mind. Play it cool, he told himself, take it how it comes. As an animal will know another, he suspected by her smell, her stance, suspected at a level below conscious thought that he was hers still if he played it right. At the gate, how she'd been.

So he looked at the last square of toast; he was full but it seemed a shame to leave it. He put it on his plate and stretched out towards the pat of butter. And then changed his mind. Start the day with control, he told himself. A good omen. You don't need the toast. He eyed it viciously. Like a dog about to yap at one's trouser legs. Stay there. You little bugger. And it did.

After breakfast he sat in the chair in his bedroom and decided to write to Alice. A quiet self-sufficient child, always more her mother's than his. A small facsimile of Helen. More academic than the twins. Lately becoming a consummate reader. He's used her once or twice this last year as a reader for the occasional children's book that had found its way into his hands. This she seemed to like, writing her opinion down in her large neat rounded hand. More communicative on paper than when approached directly.

The one perhaps most of all who would suffer if – So he looked for his briefcase and found that to his annoyance he had left it at the house. Was it a subconscious slip? he wondered. For in it were the pre-trial papers that he had promised himself he would have to look at over the weekend. But was by no means keen to. Still, bother! How forgetful he was becoming. Besides, no paper.

He went downstairs to ask at the desk for some sheets. Then returned to his room with its unmade bed on which – though he did not plan to admit it to Helen, he had not spent a comfortable night – and wrote to his youngest child.

Then he ambled towards the house.

The day had passed peacefully. His father-in-law, after his second stroke, was now bedridden. The housekeeper was away for the

264

weekend. So it was Helen who washed, cooked and did the necessary. She was making lunch when Jeremy arrived. He poured sherry and took a tray up to the old man. Later joining Helen and her mother for lunch. In the afternoon he offered to do some digging in the vegetable garden, which was badly in need of attention.

The evening meal they ate on trays in his father-in-law's bedroom. And afterwards watched television. By ten the old people were ready to retire for the night.

'Shall I walk you down to The Bull?' Helen surprised.

They were shy with one another on the walk. He determined still to keep the conversation light, immediate, slide away from anything that might cause problems.

At The Bull, 'Do you want to come in for a nightcap?'

'Then you'll have to walk me back,' she laughed.

At the white gate-post a second night running,

'Are you really comfortable at The Bull?'

'Not really,' he smiled at her, admitting, but not pleading.

'In that case would you like . . .'

In the spare bedroom lying on her back, but close enough to feel the swell of his hips and stretch of his thigh, she felt better, cleansed, steadier. She reached out a hand to him.

'Weren't you the eager one.'

'Well, what would you expect after a whole year?'

'Have you been faithful to me, this time?'

'I've been faithful to you.'

She turned over to look at him. Then gave him a peck on the cheek. 'Heavens, I'm tired from all that fetching and carrying. I don't know how Mrs Hammond keeps it up. After all, she's no chicken herself.'

'Poor old Helen. What a good sort you are.' He stroked the inside of her arm. 'When's she due back?'

'Tomorrow evening, thank God.'

Helen yawned. And turned over but kept hold of his hand, shifting so that his knees were curled into the back of hers, her buttocks against his warm tummy. So she prepared herself for sleep.

Her last thoughts were not unhappy ones. Wedged as she was between ageing parents and the demands of the children, needing her man so very much to provide some kind of acceptable balance. And so she allowed herself the thought, perhaps after all people do change, perhaps he'd learnt his lesson. Perhaps – and then she was asleep.

The trouble had set in the following day in a rainstorm. In the afternoon they had set off to take extra provisions (a coffee cake Helen had just baked, the second water container that had come to light after the twins' departure) to the children in their camping site.

The plan had pleased Jeremy. It was good to be out of the house. Too stifling, too quiet, too full of the atmosphere of age, of things running downhill. Which set his nerves on edge. The prospect of breathing some bracing Dartmoor air before his return to London that evening, pleased. It would be good, what was more, to see Hugh and Rebecca and for them to see him with Helen, all apparently happy and normal.

The sky had darkened before they left the house and Helen with foresight had thrown into the boot macs and wellington boots, of which there were just about every size in the downstairs cloakroom of her parents' house. These, when they abandoned the car and set out on foot, she insisted they took with them.

'It's only a matter of time.'

'Such a pessimist!'

But he changed shoes for boots and carried an old mac of his father-in-law's nevertheless.

They followed a long dirt track. The children were on farm land on the edge of Dartmoor. A location known to Jeremy and Helen, where the entire family had camped two years previously. The sun shone. The sweat poured from their brows as they walked, carrying cake tin, water pitcher and other last-minute inspirations.

Their visit was greeted with pleasure by their children, who were keen to show them round the set-up, pleased to act host for a mug of tea, pleased to tuck into the coffee cake, and then quarter of an hour later, itching to show their parents on their way.

Jeremy, reluctant to return so quickly, suggested to Helen that now they were more or less empty-handed, they might try a detour onto Dartmoor itself and up to the nearest of the Tors. She was agreeable.

It was whilst they were standing in the Tor itself, those uncanny pre-historic clusters of stones, looking down on the barren and impressive countryside that they saw the first streak of fork lightning followed within seconds by a violent clap of thunder.

Then the heavens seemed to open and it poured. Poured and poured.

'Thank God for the macs.' Jeremy.

'Thank God for the shelter.' Helen.

The stones actually gave little protection but they sheltered against them as best they could. The rain was soon running through their hair and onto their faces in rivers.

The thunder in that vast empty landscape seemed to Helen terrifyingly loud; the zig-zags of lightning destined for them. Unnerved, she took Jeremy's hand.

Jeremy was enjoying it: the noise, the light, the battle of the firmament. The two of them, unprotected, caught up in all of this. Yes, it turned him on. He watched water running off Helen's chin and down her defenceless neck and squeezed her fingers hard. Then opened his mac and put them against his chest.

She felt his heart beating.

'Don't do that. You'll get even wetter.'

He opened his mac altogether and pulled her to him. 'Not like this.'

It was warm there against his shirt and his hot skin. She was beginning to find it sexy too, his kissing her neck and opening the top button of her cotton blouse whilst all the time the rain beat down on her hair and shoulders and back. He put his hands inside her raincoat and fondled her wrists and her inner arms where she felt particularly sensitive. She shuddered against him. He put his hand under her skirt.

'Jeremy.'

'This is gorgeous,' he urged.

'We're behaving like a couple of kids.'

'And why shouldn't we?'

He shook off his mac, lay it on the ground in the rain and there between two of the central stones of the Tor pulled her down on top of him. And against the ebbing lightning and dying thunder she clung to him as excited as he. They made love with a sudden hurting thrusting passion. Leaving them winded, their mouths slaked and open, grateful for the rain.

He hugged her to him, 'Helen, Helen.' And she with her arms around him felt what only a few days before she never thought to again; as soft in the middle, as vulnerable as any schoolgirl. She clung to him and he pushed her hair off her cheek and bit her wet ear, for fun.

Then so sodden they were that despite the hot day they began to feel cold.

'It doesn't look as if it's about to ease off,' he said, 'so we might as well get moving.'

She got up and brushed her clothes down as best she could. Slowly they started to walk back, she holding his hand, her insides still peculiarly fragile and her legs like cotton-wool. Their boots squelched in the wet grass and she kept a firm grasp of him over many a wobbly stone.

He'd begun to feel expansive as they walked back. Telling Helen about some of Alan's tribulations at work this last week (Jeremy and Helen shared opinions on Alan Boddington), Josie's name cropped up.

Ah Josie. If Helen had hardly given her a thought it was because her own troubles had been uppermost this past month. But Josie, Sylvia's oldest. She remembered her as a wee girl, determinedly outside their flat with her new skipping-rope despite the raw blustery day and the rain. 'That must be years and years ago. I hate to think how many,' she sighed.

'Jeremy, how is she, how has she turned out? Is she anything like Sylvia?'

'In some ways, yes.'

'Well, in what ways? Come on, man, be more explicit.'

'You'll have to see for yourself.'

'Yes, I'd like to. We must have Sylvia and Josie over. Perhaps on a weekend when Daniel is with us. The twins are not likely to be of much interest to her, I suppose. How long is she staying?'

Jeremy wasn't sure.

'Do you think she and Daniel would get on? They used virtually to share prams, you know.'

Jeremy shrugged. It appeared he had no opinion on whether Daniel and Josie would get on.

'Do you want to fix something up,' she persisted, she who usually hated arrangements and shied away from entertaining, 'say, for the weekend after next? I think Daniel said he'd be in London then. I must say I'd rather like to see her myself; what a strange life she's had. Come on, Jeremy, how *has* she turned out? And what's the news of Patrick, and of the other children?'

'She's basically okay. A bit all over the place. But that's to be

expected. I don't think she'd come over with her mother, incidentally. Or rather Sylvia, according to Josie, seems to want to have
nothing to do with her.'

'You've been having chats with Josie then?'

Jeremy yawned. 'It's inevitable when you work with someone.'

'You've become quite friendly?'

'You know, uncle Jeremy's shoulder to cry on when the
atmosphere between Sylvia, Alison and Josie becomes too thick for
her to handle. Actually she's been through a few tough times since
she's got here, Helen.'

'Yes.' The cheer somehow seemed to have gone out of the
afternoon.

'Helen?'

'Sorry,' she forced a laugh. 'Bad old habits.'

'Whose?' It was a lopsided grin. He'd released her hand when the
conversation had first got round to Josie but now he took it again
and swung her arm companionably.

'Actually she's been over to the house once or twice.' It would no
doubt come out eventually. He might as well slip it in now.

'Our house. Why?'

'It's been something of a bolt hole for her.'

'I see. Why hadn't you said –'

'There's hardly been time.'

'What does Sylvia think?'

'I don't think she minds.'

'Or doesn't she know?'

'Helen, please –'

She dropped his hand. They walked the remaining distance to the
car in silence. She watched the way with his fingernails he rubbed
the bristle above his upper chin. She expected him to say to her,
'You're being unreasonable.' So often he had in the past. But this
time he didn't.

That little voice, she tried to block it out. But back at her parents'
house whilst she cooked the supper and watched through the corner
of her left eye Jeremy playing whist with her mother, it became
increasingly insistent.

'Jeremy,' she called, 'what about pouring us a drink?'

'I was just about to.'

'Some of us are in need of one.' Her laugh didn't sound like a
laugh at all.

How could she live with him, if she trusted him so little? If he only
had to mention another woman, however young, indeed, in this

case even the daughter of his colleague and friend, to make her wonder. How indeed could she continue to cope with that state of affairs? She could, of course, ask him outright.

Through the long, drawn-out meal, over the chatter of banalities she eyed him, thinking, yes, she could surely ask him. But what would that prove, would he be honest? Would he ever be? Was he any longer capable of it? And if he was, would that help? For would she any longer believe him?

So what were the options? To go on living with her jealousies, blotting them out as best she could, or, or the other: have the courage to make a life without him.

Because they had been so close at the Tor, she felt even the more crushed. She had never, she felt, been so unhappy.

He saw it in her. But was helpless against the tide. He told her to sit with her parents, offering to do the washing-up before he took off for London. And she came into the kitchen and lolled against the door.

'Don't go back tonight.'

'Not tonight?'

She didn't know why she wanted to keep him. For surely it couldn't change anything. And yet she heard herself asking, even pleading.

'You could get up and take off early tomorrow,' she suggested.

'The traffic is always so bad coming into London.'

'I know.'

And yet she was asking.

He tried to get an eye contact, to retrieve something of the mood on the Tor. But there was none of it.

'Helen, do you really . . .'

'I don't know. Not if you feel you can't.'

In the event he did.

He took a bath and lay in it for a long time, wrestling with himself. He had lied to Helen about his celibacy. Should he own up now? Make a clean breast of it. Would that help, or cause more pain? How could she possibly understand how casual the whole thing had been. How irrelevant the sexual part of it. On past performance, would she believe it?

Having asked him to stay, if that is what she had done, in bed before him, she turned away. And before he had turned off the bedside light she was crying, weeping quietly into the pillow.

'Helen, is there anything? Can I help?'

'No nothing, nothing honestly.'

And so he lay and wondered. If honesty was to be the turning point then he would gladly be honest with her. But the damnable thing was, they seemed somehow beyond that. Honesty having no credit left in the bank.

Was it because at the Tor they had drawn so close, all seemed more than redeemed, that to both in their separate ways the cold distance of the long night seemed all the more awful? Or was it just that there were this time, unlike Ruth and a year ago, no hysterics, no shouting, screaming accusations? Just between them a sense that too much had happened once too often for there to be any going back.

That was what Helen came to through the long hours of the night. And what Jeremy came to fear. For because it was so quiet, so unspoken, so nebulous, yet hard and there. It was difficult, impossible for him to deal with. Or to see a way around. He could not charm her back. That he knew. That nothing, nothing he any more said would take away. And yet there must be something.

Neither slept. She woke at hourly intervals, preparing herself for what it seemed she hardly had the strength to do. And yet what other way was there? Now they had, it seemed, come to the end of the road. Through the night she drew away from him. In waves. In silence. Every time she woke it was as if she was that little bit further. That little bit stronger.

And he sleeping as lightly as she, woke, almost it seemed every time she turned over. He could not tell if he loved her. Nor what that was. Yet he felt indelibly committed to her. They were tied together it seemed by what they had shared: the way they had made a life together, made children. He wanted to be loyal to her for the rest of his life. At this moment he wanted nothing more.

Her pain ached him. If he liked her less than he did, all this would be so much more bearable. And so the night came and went, and with the early light of dawn both looked worse for it.

'Jeremy,' she whispered. It must have been around five o'clock. 'Are you awake?'

He nodded.

'You might as well have gone back to London for all the good this has done us. I'm sorry.'

What could he say? He squeezed her hand.

271

'I rather feel like a drink. It's been such a long night,' he yawned. 'What about you, can I get you anything?'

'Yes, but let me.'

'No, honestly –'

Both were eager to be up and doing. In the end it was Jeremy who made his way to the kitchen and returned bearing a fully laden tray.

'Breakfast,' she attempted a laugh, 'at this hour!'

'We need to keep up our strength.'

She agreed that they did. They were tender with each other. But each silence hung heavy. Should he own up? Should she ask him directly, or should she try and avoid all further talk of Josie?

They'd finished their toast and tea.

'With luck we might sleep now.'

He supposed so.

'What time will you need to be making a start?'

'Don't worry about that.' He had already decided that he would be in no fit state to go into work this morning.

'Well I'm going to try and catch an hour or two.' She turned over. And was indeed only a few minutes later in a deep sleep. Jeremy tried the same but with less success. How intolerable to lie beside someone whom sleep has chosen when one has been overlooked!

By a quarter to six he could stand it no longer. He got out of bed as quietly as possible, dressed and crept out of the room. His thoughts seemed altogether too unquiet for sitting or lying. He would take himself for a walk. See if anything became clearer out there in the fresh early morning air.

He walked and walked. It was a beautiful early morning. But his mood seemed agonisingly out of joint. The poppies blowing in the ripe wheat fields, the profusion of wild flowers growing in the hedgerow and on the sides of the lanes down which he trekked, directionless, quite passed him by. Of all things how utterly ironic and downright absurd if it should be his friendship with Josie that finally drove the wedge between himself and Helen. Should he walk fast back to the house and sit Helen down, and force her to hear him out, make her see how it was.

He turned in the direction of the house. But then back again and onwards. For what would hang between them, beyond Josie, was Helen's inability now to believe anything he said. And there it lay. How then could they live together? How indeed could he live with her, and keep his self-respect? And so he walked and walked and walked. Tortured, his thoughts becoming no clearer. What to do? To that it appeared as if there were no answers. For the moment

272

there are no answers. That was the answer, he thought. There is nothing more I can do. Nothing.

Now he was sitting looking at the prolific growth of the lemon-scented geranium, whilst Helen insisted on making him at least a cup of coffee. Before he got into the car and drove back to London.

*

In Islington the clock at last was on the hour. Both Alison and Sylvia looked at it mesmerised. It was Alison who said, 'Go on then, get on the damn thing.' So Sylvia picked up the phone (literary agent she, living on the phone, there was one in every room, this one a minute, discreetly placed push-button Slimtel). She was unduly nervous. Was it the pills, the night? After all, she thought, if Jeremy really had got himself involved with Josie, then he deserved all that was coming. But still she could not believe it, and disliked imputing to him something she believed so far-fetched.

Relations with him were bad enough, and the agency she knew had suffered every way this last twelve months. She was reluctant to push things further. It was almost as if she and he could take no more. She did not, fiercely she did not want it to be true. She did not want to have to tackle her emotions if calmly he said, yes, Josie was there. If he said, for example, that he was in love with her, just as he had said with Ruth. On every level she could not bear things to go that far. Nor did she know how, with regard to Josie, she could cope with it. In fact she felt, out of the mists of lack of sleep and months of stress and anxiety, that things had generally gone too far, that she was cracking up, that she could cope with little more; despite Alison's reassuring presence there beside her. She had the notion that she would like to say to Alison, I can't manage it, you take over, you phone him. She felt that she could not face the pain that might be involved. But Josie was her daughter and somehow she had to pull herself out of the state she was in and do what was necessary. She must, for Josie.

And so having hung onto the slim cream phone for some minutes, while Alison drunk her third cup of coffee, glanced at *The Times* and waited, finally Sylvia calmed herself and got her voice under control sufficiently to phone. She knew what she was going to say. Nothing initially accusatory, simply, 'Jeremy, we seem to have had a spot of bother with Josie who has left in somewhat mysterious

273

circumstances. Of course it is nothing to worry about but we just wondered if she'd taken refuge with you, knowing what a pal you've been.'

So the phone rang loud and clear in Jeremy's house, on and on, and neighbours passing heard it through the broken window, neighbours eager to walk their dogs in Kew gardens before all the world should be there, neighbours of the type that liked to imagine what was going on in every house that they passed. And one said to the other, for want of better conversation, 'How could anyone expect the Farmers to answer the phone at this time in the morning?' and, laughing, they passed on. The phone rang on and Alison, looking at the crossword, wondered when Sylvia would finally put it down.

*

In the farmhouse on the outskirts of Edmonton it is eleven-thirty at night. The household is quiet. Patrick and Anna, preparing for bed, are anticipating the third in a row of unbroken nights. After two years more or less of disrupted sleep. It seems to them that no other baby in the world has been as much trouble as theirs. Patrick sometimes sneakily in the privacy of his thoughts thinks back to those earlier childbearing years with Sylvia and wonders why it was so different. In fairness he wonders is it just that he is older, notices more? Has greater difficulty going to sleep? Were the other children also night screamers, but he forgets? He knows, however, that it was not so. He forces his thoughts back to the present.

Then two nights ago the miracle happened. No crying. An entire night without that distraction. But bugger all, it seemed as if the habit had set in. He woke twice anyway. Difficult dreams, a struggle to get back to sleep. He woke, almost, from the absence of crying. Then last night a second night of silence. Anna, hugging him, said, 'You see it wasn't just a fluke, it's the beginning of a better stage, you wait and see.'

And he smiled at her wanly, his loyal, steady if not so exciting Anna. Last night he himself had only woken once and then returned to sleep swiftly. And today had felt better for it, so that the paper-work which he set himself to each Sunday had not been as much of a chore as usual, nor the afternoon visits to patients. In fact the day had been one of the most agreeable Sundays the family had spent in a long time. A hot day; the children and Anna had swum in the river and he had walked down to join them when he had finished his work. Then back to an early supper, hash browns, sausages and zucchini, with Anna's superb maple syrup pancakes to follow. After which he'd settled down to a game of chess with Angus, who played a rather good game now and would be competing in the local junior championships next month. All too soon he'll be beating his father hollow, thought Patrick wryly.

Then the weekly letter to Josie. Although nine in the evening, that terrible tiredness which so suffocated his spirits so that by then he'd normally be yawning and longing for bed – as a result sounding more severe, so that the children would moan, 'Oh Dad, you're no sport, any more' – was tonight not making itself felt. He wrote in cheerful spirits, managing the odd joke and lively anecdote that he knew she'd enjoy.

He'd got almost used to the idea of her being in London with Sylvia. Something that at first it was impossible in any way to deal with had become, by its mere duration, more acceptable.

On the first days of Josie's arrival, when he imagined them meeting, imagined her embarrassment, imagined again the whole turgid mess of his ex-wife's life, he found his nerves ajangle and screeching. Josie, so much part of him. He could not bear her to be hurt, he said over and over to Anna. Who counselled, 'You must let her go; it's her life now, Patrick.' 'Yes, I know but –'

Because of the past there was much that they could not say to one another. She had always deemed it best not to enquire too closely. After all, she had been there. Seen it all with her own eyes. Seen, she sometimes thought, more than Patrick himself saw. Was it because Sylvia was of her own sex? Was it because of her bravery over those childbirths or her way with the children, was it because though eccentric she had been a good employer? Whatever it was, Anna had some sympathy for Sylvia. Thought her odd. Thought it was terrible for poor Patrick, who should never have married a woman like that. But then he didn't know her true colours. Thought that Patrick was better married to her. But felt all the same in the secret place of her heart, that, whatever else, Sylvia was not as wicked, as bad, as thoughtless and as utterly beyond the pale as Patrick made out.

She thought too (whenever she did think about it, which was not often these days, now she had her own child and years had gone by, not often that is until all this recent trouble with Josie had brought it all to the surface again) that she had been handed a rotten deal, poor

Sylvia, for she couldn't help being what she was. Anna had known, at a distance, an older sister's friend in Norway, someone of Sylvia's persuasion. It had seemed slightly odd, but nothing more than that. Men, she decided, it's harder for them. They just can't face it. A man, for example, like Patrick. And you've got to account for the jealousy. And their male noses being put out of joint. There's a lot of that in it. Whatever anyone may say.

So, on the whole, she felt more mildly towards Sylvia. Sylvia who by her absence posed so little of a threat. Until Josie got the bit between her teeth. Till Josie, young woman, difficult in her adolescence, implied that there was much about Anna which was not as good as her own mother. Implied restless dissatisfaction. Then came that one time when Anna had let her own feelings get the better of her and had said certain things which should never have been said. Of course she could be forgiven, she argued. There were stresses and strains. She was pregnant. Much that Josie knew nothing of. Still Anna regretted it deeply.

Though Patrick on the surface had been supportive to her, she often felt that he had not forgotten it himself. For a time it was as if there were two camps: her and her baby to be; Patrick and the children. It had never been like that during all the period she and Patrick had been together. And though it passed, she could never quite get it out of her mind, that division.

When Patrick had read the letter from Sylvia telling of the contact with Josie and the agreement, she had not been as surprised as he. Perhaps she had been suspecting it for some time. Nor did she think, as she told Patrick, that it was such a bad idea. But Patrick was at first beside himself with rage. And with anxiety. And again at night Anna had to cradle him in her arms, he and the baby both, as Patrick remembered and relived the inconsolableness of his grief and sense of desertion.

This time, with a young child, Anna suffered more. For it was clear to her now, how little, despite the happy life they appeared to lead, he had got over it. Perhaps one never quite gets over those things, she had to accept. Perhaps she had been foolish to assume as much just because they rarely talked about it. And then the thought, just once in a while, while she pushed the baby in the pram, does he miss Sylvia, actually miss her?

So in the months that Josie had been away each of them in their own way had thought more about Sylvia than either let on. And Anna, particularly, would be pleased when Josie was back. She felt fairly confident, knowing Josie as she believed herself to do, knowing her attachment to her brothers and sisters and to the new baby and of course to her father, that this was just a crazy rebellious period. After all, hadn't she herself been through just that when she had left Norway to come to England as 'au pair', despite her parents' wishes?

Josie, she felt sure, would get over it. Josie would come home (unless she married an Englishman, but she seemed too young for that, too unready). No, she would have a fling, find out what she had to; then return to where she belonged. For Josie was a good girl, and an intelligent one. And her roots here were strong, so Anna thought.

Patrick, as he'd written the letter this evening, realised that writing to Sylvia's address a letter which would lie on Sylvia's breakfast table being read by the one whilst the two drank their coffee together (with Alison and in silence, as described by Josie) was something he was getting used to. Something which caused no longer the same pain, if pain at all.

Josie, from her letters, was clearly surviving well. Enjoying the work at the agency. Not troubled by the lesbian affair, which she described as totally in the background, the two very discreet, just like good friends: 'Really, Daddy, nothing to worry about at all.' And so the sex of it was diffused in Patrick. He began to be able to feel more warmly. She was learning a lot, Josie.

Those opportunities, for theatre, books, good conversation, the whole literary world into which she'd been plunged were lacking for her here. Maybe the visit was no bad thing. Clear also that his ex-wife had done well. Josie spoke about the agency in a way which gave it reality. He even wondered, having a little joke with himself, whether she, Sylvia, was doing better than he. And a faint admiration came into play. And he thought again of her beauty, of her vitality, as he'd known her. One day this last week when no one had been in the house, he'd done, by his own standards, an odd thing. He'd gone to Josie's room and searched out an old photo she kept. And looked at it long. She had indeed been very beautiful, his wife.

So tonight he wrote with mild pleasure. It almost gave satisfaction, to pen this letter that would make its way to the Islington table. He was aware of Sylvia as he wrote and he wrote more generous sentiments, which he imagined would get passed on. After the home news and after some thought, he wrote saying how pleased he was that Josie was getting to know her mother at this crucial stage in her life. That he had come round to believing in the good of it. And that she must try as best she could to accept what had happened, 'for we all have our peculiarities, darling' and to put it behind her and make the most of what was. To send Sylvia best wishes from him. Perhaps if the visit continued well, and if Sylvia would like it, he and Josie would discuss on her return the possibility of a meeting in due course with the other children.

Meanwhile, darling, make the best you can of this most exciting experience – being in the heart of literary London – I'm sure Edmonton is going to seem very plain beer afterwards, but we are all looking forward to seeing you and hearing your no doubt mountainful of news on your return. We feel confident that it will make it much easier to settle down to a better second year at UBC after such an exciting experience. You know, darling, after you've got your degree who knows if you felt that way inclined you might think of returning to England to work for a couple of years. And if so I won't stand in your way. We all love your lively, witty letters, you really are an excellent letter-writer. Do keep it up. And look forward to seeing you at the end of September.

So it was in cheerful spirits that Anna and Patrick ascended the stairs on the way to bed that Sunday evening. Patrick half way up the stairs rested his arm on her shoulder with affection.

'Going up the stairs to bed. Still one of my favourite times of day. Funny that one dreads it so much as a child.'

And she smiled at him. 'I hope you're not feeling randy?'

'Whatever could have given you that idea?'

And so they were undressing, both with cheerful anticipation, both more or less content with their lot, more or less sending up a grateful prayer, for it could all have been worse. When the phone rang.

'You get it,' she said to him.

'It's bound to be a patient. You answer, darling. Let me just get my dressing-gown on.'

So Anna went to the phone.

'Darling, I think you had better take it.'

'Who is it?'

'It's London.'

Patrick strode over to the phone.

'Hello, hello. Is that you, Patrick?'

Her voice over a decade's absence sounded at once the same and different, so different, she was a stranger to him echoing her hellos down the transatlantic cable.

'Sylvia, can you hear me?'

'Patrick?'

He heard, 'Oh hell, the damn thing's not connecting,' as if she were speaking these words to someone else, not into the phone. And then a click. She'd cut off. He looked back at Anna. 'Whatever —?' He did not think of danger, more of connections. The kind of mood he'd been in when he wrote this evenings's letter. Maybe she too — He was standing irresolute. Waiting for the phone to ring again. But it didn't. 'Do you think I should try?' 'You could.' Anna was in a turmoil. She didn't like this interruption in her bedroom late at night. It seemed to her ominous. It smelt of trouble. But she would not say so to Patrick. Who was opening and closing the fingers of his left hand that had recently been giving him trouble from rheumatism. 'You might as well,' she repeated, slowly.

Then they heard the first ring. Although anticipating it, they both jumped. 'There it goes,' said Anna. 'Answer it.'

'She appears to have lost Josie,' was all he would say to Anna later. 'I think I'd better fly over.'

'Wait,' counselled Anna, 'be patient, darling.' She remembered her own young days, she remembered how these things could happen that looked so extreme but were no more than storms in teacups, all the hurly burly of growing up when things seemed as if they were intolerable one day so that one had to make the most wild and extreme kind of gesture. Who hasn't said at one point, 'I am leaving home for ever'? Who hasn't felt quite differently the next day? Or the next. And there was bound to be some kind of a clash between those two, Sylvia and her daughter. All that font of hurt and bitterness must come to some kind of a head.

'Wait,' she counselled, stroking Patrick's head, 'give it at least another day.' 'That's what she said,' he mumbled grumpily. 'We'll have to see. She's promised to phone the moment she hears anything.' Then suddenly he yawned and at that moment his taut face relaxed. Maybe Anna was right. Maybe it was only a storm in a teacup. Women! Even with his patients, he thought, give me the men any day.

'Come to bed, darling,' Anna urged. 'Come to bed now.'

*

279

'Well tonight at least you'll be back in your own bed,' Helen was saying.

She was nervous whilst she poured the coffee. She couldn't tell whether she should avoid all issues or have them out. On the whole, true to her nature, she was inclined towards the latter view. On the other hand she had the sense that if she let him go now, without saying anything, then for her there would be no turning back. She found that she was already turning over in her mind the prospect of the partner in her parents' firm of solicitors with whom next week she would communicate. 'I'm afraid that between my husband and I it has come to the point . . .'

So, more nervous than usual, her hand shook around the slender handle of the coffee pot. Josie hanging as real as anything, larger even than life, suspended between them in that small (hardly four foot square) sun lounge into which the sun streamed. And yet pretending that they couldn't see her, they gingerly scouted around for other topics of conversation. Soon he must get up and go, Helen said to herself. Then it will be awful. But in another way it will be better. She watched whilst he sipped at his coffee.

His cup was half empty when the phone rang in the hall. The sheer unexpectedness of it, making him jump so that some of the remains of the coffee splashed over the rim of the coffee cup and into the saucer.

It was Jeremy who finally strode into the hall and picked up the receiver. He spoke for a good few minutes. Helen, frowning, was straining to hear what he was saying. Had something happened to one of the children? She couldn't imagine who'd be phoning at this time of the morning, here.

She took the coffee tray into the kitchen. Mrs Hammond had returned late last night but had not appeared yet this morning. Helen's father liked porridge, then a cooked breakfast. She started to gather together the ingredients. The oats were cooking when Jeremy appeared.

'Jeremy?'

'It was Sylvia.'

'Sylvia, at this hour? What did she want?'

'Apparently Josie's done a bunk.'

It was a long time before she was calm enough to say:

'Does she expect you to know where she is?'

'I don't know what she expects, Helen, but I know nothing about it.'

'No, of course not.' She tried to steady herself, to resist the temptation to pick up the porridge pot and throw it over his head.

*

'Now are you going to be all right?' Alison at the door to their flat was looking at Sylvia solicitously. Sylvia had it on the tip of her tongue to plead, 'Don't go in to work today.' She could have done with the other's reassuring presence, even Alison's wry humour, to help her through the day.

'If only there was something to be done. But I suppose there is nothing now but hold tight and wait.'

'Nothing. Phone me though if you do hear anything.'

'Of course I will. Oh Alison, you don't think do you . . .'

'No, I don't.' She put her arms round Sylvia. 'You're just an anxious Jewish mother. She'll be back in a day or two, you see. Meanwhile you've got to keep up your strength. I wish you'd eaten some breakfast. What kind of a day have you got?'

'God, I can hardly think what's ahead of me. Or how I'll manage.'

'You'll manage.'

'I should have talked to her, I should have . . .'

'We both should have.'

'Why is it so much easier to support other people who don't really matter to one, than those nearer to home?'

'We know the answer to that one.'

'Yes.'

Sylvia realised she was delaying Alison on purpose. With difficulty she moved out of Alison's embrace. 'You must go, I suppose, and so must I.'

'I must. Call me if you hear anything, or just want a chat.'

'Thanks, darling.'

Through the habit of self-discipline she forced herself out into the much overgrown garden that, despite Jeremy's suggestions the year before, was still in the hands of the landlord and still badly neglected. And picked herself a single yellow rose.

In the office the sun streamed through the window onto her back and onto the piles of paper that covered every inch of her desk. Never, since the day almost ten years ago when she'd first walked into the offices of Gideon Tickle, had she found the day of work ahead so very difficult to contemplate. Let the phone go, she prayed, let someone tell me that Josie is all right. Just that.

Sally, when she arrived with the post, was surprised to find Sylvia tearing the petals off the rose. Yellow petals were strewn all over the desk. This wasn't like her employer. And where was the automatic smile?

'Is anything the matter, Sylvia?

'Oh Sally, yes, there is.'

*

When the phone went for the second time within the hour in the Tomlinsons' house, Jeremy was on the verge of departure, even at that moment engaged in packing his overnight case and other oddments into the boot of the car. So it was Helen who answered. Helen who at all times hated the phone. Who could it be now?

'Hello, hello?'

The voice of her neighbour, Margaret Chandler, came breezily over the line.

'Is that you, Helen? What a gorgeous morning! Must be simply *wonderful* where you are. Listen, darling, I'm in a bit of a rush – just on the way to work. But thought I ought to give you a quick buzz. Neighbourhood Watch and all that!'

'Why, whatever is it?'

'Probably nothing, darling, but Jim did think – just in case you know nothing about it. We'd hate to be interfering or anything like that but there was a girl who we *think* must have broken into your home last night. The children insist that they heard the sound of shattering glass. Jim and I heard nothing but then we did fall asleep straight after the ten o'clock news. Such a hot weekend. But this morning there was definitely someone around. Not quite a squatter type. But you can never tell. One of the windows to the side of the house was broken. I sent Jim over to have a look. An attempt had been made to seal it up with tape. Of course you might know all about it, darling – one of those little mysteries which isn't a mystery at all. But we did just think . . . Portugal, incidentally, was great fun. We're all as brown as berries. I'll show you the pictures sometime. How are you? Is there anything we can do about this other business? Jeremy is on his way back, you say? Good, then he'll be able to straighten it out. I'm sure it's nothing to worry about. Maybe one of your kids' friends. Ah well, really must dash. Do phone if there is anything we can do.' She rang off.

And Helen, who had decided that reticence was no longer sufficient for the situation in hand, strode out to the car, still in her dressing-gown, her bare feet hurting on the gravel, this time once and for all to confront her husband.

Mid-morning, Helen was crouching behind a splendid oak tree in full leaf, peeing into rich earth through a network of twigs and leaves. The tree, she hoped, shielded her from the road. She herself could just see the gleam of the Vauxhall, in which, at the driver's wheel, Jeremy waited.

Her body was so hot, even those parts now exposed to the air. Her pee left her in a torrent of steam and energy, bringing relief. She took her time, pulling up her briefs and straightening her black and yellow skirt (new, bought in France with Rebecca's encouragement). Then she walked carefully back to the car and settled herself into the passenger seat beside her husband. She actually managed to smile at him. 'Home, James,' she said, an old joke, 'and hasten the horses.' Jeremy put his foot on the accelerator.

It was that conversation with Margaret this morning that had done it. The absurdity of our everyday lives, she thought. The knowledge that it is, after all, a game that we are all playing, for better or worse. And the marriage bit, well, didn't that have to be considered a game too in the final analysis? Listen, for example, to Margaret Chandler. What kind of a game did she think she was playing?

And whatever it was, did Helen really want to put herself outside all of that, the sheer knowableness of their life in Kew with its acceptable well-worn patterns of social behaviour? No, on balance she did not. She didn't want to be a loner. She doubted whether she had the temperament for it. And as to another partner, let alone the consideration of the unhappiness it would cause to her children, who was to say that she would be any better off for it?

She looked at her husband thoughtfully, his hands at a twenty-to-five position on the driving wheel (would have failed him the driving test), his eyes staring straight ahead. Listening to the engine's mild protest as it managed a brave eighty she went back over what he had said to her after her control had finally broken, when she had gone out to the car after him and there outside the house, in the open courtyard, exposed so that anyone could see, she had pummelled him in the chest, screaming that he had deceived her

283

once again, even after everything that had taken place, and that this time he had better have some reasonable explanation. Otherwise, she told him, feeling as she did, it was quite possible that she could kill him.

He had warded off her fists and tried to calm her. Eventually she had let him persuade her to move away from the overlooking windows to a spot further down the garden. They had sat on the broken bench by the duck pond where they had talked, really talked openly and freely it seemed to her for the first time in years and years.

'I fell in love with Ruth,' he'd said. 'It started by being an adventure, then got out of hand. With Josie the sense of adventure was minimal. And there is absolutely no question of anyone falling in love. It's on a different plane, believe you me. She's got quite enough on her plate with her mother. We've just been helping each other through a tough spot. And this doing a bunk now. It was nothing to do with me. I wish you could believe me.'

'And yet she slept in our house?'

'To her it's a refuge. Think about it, where else could she go if she was intent on leaving Islington?'

'And yet you say it, too, was an adventure?'

'In a way, all my goings on with women have been adventures. I need them, Helen. It's got nothing to do with our marriage, except that once, I admit, when the pace became too hot for comfort. Never again. That I assure you; never like that.'

'But why?'

'Why what?'

'Why do you *need* them, Jeremy? Why aren't – we enough?'

'I can't tell you. I genuinely can't. Maybe it's just the way I'm made. Maybe it's a difference between men and women.'

'You're not telling me that all men feel the same?'

'No, but there are lots who do. And a lot more who fantasise but never get round to doing anything about it.'

'Why?' she asked again. 'Why can't marriage be enough, and work, and the children, and . . .'

He was looking at her gently and shaking his head, '. . . After the first few years . . .'

They sat in silence. She pondering what he had said. She had thought to ask the central question, *had* he slept with Josie, but now it had somehow slipped to the side . . . if they were just pals . . .

It was depressing utterly depressing what he had said. And yet.

'Though I find it hard to accept, at least we're talking, properly talking. I wonder why it has taken so long.'

'You've always been so moral and judgemental. Heavens, there must have been times when you've been bored, when you've had dreams?'

'Yes, but not in the same way. Women are just different, I suppose.'

'Some women, not all.'

'He speaks as an authority on the subject.'

They laughed companionably.

'Look, I've really got to be getting back to London. As it is I won't be in the office much before lunchtime.'

'I think I'll come with you.'

'What about jumping on a train later? It'll take hours for you to get dressed and arrange things with Mrs Hammond and your parents. I really can't hang around.'

'No, I shall come with you. It'll take me no longer than half an hour to be ready.'

He sighed but gave in. It sounded much more like the old spunky Helen, and secretly he was relieved. Besides he was not displeased to have her with him on the return journey. God knows what kind of muddles were likely to greet them on arrival. Yes, all things considered, the conversation by the duck pond had gone better than expected, thought Jeremy.

While Helen had dressed he had wandered round the house, getting in Mrs Hammond's way, pulling at magazines from neatly made piles, re-arranging ornaments, requesting nail-scissors in order to trim the lemon-scented geranium (which Mrs Hammond considered far too ruthlessly attacked, half the plant was cut away), considering giving Sylvia another buzz but deciding against it. If he spoke to her it would be hard not to mention Margaret Chandler's call. Yet with regard to this, his gut feeling was that it would be better to stall; at least till he got to the house and had more of an idea what was going on.

Josie, what are you up to, he wondered as the car now steamed its way towards London. And now as his own troubles seemed if not patched, then temporarily diverted, he allowed himself the luxury of a general feeling of concern about her and a gentle remonstration that he had been so off-hand all this last week.

Helen broke into his thoughts. 'In the event, remark, I took exactly twenty-nine minutes to get ready.'

'I know, I timed you. That's my reliable Helen.'

'Am I always so reliable?'

When he didn't answer and they both lapsed into their own thoughts she was back with the conversation at the duck pond. She thought of her mother and the anxiety and confusion in her mother's eyes when she'd hugged her goodbye. Though little had been said, such was the bond between them that her mother knew just why Helen had spent such a long period with them this summer and intuited much of what her daughter was going through. 'Things will be all right, Mother; don't worry, they are going to work out.' So Helen had promised.

Her mind slipped back to the last time she'd said it. When Helen had been in her last year at university, her mother had been going through the menopause and bitterly unhappy. There was a year or two of hiccup in what had basically been a long and happy marriage between her parents.

Whilst she was home on vacation her mother had become distraught. 'Your father, your father –' What was it her mother had wanted to tell her about her father and never quite got round to? She wondered now if her father had had an affair. Or had at least fancied another woman to a degree which caused her mother pain. At the time she'd thought it all in her mother's head. 'Your mother's going through a rough time,' her father had said. She had tended to side with him, finding the embarrassment and inconvenience of her mother's mood changes easiest to put down to her time of life. Attempting to jolly her mother along when she was at home, and forgetting about it as soon as she was back in her university life, she had told herself that soon her mother's menopause would be over and everything at home would hopefully settle back into its normal equilibrium.

For menopause that was what it was. But only in part, she thought to herself now, seeing her own life unfolding in the same way. Only in part was it directly to do with the hormone imbalance and all that entailed. It was bound to be a bad time for women. No wonder we all feel so bloody awful. Look at it frankly. What is in store? Children leaving home. The mothering part almost over. No new challenges. No exciting sex. Husbands running after women who are younger and prettier. What did that make one feel like? It's true that men have it all.

But then, in this age of women's independence perhaps she too should take a lover? Even just for one night to see what it felt like; someone different. Nonsense, how could she possibly go about it? And then her body, would it any longer attract? It had been so many years. But it was an option. There were always options. It was going to be all right. As long as they could keep talking to one another. And after this morning perhaps they had really turned a corner.

And then as they came to the Staines roundabout and the car's speed slowed to an urban crawl, as they got nearer and nearer to the house, her thoughts came back round to Josie. Had Jeremy indeed been truthful with her this morning? Or was she once again being falsely optimistic? As they entered her own neighbourhood she became increasingly nervous. The tale-tell signs of the pain at the base of her spine were beginning to make themselves felt.

I can take so much, she said to the unknown hands who threw the dice – if it really was a game – so much. As it turns out, a great deal more than I thought I could take. Or thought I would have to take, come to that. But don't, don't let him have lied to me this morning. Don't let the story with Josie be other than what he said it was. There has to be something, some kind of a limit. This is mine.

*

In the small back kitchen at Fisk, Farmer, Sally was making coffee. She had taken the unprecedented step of popping out in order to buy macaroons for herself, Alan Boddington and Sylvia, furnishing them out of her own purse. To hell with the expense, she knew that Sylvia liked them.

As she poured the boiling water onto the granules of Gold Blend she thought with satisfaction that this was one of the small changes she had instituted. Her predecessor had economised by buying the cheapest brand. She had switched without asking Sylvia or Jeremy. One of her few moments of power. The ability to effect things; even on such a minor scale. Until today there had been precious few of them at Fisk, Farmer.

These last months she had been wondering about bestirring herself to change jobs. On and upwards. Oh, not to be anyone's secretary or assistant. To be one's own boss. And yet on the whole there was quite a lot to be said for the place. The pay was above average. Sylvia made one work, but she was generous when it came to salary and holidays. And then the work was varied. One never knew who was going to come into the office next. She enjoyed the contact with the clients – most of them. The trouble was that in a small agency there was no hope of promotion. And she'd been feeling that she just couldn't remain Sylvia's assistant for ever.

She'd arrived at work resolved to ask for an extra half an hour at lunchtime in order to go into town and put her name down with two of the employment agencies who dealt with jobs in the media. But now there was no question of it. In the middle of all that was going on, no, she wouldn't do that to Sylvia. Not now. Maybe later in the autumn. Give it another three months and then see.

She stirred the one and a half teaspoonfuls of sugar into Alan's coffee. Of course she'd sensed it all along. Sylvia and Alison living in that flat together. She'd often wondered. Not quite quite certain; on the other hand not surprised either when Sylvia told her. And that other stuff, about her marriage and the children and why Josie hadn't seen her for so many years. Of course it all made sense, it all fitted into place. Many things made more sense, even Sylvia's present irascible moods. She was clearly going through one hell of a lot.

'And are you not shocked then by what I have said?' Sylvia had asked.

'Shocked, why ever should I be? Quite a number of my friends are that way. Or a bit of both, you know. There's no big deal to it. People make such a fuss,' she'd replied.

If there was any kind of surprise this morning it was that her employer had been prepared to reveal so much about herself. Which Sally appreciated. It made Sylvia more accessible, put the whole relationship between employer and employee on a different level.

'And have you any ideas about what we should be doing to find Josie?' Sylvia had ended up asking. 'You're more her age. You might have some suggestions. Has anything she's said to you given you any clues?'

'I wish it had. I wish I could help.'

'You can think of nothing?'

'It'll turn out okay. You see. I don't think Josie is likely to do anything too screwy. She doesn't strike me as the type. Try not to worry. I know it must be awful for you.'

Yes, she'd been feeling quite pleased with herself as she left Sylvia to get on with her work, telling her not to worry, and had gone off to buy the macaroons to go with the coffee. She had even told Sylvia that she herself would handle the two difficult calls that they were expecting this morning.

'Thank you so much. You're a good girl, Sally.'

Like a lamb. Why had she ever been scared of Sylvia? she wondered. Perhaps she should have pushed for more responsibilities earlier. Perhaps it was up to her to take the initiative. Despite

Sylvia's efficiency she's human like the rest of us and one thing's for certain, I'd prefer my problems to hers, any day of the week.

Moments later she actually found herself snapping at Alan when he, whilst munching the macaroon (with not quite enough appreciation), asked if Sylvia had got round to thinking about the note he'd left on her desk.

'She's got quite enough on her plate as it is. And those meetings aren't till next week, are they? Surely it can wait till tomorrow? Or if it can't, perhaps Jeremy and you could sort it out for yourselves.'

'No panic. I was just *asking*. Really!' expostulated Alan under his breath.

'Really!' echoed Sally tossing her head and marching back to the office. After that she found herself fielding calls and working like a Trojan despite the heat. It was one of those mornings that zipped along. There was hardly a moment to look at the sun and wish she was outside enjoying it.

*

At eleven fifty-two Jeremy drew the Vauxhall to a halt outside his house. Later, he would have been able to record the time with precision because before taking the key out of the ignition he had pointed to the clock on the dashboard and remarked to Helen that with any luck he'd be just in time to catch the 12.01 in to work.

She had thought this unrealistic but had kept such thoughts to herself. Besides, what time Jeremy would get to the office was not paramount in her mind. Far from it, as with heart beating far too fast for a day as sweltering as this, she silently stood staring up at the broken window pane. Why did the criss-cross of tape seem so ominous to her?

Silently they stared. Both rooted to the spot. It was she who trying in vain to make her voice sound normal, finally said:

'Hadn't we better go on in?'

'Ah, yes.'

Together they stood on the porch while he fumbled in his pocket for the door key. It was unbearable to her. Such an intrusion. *And in her own house*. She gave a little gasp. Wanting to run back to the car, drive away, not face whatever was in store.

But now he had found the key and was slowly twisting it in the lock. Why were all his movements *so slow*. She could scream, but held on to herself. He was never normally like this, she thought. He must know something.

Now they were inside. Together they stood in the hall and looked for signs of a recent presence. Together they stepped into the sitting room.

'Ah, the paint!'

'Do you like it?'

'Yes I do. . . . Jeremy?'

'Yes?'

It all looks much as normal. Why was she whispering?

'But you like the paint, you're happy with the colour?'

'Oh yes I am. The kitchen –'

'What about the kitchen?'

'We ought to look.'

Together they opened the kitchen door. So sure had Helen become that *she was inside* that she jumped as the door creaked on its hinges and the room revealed its emptiness. In which the red, purple and white of the garden flowers made a splash of colour.

'But why did you put them in a milk bottle, Jeremy?'

'Not I –'

At the same moment their eyes focused in on the small square of neatly folded paper that lay at the base of the bottle.

JOSIE

Some hours later I was on the beach at Brighton, my jeans rolled up, paddling in the sea. I was waiting. Killing time. In about half an hour I was going to make my way to the address in Hove. My grandparents I hadn't set my peepers on since we left England, since Dad took us down to say a tearful and constrained 'goodbye' just before we travelled.

I had happy memories of the house in Hove, and of them: of my grandfather tall and lean, taking me and Angus and William in turn for rides on his shoulder round the house and gardens; of my grandmother taking an interest in my school work and urging me to bring my 'projects' down for her to look at. I remember sitting in her sewing room, poring over old picture postcards of holidays they'd taken, and loving it; my first whiff of the rich and exotic East and the art treasures of Europe. As we examined pictures of castles and cathedrals she would speak to me as an equal, or so it felt, eager to unload her store of knowledge on a receptive mind. We always used to laugh together at the leaning tower of Pisa. That was a card I insisted on seeing on every visit. 'But when will it fall?' I would ask. 'When, when?' Angus would mimic.

Geeze, it was hot. I splashed the water over my jeans and shirt, knowing it would dry in no time at all. Around me toddlers in bathing suits were playing, people were getting in and out of the water, lots of swimmers. And further out sailing-boats and wind-surfers. I'd never seen a beach with so many stones. None of your wide white sands lark. But I liked it, the backdrop of Regency buildings, the funny old pier going right out into the sea.

I remembered being here as a kid with Sylvia and Dad, Grandma and Grandpa, us kids with the obligatory buckets and spades. Dad and Grandpa building us a moat, here on this beach. Waiting, waiting for the sea to come up and rush into the moat. The first day I learnt to swim, all of three strokes, and Grandpa telling me that soon I would be swimming from one pier to the other, just like he did.

Memories flooded back, overwhelmingly strong. I wanted to thrash with my arms and throw them off. I walked back and forwards along the beach splashing myself with the icy water. It was mid morning now. The beach was filling up; people arriving in their swarms. Must be the hottest day yet. My shoes, and a sweater for later in the day, I'd left higher up the beach. In my jeans pocket my purse, toothbrush and flight ticket. My case was in the left-luggage at Victoria. I was travelling light, you could say. Just had this crazy idea that I'd visit my grandparents before I went home. It seemed a day for a last final gesture, that was what was needed.

It was scary waiting. Old people are scary. Maybe they wouldn't remember me. They could have lost their memories entirely, or be crippled, or have died even. Though then I think Dad would have said. The last time they sent presents was at least a couple of years ago. Dad never wanted to talk about them, because they were 'her' family, best forgotten. Maybe they'd be bedridden or not have any teeth or something. Maybe they'd see me and cry and embarrass me with all that stuff. Maybe I'd cry. That would be worse. And I was still in a pretty funny state of mind after last night.

Only holding onto my onions. More calm though. More together.

I could have left a note for Jeremy and taken off straight for Heathrow. I did think of doing that. Probably if I'd waited long enough I'd have got a plane seat today. But it wasn't a day to be on a plane. And anyway I wanted to see them. Wanted to see for myself, just as a last gesture. There are days like that when you have to do something extended, something kind of crazy, like taking off into the unknown.

Calmer I was. It was all that stuff with the windows that helped. The nosing around the sheds and garage in search of putty. And concentrating on making a neat job. One I thought, when I was through, that Dad would have been proud of.

Then I couldn't find any tape for that broken pane. So it had to be Elastoplast in the end. Rifled the entire contents from the box in the medicine cabinet. A temporary measure. Till Jeremy got back. Picked Michaelmas daisies and lupins from the garden (the flower beds were thick with them so I reckoned it would be okay) and left them in a milk bottle on the kitchen table with my note of apology and explanation – 'Things got somewhat extreme back in Islington and needed somewhere just for one night.' I knew Jeremy would understand. I promised him that I would write more fully from back home, brilliant scintillating letters, 'So good you'll be thinking about becoming *my* agent soon,' I told him. Then I was ready to quit.

But before I quit, just before, I went back into the sitting room and looked at the phone. Felt drawn to it. Like waiting for it to ring again. I said to it, 'I know you're going to ring, so sod it, do so.' I said to it, 'Who were you, causing trouble, who were you, needing something?' I said to it, 'Tell me; I've needed things myself, geeze, lots of them.' I said to it, 'Here is your chance, your last chance. After that I'm gone.'

I suppose that is when I must have made a conscious decision to start searching the house for any correspondence relating to Ruth. It was crazy, I know. And I came to think, geeze, this story of Alison's has hit deep. So I never did just leave Jeremy's house. Not like that, not like I'd intended after I'd left my note with the Michaelmas daisies. The kitchen door was already open, the glorious morning sun shining in. All I had to do was collect up my case, lock the door and throw the key back through the letter-box. Then away.

Instead of that I was back inside, hunting through Jeremy's papers. He didn't have a study or anything like that. Just a mahogany table in his bedroom, littered. I rifled it. And all the places downstairs where books and correspondence were lying; the kitchen table, the mantelpiece, the sitting room floor, and eventually back to the bedroom again, and there I opened his briefcase. Last, because it seemed to me the most personal. Also I didn't think, not a year later. Not in his briefcase, now. It linked it too much with the present. The present in which I'd been involved. And I didn't want to think of that, I wanted rather to think of it, if it did indeed happen (this morning all of what Alison said seemed far more real), as far away in an almost forgotten past.

But there in his briefcase, unlocked, open to the world, there in his bedroom for Helen to come back to and find, for Christ sake, was a whole bundle of papers, splendidly tied in a pink ribbon – pleadings in the case of *Fisk* v. *Flowert*.

I read one letter. It was the last, or rather a copy of the last: the one written to Jeremy last October. She said she couldn't bear it any more, herself in London with the child. She didn't know, she wrote, if she could bear anything any more. Had been taken in by friends in the country 'kind friends', she wrote, 'sculptor and his wife, very kind'. 'I don't mean to blame you,' she wrote, 'only to describe, in the hope that it will relieve my burden, the anguish I'm living under.'

Then I did leave. Didn't stop to read all those letters and all that other stuff, didn't stop to find out if Alison had been right or wrong. Geeze, no, we all have our troubles and mine are what I'm coping with. You've got to be okay, do you hear me, Ruth? *You have got to be okay*. You are older than me. You've got kind friends who sculpt. Geeze, no, you've got to be okay. Anyway that was almost a year ago.

So great my concentration I'd hardly noticed how far I'd wandered along the shore out of sight of my shoes and sweater. I got out of the water and ran along the thin strip of sand back to where I hoped they'd be. A couple were laying out a picnic lunch, couples, families, dogs, children, girlfriends and boyfriends, the lot. The whole seething mass of humanity there on Brighton beach.

My sweater and shoes: such a small pile. I kept looking and looking, getting more panicky. But eventually there they were between two groups of picnic-makers. The face of the beach had changed so, just in the time I'd been paddling in the sea. I felt down into the toe of my right-hand shoe where my watch was. Twelve fifteen. Seemed about right. The kind of time you might call on old folks like them, the kind of time they would have got up by, if they were going to get up for lunch. Okay then. Taking a deep breath, carrying my shoes, for my feet were too wet to immediately put them back on, I made my way painfully over the stones towards the esplanade.

Half an hour later, by dint of many stops to solicit directions, I was walking up that wide road that had always intrigued me because they had explained that it divided Brighton from Hove. And I remembered, as a kid, being bothered that there was no dividing mark; wondering where, at what exact spot in the road the division came.

I couldn't remember the number of the house, only the name of the road. Still, I knew it was on the Hove side, also that the house faced down over the sea, jogging memory easily. I seem to remember that it was a long way up the road, almost at the top, at the brow of the hill; almost at the end of the town itself and where suburbia made the transition to wild downland.

It was sweltering hot. I was quite dried out from the splashing but sweating like a pig. It was almost unbearable holding my woolly sweater, but more unbearable still wearing it round my waist. I'd rolled my jeans again up to my knees and the sleeves of my shirt back as far as they would go. My hair I'd tied back with a rubber band but wished to hell it was on a knot on top of my head. I wanted it nowhere near my neck and shoulders. I'd stopped for an ice before finally leaving the beach. Money was getting short now. Only a few more pounds left. I had my return ticket to London. But somehow I'd have to get myself to Heathrow. Could perhaps borrow from my grandparents. Nope, not such a hot shot idea. The ice had been just irresistible. But now it was making me thirstier than ever and I was regretting it like mad. What wouldn't I give for a glass of iced water.

I knew I hadn't come far enough to seriously start inspecting the houses. As I made my way slowly uphill, panting and stopping in the shade of a tree or wall when it got too unbearable, my mind was mostly a blank. I couldn't imagine what would be ahead. So it was like something I didn't want to think about. Every now and again I thought about Jeremy coming back and finding my note with the Michaelmas daisies. I also thought of Sylvia. But thought, sure she'd just survey that message of mine with that cold impassive face of hers, ask Alison what it was all about; Alison would lie madly, naturally. Then Sylvia would shrug and say something like, well it's her business anyway, and get on with her life. Forgetting all about me. That's what she's done all the way along the line. All the way since – Still, I can handle it now, I told her silently, just get along with my own life. As long as I don't have to see you any more, the seeing you is what is so painful.

Once or twice I thought about Ruth and the sculptors. A week before her case came before the court. But blotted it out. Like I told

Ruth, I had enough on my mind without her problems. Frankly I just didn't want to know. I'd climbed so far out of the town that I could feel the beginning of a breeze blowing off the Downs. And geeze, wasn't it just welcome. I must be getting nearer.

The houses were becoming grander now. I started to inspect them more rigorously. All were low and stretched out, so unlike London, lots rather ugly, solid-built in red brick. Some modern single-storey ones. I was searching my mind hard for features I remembered. A kind of drive that has an entrance and an exit. I remembered playing with Angus that we were the cars, racing round and round and having the most almighty crashes. I remembered formal gardens in the front. A huge garage which housed Grandad's three cars. He loved cars, loved having different ones for different occasions. I tried to remember the colour of shutters on the windows. I shut my eyes and tried to think back. Usually I'm good on colours. Green, yeah. I think that's what it was, green. Don't be daft, I told myself, they're probably bright orange now.

And so I began to creep along, not only because of the heat, which was less intense now, far better with the breeze blowing, but because at any moment I might really come face to face with this house that I was picturing. As my steps became slower and slower, I was aware of the stillness round about. This was one of the poshest areas in the town, I guess, no kids playing or babies squalling. A few tradespeople discreetly bustled by. Hardly any activity at all. Like everyone was inside their houses, lying down in the heat or waiting for death or something. All sound muffled by heavy curtains and thick carpets. Spooked me. What was I doing?

As I drew nearer – I could see the top of the hill now, where the road spilled out into the countryside, so it had to be soon – I began to wonder more seriously about old age. Tried for a start to reckon their ages, but couldn't get along too well there. So little has ever been said. They could be in their seventies, could be in their eighties. I don't think they'd be in their nineties.

I tried to imagine them inside their house, not expecting anything like what was going to happen to them in a few minutes. I hoped the shock wouldn't kill them. Tried to imagine inside their heads. What would they be doing exactly at this moment? All I could think of was two little old people, shrunk and frail because of Sylvia and my uncle Timmy, shrunk and frail, wrapped in rugs even on a day like today, sitting upright in opposite chairs in the sitting room facing the garden. He would be in his dressing-gown; but still correct, still stylish like I remembered him, with a rose in the lapel of his dressing-gown. She would be in a silk dress and cardigan. She would have a hearing aid. Her hair would be white; she had a white streak, I remember, before. Yes, totally white, but lovely and soft like old people's hair sometimes is, and someone would have driven her to the hairdresser so that it would be set and looking immaculate.

They would be reading the papers, or listening to the radio, yes, that is what they'd be doing. Listening to the radio and quietly waiting. Waiting for the cook. (They'd still have a cook, though no one else does any more, I reckon. And quite right too. Folks should cook for themselves. Except when they're old; that's different, I suppose.) They'd be waiting for the cook to say, 'It's lunchtime.' At least, they'd be thinking that is what they were waiting for. But really they'd be waiting for me. They wouldn't know it but they wouldn't be waiting for death, nor for lunch; they'd be waiting for me.

Then there was the house. The shutters were indeed green. Though much in need of new paint. In the front garden a valiant display of dahlias, pansies and anemones waved in the breeze. There were things I immediately recognised and wondered how I could ever have forgotten, like the salmon-pink step up to the front door. The wall against which I'd practised throwing a ball, careful to miss the aubrietia of which my grandmother had been so proud. The wall was there, dividing their territory from the next. The aubrietia was no longer. 'It's a miracle,' she'd said to me, 'that it grows here, the gales are so fierce.'

I ran the last steps, all doubts as to what to expect blown to the breeze, in a fury of expectation. Tears started to pour down my cheeks – Grandma, Grandpa – and I fought them back. No, this wouldn't do. I wiped my face best I could with my sweat-sodden shirt and took some deep breaths, trying to compose myself.

It was my grandmother who answered the door. She stood looking at me for what seemed like for ever. And then I did start to cry. And then she took me in her arms. And then she cried too. And my grandfather, hearing the commotion, limped out of the sitting room. He was leaning on a stick but properly dressed, not in a dressing-gown at all and as lean and upright as ever.

'Grandpa.' I left my grandmother's arms and raced towards him.

'Wait a moment,' he said to her, 'who is this?'

But I knew that he knew. Just needed time. We all needed time.

There was no cook. We were eating ham and salad, my grandparents and me. My grandmother must have been in her early seventies. She still moved vigorously. She had prepared the meal with quick capable hands whilst I had stood around in the kitchen watching and talking. I had asked if I could help and she had set me to making mustard, like I remember it as a child, a little pot with grains of pure yellow mustard which had to be mixed to a paste with water. She was not as tall as I remember. Or perhaps she'd shrunk. More or less my height now. She'd grown stouter, but only around the middle, her arms and legs were thin. He was older, my grandfather, thin, almost gaunt. His hands were rheumatic and trembled ever so slightly. He was less alert than she, perhaps a little deaf, I couldn't tell yet. Slower. From time to time he asked her what I was saying. As if he had got used to speaking through her. My grandparents.

We sat eating our ham and salad. Time seemed to be something they had masses of. Though I of course was in a rush. I wanted to tell them everything. Between mouthfuls of ham and salad to retrace the steps between now and the warm intimacy of the contact of my childhood as quickly as possible. I found myself catapulting into phrases, tumbling down avenues of thought, guilty of eating with my mouth open – and far more. I drew a picture of our life in Canada, gave a thumbnail sketch of each member of the family exaggerating for effect and laughs. I wanted to get it over as quickly as possible and come down to the real business of them and me.

My grandmother listened and each time I stopped to gobble more ham, plied me judiciously with further questions. I was never quite sure how much my grandfather understood. Or indeed heard. From time to time he would put up his hand imperiously to halt the drift. 'What is she saying?' he would ask Grandma. Who would do her best to repeat all I was saying.

They spoke of Dad with affection. And that gladdened me. 'He was a dear boy, such earnestness, such a fire for his profession.' 'And that "au pair", now your stepmother. . . ?' They seemed worried. I tried to reassure. 'Oh she's great, really great Anna. And makes Dad ever so happy. She's got a baby of her own now, you know. My half brother.' Here they frowned and I realised how close I was to dangerous ground.

At one point my grandmother stretched out a hand. 'Stop talking now and finish your ham. There is so much we want to know; but all in good time.' I ate in silence but with no interest in the food. Like a child dying to finish my plateful so that I could get down from the table, only in this case it was so I could continue with the communications that were beginning to flow. I had so much to tell.

While I ate and she fussed about him, I thought about the difference between this lot of grandparents and those other, Scottish ones. Dad's parents. She who knitted me thick sweaters for the winter and sent us homemade shortbreads and other goodies. They who came to stay and disapproved: of Anna (overtly) and us (less overtly). They who always implied that things had been better in another age. That Anna and Dad were too soft with us, that it was a pity children weren't still seen not heard. That Canada was mostly a wicked influence on us all and that Dad having made the decision to emigrate (which they managed to imply wasn't exactly their son's fault but had something to do – much – with our terrible mother) the least he could do was fight to keep going as much of the Scottish/English tradition as possible. Always there was the implication that everything was better back home than in Canada. Always the impression that everything had been better in their day than ours.

When we started to groan, 'Oh no, not another visit!' Dad mournfully urged, 'Can't you just try and be nice to them? They are your grandparents, you know, and they love you dearly.' So we gritted our teeth and wrote the obligatory letters every month (which Dad said helped to further our letter-writing ability – 'mostly becoming a lost art in this country: you and all your peers for ever on the phone') and were more or less amenable when the dreaded visits occurred.

Ever since I started thinking about them at all, I wondered about their kind of love. I thought it had more to do with inherited traits that reminded them of their own parents, or brothers and sisters; a sense of family blood, of it being renewed down the ages. The hope that in its most recent form (us and our Scottish cousins) it would still be something they could be proud of. Continuation, something to buoy them up. They hated our Canadian accents and all that made them think not of sameness but of differences.

In the same way, disapproving of (despising might not be too strong) our mother, they were closed to anything that might smack of her genes. My winning essay-writing competitions, Angus having his art-work in the school magazine, were looked upon coldly as being altogether attributes too arty by half for 'their' sort of family. And it was the same with anything that might be considered too Jewish a characteristic.

Jewishness was not something much mentioned in our household. It was only in my late teens that I began to be aware of myself as half Jewish (completely Jewish, the Jews would have it, since the religion is taken from the mother's side) and to secretly try to figure out what all that amounted to. And I don't even know if the others thought of it at all. By that time I had become acutely aware that Jewish traits were looked on askance by my Scottish grandparents. My sister Karen for example is a real neat-looking kid. She has large brown eyes, wavy brown hair, a dark ruddy skin that makes her always look like she's glowing with health. 'She is obviously flourishing,' I once overheard them saying, in response to a comment of Dad's, 'but what a pity her skin is so sallow.'

No, they didn't seem to me to be on our side and the older I grew the less I liked them. Often in my mind I compared them to the grandparents I'd lost, who I secretly thought of as my real grandparents. Who seemed to have been truly interested in me. In each one of us. Who wouldn't, I knew, have responded to comments we would make about our school subjects or activities so disappointingly. 'Tell Granny about your History project, darling.' 'Tell Grandad about your music class.' But whatever you said they never seemed to listen. Not really. They'd listen for a moment or two, just enough for politeness. Then in they'd come with how it was a shame that History was taught in this way in Canada, now in their day . . . It was all like that.

They thought the young had a duty to listen to them, to their old nostalgias. They thought we'd be interested. They looked on the modern world, as far as I could see, with sadness, their favourite expression – what a shame . . . About our school work, our manners, our hairstyles, the clothes we wore, the way we talked. You name it. They couldn't see anything good, it appeared, about any of it. Yet we thought that it was wonderfully exciting, whatever we were doing, and couldn't see why they didn't.

Between us a hostile divide that grew and grew. And when I used to go to bed angry and saddened once again, at its worst when they criticised us to Dad, poor Dad who had enough on his plate as it was, especially after Anna got pregnant, I'd grit my teeth and say to myself over and over, 'Never mind they're not my *real* grandparents.'

These were my real grandparents then. These old, dignified people. Sitting so upright, so quietly as they ate their summer pudding.

I started again to babble, but again my grandmother, with a smile at my impulsiveness, halted my flow. 'Gently, gently, your grandfather can only take in so much at a time. And yet we want to hear everything you've got to tell us. But all in good time. We're not going anywhere. And I hope you're not either. So eat your pudding and then I'm sure your grandfather would like to show you the rose garden. Do you remember playing in the summer-house there?' Indeed I did. 'The roses are quite at their peak this year. We've extended the garden considerably over the last years and recently invested in two enormous greenhouses. All of which helps dear Sarah.' Who was dear Sarah?

Later in the kitchen as I stacked the dishes and my grandmother made the coffee she was more expansive than in front of my grandfather, and with some prompting told me the following. 'After your mother went out of our life, and we lost touch with you little ones, we felt a very great loss, naturally. We were devastated, Josie, I hardly need to tell you. It was my idea to approach the Home. We were completely honest with them. We had no illusions that it wasn't just as much for our benefit as for that of any children we might take on. We did, on the other hand, have a certain amount to offer, candidly, money, a good home, time to devote. Michael and I both hoped that we could help perhaps some other less fortunate children. As it was, it was they who helped us, Sarah and Tony. I think it is true to say that without them I don't know quite what would have happened to us.

'Sarah was fourteen then, Tony just coming up to thirteen. It was a bare three months before his Barmitzvah. They were casualties of the war. Both their parents were born in concentration camps. The father, never very well, died young of a mysterious illness and the mother a year later committed suicide. The children were eight and nine respectively. The authorities could trace no relatives who would take them in.

'We decided we were too old and set in our ways to foster them. But we took an interest. They started by coming to the house after synagogue every Saturday, and then took to staying over for the weekends. We were able to afford things for them that otherwise would have been impossible. Extra lessons for example, and holidays. They were devoted to each other. They were also most warm and loving to us. As I say they've helped us through, Josie.

'Of course they're both grown-up now. But we still see a great deal of them, of Sarah particularly. When she left school her idea was to become a florist. Then it turned out that she had a real talent for arranging the flowers. She went on a training course, then last year we decided to set her up in her own business, and extended the gardens and greenhouse for that purpose. Most of the flowers she uses are grown here. She in return keeps us gloriously stocked.'

'And Tony?'

'Tony is just about to take his qualifying exams as an accountant.' She spoke with pride. She must have seen the expression on my face for she touched my arm lightly. 'Of course it's not the same as family, Josie, real family. Now let's take this coffee in to your grandfather.'

He had moved into the sun lounge. The doors were opened into the garden. From hanging baskets plants cascaded into the room, rivulets of colour. Huge mixed bowls of plants were decoratively arranged on low tables. Framed by blooms of every colour, my grandfather at first appeared asleep. Outside the sun lounge a blue awning had been pulled down casting his face as low as his chin in shadow. But the sun shone bright on his jowl and neck.

'Is he asleep?'

'No, just resting.'

It made me nervous the way his breath came in staccato-like jerks. Was he really 'just resting'. But as she put the coffee cup down beside him, he opened his eyes wide. Good clear blue eyes. Very direct. Like they knew lots that I didn't. All the mysteries of the universe – was it just his nearness to death? – and said, 'Well what have you been doing with yourself, lass?'

I was caught off guard. 'In the last few minutes, do you mean? Or – or, since I've come to London?' Those eyes looking at me.

'Have you been with your mother, then?'

'That's right, Grandpa. I came over for a visit, to see her.'

'How long are you staying in England, Josie?' came in my grandmother. 'We're throwing an engagement party for Sarah, you know. She's recently got herself engaged to such a nice . . .'

'Your mother. We've never been able to understand her. She broke her own mother's heart by what she did. Do you know that?' My grandmother was rattling saucers on the tray. 'Well?' he demanded.

It had never occurred to me that I would be called to account for my mother.

'Well?'

'Leave her alone, Michael.'

It seemed to me that at that moment I had to rush in with flag waving. Or otherwise it would be too late. My grandfather would be dead. I would lose energy. The moment would pass. It had to be now.

'I think that she's suffered a great deal,' I blurted out.

301

'Ha! Suffering.'

'She has a lovely home. And then this agency of hers, she looks after ever so many writers, they're all phoning her all the time, Grandpa, and crying on her shoulders and she's ever so good with them.' I couldn't believe I was saying these things. Defending my mother. 'She's an important agent, really she is. She makes masses of money.' Grandpa snorted. 'No, honestly, Grandpa. She supports herself entirely and does all sorts of good things with her money.' I hoped this was true. 'Jeremy Farmer, that's the bloke who works with her says she's a literary agent extraordinaire. How about that?'

'Jeremy Farmer, eh?'

'Yes, Grandpa, when he got turned out of his publishing firm, she gave him a job. So you see –'

'What do I see?'

I faltered.

Suddenly. 'That scandalous relationship. I just cannot understand. It's a wonder she has time for anything else. And that she isn't too ashamed . . .'

'Oh it isn't like that, honest. They're just – ordinary. Just like anyone else, you know.'

'Are you telling me that you can understand it?' His eyes, boring into me it seemed, demanded honesty.

I shook my head. I tried to speak with the same certainty, but my voice let me down. I said it anyway, 'Haven't we got to try?' I went over and held his hand and couldn't prevent my tears, but tried to restrain them, not wanting to cause these elderly people more distress. As I sniffed he looked at me with those bright eyes of his.

After a time.

'There, that's enough of that.' He patted my hair as one would a child. 'Help to pull me up,' he said, 'and we'll go and have a look at the roses.'

'Grandma . . . ?'

'You go with him.'

I looked at her uncertainly. 'Go on,' she encouraged. Then mouthed, '*It will do him good.*'

He took my arm, his stick in the other arm. The breeze quivered through the garden, making the tufts of short manicured lawn and the well-stocked flower-beds restless. The garden was on a decline, with steps from each level to the next. These my grandfather took slowly and painfully. While I waited uncertainly, quickly learning that there was only a limited amount of help he would accept, I looked down through the many tiers of Brighton and Hove, all stretched out there in the sun, to the deep blue sea on which I could now see the white of sea horses.

'I love to look at the spray,' I told him. He nodded, more intent on the garden. We were walking now through a covered pathway made up of a mix of honeysuckle and wild dog-roses. The yellow and red was a glorious mix. But mostly I was grateful to be out of the sun, which I feared might prove too strong for my grandfather. For the moment he appeared oblivious, intent on his task. With his arm through mine he hurried forward with determined steps. The determination of all Fisks, I thought. And of myself. I felt glad as I walked beside him. I loved it that he rested his arm against mine.

Through the stone wall into the walled rose garden we went. In the middle of the rose beds there was now a miniature fountain, the water erupting from a cone held in the chubby hands of a small boy. He pointed with his stick, 'In memory of Timothy,' he said gruffly. 'Yes,' I said, 'of course.'

The roses, as he'd claimed, were at their peak. He took me round slowly, talking of each strain, its history, its origins. They were a riot of colour, of reds, oranges, yellows, creams and whites. Their scent overwhelming.

'Which are your favourite?'

It only took me a moment to decide.

'How strange. Those are mine too.' Then it occurred to him; he looked at me craftily. 'Did she tell you?'

'No, honest she didn't. Of course she didn't.' He seemed satisfied.

I would have liked to have looked in the garden house but was reluctant to keep him out too long. So we moved on to the greenhouses which we popped our heads inside for long enough for me to view the tomatoes, soft fruits, carnations, even orchids.

'Grandpa, how exciting to have all this going on.'

He looked thoughtful. 'Back now,' he told me.

As we made our leisurely way back to the house he said little. Then just as we were about to step inside:

'So you've been staying with her, eh?' As if it had never been out of his mind.

'Yes, Grandpa, I have.'

He looked at me once more with that same intent look. Then nodded.

'Well what are you waiting for?' he said briskly. 'Come on into the house with you, lass.'

Inside, he moved away from the sun lounge, which was hot even with the awning down, to the cooler back drawing room. With its

303

serious ornate furniture and stuffed cushions, it was a room that was just as I remembered it. Grandma, watching him trail across the room to a large armchair at the far end, said to me:

'Now he most probably will fall asleep. This is the time for his afternoon nap.'

'I hope I didn't tire him out.'

She shook her head, smiling. Then she embraced me.

'Now don't start crying again. The older you are, the harder it is to take tears – particularly of the young.'

'I don't think I'm going to. It's just that, geeze, I'm so glad to be here.'

Some time later she excused herself, went off upstairs and never came back down. I guessed that she too was taking a sleep. It was that kind of day. Scorching in the still afternoon. The sort of day when everyone should sleep now and wake up again as the moon comes up. Then dance the night away. But I couldn't have slept if I'd been paid. I retraced my steps across the garden towards the summer-house: treasure-trove of memories.

Glad to be here. Glad to be accepted by them, I could have said. The swings of mood in me seemed to be extreme. As if after the weekend all the emotions were dangerously pushed to the front. Just under the skin. As if at any moment tears or laughter would surface, difficult to know which. It didn't seem like the real stuff of me, didn't seem what I was used to tackling in myself, and it unnerved me.

I retraced my steps to the summer-house in the dead of that hot afternoon while both my Fisk grandparents napped. Making towards that room in which I'd more than once dressed up in my forebears' clothes, hats, trinkets, jewellery, I was giddy with what had just taken place. To which the heady perfume, trapped in the still hour, of all those many thousand roses, added its part. We had found each other, they and I. 'I'm alone, alone,' I heard that other voice, crying. 'No, I don't want to hear you. I'm thinking about my grandparents. *Go away.*'

Thinking about my grandparents. The reality of what I have been party to. The possibility too, that a bridge has been formed, as yet rickety like a rope bridge over a high gorge. The kind where one has to pass in single file, treading with great attention, possibly even on hands and knees: but a bridge all the same over which there might follow other traffic; my brothers and sisters, Dad ('that nice young man'), and not quite out of the question, Sylvia herself. Because of me. Maybe then she would – But that was taboo ground. Hadn't I settled it once and for all? I wouldn't allow myself to hope any further. Not even to want.

'You're not rushing off anywhere, I hope, Josie,' my grandmother had said. 'We're getting on now. Something like this comes as a shock. You must allow us time to get used to it, and used to you. There is so much your grandfather and I want to ask. But not now. Not in a rush.'

As I wandered round the now empty summer-house, empty except for old deck chairs and an assortment of outdoor furniture, looking for traces, items to which would cling the memories of childhood romps, and finding none, I thought dreamily of the days ahead. Of course somehow I'd have to retrieve my luggage from Victoria station. But then, then . . . The cosy chats over light lunches, the daily walk in the garden with my grandfather, the occasional jaunt out into the countryside, the small acts of spoiling by my grandmother. Perhaps the two of us would sit together in her sewing-room as of old, whilst downstairs my grandfather read yesterday's papers. And perhaps she would tell tales from her youth and of our various ancestors, of whose lives I was so abysmally ignorant. Perhaps she would tell me the secrets of her own life, which she had told no one else . . .

'God damn it, Ruth,' I said. 'Don't come peeping into my thoughts now. Away with you. Leave a person to have a bit of peace, will you.'

But she wouldn't. She came in on the scent of the roses, I reckoned. She seemed to be there more and more like a lone violin that no amount of noise from the orchestra will blank out. This other woman with whom Jeremy had also. This other woman with her young son who wretchedly needed a father, she had written. This other woman to whom I felt bound because – because. This other woman who had written from the house in Plumpton last Fall saying . . .

Plumpton. And then, there in the garden-house, out of the recesses of my mind the name conjured up something it had not when I was in London. All of a sudden it became frighteningly clear to me why I had made the journey down here. It wasn't at all as I thought.

*

305

'Now are you quite sure you can manage?' Sylvia said to Sally.

Jeremy, Sylvia and Sally were in the reception area of Fisk, Farmer. On Sally's desk, Jeremy, leaning over her shoulder, was making a volley of attacks on the book in which the stamps were neatly housed. So many 1st class ones when really, wouldn't 2nd class do? A look passed between Sally and Sylvia.

'Are you ready then?' Sylvia said to Jeremy with mock gaiety.

'What do you think I'm standing around for, woman?'

'And Sally, if Alex Boyd phones . . .'

'Yes, I've got it all written down, Sylvia. Honestly, don't worry about a thing.'

Sylvia couldn't quite believe it. She looked around for something more to concern herself with. Maybe to put off the moment of leaving the office; a last-moment attempt to distract herself from what lay ahead. But Sally was having none of it. She was brisk with her employer. Standing up she began to flap her arms about. At one and the same time shielding Sylvia from the sight of the neat piles on Sally's desk that might give rise to more last-minute instructions – or further explanation; and by her body movements driving Sylvia and Jeremy towards the door in the same almost imperceptible way that she had seen Sylvia do to clients who were taking too long over their departure.

'What a perfect day for Brighton. Wish it were me. But I'm sure you should try and get off quickly; before the rush-hour traffic builds up.'

'She's right,' said Jeremy, looking at his watch (it seemed to be a day for time checks). 'Come along, woman.'

Sylvia preferred 'woman' to 'darling'. He'd been in that kind of mood ever since he'd phoned her from the house to tell her about Josie's overnight stay and the substance of her note.

'My parents, Jeremy. Oh heavens! What a mess this all is. I do hate to think of them being dragged in.'

'Dragged in. Nonsense. She probably just wants to see them.'

'Them and her. After all these years. I can't imagine what it will be like. But thank goodness she's safe. Did you get any idea of what kind of a state she's in?'

'Not much, no. I do think she's feeling terribly let down by you. By all of us. She's quitting, you know.'

'Quitting?'

'Planning to fly home.'

'What can I do, Jeremy? I've handled all this so badly. *Something* must be done. She can't go back. Just like that. I'm at my wits' end.'

'Pull yourself together, woman.'

He'd said it then. She'd found it strangely comforting. As she did now. It was he too who had suggested the step they were just about to take. On the stairs she turned to him.

'It really is extremely kind of you to offer to come too. Especially after all the driving you've already done. Are you sure . . . ?'

'Of course I'm sure. We'll just have to stop off at the house and explain to Helen what's going on. And so I can change shirts. Talk about suffocating; I'm soaked in sweat. It shouldn't take more than a couple of seconds.'

JOSIE

It was near on five o'clock. At last the scorching heat had gone out of the day. In my grandmother's blue Austin the two of us were being bounced up and down as we proceeded at quite a pace down narrow country lanes.

She slowed down and turned at right-angles. I saw the sign, Plumpton racecourse one mile.

'You can't remember much about those times, surely, Josie, after all you were still a very little girl. I can't think what makes you want to come –'

'Grandma, can I ask you something odd?'

'What is it?'

'Just drop me here.'

'Drop you?'

'Yeah. I've got to visit someone, Grandma. Don't look worried. It's kind of odd, I know. But I'll explain everything later. I promise. You just get back to Grandpa.'

She continued undecided. A shut-mouth look, as if life had dealt her so many surprises, why should she query this one.

'I'll be back later, I promise.'

Practicalities. How? Would I need a taxi – did I have money? I admitted to having only a pound or two.

'Here.'

'That's far too much.'

'Take it.'

'Geeze, I really can't.'

307

'If you don't use it, give it back to me later. But hold onto it for the moment.'

'Grandma, you're great.' I gave her a peck on the cheek and was out of the car. Soon I was waving to her through the driving mirror.

After the sound of the motor had died in the distance, I became intensely aware of the surroundings. Of the quiet. Of the first traces of vivid pink in what had been a blue, blue sky. Of the Downs rising dramatically, almost at my feet. Of their switchback contours stretching way into the distance. Of a patchwork of different colours, fields every shade of yellow and brown, minute, like pocket handkerchiefs, each divided by hedge or fence. It was a toyland compared to the prairies, the breeze just great, the smells gorgeous: country smells, cows, horses and I don't know what all else. All around the birds, lethargic in the middle of the day, were now singing their heads off. It was countryside you could feel comfortable in.

Despite that I still felt unreal to myself, like so much – too much – was happening. Like I was floating. Like I was outside my body. Like I was driven. I had to go and see her, though it was crazy. What after all, when I found her, would I say? I sat on a pile of rubble by the roadside, to get my breath and my bearings.

A guy came by on his bike. I asked him the way into the village. He pointed up the road. I half believed that she'd no longer be here. The letter had been sent last Fall. She could have returned to London. She could have moved a hundred times since then. Would I chase her all the way?

In the village store I found out that I wouldn't have to. She lived with the Spurlings, I was informed, up at West Lodge Farm. A few copies of *Wasted* and of an earlier novel, *Good Terms*, were even displayed on the shelves amongst the more popular paperbacks. The woman behind the counter talked about Ruth's son Toby. 'A fine little boy,' she said, 'one of my favourites. Of course he's in here often with his mother or Mrs Spurling, buying his sweeties and that.' She wanted to close up, she indicated. I bought a packet of marshmallows.

'I'll be on my way then. Thanks again. Third on the right, you say?'

'Then after the bridge, take the dirt track on the left. Then right to the end as far as you can go. There's a fork off to the left. But don't have anything to do with that. Carry straight on. You shouldn't have any difficulty. It'll be near enough in front of your nose then. And sign-posted.'

The easy part, I told myself. What was hard was what the hell would follow. The woman was standing with one hand on the door. Okay, Ruth, I'm coming.

A kid, about four years old, was sitting on the gravel at the gatepost, legs splayed out, in one small fist a miniature fire-engine, in the other a lorry. The cars were being revved up, as if in preparation for a race. He was dressed in khaki-coloured shorts and open-toed sandals. The rest of him was exposed to the sun. A skinny little guy with auburn hair, a small pointed face, large ears, and deep penetrating amber eyes that as I drew up level seemed to be searching right through me into my soul.

'Hello.'

He bent back down to his cars.

'Are you Toby?'

Some two feet above his head, a sign in fine script read 'Concealed entrance. Approach carefully. Keep a look out for children.' The house was quite a distance away. I wondered about him being out here, so near the lane, on his own.

'Oh, I brought something for you.' Fumbling in the pocket of my jeans for the marshmallows I brought out two of them and placed them in front of him.

'Here, these are for you.'

He picked up a handful of gravel and stuffed it between his toes, still bending his head away from me. I crouched on my knees beside him. But not too near.

'Of course these aren't for eating. They'd be horrid to eat. But they're great to play with, they're so squishy. I bet one of them could be squeezed into your lorry. Then you could pretend it was carrying a sack of potatoes. Or if I ate half of one – you wouldn't want to do that, would you, Toby? But I wouldn't mind, just to help – and then we sent the cars crashing in to it, they'd stick. It would be a great laugh. Do you want to try?'

'How do you know?' Still he wasn't looking at me.

'Know, sure I know. I did it with my brothers. And other much more fun things.'

'Like what?'

'Well,' I grinned, liking him, 'you'll have to find out in time. Now, do you want me to bite it in half, or you?'

'You.'

'Right. Here goes.' I bit into it, then made exaggerated faces of delight. 'Perhaps to set it up properly we'll need two. Shall I bite into the second one?'

'Me, me.'

'You'd like to try it, would you? Okay then. It's half the fun, you see. Do you like the taste?'

He obviously did.

'Another one.'

'Another? Let's leave the others for later. Now what about these cars. Look, if I set up the marshmallows like this. And you revv them up like mad then push them with all your force –'

Soon the remaining marshmallows were gone and he was telling me a long convoluted story of what had happened when his friend Gregory had come to play, something to do with tractors but I could only understand one word in four. All the same I listened carefully, real pleased to have won his confidence. With a great woosh of happiness I was experiencing the pleasure of being with a kid again in a world that seemed altogether more easy. More accessible. I thought of my brothers and sisters. I almost looked forward to being home now.

'Toby, I know your name but you don't know mine. It's Josie. I'm a friend of your mother, kind of. I'm real pleased to have met you and now I want to meet her. Is she in the house? Will you show me the way?'

Again he gave me that strange look as if he was seeking God knows what.

'Not here.'

'Your Mum isn't here? Where is she?'

'Up there.' He pointed up the lane, towards the village.

'Has she gone to do some shopping?'

He shook his head.

'I expect she'll be back soon. Are Mr and Mrs Spurling at the house?'

He shook his head.

'Come on, Toby. Someone's at the house. Will you take me up there, please?' I held out my hand to him, 'I need you to show me the way because it's such a long long drive, isn't it, and I might get lost otherwise.'

'Stay here.'

'You want to stay here?' He nodded. 'To wait for Mummy?' He nodded again. And then that look. To make quite, quite sure I understood. I did.

'Well what if we both go to the house together. I'd like it if you came too, Toby. And then I'll come back here with you later.'

'Promise?'

'Promise.'

He groped up towards my hand. It gave confidence to have Toby's hot fingers in my own. Whatever was I going to say when finally I came face to face with Ruth? Just how was I going to explain why I had come? Yet more than ever, with Toby's fingers wound round my own, I was certain that there was no going back.

Outside the house Toby hesitated, scuffed his toe in the gravel; withdrew his hand from mine.

'Where to now, Toby?'

He drew a semi-circle in the gravel.

To the left a long low outbuilding showed signs of having been converted into a studio. From where I stood I could see through the half-opened gable door to a massive piece of yew wood which two men, one young one older, were in the process of persuading into a girl's shape. Moving quickly out of their range of vision I turned around and contemplated the house. Part-tiled, part-thatched, it too was low and extended intriguingly in a number of directions. The front section was entirely covered with Virginia creeper, whose luscious green leaves reflected the sunlight.

As I was contemplating my next move, the front door opened and a black and white Collie came out excitedly wagging its tail and sniffing at Toby's bare legs.

'Off, Jasper, off!' he cried.

The open door revealed a long passageway with stone floor, on the sides of which shelves were stacked with pots of every size and colour.

'Is that the way in? Shall we go and find Mrs Spurling, Toby?'

'She's working. Dick's working. Mummy's working,' he said sadly.

'What a world! Poor Toby. Never mind; I'm not working. And I can play lots of games with you. But I think I ought to just say hello to Mrs Spurling. Can you lead the way?'

He shrugged his shoulders and set off with determined little steps down the corridor. I followed. The inside was a network of inter-connecting rooms. Passing through them, each one dark, cool, offered shelter from the tremendous glare of the sun. The walls were painted in bold colours, brick red, deep blue, mauve, brown. The objects they harboured were exciting. Such individual things. I

311

slowed to inspect in more detail a wall hung with masks, crucifixes, old prints, framed poems.

'Come ALONG,' urged Toby.

'Okay, okay; I'm coming.'

We went out of a side door into a yard where chickens wandered freely. Two large ginger cats lay stretched out asleep on a stone table.

'Goodness!'

'What?'

I'd just noticed the peacock.

'He's nasty.'

'Bad-tempered. You bet he is. Still I'd love to see him open his tail.'

Toby shrugged as if it meant nothing to him. 'He's mean,' he asserted. 'But Malika and Woolly Socks are nice.'

'Who are they?'

He pointed at the cats.

I was gazing about again, taking it all in, this habitat which Ruth and her son had inhabited this last year. What a far cry from London. The garden was extensive, lawn and flowerbeds, giving way to vegetable garden and orchard. Here and there a sculpture was placed. Some in clay, others in wood. One magnificent bow and arrow effect, more abstract than the rest, was in bronze. At the bottom of an avenue of splayed fruit trees, was a gush of water from a bubbling stream. Beyond which the garden gave way to fields as far as the eye could see. In two of the nearer fields a herd of creamy brown and white cows clustered. In the distance a couple of dogs were rounding up the sheep.

Turning round again towards the house, I traced the line the Downs made against the very blue sky. It was so still. I listened to the farmyard noises, somewhere a tractor, the bark of a dog, the breeze in the long grasses, the chirping of birds. It was idyllic. An idyllic spot. And yet.

'Come on,' the little boy said again.

Coming in out of the glare it took me a moment to adjust my eyes. A large fair woman with hair pinned on the top of her head in an enormous bun was sitting with her back to us at a potter's wheel.

'Caitlin –'

'Just a moment, Toby.'

I remained at the entrance, my eyes resting on the pots and bowls stacked all around, my heart beating uncomfortably.

312

When she turned I immediately felt better. Such a great under-standing face she had.

'Hi. I'm Josie,' I told her, 'a kind of friend of Ruth's. A kind of a friend of a friend. Toby says she's not here now. Can I wait for her?'

'Of course you can.'

She got up, and went to the sink at the back of the studio.

'You came at the perfect moment,' she said whilst she scrubbed her clay-covered hands. 'I was just thinking of packing it in for the day. What about you, Toby? You must be ready for your tea?'

Toby jumped up and down, nodding and shaking his head alternately. 'Do you know what that means?'

'I think it means you're very hungry indeed.'

'No. Sort of. It means . . .'

'Come along. We've got a visitor, Toby. Isn't that nice. A friend of Mummy's. Perhaps she'll let you do your puppet show for her after tea. Have you met Dick yet?' she said to me.

'No, I –'

'No doubt he'll be in soon. Are you American?'

'Canadian.'

'Ah. Well I must say this is a pleasant surprise. A friend of Ruth's.'

Walking back over the yard with her towards the house, with Toby pulling at my hand, the setting sun turning the sky above the Downs to a wonderful pinky hue, I was lulled into thinking this was all going to be okay, this was all going to be just great.

I was still in the same frame of mind half an hour later while we were munching our tea. The dining room in which we sat was square and looked out over the garden through small latticed windows. Much of the room was taken up by the large round mahogany table around which we sat; Caitlin, Dick, his assistant Aaron, Toby and myself. They had just kind of accepted me, that I was waiting there for Ruth. Hardly asked me any questions. From the time Dick breezed in, which was minutes before we reached the kitchen, the talk had just flowed.

He was great, Dick, a large thin man with a magnificent flaming red beard. Could he just talk, geeze, on any topic you could care to mention. I'd never met with such a conversationalist. Poetry, history, music, travel, art; he was one of those types who was interested in just about anything. Never stopped. He was full of vitality. He seemed to have an obsession about Trollope. Went on and on. Kept coming back to him. I suppose he assumed that being a friend of Ruth's I'd be one of those literary types. The talk seemed to flow out of his beard. He was really great. I thought Ruth lucky; I thought she must be okay living here with them.

Toby gobbled down his food: scones, bread and jam, flapjacks, fruit cake; then scampered off to prepare his puppets.

'He's so delighted to have a new audience,' said Caitlin to me, 'I hope we're not imposing on you?'

'Geeze, no. I love puppets.'

'Ruth ought to be back soon. She works up at the forge,' Dick explained. 'Finds it easier out of the house. But she normally gets back around now; in time to bath Toby. You won't have to hang on too long. You'll stay and eat with us tonight?' He looked at Caitlin for confirmation. 'You know, Ruth hasn't had a person down here, or a phone call, the whole time she's been here. I was under the impression that she hadn't given anyone our address. Something of a hermit, Ruth. So you're quite a surprise. But I'm pleased. This last week we've been — well, I wouldn't exactly say worried, but she has been unusually withdrawn from us and the boy. It will probably do her a power of good having a visitor. If she'd like you to stay over for a day or two, of course you're welcome.'

'Oh I couldn't do that. Actually I'll have to be getting back to my grandparents before it's too late. They live in Hove.'

'Then we'll drive you in after supper. But what a shame. I was hoping to persuade you to pose as model for me. I'd rather like to sculpt your head.'

'Thanks, but no, well no I couldn't stay.'

Geeze, just listen to that, Jeremy.

'That was great.' I was hugging Toby later. 'Really great. I loved it. Especially the bit where Badger bonked the Policeman over the head.'

'Shall I do it again?'

'Yes, do.'

'All of it?' His serious little face looked at me hopefully. He was peering out from behind a large armchair the top of which he was using as a stage. Strewn on the floor to the left and right of the chair were a number of glove puppets.

'Go on then, Toby; I'll have the whole show again.'

'Really?' He was grinning from ear to ear.

It was a different version this time with more larking around, the characters having violent fights and then great huggings and kissings to make up.

After I'd given the most convincing version I could of sustained applause, I went round behind the sofa and together we mucked around, making the puppets crawl up each other's backs and pull one another's hair, and so on.

I seemed to be sustained out of time, completely happy in this house with its sculptures, its colourful paintings, its pots, its wooden floors and mauve and brown walls. It came to me that it was like a house I'd visited in another life, a house I already knew. The house, of dark and light, of mysterious corners, a house with a history, with parts that unravel slowly, the house I had dreamt of, in my restless disturbed adolescent days in Edmonton. How crazy that it wasn't my mother's house at all: but this house.

What a fitting end to my stay, I thought; and then I can go back. It's okay now. I can go home, home. I wanted to see the others again, even little Paul.

Caitlin came into the room. 'What about your bath now, Toby? Mummy's late today. Are you going to be a big boy and bath yourself?'

'No.'

'What if I come with you?' I offered.

'Wait for Mummy.'

'Let's give Mummy a surprise. Have you in your pyjamas, all scrubbed and clean. She'd like that.'

He considered it. Then put out his hand to me.

'Josie's my second Mummy now,' he said to Caitlin, who laughed.

So we went up to the bathroom. I don't think I was worried any more about meeting Ruth. It no longer seemed to me crazy that I was here. Perfectly, perfectly natural. Helped by Caitlin and Dick's welcoming hospitality, and by Toby, it seemed certain that the evening would flow smoothly.

I trailed my fingers in the luke-warm water of Toby's bath. We sailed boats. I made up stories for him.

My body had stopped doing strange and unnerving things. The connection with Toby, real and very much in the present, making me more solid. Soon I would see his mother and whatever it was I had come for would be brought out into the open. Then it would be over. I'd go back to Grandma and Grandpa and spend a few days there. Then home. Home.

315

It no longer sounded like failure. You go on an adventure, expecting some things, and you find others. I couldn't exactly say what I'd found, but the thought of home no longer sounded like failure. So I sailed Toby's boats and told him more and more stories till we both became quite giggly and there seemed to be more water on the bathroom floor than in the bath itself.

'Geeze, this water is just about cold, Toby. We must have been ages. Come on, out you pop.' I took a towel from the rail. 'Jump into this.'

'That's not mine.'

'Never mind.'

'You dry me.'

'Come on then. Jump.'

I sat on the loo with him on my lap.

'Give me a kiss, Toby.'

He put his arms around me and kissed me on the nose.

'You've got a funny nose.'

'A distinctive nose. A nose that shows character.'

'What's character. Have I got it?'

'Masses.' I hugged him. Two waifs and strays, us. Through the high windows I saw that the sun was a red ball of fire as it set over the fields in the far distance.

I was rubbing the towel over his warm little body when he shifted on my lap.

'That's where it is!'

'Where what is?'

He leant over and from the floor beside the loo picked up a half eaten chocolate biscuit. With an air of triumph he held it up. 'There it is!' He fought his other hand free of the towel, turned the biscuit over, then crammed it into his mouth.

'I wouldn't do that. It must be filthy.'

'But I've MISSED it,' he said with his mouth full, 'all day, since when I woke up.'

'What are you talking about, Toby? Here, let's get your pyjamas on you. You're dry now.'

Since the biscuit was making its way down his digestive system my mind leap-frogged need for further explanation but he went on:

'I was hungry. She said I could have a biscuit. We went to the tin. There was only one chocolate one. She gave it to me. Then I lost it. I cried. She cried too. Now I've found it. I want to tell her. Where is Mummy?' he said, his voice becoming more and more agitated. He

316

jumped off my lap, 'I want to go to the gate and see if I can see my Mummy.'

I tried to keep him still for long enough to do up the buttons on his pyjamas but he pulled away from me.

'I want my Mummy. I've found it. I must tell her NOW.'

He started running along the corridor and down the stairs calling at the top of his voice, 'Mummy, Mummy.'

Half way down I caught up with him. 'I'll come with you to the gate, Toby, if Mrs Spurling says that's okay. But don't worry. Don't get in such a state. It's only a biscuit. I'm sure she's not worrying about it now.'

'But she was crying, you see. Crying and crying. She wanted to phone but nobody wasn't there.'

'To phone whom?'

'You won't tell?'

'No.'

'Jeremy,' he whispered, 'but now she'll be happy –'

Oh geeze, no.

*

Peas Pottage, Slaugham, Goddards Green. Sylvia watched the names speed past as the Vauxhall rushed down the dual carriageway getting closer and closer to her family home. It was years since she'd last driven this road south. Yet the first sighting of the Downs brought the familiar lump to her throat. Some things don't change. Though others do. She recognised changes in herself this last decade. Was it only a decade ago that she had left Patrick? How would it be? How would she find them? How they her? I'm my own woman now, she thought. They can't push me around. Maybe they'll not want to. Whatever, there must not be a scene in front of Josie. I'm sandwiched between the one generation and the other. But it is up to me now. She thought of what Alison had said when she'd told her that she was going down, 'Play it the best way you can; summon up *all your wisdom*, darling.' All my wisdom, thought Sylvia, pray God.

In the back of the car, curled up on the seat lay Helen, sleeping with her mouth open. The sun, low in the sky, shone in through the back window full onto her face. The heat disturbed her; every now and again she made a grunting sound and shifted position. Though uncomfortable and hot, however, she was too dog-tired to let go of sleep.

Jeremy and Sylvia had been taken aback at her insistence that if it was to Brighton they were to go, she would accompany them. 'I think I've had *quite* enough of being out of things,' she'd asserted. But so many emotions. So much travelling. So many wakeful hours last night. All that was beginning to take its toll. So that a time came when abruptly sleep made its own demands.

Jeremy was bothered by the glare on his side window. He wished he'd remembered sunglasses. He blinked his eyes and held the wheel tightly. It was with difficulty that he kept his eyes focused on the road ahead.

They were going well over the speed limit. Sylvia wondered if she ought to mention it; but didn't.

Jeremy was thinking about Ruth Flowert. Finally in the baking office that afternoon he had gone through the bundle of documents including a copy of Proof of Evidence. The whole made painful reading. Forced to bring his mind to bear on certain central issues, he had to admit to himself that it was a part of his life of which he was not proud. In re-reading the letters he could hear Ruth's voice – its particular poignancy. She had written of the happiness they had had. It was painful, painful. Poor old Ruth.

'Sylvia, open the glove compartment, will you? There could just be a pair of sunglasses in there.'

Sylvia took out Kleenex, old AA books, a packet of sweets, a duster.

'No sunglasses.'

'Damn!'

'Is the glare getting to you? Would you like me to drive?'

'It's okay. I've been meaning to tell you. Harold phoned this afternoon. Apparently Robert Jeffries wants to have a meeting with us before the court hearing. How are you fixed for tomorrow afternoon?'

'Without my diary how can I tell?'

'Just wondered –'

'Jeremy, I too was just wondering. It struck me that maybe we should phone and prepare them.'

'Who?'

'Where are you? My parents. Give them time to adjust. What do you think?'

'Maybe it would be for the best.'

318

*

Josie: With Toby it was impossible to do anything more than walk slowly: and that suited me. I didn't like it. Geeze, I didn't like it at all that he was coming along.

'Mrs Spurling, I was thinking of making my way up to the forge and saying "Hi" to Ruth there,' I'd suggested, after Toby and I had been hanging on at the gate for what seemed like a long long time. 'Perhaps I'll meet her on the way down.'

'Yes, you go on up. What a good idea. She must have lost all track of the time. What about you, Toby, are you going to let me put you to bed? Then Mummy can give you a kiss later. Come along.'

'Want to go with Josie.'

'It's rather late for that.'

'But I want to go with Josie.' He was whimpering and holding onto my hand as tight as he was able.

'Stay with Mrs Spurling, Toby. I'm sure you'd get tired now going up to the forge.'

'Wouldn't.'

'I think you'd best stay here.'

'I want to come. I'm coming. You can't stop me.'

I looked at Caitlin for support. But she didn't understand. How could she?

'Perhaps it's best not to upset him. Besides, he can show you the way.'

He had already started out.

Sylvia: The timelessness of her voice is quite striking. Her lack of surprise, surprised me. 'Since Josie has arrived it hasn't seemed so impossible. How wonderful to hear you, my girl. Your father? Yes, he's in excellent health and tickled pink by Josie's arrival. By the way, she isn't here at the moment if it was her you wanted to speak to.'

'No?'

'Around about teatime she suddenly took off. Or more accurately, persuaded me to take her. Got a bee in her bonnet –'

'But what friends could she have? Plumpton, you say?'

'Yes, quite distinctly Plumpton. I dropped her by the racecourse. She was most determined. It was as much as I could do to persuade her to take the money for the taxi fare back.'

I opened the door of the phone booth. 'Jeremy, she's gone to Plumpton. What in the world – ?'

It was Jeremy who put two and two together.

Josie: But now. Was it only I who lagged? We stopped by the water. Above the pond, in the highest branches of tall trees, ravens wheeled around their nests. Looking at our two reflections in the patches of clear blue water I wondered why it had to be so much more complicated for human beings.

'It's just over there,' Toby pointed. But neither of us made a move. I felt in my pocket.

'How about another marshmallow?'

Sylvia: Jeremy most certainly is driving too fast. Which is one matter on the motorway, another along these narrow country roads. But he is quite beside himself. I fear remonstrating will make it worse. Nothing for it but to sit tight and hope for the best. I'm astonished the last swerve didn't wake Helen.

I must say I hadn't expected it to be like that. Hearing her voice. I'm glad it was her and not him. We'll take Josie back there afterwards. What a strange way it has come about. And yet I'm not sorry. If only he would ease the pace; anyone would think we were in the Grand Prix! At least the sun is no longer worrisome. Luckily we'll have to stop for petrol soon.

Josie: Situated on the ridge were a cluster of houses. Toby pointed to the last.

'See at the side there, that's the forge.'

'We've almost made it then.'

'She wasn't walking home,' he shook his head sadly.

'Well let's surprise her.'

Toby, knowing what I know how can I let . . . I shouldn't be here. I shouldn't be in this.

But it was he again who diverted us by insisting on showing me the churchyard.

Sylvia: The stop at the petrol station woke Helen up. Jeremy explained what had happened. 'But what exactly are you frightened of, Jeremy?' she asked.

'She shouldn't be in this,' he said. 'It is one matter going to see her grandparents but this is quite different. I'm the only one of the three of us to know anything about Josie; and you can take my word for it she might be a very nice kid, in many ways she is, but she's bound to make a cock-up of this. I can see her jumping in with two gallumphing feet and saying all manner of inappropriate things. She's crazy even to think of becoming muddled up in this. Good God!'

'But why has she? I wish I understood.'

'It's my hunch, Sylvia, that your daughter is doing it for you.'

'For me!'

'I'd lay my bets on it that she's got into her head some benighted scheme of persuading Ruth to give up her case – even at this late stage.'

'But Jeremy . . .'

'Don't "but Jeremy" me. The sooner we get there the better. And incidentally when we do, I'll park the car some distance from the house, leave you two in it and go up myself. We don't want to cause even more trouble. Christ almighty, what can have got into her to do something so stupid?'

'Perhaps, Jeremy,' I started to say.

'There aren't any "perhaps's" about it. Now if you could just check the map again.'

Josie: It was a small graveyard. Peaceful. The darkening Downs giving such splendour as a backdrop. Toby had looked at each one of the tombstones. There was nothing more to keep us. But still he hung back.

'This poor grave has no flowers. I'll just pick one daisy for it.'

'Okay, you do that.'

I sat on the bench waiting.

The sun had disappeared now beneath the horizon, leaving the sky apple-red. I wondered if it would be the same colour in London. Where Sylvia would just be leaving the office to go upstairs and have her drink with Alison.

Then it all happened so quickly. Toby seemed to have made up his mind. He came over to the bench and pulled me up.

'C'mon.'

'I'm ready when you are.' Ready as I'll ever be.

Now he held my hand more purposefully. His strides were enormous for such small legs. At the entrance he let go of my hand and went in first. I think I was still looking at the sky when I heard.

At the entrance to the forge he let go of my hand.

The sky. The colour of the sky. I must hold onto that. Some things, those things won't ever be taken away.

Sylvia: 'This is madness,' I said to Jeremy when he got back into the car and started the engine once more. 'Wherever to now?'

Helen, sitting up now, leaned forward, resting her arms on the back of his chair:

'Yes, tell us, wherever next?'

But Jeremy was as silent as I'd ever known him.

Josie: Inside I knew what I'd find. I suppose I've known it for a long time now. But I couldn't quite. Oh geeze. Apple red. Red red red.

Sylvia: Over the birdsong came the noise, horrible, ugly. A wailing only half human. Jeremy had stopped the car and leapt out. He was running. Helen and I ran after him in the direction of the noise. Once he turned to shout, 'Don't', but on we ran. The noise was half human, half animal. It was dreadful. I couldn't imagine. It was a child. A child caught in an animal trap, perhaps. No, it was my daughter. Then the noise was everywhere. The noise was Timmy, the noise was loss. Timmy, loss, me, my noise; my child, my children. The noise was everywhere. I ran fast, outstripping Jeremy. Josie. Josie

Josie: 'Oh, geeze, oh, Jeremy –'

'Get an ambulance,' he said. 'For God's sake, one of you phone for an ambulance.'

'It's too late,' someone said, 'she looks as if she's been dead for hours.'

'Don't argue, any of you. Helen, for Pete's sake, run up to the phone box or go next door and use theirs. Quickly, woman, quickly.'

'Jeremy, Jeremy,' screamed the little boy, clinging to him.

'So much pain, I can't bear it,' I sobbed. 'Why did she have to –'

'I thought it was you,' said Sylvia.

'What?'

'Dying.'

I went to her and sobbed against her narrow chest. For a brief second I thought, even now I can do it, climb right back inside there. Be the child again. Down, down to some eternal and lost place. And so I clung, trying to blot out.

'She was such a lovely person,' she was saying. I felt her chest heaving with her own tears. 'The court case, the strain. I should have known.'

'No, you mustn't, mustn't blame yourself.'

I looked at the little boy whose head was buried in Jeremy's paunch, his little fists making balls of Jeremy's shirt, his howls filling the empty spaces of this strange room. I looked at Ruth lying on the floor, her speckled eyes seeing nothing. We cried together, my mother and I. And then a moment came when I recognised that I wasn't clinging to Sylvia, but she to me.

*

When Ruth's body was removed, the note was found lying underneath. She had been lying on it when the pills took effect. Josie who went forward to pick it up commented that it was still warm. She asked the others if they would like her to read it out and the consensus was that she should.

Jeremy listened from his position on the floor with Toby attached to him as if he would never agree to be parted. Helen, at a distance,

323

rested against one of the walls with her hand over her mouth as if she threatened to be sick at any moment. Sylvia was sitting on the single chair, her head supported by her elbows that rested on Ruth's writing table. Even at a moment like this, Josie thought, she can be so absolutely graceful. Sylvia noticed Josie looking at her and signalled for her to come near. Josie went over and stood beside her. Sylvia slipped an arm round Josie's waist.

Ruth wrote that she could not battle further in this life and hoped that the next would not be so turbulent. She said that for choice, though she doubted that there was such, she would wish to be reincarnated as a cat or a tortoise. That she had a particular preference for the tortoise's long periods of hibernation. She said she had written a letter to Toby which was lodged with her solicitor and was for him to read when he was older. Meanwhile, she had suggested that she would like Jeremy to act as guardian, 'I can think of none better,' and that she hoped Sylvia and Alison would agree to being joint literary executors. 'There is no point going into the next life with battles still unresolved in this one.'

For a long time there wasn't a sound in the room.

It was obvious to Helen what was to be done. How utterly extraordinary, she thought. For the whole of the weekend she had tortured herself as to how the remainder of her life could resolve itself. Never could she have imagined that it would resolve itself like this.

'Toby will come and live with us,' she announced, 'if he'd like to, and his relatives agree.'

'Helen, that's splendid,' exclaimed Sylvia.

'You're a saint,' said Jeremy to his wife.

'That's right,' she told him. She smiled, imagining with pleasure more years of a child's laughter, hopefully he would laugh in time, the children's toys being used again, another one to read to, to mother. When she'd thought it was all over. She didn't even mind that it was Ruth's child now that Ruth was dead. 'Yes, a saint,' she said to Jeremy, 'and don't you ever forget it.'

'I tried, I did try,' said Josie to Jeremy. 'I was just too –'

'I know.'

'Still maybe –'

'Maybe,' said Helen and Sylvia in unison.

Jeremy stroked the little boy's back. 'Can you hear me, Toby?' But Toby said nothing. Just clung for dear life.

FOR THE BEST IN PAPERBACKS, LOOK FOR THE

In every corner of the world, on every subject under the sun, Penguin represents quality and variety – the very best in publishing today.

For complete information about books available from Penguin – including Pelicans, Puffins, Peregrines and Penguin Classics – and how to order them, write to us at the appropriate address below. Please note that for copyright reasons the selection of books varies from country to country.

In the United Kingdom: For a complete list of books available from Penguin in the U.K., please write to *Dept E.P., Penguin Books Ltd, Harmondsworth, Middlesex, UB7 0DA*

In the United States: For a complete list of books available from Penguin in the U.S., please write to *Dept BA, Penguin, 299 Murray Hill Parkway, East Rutherford, New Jersey 07073*

In Canada: For a complete list of books available from Penguin in Canada, please write to *Penguin Books Canada Ltd, 2801 John Street, Markham, Ontario L3R 1B4*

In Australia: For a complete list of books available from Penguin in Australia, please write to the *Marketing Department, Penguin Books Australia Ltd, P.O. Box 257, Ringwood, Victoria 3134*

In New Zealand: For a complete list of books available from Penguin in New Zealand, please write to the *Marketing Department, Penguin Books (NZ) Ltd, Private Bag, Takapuna, Auckland 9*

In India: For a complete list of books available from Penguin, please write to *Penguin Overseas Ltd, 706 Eros Apartments, 56 Nehru Place, New Delhi, 110019*

In Holland: For a complete list of books available from Penguin in Holland, please write to *Penguin Books Nederland B.V., Postbus 195, NL–1380AD Weesp, Netherlands*

In Germany: For a complete list of books available from Penguin, please write to *Penguin Books Ltd, Friedrichstrasse 10 – 12, D–6000 Frankfurt Main 1, Federal Republic of Germany*

In Spain: For a complete list of books available from Penguin in Spain, please write to *Longman Penguin España, Calle San Nicolas 15, E–28013 Madrid, Spain*

FOR THE BEST IN PAPERBACKS, LOOK FOR THE

A CHOICE OF PENGUIN FICTION

Monsignor Quixote   Graham Greene

Now filmed for television, Graham Greene's novel, like Cervantes' seventeenth-century classic, is a brilliant fable for its times. 'A deliciously funny novel' – *The Times*

The Dearest and the Best   Leslie Thomas

In the spring of 1940 the spectre of war turned into grim reality – and for all the inhabitants of the historic villages of the New Forest it was the beginning of the most bizarre, funny and tragic episode of their lives. 'Excellent' – *Sunday Times*

Earthly Powers   Anthony Burgess

Anthony Burgess's magnificent masterpiece, an enthralling, epic narrative spanning six decades and spotlighting some of the most vivid events and characters of our times. 'Enormous imagination and vitality . . . a huge book in every way' – Bernard Levin in the *Sunday Times*

The Penitent   Isaac Bashevis Singer

From the Nobel Prize-winning author comes a powerful story of a man who has material wealth but feels spiritually impoverished. 'Singer . . . restates with dignity the spiritual aspirations and the cultural complexities of a lifetime, and it must be said that in doing so he gives the Evil One no quarter and precious little advantage' – Anita Brookner in the *Sunday Times*

Paradise Postponed   John Mortimer

'Hats off to John Mortimer. He's done it again' – *Spectator*. A rumbustious, hilarious new novel from the creator of Rumpole, *Paradise Postponed* is now a major Thames Television series.

Animal Farm   George Orwell

The classic political fable of the twentieth century.

A CHOICE OF PENGUIN FICTION

Maia Richard Adams

The heroic romance of love and war in an ancient empire from one of our greatest storytellers. 'Enormous and powerful' – *Financial Times*

The Warning Bell Lynne Reid Banks

A wonderfully involving, truthful novel about the choices a woman must make in her life – and the price she must pay for ignoring the counsel of her own heart. 'Lynne Reid Banks knows how to get to her reader: this novel grips like Super Glue' – *Observer*

Doctor Slaughter Paul Theroux

Provocative and menacing – a brilliant dissection of lust, ambition and betrayal in 'civilized' London. 'Witty, chilly, exuberant, graphic' – *The Times Literary Supplement*

July's People Nadine Gordimer

Set in South Africa, this novel gives us an unforgettable look at the terrifying, tacit understanding and misunderstandings between blacks and whites. 'This is the best novel that Miss Gordimer has ever written' – Alan Paton in the *Saturday Review*

Wise Virgin A. N. Wilson

Giles Fox's work on the Pottle manuscript, a little-known thirteenth-century tract on virginity, leads him to some innovative research on the subject that takes even his breath away. 'A most elegant and chilling comedy' – *Observer* Books of the Year

Last Resorts Clare Boylan

Harriet loved Joe Fischer for his ordinariness – for his ordinary suits and hats, his ordinary money and his ordinary mind, even for his ordinary wife. 'An unmitigated delight' – *Time Out*

A CHOICE OF PENGUIN FICTION

Stanley and the Women   Kingsley Amis

Just when Stanley Duke thinks it safe to sink into middle age, his son goes insane – and Stanley finds himself beset on all sides by women, each of whom seems to have an intimate acquaintance with madness. 'Very good, very powerful . . . beautifully written' – Anthony Burgess in the *Observer*

The Girls of Slender Means   Muriel Spark

A world and a war are winding up with a bang, and in what is left of London all the nice people are poor – and about to discover how different the new world will be. 'Britain's finest post-war novelist' – *The Times*

Him with His Foot in His Mouth   Saul Bellow

A collection of first-class short stories. 'If there is a better living writer of fiction, I'd very much like to know who he or she is' – *The Times*

Mother's Helper   Maureen Freely

A superbly biting and breathtakingly fluent attack on certain libertarian views, blending laughter, delight, rage and amazement, this is a novel you won't forget. 'A winner' – *The Times Literary Supplement*

Decline and Fall   Evelyn Waugh

A comic yet curiously touching account of an innocent plunged into the sham, brittle world of high society. Evelyn Waugh's first novel brought him immediate public acclaim and is still a classic of its kind.

Stars and Bars   William Boyd

Well-dressed, quite handsome, unfailingly polite and charming, who would guess that Henderson Dores, the innocent Englishman abroad in wicked America, has a guilty secret? 'Without doubt his best book so far . . . made me laugh out loud' – *The Times*